THE LAST GOODBYE

ALSO BY REED ARVIN

The Will

THE LAST GOODBYE

A Novel

REED ARVIN

HarperCollins*Publishers*

HarperCollins books may be purchased for educational, business, or sales promotional use. For information, please write: Special Markets Department, HarperCollins Publishers Inc., 10 East 53rd Street, New York, NY 10022.

FIRST EDITION

Printed on acid-free paper

Library of Congress Cataloging-in-Publication Data is available upon request.

ISBN 0-06-055551-3

04 05 06 07 08 ❖/RRD 10 9 8 7 6 5 4 3 2 1

For Dianne
Bella como la luna y las estrellas

ACKNOWLEDGMENTS

MY GRATEFUL THANKS for technical advice are extended to the brilliant Dr. Richard Caprioli of Vanderbilt University. If I had known research scientists got to drive Ferraris, I might have made different career choices. Any technical errors are entirely my own. Also due thanks at Vanderbilt are Vali Forrester, Joel Lee, and Dr. Mace Rothenberg. Thanks also to Ron Owenby, tour guide and lunch companion. Thanks to the Atlanta Opera for its kindness and access, and to Kelly Bare for her good-natured handling of many details.

As always, sincere thanks to Jane and Miriam at Dystel and Goderich Literary Management.

To Marjorie: your faith means much. I will try to live up to it.

THE LAST GOODBYE

CHAPTER ONE

SO I'LL TELL YOU. I'll tell you because confession is supposed to be good for the soul, and when choosing between the tonics available—from religion to Tony Robbins to the friendly late-night chemist—this unburdening seems to present the least risk. When it comes to my soul, I have adopted a doctor's attitude: *First, do no harm.*

The complete overthrow of my principles. That was what I had done. A moment in time, and my life—previously not lived to the highest standards, but plenty respectable—blew up. The distance between integrity and the loss of innocence proved to be razor-thin, a handful of decisions, frictionless, greased with desire. I thought I was choosing a woman. I thought—and I have to swallow this back, but it's the truth, and this is the unburdening, after all—I had *earned* her. And now she is my ghost, come to judge me.

This is the beginning of moral collapse: to be held captive by a woman's eyes. Looking into hers, my mind went blank. All I knew was that she was in my office, and she was crying, and at some point I asked her to sit down. Her name was Violeta Ramirez, and I ignored her faux leather pocketbook, her Wal-mart dress, the run in her stocking. These were signals that she was in the wrong office, of course, in the same way that a Timex is the wrong watch in a store that sells yachts. But I was looking at her flawless, caramel skin, the deep, black hair pulled back, the fathomless, brown eyes. The familiar script in my body began to play, this hormone washing over these cells, neurons lighting up, a million years of evolution lining up my thoughts like little soldiers.

The clients of Carthy, Williams and Douglas did not generally cry in my office. They were far more likely to rant, curse, or even, when I was lucky, to intently listen. But having paid four hundred dollars an hour for the privilege of occupying the chair opposite me, complaints about their manners were not welcome. A crying woman was something else, however, and I found myself leaping up, asking her if I could get her anything. She was exquisitely beautiful, she was crying, and she could not be ignored.

Caliz was the father of her child, she said. There had been a mistake; he had aggravated the police; they had planted *las drogas* on him. He was good, if only people understood him. He had a smart mouth, and the police had made him pay. He was no choirboy, she knew that—was that a bruise hiding underneath her dark makeup?—but of this, he was innocent.

I don't know if she was aware of the effect she was having on me. I watched, mesmerized, as each tear slipped down her cheek. She crossed her legs, and I caught my breath. It's not that I didn't appreciate most women. I have appreciated them from my earliest memories, from the bosomy warmth of my mother to the incisive intelligence of the female associates at the firm. It's just that feminism doesn't mean anything to the human body, and there was something so uncomplicated and vulnerable in her that I couldn't stop my entire soul from wanting her.

There were obligations, which I met: I explained the firm didn't do drug cases, or for that matter, criminal law of any kind. The crying had gotten worse then, and in the end I couldn't even bring up the obvious impossibility of her paying my fee. But it wouldn't have mattered, because Carthy, Williams and Douglas would sooner invite the archangel of death into their offices than defend a drug dealer. So I simply said that my hands were tied, which was true. I did not have the power to change the rules of the firm. She rose, shook my hand, and crept from my office in tears and humiliation. Hours after she left, the image of her lingered. I stared at the chair where she had been, willing her back. For two days, I couldn't do a thing at the office. At last I called her, telling her I would see what I could do. The truth is, I would have moved heaven and earth to see her again.

It was work selling the idea to the firm. By meticulous design, Carthy, Williams and Douglas was as far away from legal aid as it was possible to get. Its offices occupied three floors of the Tower Walk building in Buckhead, the part of Atlanta where it's a crime to be either old or poor. And if anybody was going to go play in the slums for a few days, it wasn't likely to be me, Jack Hammond. At three years out of law school, I had just moved to Atlanta—the magnet that pulls together the shards of humanity from all over the Southeast—was working seventy-hour weeks, and generally outspending my salary with a vengeance. I couldn't afford any detours. But in spite of this, I made an appointment with founding partner Frank Carthy.

Carthy was seventy years old and had come up when pro bono work was a part of every big firm's responsibility. Until the early 1980s it had been expected, and judges had handed it out as a part of the obligation of the profession. That had suited him fine; he was an old-school southern liberal, with a soft spot for civil rights cases. He still told stories about getting protesters out of jail in the 1960s, mostly for things like being the wrong color to sit at a particular place in a restaurant. So even though he would resist a drug case, he might be attracted to a case about a crying girl and false arrest based on race.

I didn't see Carthy much; within the hierarchy of the firm he occupied Mount Olympus, rarely descending into Hades two floors below him where the new associates worked. In spite of working my ass off—mostly to live down growing up in Dothan,

Alabama, with an adolescence so ordinary it could have been cut out of cardboard—my access to the gods of the firm was limited. I had arrived with the impression that I was in possession of a significant legal gift. What I discovered at Carthy, Williams and Douglas was that being the smartest little boy in Dothan, Alabama, was like being the shiniest diamond in a pool of mud. So in a way, just having something to talk about with a founding partner was a boost to my prospects.

I knew the second I told him I had hit a nerve. For a while, I was actually worried he would volunteer to try it with me. For Carthy, a millionaire several times over, taking a case like this was the equivalent of standing outside a grocery store for a couple of hours with a red cup for the Salvation Army, except he wouldn't risk getting wet: it was good for the soul. He probably assumed that this expression of legal largesse would be a minor diversion, likely taking only a few hours. Drug court—a tiny courtroom attached to the police station, with seating for only ten people—was little more than a revolving door.

I went to meet Caliz the next morning, which required a trip to the inner recesses of the Fulton County Jail. The smell of that place is the atmospheric accumulation of everything unpleasant when things go horribly wrong. It is composed of equal parts human misery, sweat, and indifferent bureaucracy, of metal filing cabinets and the homeless and overweight cops and fluorescent lighting that has never been turned off. I followed a wordless guard to a nondescript room with two metal chairs and a long table.

Caliz came in a couple of minutes later, and it took me no time at all to dislike him. Still in his early twenties, he already had the insolent, blank stare of the small-time thug. His eyes were pools of detached anger, precursors to sociopathic behavior. Whatever he lacked in that department, he would certainly find after a couple of years at the school for cruelty known as state prison. Getting a straight story out of him was impossible, his ability to lie having already become effortless. He looked right at me, expressionless, and said, "No, *la policía* put *las drogas* in the car. I never take *las drogas*. Bad for you. I stay away."

Horseshit, I thought, which wasn't strictly the point. The real question was why his car had been pulled over in the first place, and why, after a brief but unfriendly conversation, the backseat of his car had been removed, disassembled, and his trunk thoroughly searched. Bad attitudes didn't void the Constitution.

Pitting the word of Miguel Caliz against the Atlanta Police would not be a walk in the park, except I met the arresting officers later that afternoon, and they were exactly as Caliz described. That was the moment I knew for certain that Caliz would walk, whether or not he was guilty. The two policemen were a couple of mean-spirited assholes who couldn't keep their dispositions off their faces. They reminded me of Caliz himself: they were bullies, making their living off the pain of society. It was simple human nature, therefore—people despising being reminded of their own short-comings—that Caliz would bring out the worst in them. I could see it in their eyes: they didn't like Latinos, they didn't like Caliz, and above all, they didn't like people they couldn't scare. If I put together a jury with the right disposition, just looking at those officers would be all it would take to spring Caliz.

None of that explained what happened, how I took his girl-friend to dinner, how for three or four hours the conversation drifted easily into areas she knew nothing about: law school, the summer I had backpacked across Europe—it was only three weeks, but we were a couple of drinks into it by now—how the cost of a really good bottle of wine wasn't something to compare with other, lesser things. In fact, I knew very little of these matters, but she had watched me with those shining, dark eyes, which was enough. It was a wet fall evening, and she had huddled close to me as we walked past the shops in Buckhead, a world she couldn't reason-ably expect to ever call her own. She was wearing what ghetto girls always wear when they go someplace decent—something black, a little too tight, a little too short.

The word *seduction* implies a victim, and there is too much con-fusion about what happened next to assign the word here. Cer-tainly, I found myself wondering what it would be like to lose myself in her beauty, to see myself in her dark, shining eyes. And

after a few hours I invited her home—I fumbled the invitation a little, but she didn't seem to notice—still telling myself we were only
going to talk, to spend some time together. But inside my apartment she brushed against me, bringing her breasts against my chest,
and I pulled her to me, determined to treat her like the angel I wanted
her to be. My sin was not lust. My sin was the sin of Satan, who
wanted to be like God. I wanted to be the savior of the earthbound
Violeta Ramirez, and I wanted her to worship me for doing it.

The next morning there was a rustle of sheets beside me, her
exquisitely feminine scent creeping over me as I woke, making me
dizzy. She sighed deeply and turned over, her light brown backside
coming up against my hip. I closed my eyes and felt something like
euphoria, only deeper, earthier. Her sleeping was so deep, so
untroubled, that I marveled once again how God, with His infinite
capacity for irony, so often paired angels like Violeta with losers
like Caliz. Maybe I was romanticizing. I'm certain that I was,
because at that point in my life I still had that capacity. Maybe she
had a bad-boy complex. Maybe she was working through some
father issues by dating a guy like Caliz. Maybe she was like me, and
just wanted someone of her own to save. Caliz certainly fit that bill.
The mind is infinitely complex.

Lying awake beside her in bed, I didn't know if what happened
between us was romantic or cheap. There was so little context, and
I never had the chance to find out. One of God's tricks is to cloud
the human mind at the moment of mating with so much angel
dust that it's only in looking back at things that you can discover
what they really meant. We fall in love and then, on the fourth date,
we wonder who the hell we're with. I do know that when Violeta
finally awakened and started to dress, she looked even more beautiful to me than the night before. It hit me how extraordinary sex
was, that she was walking around with me inside her, every strand
of genetic code containing the purest essence of myself. Inside her
warm body was every detail of who I am, and I felt extravagantly,
marvelously happy.

We didn't speak much before she left. She dressed and slipped
away gracefully, without imposition or demand. She left me with

my task: in other words, to get Miguel Caliz out of jail. If nothing else, I owed her that. And after what had just happened, I owed *him* that.

I had to buy him clothes. I paid for them myself, probably out of a sense of penance. I knew I had crossed an ethical line, although lately the lines were moving so quickly that I wasn't sure where they were. I only knew one thing for certain, that winning was the most ethical thing of all.

I met Caliz at the jail to give him the suit, and he accepted it without a word. I waited for him to dress to go over his testimony. He looked good, but not slick, which was the idea. I didn't want the jurors to know I had dressed him, so the suit I brought was cheap-ish, nothing too stylish.

Ten minutes into the trial, I realized it didn't matter. I had planned carefully, ready to cite the most cutting-edge legal opin-ions on constitutional law, from search and seizure to racial profil-ing. I never had the chance. Everyone in the courtroom was spellbound as they watched the police officer on the stand blowing up, his face covered with ill-concealed loathing for all things brown in the inner city of Atlanta. I actually wondered how long the pros-ecuting attorney would let it go on. But she had no choice. The policeman was the arresting officer, and without his testimony, there was no case. In spite of his angry, narrow eyes, sarcastic tone, and generally hate-filled countenance, she had to keep asking him questions. The jury—there had never been a question in my mind whether or not to ask for a jury—was more than half Latino, and they were hating him back with a combined hundred years or so of built-up resentment.

Caliz himself had helped; like a lot of cons, the kid could act. His expression, with me suspicious and dangerous, transformed itself into victimized fear. His voice trembled. The officers had pulled him over because of his skin. He was humiliated. They had searched him because they didn't like his accent. Of course he knew about drugs. Everybody in his neighborhood knew about them. But he had never taken them in his life.

It took less than an hour for the jury to acquit. There was some satisfaction in that, I suppose. I had to take satisfaction where I could get it, because I didn't get any from Caliz. He didn't shake my hand when he heard the verdict. Instead, he turned and looked at Violeta, who was sitting quietly behind the two of us. Which was the moment I began to wonder who was driving the train I was on.

I thought about her that night, missing her. I was confused, wondering what she was doing. Was she flat on her back, happily letting Caliz replace my heritage with his own? Or was she declaring her independence, telling him having her man in and out of jail wasn't acceptable anymore? I wanted to will her back into my bed, to feel her legs wrapped around me, to lose myself again in her dark hair and eyes. The next morning, submerged into my normal life, she floated in and out of my mind, coalescing in my memory. I very nearly called her, formulating some banal question to ask, some bit of paperwork needing to be signed.

I did not yet understand the chasm between normal and criminal thinking. To Caliz, it didn't matter whether or not Violeta had sacrificed herself to get him the kind of legal expertise he could never afford on his own. It only mattered that he was the kind of angry young man who beats the woman in his life. If she had seduced me on his orders, maybe he just suspected that she had enjoyed herself too much. I never found out. I only know that two days after I got him out of jail, he beat her to death.

The coroner explained to me that when he broke her jaw she would have stopped begging him for mercy. But it was when he broke her ribs that she stopped breathing. Respiration wouldn't have continued for long, what with the punctured lung, the rapid and inevitable buildup of fluid around the heart. He testified that she would have survived between four and six minutes.

No one was able to testify what Miguel Caliz had on his mind while he was beating the hell out of Violeta Ramirez. He might have been taking revenge on her for breaking the foremost rule of dating a thug: never cheat. He might, on the other hand, have felt nothing at all. He might have been as calm as a hot, airless Atlanta day in summer. But either way, Violeta Ramirez was dead.

I learned what happened when I was served witness papers in

the middle of a lunch with clients at 103 West, a trendy and expensive restaurant in Buckhead. I smiled apologetically for the intrusion, set down my glass of pinot noir, and read the handful of lines that were to blow up my world. Caliz's lawyer this time was cheap—I had never heard of the firm—but not so cheap that he didn't know there was sympathy for his client in the fact that I had just slept with his girlfriend. So my deposition would be required.

Some weeks later I put my hand on a Bible and swore that my name was Jack Hammond, and these were my sins. But a judge isn't a priest, and he didn't offer any penance. I would have to find that on my own. He did, however, use the word *reprehensible* in his admonishment to me before I was excused. That word was powerful enough for the firm of Carthy, Williams and Douglas. They did not desire to have a person who committed that word in their employment. The tawdriness of what happened to the girl was not a positive reflection on the firm, and I was on the street.

For several weeks, I didn't turn off the lights in my bedroom. I simply sat, watching the hours click by slowly. Eventually, my body demanded its due, and I closed my eyes. But it was a dangerous sleep, and there was no protection in it.

It means nothing at all to me that Miguel Caliz will spend the next several decades in a federal penitentiary. Locking up Caliz did nothing to restrict the memory of Violeta Ramirez. That memory continues to haunt me, both in daylight and dark.

The complete overthrow of my principles. That was what I had done. And here I make confession, for the benefit of my soul. But even as I confess, I know that the scar remains. Until I make this one thing right in my life, I will have no peace.

CHAPTER TWO

Two years later

MY EYES WERE CLOSED, and I was remembering. The venerable Judson Spence, professor of law, was repeating his ceaseless plea, beating into our young, idealistic heads his most fervent bit of advice: *Avoid criminal law like the plague. It is one of the principles of life that once you get involved in the shit of another human being, you become magnetically attractive to the shit of others.* Again and again, he steered his most talented students toward the vastly more profitable, and sanitized, world of torts. He made his entire class memorize a little aphorism: "Spend your time around the successful, and you will be successful." Otherwise, he cautioned, a huge codependent cycle of human excrement would rain down on us, as the damaged of the world flocked to the enabler.

I, Jack Hammond, am living proof that Judson Spence, professor of law, was an absolute genius. After a considerable tour of duty in the world he warned against, I have discovered my own magnetic powers to be considerable. Not that this has made me rich. My law offices are utilitarian, beginning with the location—a mostly vacant strip mall in a spotty part of southwest Atlanta—and continuing to the furniture, which is cheap, leased, and unsupportive. The paint scheme of the walls—a semigloss eggshell with an unfortunate tendency to reflect the harsh overhead light onto the linoleum floor—is so uniform across doors, walls, and ceilings as to give a visitor vertigo.

There is a sign on the constructor-grade, single-frame door that says, "Jack Hammond and Associates." This is an embellishment, since other than myself, the firm's only employee is Blu McClendon, my secretary. Having associates makes the phone listing look better, so I do it. This is not the time in my life to be overly scrupulous about details. This is the time in my life to survive.

To be honest, describing Blu as a secretary is itself a kind of embellishment. Although she is nearly devoid of skills, she is happily provided with both a living wage and a very comfortable chair in which to sit and read *Vogue* and the catalog for Pottery Barn. How can I describe her? She is the love child of Marilyn Monroe and somebody who doesn't speak English that well, like maybe Tarzan. Her hair—dark blond with highlights, although only at the moment, this is an ever-evolving thing—frames a face of mystical symmetry. The way the gentle, downward curve of her back meets the rounded uplift of her backside is capable of cutting off a man at the knees. Only one pair of knees is essential for the survival of Jack Hammond and Associates, however, and those are the knees of Sammy Liston, the clerk of Judge Thomas Odom.

The words that enable me to pay three dollars more than minimum wage to the beautiful Miss McClendon are these: "If you cannot afford an attorney, the court will appoint one for you." Although the drug problem in Atlanta is thoroughly equal opportunity, the criminal justice system is not. It specializes in low-income, black defendants. Because the court of Judge Thomas Odom—the very cesspool where I destroyed my once impressive career—is overwhelmed with such cases, the good judge is forced to utter that beautiful, rent-paying phrase several times a day. He leaves the actual appointments to Sammy Liston, his trusty clerk, and the unrequited lover of my secretary. Sammy and I have a deal: I am unceasingly available, I am affably predisposed toward plea bargaining, and I look like I believe him when he tells me he has a chance with Blu. Sammy's love for her is all-consuming, impressively one dimensional, and utterly hopeless. Blu McClendon wouldn't date Sammy in a post-nuclear holocaust. In exchange for ignoring this fact, I am free from the burden of putting my face on bus stop benches, and I will never have to figure out how to make my phone number end with h-u-r-t. Let me put it plainly: when the phone rings at Jack Hammond and Associates, I always hope Sammy is on the other end. A phone call from Sammy is worth five hundred bucks, on average.

At about ten o'clock in the morning on a day in May hot enough for July, the phone rang. Blu twisted her perfect torso and said, "It's Sammy, down at the courthouse."

I opened my eyes, left behind my memories, and came back to reality. "Our regular delivery of government cheese," I answered. I picked up the phone and said, "Sammy? Give me some good news, buddy. I got Georgia Power and Light on my ass." Other than the fact that Blu thought he had a face like a horse, I kept no secrets from the clerk of Judge Thomas Odom.

Liston's southern-fried voice came across the phone. "You hear the news?"

"News?"

"So you haven't heard. It's one of your clients. Actually, he's more of a former client. He's dead."

I have a mantra that I repeat to myself for news like that; lately, I had been using it more often than I liked. *Strip it down, Jack. Let it go.* "Who is it?" I asked.

"You aren't going to like it."

"You mean there are some of my clients I wouldn't mind finding out they're dead?"

"If most of your clients were dead, the entire justice system would be grateful."

"I'm waiting."

"It's Doug Townsend. He fell off the wagon, big time, and ended up in overdose."

And so the irony that is my life cranks up a notch. Doug Townsend, the very reason I became a lawyer, is no more. "Overdose?" I asked. "Are you saying he tried to kill himself?"

"Who knows? You know how it gets, Jack. The body readjusts after a while, and they can't take the whack."

"I just spoke to his probation officer three days ago, Sammy. The guy was glowing."

"I'm sorry, Jack."

"Yeah."

"Listen, Jack, the old man wants to know if you'll stop in on Townsend's place."

"To do what?"

"Go through his stuff. See if there's anything to salvage for the estate."

"Does he have any family coming? He's got a cousin in Phoenix, I know that."

"Just got off the phone with her. She doesn't want to know."

"Charming."

"What can I tell you? You get a black sheep, family gets scarce."

"All right," I said, "maybe there's something of his I can salvage. I'll make sure to send it to his loving cousin, who can't be bothered to get on a plane and bury her relatives."

"They probably weren't that close, Jack. The guy's a junkie."

"Was a junkie, Sammy. Was."

"Stop by the courthouse on the way over and pick up a key. And listen, Jack, take it easy over there. It's not exactly a great neighborhood."

That was putting it mildly; Townsend had traveled the well-worn path, spiraling downward to pay for his habit, eventually landing in a crap apartment building called the Jefferson Arms. "I know, Sammy. I'll be in touch."

A pointless, futile death for Doug Townsend was laced with irony, because ten years earlier, I had watched him do the bravest thing I had ever seen. We met in college—I was a freshman, he was a senior—through the intracampus tutorial service. Doug tutored me through calculus, about which I had little aptitude and less interest. But it was a hoop to jump through, so I had to buckle down. We were both busy during those days—I, grinding through the freshman flunk-out courses; Doug, who was three years older, with his computer science classes—and we usually met late at night, around ten.

Doug had confided to me that he had pledged every single fraternity on campus his freshman year, and been turned down by them all. He had the kind of overeager, wide-eyed social style that doomed him to loneliness. He was as well-rounded as a ruler and as awkward as a one-legged bird. But he could be brilliant in a narrow range of subjects. Chief among these was the application of computer technology. He loved computers, adored them, opened them up to expose their inner workings. They were, for him, friend, lover, and savior. It was just as well, because his human friends could be numbered on a single hand.

Late one night, Doug having finally explained to me the difference between tangent and secant lines, we were walking back across campus toward the dorms. I was staring down at the concrete, trying to work out what he was saying, when Doug sprinted out ahead of me. What Doug saw, and I did not, was a girl involuntarily vanish into the bushes beside the walkway. While I was still trying to figure out what was happening, all 130 pounds of Doug Townsend leaped into those bushes with a high-pitched, blood-curdling wail. He was all arms and legs with no particular strategy, but it was impressive to see.

There were two frat boys in the bushes with the girl. Under ordinary circumstances, it would have taken them about ten seconds to waste Doug Townsend. Because they were drunk, it took about twelve. By the time I got there—and believe me, I was hauling—Doug had already taken a couple of significant clips to the body.

I dropped one of the frat boys with a decent right. I turned to see what was happening with Doug, and saw him take a smack to the side of the head. On the point of impact he had a strange, almost detached smile on his face, like a baby held in his mother's arms. There was the crunch of bone on bone, the peaceful, satisfied smile, and Doug crumpling into a little heap at his attacker's feet. Who then leaned over, vomited into the bushes, and passed out, saving me the trouble of finishing him off.

The girl was no more sober than the frat boys. She crawled back out onto the sidewalk in a drunken, four-legged, crablike move and fell to one knee. I tried to help her up, but she refused, eventually righting herself. She muttered something incoherent and careened down the sidewalk toward the dorms. Strictly speaking, I should have seen her home. But I didn't, because Doug Townsend, her forgotten, damaged hero, was groaning at my feet, and between the two of them, I knew who I was going to help.

No charges were filed. The girl let the bastards off, which wasn't a big surprise. But that night was a watershed for me. It was the moment adult concerns first entered my young mind, the time when my adolescence ended and I discovered that some things were truly important and worth fighting for. On that night I left Dothan and high school behind, and I decided that if there were frat boys and drunk girls and people as weak and brave as Doug Townsend in the world, there were going to be quite a few thorny inequities to be made right. In a fit of hubris that makes me wince to remember, I decided there and then to become a lawyer, and I've been trying to save people ever since.

We stayed friends through Doug's last year, but we lost track of each other when he graduated. I plowed through my prelaw classes, went to law school, and ended up in Atlanta. I had nearly forgotten about him, until from out of the blue, he called me. He sounded changed—agitated, like he had drunk too much coffee—but a lot of time had passed, and for all I knew, I sounded different, too. We agreed to meet for lunch. The man who walked into the restaurant that day was a shell, a thin capsule of skin barely capable of holding a human soul. Thanks to my new, inglorious line of work, it took me about ten seconds to recognize his problem: Doug Townsend had become a drug addict. From his amped-up, frazzled look, the problem was some kind of uppers.

The first question was how, and he refused to answer. He had more immediate needs: he had been arrested. Bail had been set at two thousand bucks, and scraping his ten percent together for a bondsman had tapped him out. He had nothing to pay an attorney, but I agreed to defend him. He was, after all, the reason I became a lawyer in the first place.

It was a first offense, and I pled him down, like most of my clients. There was time served, a stern lecture, a hand-slap. None of which served to slow down his wicked meth habit. He relapsed; he relapsed again, risking serious incarceration. But a few months later he had made a turnaround. He had reached the all-important bottom, and, having discovered himself doing and thinking and feeling things he would have previously considered unimaginable, he was determined to live. Weeks had gone by, his resolve taking root. The last few times I had seen him, he had seemed like his old self again; full of dreams and optimism. Now, inexplicably, he was dead.

All of this was on my mind as I drove across Atlanta toward Doug's apartment. I exited off I-75, making sure I didn't miss the Crane Street flyover. If you miss it, you and your formerly valuable car are dumped into one of the largest public housing developments in the Southeast: the McDaniel Glen projects. I took the flyover and looked down on the Glen—as it's referred to by its lamented residents—as I headed farther south. I had been there a few times with a uniform, looking for testimony on a drug case. But I never went there without a good reason.

Townsend's place was only two streets past the Glen, which gives you a good idea of where it stood on the desirability scale. It was called the Jefferson Arms, but it sure as hell wasn't Monticello. It was a sad, two-story brick affair, and the row of beat-up cars out front in the middle of the day told me welfare checks paid a lot of the rent. But even at the Arms there were better and worse units, and Townsend had told me how he had swung a second-story, corner two-bedroom: wiring up the manager with untraceable cable TV. A lot was possible in the black market economy if you had skills.

I pulled into the lot, parked, and looked around. Doug had drifted a long ways down from the college kid with dreams I remembered. He had started and failed at a couple of small-time computer businesses, but his bad habits undermined any chance of success. I pictured him fighting his demons, struggling against the compulsion, then giving in at last. I could picture him going out and making the buy, or worse, uncovering the secret stash he had kept around. I could see him talking it over with himself, going through the self-justification, the delusion. Then the whack, the horrible surprise, the struggle to breathe.

I stepped out of the car and walked up to Doug's door. I took a breath, turned the key, and walked into the very still, very quiet airspace of a dead man. I looked around cautiously. The first thing I noticed was the neatness of the place. The police usually left a place worse than they found it, but Doug's apartment was immaculate. There was something defiant about how everything was in its place, especially so close to the chaos of the Glen. I could picture Doug straightening the magazines on his table, just before he decided he couldn't live another second without meth.

The furniture was predictably worn: a sofa, a couple of chairs, a coffee table. I opened the miniblinds, standard apartment issue. The window unit air-conditioning snapped on, probably from the blast of warm air when I opened the front door. I'd have to get the electricity turned off, one of the little details nobody thinks about when a loner dies. Electricity, phone, cable, magazine subscriptions, all continuing on, oblivious, all assuming that the body of Doug Townsend was still warm, still filled with moving fluids, still dreaming up business plans for his little company.

I walked into the kitchen, looking at the three dishes and the silverware resting upright in the drying rack. I opened up a cabinet: Rice Krispies, Ramen noodles, couscous—which made sense, because Townsend, like a lot of computer geeks, had been slightly built, as thin as a blade of grass. I moved through the apartment, switching on lights. The first bedroom was fairly large, and doubled as his office. The bed sat simply on a frame, no headboard, but the covers were pulled taut. At the other end was a desk with a computer, a file cabinet, a couple of phone lines. It dawned on me that the phones were probably not in the database of Southeastern Bell; or if they were, they were being paid for by some company that had never heard of Townsend. We had talked a few times about hacking, and Townsend had played it down, but like I said, he had skills.

I opened the filing cabinet, flipping through the index tabs of projects. I knew Townsend had been busy; as a part of his defense we had discussed his business prospects at length. Townsend was pure geek, down to the cheap rayon shirts and the black-frame glasses: he once told me he could write programming code like some people hum melodies; almost improvisationally. As expected, there were a good number of folders, and I opened a few at random. Most were bids for programming work: small-time stuff, customizing databases or a networking job for a small business. Townsend could have done far better working for a company that could handle the business end, letting him be free to create. But he kept dreaming about a big score, coming up with something revolutionary enough to flip or turn into an IPO.

Junkies fall off wagons. It happens every day. But after two years of defending small-time drug offenders, I had acquired a nearly infallible sixth sense about that. Not just me; everybody who works in Odom's court gets it. We wonder: *Is this guy fucked? Or will he look back on this as his dark hour, secure and comfortable on the other side?* I can see it in a defendant's eyes, in his posture, in his damaged, unredeemable soul. Judge Odom could see it, that was certain. He was doing his best to hang on to a shred of humanity, a pretty considerable task for somebody who spends eight hours a day sending people to hell. But the fact was, for some defendants, he and everybody else knew he was merely delaying the inevitable. Maybe there's a value even in that.

Doug Townsend was as firmly on the side of life as anybody I'd seen. For one thing, he had something other than drugs that he was passionate about, a key survival ingredient. Watching him talk about computers was like watching Sammy Liston talk about Blu McClendon. I used to buy Doug coffee just to listen to him rattle on about what the future would look like. He saw a world where computers were in everything, even people, making sick people well, making old people young.

I cast off the memory and went back through the living room to the remaining room, the back bedroom. I opened the door and stopped cold. Most of the opposite wall was covered with pictures of a woman. I walked in, drawn forward by the photographs. The woman was black, late twenties, and strikingly beautiful. *What the hell is this?* The pictures were a mélange, some professional, others cut out of magazines and newspapers. At first I thought she must be an actress, because several of the photographs had been taken on stage, the woman dressed in a variety of ornate costumes. But one picture was a simple headshot, and there was writing beneath the photograph: *Michele Sonnier, mezzo soprano.* I stared at the photo, thinking. *Michele Sonnier. Sounds French, upper crust. Or maybe a stage name.*

I tore myself away from the pictures to get a handle on the rest of the room. There was a twin bed, a small chest of drawers, and an old, wooden desk and chair. I pulled out the chair and sat down. There were some papers on the desk, business ideas, mostly, and some printouts of what looked like computer code. To my surprise, there was a framed snapshot of the woman—casual, with a lot of people in the background. She was smiling, although it wasn't clear if she was smiling at whoever took the photograph. I looked for an inscription, but there wasn't one. I tried to place the face, but I drew a blank. *If you had ever met this woman,* I thought, *you would definitely remember.* I set the photograph down and opened the main drawer of the desk. Inside were the usual paper clips, rubber bands, and pens. To the left was a row of three more drawers. The first had more nondescript papers; the second was nearly empty. I opened the third, the deepest one, and saw it was nearly full; on top was a stack of rectangular papers tightly bound by a rubber band. I picked up the packet and pulled off the bands. *Airplane tickets. A lot of them.*

I fanned out the tickets on the desk before me. *Baltimore. New York. Miami. San Francisco.* I counted the tickets, then sat back, stunned. Townsend had made more then twenty trips in the last year, all paid for in cash. After defending him so many times, I was intimately aware of his finances; basically, there weren't any. *What is this? And how the hell did he pay for it?*

I reached down into the drawer, pulling out the rest of the papers. On top were at least twenty more photographs of Sonnier, again, from a variety of sources. I looked through the remaining papers: more Sonnier, everywhere I looked. Beneath the photographs were press clippings and performance reviews, almost all of them glowing. Mixed in was a set of playbills, all apparently originals. I glanced back through the plane tickets, mentally calculating the cost. *Maybe the guy was stealing for* this, *not meth. Maybe she was his real drug.* Eventually, I was just seeing more of the same; not content with one photograph, Townsend had accumulated several copies of each. I stuffed the plane tickets and photographs in my valise and stood up. *This is beyond being a fan. This is definitely some kind of obsession.*

The computer equipment was the only thing of obvious value, so I loaded that into the trunk of my car. Knowing Doug, it would take a security expert to find out what was inside it, and I didn't have those skills. I walked back to the apartment and stood in the doorway, taking a last look. *Opera. Rich people's music.* Connecting that world to the world of Doug Townsend was a problem I had no idea how to solve. I locked the door, recognizing it as a gesture of futility. It wouldn't take long for people to figure out Townsend wasn't coming back, and his place was certain to be looted.

I got back in my car and started the drive back toward town. *Presumed suicide.* That was what Sammy had said was on the police report. Which brought me back to why Doug would have picked that moment to throw his life away. No matter how hard I tried, I couldn't make that make sense.

The thing about cops is that half of them are crooked. I don't mean bad crooked, just bent a little. I'm not judging them. And I'll tell you who gave me the fifty percent figure: a cop. But here's the deal: they're so underpaid that most of them work extra security jobs just to make ends meet. Say you're young, you've got some school loans, and you can choose between a hundred hours of babysitting the parking lot of a rowdy bar in the middle of the night, or just picking up the two thousand dollars in cash that's staring you in the face in the crack house you just busted. Like the man says, you do the math.

Which is not to say there aren't good ones. Billy Little, who was handling the paperwork for Doug's death, is one of those. Here's how much I trust him: I'd pour him two bottles of Scotch, tell him I'd screwed his mother, hand him a loaded gun, and beg him to shoot me. Billy Little plays by the rules.

Don't let his name confuse the issue. He's Samoan—the whole dark hair, slightly wide face thing—and six-two, every bit of two thirty-five, and percent body fat of six, maybe. He could subdue the average man while calmly eating a cheeseburger. He started in the projects, on the bike squad; incredibly enough, they patrol those monstrosities on bicycles, at least during daylight hours. That way they can haul down alleys that cars would never make it through. After about three years of that, Billy finished college at night with a business degree and made lieutenant. He made detective four years later. He was barely thirty, and as far as I was concerned, he knew more about the Atlanta drug trade than anybody in the department. He was, as they say down here, the shit that killed Elvis.

Billy worked at the Atlanta PD headquarters in the City Hall East building, which is where I went from Townsend's place. He always looked impeccable, and when I went to see him about the Townsend case it was no different. He looked like he was ready for a screen test, in nicely pressed tan slacks, a green golf shirt, and brown leather shoes. Predictably, he was also up to his well-muscled arms in paperwork. When I walked into his office, he looked up and smiled. "What brings you to the slums, Jack?" he asked.

I shook his hand and took the chair opposite his desk. "Sammy Liston tells me you're handling Doug Townsend's case," I said. "Anything special I should know about it?"

"Other than the fact he's dead?"

"Townsend was a friend."

Billy's smile faded. "Sorry, Jack. I didn't know that. Were you guys close?"

"We were friends in college. I lost track of him, until recently. His life took a bad turn, and he needed a lawyer."

"So you were representing him?"

"Yeah."

Billy nodded. "Well, it's still provisional, but it looks like he killed himself."

I reached in my pocket and pulled out the picture of Michele Sonnier. "Does this ring any bells?"

Billy glanced at the photograph. "Yeah. I heard about that. Lots of pictures, apparently."

"You know her?"

"The lady's an opera singer. Supposedly she's some big thing in the music world. She's also the wife of Charles Ralston."

I looked up, surprised. "Charles Million-Dollar Ralston?"

"No, Charles Hundred-Million-Dollar Ralston. But yeah, he's the one."

"No kidding." I stared at the picture. Ralston, founder and CEO of Horizn Pharmaceuticals, was a poster boy for the new African-American South. Pick your stereotype, and he blew it up: he was a superbly educated scientist, an impressive speaker, and a brilliant, hard-nosed businessman. And he was just as aggressive about solving Atlanta's social problems, even when it bought him controversy. He had achieved near-sainthood with the city's peace-and-justice activists by instituting—and eventually paying for with his own money, because he couldn't find anybody with the guts to push for it in city hall—a clean-needle exchange program in the projects of Atlanta. Considering he had made his fortune with a hepatitis treatment, there wasn't much point in arguing about whether or not his motives were pure. Every addict he saved cost him a potential patient, and that wasn't the kind of behavior most people expected from pharmaceutical companies. Not content with his millions—the kind of money most people find sufficient—he was preparing to take his company public and walk away with something under a billion. Everybody decent in Atlanta business was pulling for him to make a killing, simply because he had a superb track record of reinvesting in the cultural and social life of Atlanta. Billy was eyeing me warily. "So what's his wife got to do with Doug Townsend?"

"Her picture was all over Doug's apartment." I pulled out the plane tickets and tossed them on Billy's desk. "These were in a drawer. There's about twenty of them."

Billy looked through the tickets a moment, then back at me. "That wasn't in the report."

"Tell me something, Detective. Can you get your people to give a damn about the underclass in this city for a change? You know, actually do a real investigation?"

"Don't start with me, Jack. The city's broke, and I'm doing the best that I can."

I let it go, out of respect for Billy. "The trips correspond with her performance schedule," I said. "They were all paid for in cash."

Billy drummed his fingers on his desk. "Looks like he was a fan."

"You could say that. He had built a chapel to Saint Sonnier."

"My daughter's got four pictures of some rap group up on her wall."

"Come on, Billy. This is a little different."

Billy leaned back, considering. "Are you saying your friend might have been harassing her? Trying to get too close?"

I thought back, remembering Doug getting decked by frat boys for trying to protect a woman. "Doubtful. Not his personality."

"Okay. Then unless it's illegal, it's not really my problem. People have weird passions."

I paused, thinking. "What did pathology say?"

"The EMTs did a Valtox on the scene, confirmed the cause of death. The medical examiner on call came out and saw no reason to contradict."

"So that makes it a suicide?"

"No, the formal victimology report we get back in about a week makes it a suicide. Believe it or not, we actually have procedures for that kind of thing."

I nodded. "So until then he's in the morgue?"

"We'll hold the body until the report's final. But look, Jack, I've read the preliminary. There was depression, a long history of drug abuse. There was the failed businesses, no apparent social life. Frankly, not a lot to live for."

"No suicide note?"

"Big myth, that. Suicide notes are pretty rare. More likely it's a DBS."

"DBS?"

"Death by stupidity," Billy said quietly. "Accidental, in other words. Happens all the time." He opened a file and flipped to the EMT report. "No evidence of foul play, no body trauma. No forced entry, no upset furniture, items of value left in place. So sure, we're going to jump through the hoops. But unless you have some connection between these tickets and your friend's death, I'd say you're back at square one."

"Did your guys take anything from the scene? Any papers or anything?"

"Lemme see." Billy flipped further through the folder. "Yeah, a few things. The drug stuff, obviously. But papers . . . yeah, a notebook. It was on the floor, right by the body."

"What's in it?"

"Blank, except for one page." Billy pulled a cheap notebook out of a plastic bag. He opened it up and showed me the first page. There were three letters printed near the top.

"What's that?" I asked.

"'LAX.' Los Angeles Airport. Makes sense, considering how much flying he was doing."

I looked at the letters, thinking. "Whoever wrote it didn't have the best penmanship in the world. Pretty bad scrawl."

"Yeah."

"So are you following up on it?"

"Follow up on what? Last time I checked, the airport's still there." Billy looked at me sympathetically. "If the final victimology report turns up something, you'll be the first to know." He rose. "Let's you and me get a beer sometime, okay, Jack? Maybe over at Fado's."

I rose with him. "Yeah, we'll do that," I said. I started to leave, then turned back. "You said they found drug stuff," I said. "What kind?"

Billy looked back down at the folder. "Looks like the usual stuff, couple of vials, a needle . . ."

I stiffened. One thing Townsend had told me repeatedly: he had never shot up in his life. "What did you say?"

"A needle."

"There's got to be some mistake there. Doug was terrified of needles. He told me that himself. About a hundred times, actually."

"A lot of people get over that when they're addicts," Billy said, shrugging. "Anyway, maybe it's all he could get his hands on."

"He lived a block from the Glen, Billy. He could have just stuck his head out of the window and yelled, 'Drugs, please.'"

"Look, I'm not arguing with you, but the fact is we found the guy with a hole in his arm and a needle."

I shook my head. "It's like a phobia, Billy. If a guy's going to kill himself, he doesn't pick that moment to get over a lifelong fear. And anyway, Doug was a meth addict. You don't even have to inject it, for God's sake."

Then Billy Little looked up in surprise and said five words that changed everything. "Who said anything about meth?"

CHAPTER THREE

"TWO THINGS CAN LEAD A MAN to make a commitment."
Sammy Liston, clerk of the court of Judge Thomas Odom, was
chewing steak, which always put him in a good mood. He was not
yet seriously hammered, the place where his brain became inert;
instead, he was in the in-between state, which made him philosophical. He was holding forth on why I should follow up on Doug
Townsend's death. "Number one: intuition."

"You mean like, 'The second I saw her, I knew she was the girl
for me'?"

"No, I mean like, 'The second I saw *it*, I knew *it* was the right
pickup truck for me. Or maybe the right dog.'"

"What's the second thing?"

"Huh?"

"You said there were two things."

Sammy cut a perfect slice of sirloin off his plate and held it on
his fork up to the light. "Beef," he said. "It's what's for dinner."

"Sammy."

"Oh, yeah. Loyalty, Jack. The code of honor."

"The guy thing. Somebody messes with your friend, you got to step in."

"Damn right." Sammy took the bite, chewing slowly, savoring the taste. Suddenly, his face turned serious. He chased the beef down with a swallow of Seagram's. "But how do you know?" he asked. "That he got messed with, I mean. The guy was a junkie. Bad things happen."

"It was fentanyl, Sammy. Fentanyl."

Sammy whistled. "No shit. I didn't know that." He took another bite. "What's fentanyl?"

The trouble with alcohol—and I say this with considerable personal experience—is that it makes people feel like they're getting more brilliant, when it's actually having the opposite effect. "Fentanyl," I answered, "is the place where man's capacity for greed and disregard for human life reach their current apex. Some pharmacist figured out that by subtly changing the molecular structure of morphine, he could make something four hundred times stronger. It's so powerful there's only one legitimate use for it, and that's anesthesia."

"Wow. You mean it just knocks your ass out."

"Yeah. But then some inventive little bastards started cutting it down for recreational use. You know, playing with the parameters. And what they got was real smooth, both up and down. No jagged edges. The perfect drug, especially since you didn't have to deal with any of those nasty people in South America to sell you the raw materials."

"The ones who kill you if you piss them off," Sammy said.

"Yeah, those."

Sammy shrugged. "But?" he asked.

Sammy was referring to the one immutable law of pharmacology: there is always a "but." No matter how perfect a drug seems, a down side always lurks. It's as if God has decreed that pleasure and pain must be kept in a cosmic equality. The more beautiful a drug makes you feel, the more certainly it will crush you in the end. "But," I said, "it's so powerful that a typical dose weighs about the same as a postage stamp. It's almost impossible to cut accurately, especially by somebody who's probably an addict himself. And if you get too much, it does the damnedest thing."

Sammy shrugged. "It kills you?"

"If you take enough. Mostly, it just makes you wish you were dead."

"Which means?"

"It gives you an instant case of advanced Parkinson's disease."

Sammy stared. "Jesus, Jack. You serious? What is that, some urban legend, right? Like a street myth?"

I shook my head. "Billy Little laid it out for me. People are screwing around with the universal elements, Sammy, cosmic forces. They're going into labs and making things the human body never encountered before. All hell is breaking loose."

"Yeah, but, shit, Jack. Parkinson's?"

I nodded. "The whole range of tics and tremors, the uncontrolled bodily functions. Everything. Nobody knows why, except maybe the bastard who invented it."

"That sucks."

"There's more."

"Than that? Jesus, Jack."

"You can't tell it from heroin by looking at it."

"It looks like heroin?"

"Not like heroin. *Exactly* like heroin. But it's between four and six hundred times more powerful."

"So if you think it's . . ."

"If you think that, it's over before you get the hypodermic emptied. Billy told me he had personally seen some very dead, very rigid, bodies with the needle still stuck in the arms."

"You think that's what happened to Townsend?"

I shook my head doubtfully. "I don't buy it," I answered. "He'd never done heroin before, so why start now? Doug had turned his life around. He'd been clean for months. And anyway, he was terrified of needles."

"What do you mean?"

"I mean he had a pathological fear of them. So nobody is going to tell me that he did that to himself."

Sammy picked up his glass of whiskey. He stared into the amber liquid thoughtfully, turning it in the dim light of the restaurant. "Jack," he said quietly, "your buddy got messed with."

I leaned back in my chair. "Damn right."

I showed up at work early the next day, determined to find what I could about Doug's last few days. To me, the issue of intentional suicide was almost incidental; break it down far enough, and nobody takes fentanyl who doesn't, somewhere in his damaged subconscious, want to die. And obsessed or not, I didn't believe it about Townsend. I was no expert on suicidal tendencies, but Doug had been more upbeat the last few weeks than I had ever seen him. And besides, I knew enough about depression to know that the biggest impediment to killing yourself is fear. Doug would have chosen another way, rather than try to conquer his lifelong phobia of needles at the very moment he was working up the courage to end his life. So when I got back to the office, I knew I was going to find out more about Michele Sonnier. Not that I thought she had anything to do with Doug's death. She was about as far away from fentanyl and the Jefferson Arms as scented candles. But that didn't change the fact that she was all I had.

I looked over at Blu, who was staring intently at a magazine. It seemed unfair to disturb her. She appeared perfectly content and still, filling her head with horoscopes and articles like "When Sisters Want the Same Man." For a while, I was going to just let her indulge herself at ten bucks an hour. It seemed glorious, in a way, making someone happy at such a small cost. But after a while I said, "Blu, do me a little research, will you?"

My secretary looked up at me, all shiny hair and perfect skin. "About?" she asked.

"About an opera singer. Michele Sonnier."

Blu tilted her head. "I don't really picture you at the opera."

I blinked several times to prevent myself from staring. The truth is, I could never tell if she was secretly a genius, or a spectacularly beautiful kind of blank slate. Sometimes, I pictured her walking out of my office, lighting up a cigarette, and saying to herself, *Damn, I was great today.* "Okay," I asked, "where do you picture me?"

Blu scrunched up her face in thought. Even scrunched, it was still beautiful. "More like at a baseball game," she said.

"Baseball game."

"Yeah. Eating a hot dog."

We lapsed once again into silence. Blu, satisfied with her contribution, looked back down at the magazine and flipped the page. I watched her for a moment, started to speak, shrugged, and walked into my office. I flipped on my computer and typed Sonnier's name at a search site. The page disappeared, and after a few seconds I saw the results: 639 matches. *Mrs. Charles Ralston definitely gets around.* I glanced over the lead lines until I saw what I assumed was the singer's home page, MicheleSonnier.com. I clicked on the URL and watched a photograph of the singer scroll down across my screen. It was one of the photographs I had seen at Townsend's apartment, Sonnier in a long, flowing, lamé dress, very elegant. I flipped down the screen to the bio and started to read. *Michele Sonnier is the most exciting female voice to have emerged in the opera world in the last ten years. The only child of a doctor and a teacher, she demonstrated her prodigious talent at an early age. After graduation from the Juilliard School, she debuted by winning the Metropolitan Opera Competition at 21. The prize, a solo concert at Carnegie Hall, began her storied career. Her operatic premiere a year later with the San Francisco Opera was a triumph. In defiance of her age, she has performed principal roles at the Metropolitan, La Scala, and the Kirov. In a recent European tour she was compared to her idol, Marilyn Horne.*

Together with Ralston, they would make a hell of a power couple. Ralston's money would give them entrée to the new social elite, while Sonnier's artistic endeavors would give them entrance to the old. I flipped down the screen to Sonnier's schedule. I scanned down the list of concerts for that year, comparing the dates with the plane tickets I had found at Doug's apartment. *January 17, Portland, Oregon.* I riffled through the tickets, eventually landing on a Northwest flight from Atlanta to Portland. I checked the date: *January 17.* I went through several other dates—two in February, the first in

New York, the second Miami. Both corresponded to Townsend's tickets. After confirming a handful of others, I leaned back in my chair. *What the hell is this?* I scanned Sonnier's schedule into the future; one date in particular caught my eye: *June 15, Atlanta Civic Opera.* It was four nights away. After the Atlanta date there were some scattered concerts, but all far away. I called the contact number. A nice-sounding woman answered, very polite and educated. "Atlanta Opera."

"You've got a concert with Michele Sonnier coming up, is that correct?"

"Yes, sir. Bellini's *The Capulets and the Montagues.*"

I paused. "Like Romeo and Juliet?"

"Yes, sir."

That sounded promising. At least I knew the story. "In English?" I asked.

A slight pain crept into the woman's voice. "No, sir. In Italian, with English supertitles."

"Is Sonnier singing the part of Juliet?"

"Ms. Sonnier will be singing the part of Romeo."

I paused, playing back the sentence in my mind. "Romeo?"

"That's correct, sir. It's a trouser role." The voice on the phone explained, "In certain operatic scenarios the roles of men are sung by women. Bellini's opera is one such scenario."

I paused, thinking about how much I didn't know about opera, and how little interest I had in changing that fact. I don't have anything against heartache music, but I don't see why it has to be two hundred years old. Give me a beat-up John Prine cassette and a full tank of gas, and my musical needs are pretty much met. "How much are tickets?" I asked. "In the lower range, I mean."

"Well, the less expensive seats are sold out."

That could be a definite problem; I was scraping by as it was. "So what's left?"

"The least expensive seats available are forty-six dollars."

I did some quick math: ninety-two dollars, plus parking and dinner, that was a couple of hundred bucks for an evening. There was a time when spending two hundred bucks on a night out was something I did just to remind myself I could afford it. Those days had never seemed so distant. But just going to the opera wasn't enough; I wanted some personal contact. "Will Ms. Sonnier be signing any autographs?" I asked.

"Sir?"

"If somebody wanted to get his program signed. Ask her about opera, that kind of thing."

"We are offering a special opportunity for serious fans of Ms. Sonnier."

"What's that?"

"Are you a serious fan of Ms. Sonnier, sir?"

I looked down at my screen and read out loud, "Ms. Sonnier is the most exciting female voice to have emerged in the opera world in the last ten years."

The voice seemed pleased. "Excellent. Ms. Sonnier has been kind enough to agree to a private reception after the concert for a select group of her most devoted admirers. It's a fund-raiser for the opera company. Champagne and hors d'oeuvres will be served. I feel certain she would agree to sign your program."

"What does something like that cost?"

"Two hundred and fifty dollars per person," the woman answered. "However, this price does include premier seating for the concert."

"Two-fifty. Each."

"That's correct."

I very nearly thanked the woman and got on with my life. If I had, everything would be different. Life can turn on a dime. But I had just found out that what looked like the most important thing in Doug Townsend's world had been a woman I didn't even know existed. Looking at Sonnier's schedule, she wouldn't be appearing in Atlanta again for at least a year. I made a snap decision. "Hey," I said, "you guys take Visa?"

The first thing to do was to get a date. I needed a foil, someone who could help me blend into conversation. You can't go to a high-roller opera event alone. My social life at that point consisted of drinks with Sammy Liston. The reason that I hadn't dated anybody since losing my job was simple: there was nothing in my life that I needed to keep more completely under control. I learned that lesson the hard way, because it was letting my feelings go that had cost two people everything they had.

I looked out at the golden expanse of hair that was the back of Blu McClendon's head. *Notlikely.com*, I thought. Although she would be perfect. Young, gorgeous, and certain to wear the kind of dress that made women over forty nostalgic for their better days. I thought about a girl who worked down at the courthouse; not bad, but lacking a certain ability to impress . . . I looked back at Blu.

Although I was almost as deeply enamored by looking at Blu McClendon as Sammy Liston was, I had never laid a hand on her. I called her "baby" and "sweetie" on occasion, Neanderthal epithets that she accepted with utter aplomb. The great thing about Blu was she understood that kind of thing. Calling a woman like her "baby" kept me alive in a way, while I figured out that I was still a man, even though I was starting my life over. Nevertheless, asking her out on a date was new territory. It would be confusing, out of character. I wouldn't want her to get the wrong idea. Although I'd never seen her out, I had to assume that if I wasn't rich I would at least need to be a bodybuilder. Of course, in the back of my mind I also thought that if she got the wrong idea and said yes, that would be even worse. A love affair between the two of us would devolve into a soap opera by lunch the next day. But the truth was I needed her. My days at Carthy, Williams and Douglas taught me that a girl like Blu is the definitive ice-breaker. You can walk up to any group of men you want, and they are certain to open their little circle, smile, and immediately start to figure out what the hell you have going for you. I sat there and worked on the problem for a little while, until the obvious hit me, and I thought of an invitation for the gorgeous Miss McClendon so perfectly conceived it could have come from Michelangelo's chisel. "Blu," I asked, "how would you like to meet a lot of very rich men?"

CHAPTER FOUR

THE DAY BEFORE THE OPERA, it suddenly occurred to me that something like a private reception for a famous diva was probably a black-tie affair. Thanks to an unfettered ability to spend during my days at Carthy, Williams and Douglas, I possessed a nice Hugo Boss tuxedo, which I had worn exactly twice. I put it on and stood in front of the mirror in my bedroom. I always dressed up well, which is a genuine asset for a lawyer. Some guys put on a suit and still look as if they just got back from recess. But in the halls of Carthy, Williams and Douglas, it was look sharp or get lost. I resolved on the first day to look like I'd never heard of Dothan, Alabama, much less grown up there, and I was fastidious about getting my off-the-rack suits tailored to perfection. I stood there gazing at myself, but it was a long ways from narcissism. It was more a deep sense of the incoherence of the moment. If I closed my eyes and suddenly opened them again, I could almost believe I was still at Carthy, Williams and Douglas. I looked just as rich, just as successful, and just as dangerous.

About six o'clock I drove over to Blu's place, Hunter Downs.

Hunter Downs is the kind of apartment complex that is full of people who aren't rich yet but have good enough credit to create a reasonably convincing facsimile. It's a gated complex, and all the buildings are built on a grand scale, like divided-up southern mansions. The parking lot was a sea of shiny, waxed, depreciating debt.

I knocked on Blu's door, and after a few seconds, she opened it. Something transforming happens to a woman when she dresses up, even to one who starts out looking like Blu. Her gorgeous hair was up, little wisps of blond falling down onto her smooth neck. She was wearing pearls, which tapered down into the most perfect, restrained view of mother Mary's cleavage you ever saw in your life. And the dress—if you can imagine rich, azure satin painted on the ideal woman to cut your hair, especially if she did a lot of leaning over you when she did it, you get the idea.

At dinner she prattled on about Romeo and Juliet, which pleased me. I didn't even lament her insistence on a thirty-four-dollar bottle of wine that I had seen two days earlier for twelve bucks in a liquor store. Refusing her would have upset her worldview, and I didn't want to do that. "I just love Romeo and Juliet," she was saying. "It's the most tragical thing ever." She sipped her thirty-four-dollar wine. "Why can't people just let other people love the people they want?"

"I know, baby. How's your fettuccine?"

"Yummy."

"That's good."

"Jack, don't you just love Romeo and Juliet?" Blu asked.

"I suppose."

"You suppose?" She seemed offended by my indecision.

I shrugged. "These days Romeo and Juliet would just go to Vegas and get it over with. They'd tell their parents to go jump in a lake." Blu looked crestfallen, and I started to feel bad I had popped her romantic balloon. "Your hair's beautiful tonight," I said. "How do you get it to do that?"

She smiled and forgave me. "So why the opera?" she asked.

"A case," I said. "We're here to learn about the main singer, the great Michele Sonnier."

"The one you said is singing Romeo."

I nodded. "Listen, Blu, you've got a lot of men asking you out, right?"

"Um hmm."

"Let me ask you something. What would you think if you went into some guy's bedroom and discovered a bunch of pictures of you?"

Her expression clouded. "How many pictures?"

"Maybe, like, twenty."

She grimaced. "I wouldn't like that."

"But wouldn't a part of you be flattered?"

She shook her head. "Two or three, maybe. Not twenty."

"How about those guys who have seen *Cats* four hundred times? They're harmless, right?"

"I don't know," she said. "I wouldn't want to talk to somebody like that. There's got to be something wrong in the head."

We talked through dinner, Blu sharing her insight into male obsession, which was probably a topic she knew something about, judging by the attention she was receiving at the restaurant. We finished up and I paid the bill. Then we made the short drive to the opera, which was at Atlanta's grand old theater, the Fox. There was a group of impeccably dressed people milling around outside, mostly smokers getting their fix before the three-hour show. I gave my $250 tickets to the usher, and he led us down the long aisle toward the front.

The Fox is an Atlanta landmark, a tribute to the whimsy of people who can afford to pay artists to adorn their world. Walking into the hall, you are transported to a Moroccan castle, and the stage is surrounded with turrets and stone walls as high as the ceiling. Above you stars twinkle, as though you had come upon the place in the midst of an Arabian night. In other words, describing the distance between the world inside that theater and what was happening on any given night in the worst parts of Atlanta was a problem for a theoretical physicist. I'm not saying it was wrong to spend so much on making a place like that beautiful. I'm just saying that if you grew up in the projects and somehow, lost in that desert sunset, you found yourself inside the Fox, you would have had your worst fears confirmed about what life was like on the other side.

Thinking about Doug at an event like that bothered me, in a way. I didn't mind my junkies hard and pissed off; you pled them down, they did some time, life went on. But opera was rich people's music, and I figured Doug would have been as enamored with that whole cultured life as he was with Sonnier. I pictured him at all those concerts, dressed up, in the one decent jacket he owned, walking through the lobby, taking his seat, feeling for a couple of hours like he didn't live in the Jefferson Arms. In my mind I could see him trying to engage somebody at intermission in one of those concerts, saying, "Isn't it thrilling?" It made me want to weep.

Blu and I sat down in red velvet seats and waited for the show to start. In view of how little I could afford the evening, I was hoping at best not to be bored out of my mind. But for two hundred and fifty bucks you get to sit so close to the stage you can almost feel the air vibrate from the singing. The orchestra played an overture, and suddenly there were a lot of people on stage in beautiful costumes. The set—a villa in Italy, represented by faux structures and enormous background paintings—was effective, too. I settled in for the performance.

It was a few minutes before Sonnier walked on stage, and when she did, she got a huge ovation. She didn't acknowledge it; she was locked into her character. This was my first chance to look her over, and at least for this role, she seemed very different from her pictures. For one thing, she was dressed like a man, with her hair combed back, wearing pants, and a vest to hide her breasts. To my surprise, she had it down; even the walk looked real. Most women, when they try to walk like a man, fall into some exaggerated John Wayne swagger. But Sonnier understood the nuance of it: acting like a man isn't sticking out your chest. It's subtler, and comes from below the waist. So I could almost buy it, until she opened her mouth. Then she just started making the most beautiful, most spectacularly female sound you can imagine. Bellini didn't even

try to write low notes for the character to make her sound more
masculine. So Sonnier just sang away, making love to Juliet,
but sounding like the most beautiful woman in the world.

It was a long ways between that opera and where I grew up in
Dothan, Alabama. I admit I have no idea what I was supposed to
feel, sitting there watching actors in painted faces and Renaissance
costumes sing to each other. At first, hearing Romeo sing like a
woman was disorienting, but after a while, I started to think about
him in a new way. That high voice made him sound like a kid,
which is what he was in the real play. For some reason he's never
played by sixteen-year-old boys. Usually there's some guy in his
twenties or even thirties up on stage. That makes a big difference.
Because listening to this high voice come out of Michele Sonnier's
exquisitely fine, delicate face, I started thinking that Romeo was
just a victim of the system, powerless and naïve. He wasn't any
stronger than Juliet, really, because they were both just children. He
was fighting forces a lot bigger than he was, and he didn't even
know it. Every time he opened up his mouth you realized right
away that he was doomed. They gave the part of Romeo's dad to a
big man with a booming, low voice, which made it worse. When
Romeo tried to argue with him about how stupid it was that the
Capulets and the Montagues were always fighting, it was like
watching a pebble bounce off a wall. There was no way in hell
Romeo was going to get Juliet. It was the perfect story, as far as I
was concerned. All that misery—they endured every bit of it just
because they couldn't let things go. If they had stripped things
down, probably something else would have come along. They
would have hurt like hell for a while, but eventually married somebody else and got along fine. But they couldn't do it, so two people
died.

Even though everybody knew the story, a lot of people broke
down when Romeo drank the poison. Sonnier was more than just
a singer; she was a brilliant actress. Her Romeo was so fragile and
vulnerable that it was like watching a real person face his moment
of death. There were no histrionics, no ham-fisted overacting. She
was singing with deadly seriousness, her voice a candle flame in the

hall. She was facing the sober realization that there are times when so much has gone wrong that life is no longer worth living. That's the real point of that story, in my opinion. Even when the cost of believing is everything, some people just can't help themselves.

Then it was over. Blu had completely broken down, so I gave her a couple of minutes to collect herself. Most of the crowd was moving back out into the lobby, except for the people like us with the expensive tickets. We were led out a private exit to the parking lot. I led Blu in the dark to the car, and we drove over to the Four Seasons for the reception. It was only fifteen blocks, so we got there in about five minutes. At that point, I did Blu a favor: we didn't valet park. I didn't want to shortchange her, because she looked fantastic. It would have dampened her entrance for everybody to see her climbing out of my dented LeSabre.

We followed the crowd up a big staircase, and I could feel Blu getting excited looking at all the rich guys. They were looking at her, too, I can tell you that. You never saw so many men casually looking over the tops of their drinks in your life. We moved off into the sea of tuxedos and evening gowns.

Everybody is very polite at these kinds of soirees. They're also cliquish, but not necessarily from bad intentions. It's more an inevitability. The people in that room were the financial backbone of Atlanta, so they had a lot in common. You could feel it when they greeted each other. A million golf games, cocktail parties, and bank loans were silently implied with every handshake. The wives—about ten years younger than their husbands, on average—didn't fit the trophy girl stereotype, either. They seemed gracious and accomplished. But I wish you could have seen the McClendon effect that night. It was magical, let me tell you. I never had so much small talk in my life.

Even though I had nothing against it, I wasn't there in order to present Blu to Atlanta society. What I really cared about was finding out everything I could about Michele Sonnier. It was surprisingly hard to get the conversation onto that topic, mostly because the women wanted to know about Blu's dress and the men were working out how to get it off her. All I could pick up was that

Sonnier was big stuff in the opera world, groomed for success from her earliest beginnings. She had grown up in Manhattan, entered Juilliard as a prodigy, and left two years early to pursue her singing career. She had been a star from the second she set foot on a stage. There was one hell of a lot of conversation about something else, though, and that was Charles Ralston and Horizn. The men were talking strategy about how to get in on the Horizn IPO at the offering price, something only the true insiders could pull off. The consensus was that getting in early was going to be richly rewarded. They all had their brokers poised on quick-release triggers.

Eventually, I felt obligated to cut Blu loose. She couldn't really troll with me around, and she'd done everything I could have asked. So I patted her arm and she moved off, smiling like a fisherman who's just discovered a stocked bathtub.

The food table wasn't bad; there was a nice spinach pasta in pesto, stuffed mushrooms, and little shapes of things wrapped up in tortilla. I milled around for a few minutes, then grabbed another glass of champagne. After a while I spotted an impeccably dressed man circling Blu. He was plainly working up an approach to speak to her. I started counting down from ten. When I got to seven, the man slickly sidestepped a slow-moving waiter; on five, and I have to admit he did it beautifully, he picked up two glasses of champagne without breaking stride; on one, he touched her arm and handed her one of the glasses. *Touchdown.* Something about him looked familiar; I had the vague recollection I had read about him in the newspaper, and that he had been doing something unpleasant to someone, but I couldn't remember what. What wasn't in question were his intentions toward my secretary: he was a player, in every sense of the word. I could see it all over him as he stood chatting amiably with Blu. He was smart, and he was probably a hell of a businessman. But no matter what else was going on in his life, it was less important to him than getting laid.

I stood watching them for a while, fascinated. Even though I figured Blu could pick up on the guy as well as I could, context is everything. Here, at an opera party wearing a two-thousand-dollar suit, he came off like a slightly miniaturized James Bond. Millions of dollars have that effect. Without the money, he was just a guy in khakis with a five-year-old Corvette hitting on girls at an airport bar. I gave Blu a couple of minutes to be adored and walked up beside them. The man's smile transformed itself into plastic. "Jack Hammond," I said. "Nice to meet you."

"Derek Stephens," the man answered. He was about forty-five and smelled vaguely of cigars. "I was just talking with your—"

"Cousin," I said. "Blu McClendon, my dear cousin from Arkansas." Stephens narrowed his smile and moved incrementally closer to my secretary.

"Mr. Stephens here was just telling me he's an attorney, like you, Jack," Blu said. "He works for Horizn Pharmaceuticals. They're sponsoring Ms. Sonnier's tour."

"So this is a big night for you," I said.

"It's a big night for the Atlanta Opera, Jack," Stephens answered. I could feel him sizing me up. "So you're a lawyer as well." The accent was New England, upper crust. "Which firm?"

There were only about four correct answers to that question for a guy like Stephens, and Jack Hammond and Associates wasn't one of them. "Solo practitioner," I said. "Criminal law, mostly."

At that moment, I could feel Stephens starting to work out how to get Blu away from me with the minimum of fuss. People can look right at you, acting like they're interested, but if you look deep into their eyes, you can see wheels turning while they work out some completely different problem. Even though he didn't give a damn what the answer was, he asked me, "Are you a fan of opera, Jack? Or of Michele in particular?"

"New to both," I answered. I was actually sort of enjoying talking to the guy. He had so much fast track all over him he smelled like a race car. "How about you?"

"I serve on Atlanta Opera board," Stephens said. "Which is amusing, since I know nothing about opera."

"Apparently, you had other qualifications."

Stephens reluctantly pulled his gaze off Blu and put it back onto me. "A redneck hillbilly could get on the board of an opera company, Jack, if he was willing to write a sufficiently large check."

He looked over at Blu's glass, which was not quite half full. *Time's up,* I thought. "Ms. McClendon," he said, "let me get you a refill."

"I'll go with you," Blu said, beaming. "I'm dying to try those little squares with cheese in them." And like that, they were gone.

I felt protective over Blu, but I didn't, strictly speaking, know enough about Stephens to worry. And I had never discussed Blu's dating life with her, mostly because it was more pleasant to imagine she didn't have one. But I didn't get a chance to think about either, because at that moment, the atmosphere in the room was disturbed.

I turned, feeling something behind me; there was a round of applause, and then the seas parted. Sonnier and Ralston entered the room like royalty. Ralston was tall, at just over six feet, with a lean, athletic build. A slight peppering of gray in the hair was the only clue to his age; I had heard he was in his early fifties, but he looked considerably younger. His skin was dark but smooth, a gift from spending most of his life indoors. His wife, however, had been transformed. The tragic figure of Romeo had revealed herself to be an absolutely gorgeous woman who was ignoring the dress code with sublime indifference. She was dressed in the ersatz-ghetto fashion favored by twenty-something designers looking to make a name for themselves: in other words, in two thousand dollars' worth of clothes designed to look like twenty. Surrounded by tails and evening gowns, Sonnier appeared in the ballroom of the Four Seasons in tight, low-rider black pants, a tight-fitted tangerine top cut low to show a modest but perfectly formed cleavage, bare arms, and a thin slice of midriff. Her hips were encircled by a silver chain belt, each link carefully given an aged, dull patina. Her belly button was pierced, and her left ear had three small hoop earrings, all the same distressed silver as the belt. The effect was edgy, but she pulled it off with so much insouciant confidence that everyone else in the room seemed overdressed, as if she alone had read the invitation correctly. And her skin: my impressions from her photographs at Townsend's place had been right. She was chocolate and luminous in the lights of the ballroom. Standing on black platform shoes, she couldn't have made more of an entrance if she had ridden into the Four Seasons on a Harley.

Ralston was instantly waylaid by a bunch of suits; the money in the room was the hungry variety, always ready to attach itself to a rising tide. Ralston shook hands with a vaguely interested expression, clearly aware of his position. This was the new black elite: the wife, nonconformist and artsy, the husband, impeccably dressed in Armani, playing the white games to perfection.

The couple separated quickly: a handler led Michele into the crowd, while Ralston headed in the opposite direction. The crowd near her fell on her in that polite way rich people have who are in awe of artists, especially when they've paid two hundred and fifty bucks for the chance to demonstrate they have good enough taste to deserve being wealthy. I let Ralston go; I was there for Sonnier. I followed from a distance, watching her greet people who were loving her safe, calculated funkiness.

Of course, from my perspective, that of the Fulton County Criminal Court system, Michele Sonnier was about as street as Girl Scout cookies. Nobody who sings opera is going to carjack you, if you see what I mean. And being black, I figured she knew that as well as I did. Which made me figure that what I was watching was a little bit like opera itself. She could have broken out into song right where she stood, something about liberal white guilt and a mule and forty acres. But instead, she just worked the room, letting her new best friends tell her how great she was.

I watched her for a while, wondering about Doug Townsend and his obsession. In her shoes she seemed tall, but I estimated she was only about five-six without them, with slender but well-defined arms. She had fine features, delicate and precise, with dark brown eyes, and spectacular hair—brunette, with reddish-auburn highlights—swept back into a ponytail. *My God,* I thought. *Poor Doug never had a chance.* Finally, she made it around to where I was standing, and she stopped in front of me. Her handler was speaking to someone a few yards away; for the moment, we were alone. She put out a beautiful, smooth hand. I took it and introduced myself. "Jack Hammond."

"Hello, Mr. Hammond." Her voice was cultured, educated.

"Quite a soiree they put on for you."

She smiled. "I hate all this fuss."

"At least it's in your honor."

Her smile softened. "I suppose."

"So how do you like playing a man?"

"A challenge, but well worth it in this case."

"Because of the music?"

She shrugged. "The music's alright."

That was a little bit of a surprise. "Just all right?"

Sonnier leaned forward. I couldn't place her scent; it was citrus, subtle and clean. "I'll let you in on a secret, if you promise not to tell," she said.

"I think I can manage that."

"This particular opera's not one of my favorites. I do it for another reason."

"What's that?"

"The rather delicious irony, obviously."

"I'm a little new to the opera thing," I said. "Maybe you could paint me a picture."

She leaned closer. She was being confidential as hell. I had to remember to ask Blu what that scent was. "That surprises me, Mr. Hammond," she said. "You have the air of an expert."

I smiled, I was also slightly annoyed, because even though I knew she was playing me, I couldn't help falling for it. She knew that I knew, too, and it didn't make any difference. Really beautiful women get to break all the rules. I couldn't take my eyes off her glossy, soft mouth. She was actually starting to piss me off, until I realized it was Charles Ralston I was hating, simply for being the guy who got to kiss her. "In Shakespeare's time," she said, "Juliet was played by a man. All the roles were. Women weren't allowed on stage."

"Yeah, I'd heard that. So that balcony scene . . ."

"Two Englishmen pretending to be Italians making love."

"Right."

"So naturally Bellini, who really was Italian, evened the score. He wrote Romeo played by a woman."

"You're saying it was some kind of art-world revenge?"

Sonnier laughed, and the pure loveliness of her voice sent a shiver up my spine. She leaned closer and whispered, "Mr. Hammond, if you're going to understand anything about opera, there's something you should remember. No matter what else is going on, the theme is always revenge."

Before I could respond, her handler appeared. He took her arm and started to lead her away. It was now or never as far as Doug Townsend was concerned, so I put out my hand and stopped her. For a second, she was suspended between the two of us, an arm extended in each direction. "Yes, Mr. Hammond?" she asked.

"I was just wondering if you had heard the news about a mutual friend of ours."

She looked surprised. "Who's that?"

I knew this was it. If the name didn't register, it was back to the office with nothing to show for my five hundred bucks but some crab cakes, a night of Italian music, and my first crush on a black woman. I looked her in the eyes and said, "Doug Townsend."

Nothing altered in her face. Not a muscle moved. Her smile was just as inviting as ever. "I don't believe I know anyone by that name," she said. "I'm sorry."

"No, that's okay," I answered. "Actually, it's a good thing."

The guy pulled on her again, but I could feel the muscle in her arm tighten. It was subtle, but it's the kind of thing you pick up on when you're surrounded by liars every night and day. At least for the moment, she wasn't going anywhere. "And why would that be?"

"Because he's the former Doug Townsend," I answered. "Sort of a messy drug overdose, four days ago."

Her smile, which one second earlier had been warm flesh and blood, was set instantly in concrete, freeze-framed into a pleasant deadness. She knew him, alright. The great Michele Sonnier knew Doug Townsend just like I did.

CHAPTER FIVE

AFTER TWO YEARS IN Judge Thomas Odom's court, I can state one thing with utter certainty: people do not lie to hear themselves talk. They lie because there's something they don't want you to know badly enough to trade a little bit of their integrity to keep you from finding that thing out. So when I showed up at work the next day, the central question on my mind was what that thing was for Michele Sonnier, and exactly how much of her integrity was she willing to exchange to keep it private. Of course I hit an immediate wall, namely, that Doug's life and Michele Sonnier's were separated by an insurmountable cultural and financial gulf. She spent her time with European-born conductors who spoke four languages, and Doug spent his living next door to hell, trying to avoid jail. But the fact remained that more than twenty times he had crossed that gulf with plane tickets, each one paid for in cash. That, combined with my absolute certainty that Sonnier had lied about knowing him, was more than I could ignore.

Wanting to unravel the connection between Sonnier and Doug

would not, however, find me the money I needed to pay Blu's salary at the end of the month. So in spite of how much I wanted to spend time finding out what happened to Doug, the fact was I was grateful to head to the office to get ready for court. Thanks to the largesse of Sammy Liston, I had two cases on Judge Odom's docket that morning.

As usual, I met both clients shortly before trial. The first, a second offense for simple possession, earned the girl—twenty years old, pretty, with the nearly ubiquitous sad eyes of most of my clients—time served and a stern lecture from Odom, which consisted of such classic lines as "I don't want to see you in my courtroom again, Miss Harmon" and "If I hear that you've missed one of your drug tests, I'm going to have to send you away." All sleepwalking stuff.

It was an indication of the sheer repetitiveness of my practice that I looked forward to representing Michael Harrod, my second case of the day. His crime was utterly forgettable—petty larceny, otherwise known as shoplifting—but for once, it wasn't about drugs.

His appearance caused a bit of a stir, which is an accomplishment, considering who gets dragged through Odom's court. Harrod had spiky hair, like Joseph's famous coat: a haircut of many colors. Piercings were numerous and painful-looking. His T-shirt, emblazoned with the logo of the band Nine Inch Nails, was badly in need of washing. But in spite of all this, he was about as scary as an altar boy. At five foot six and 130 pounds, the T-shirt covered a nearly concave chest. His skin, having apparently been deprived of sunlight for the last several years, was as pasty-white as unbaked bread. He looked nervous, like a sharp noise would lift him off the ground. I met him outside the courtroom about an hour before his trial.

"Jack Hammond," I said, introducing myself. He looked at me warily, not returning my handshake. "You're Michael Harrod, correct?"

"Call me Nightmare," he said.

I laughed. I didn't mean to, but the comic effect of combining his name and his appearance was irresistible. "Is that Mr. Night-mare?" I asked. "Or is Night your first name and Mare your last?"

Harrod gave me a narrow, suspicious look that was, I suppose, what he could muster up for arrogance. "Look," he said, "what do I have to do to get out of this? That's what we're here for, right?"

I have nearly infinite patience with smart-ass clients. I simply remind myself that most of them have never had a father, and that they are minutes away from meeting Daddy. Daddy, in this case, is Judge Thomas Odom. The judge is a decent man but he can turn on the gruff act when appropriate, and coming as it does from a man with the power to send you to hell, it's usually fairly effective. It usually takes about two minutes for a first-timer's expression to be transformed from detached asshole to abject, whimpering baby. They crawl back through time, past their victimized adolescence, right back to the moment when a real father would have smacked their butts a little bit and put an end to their insolence problem. "Well, Nightmare," I said, "even though I personally find you charming, you might start off with a little attitude adjustment. Judge Odom likes his victims a little more contrite."

Nightmare looked me over again, thinking. I could see him putting some things together. "I can smile," he said. "I can bow and scrape for the man."

"In that case," I said, "now would be the time." I opened up his folder. "I've been looking over your file. Apparently you got confused about the correct time to pay for some items in a Radio Shack."

Nightmare shrugged. "I needed 'em," he said. "They weren't worth much."

"Then why not pay?"

"I didn't have it. Anyway, that's old economy."

"Old economy?"

Nightmare gave me a tired look. "Look, you're old economy. You're a dinosaur." He gestured around him at the walls of the courthouse. "This whole system is."

"Dinosaurs, are we?" I was starting to seriously dislike this kid.

"All of this, governments, court systems, armies, wars. It's all old economy. It's dying, and you don't even know it."

"I guess not paying for things, that's new economy?"

"Do you have any concept of how fast the world is moving? You think I should shut down my whole world over five bucks' worth of electronic parts?"

I looked down at the folder. "That's what this is about? Five dollars?"

"Yeah. Five bucks' worth of connectors for an autodialer."

"What's an autodialer?"

"It dials. Automatically."

"Computers, you mean."

"Maybe," he said.

At that moment I realized that Nightmare was really just a thief, the only difference being that his breaking and entering was electronic. Ten seconds after that, a little plan hatched in my head, most of which entailed getting him as far into my debt as possible. After last night, the particular expertise I suspected he possessed I needed very badly. Since he didn't look like the type of kid who would do me any favors, I would have to make him owe me. I figured that would take about five minutes.

I looked across the hall at the assistant district attorney assigned to the case, who was talking to an overweight, dark-haired man of about thirty-five. I watched them for a couple of minutes, thinking. I stood up, and Nightmare flinched back about six inches from the sudden motion. I stared down at him, thinking about how many times he must have had his ass kicked in grade school. But I had no doubt that he was as dangerous with a computer as a prizefighter was with his fists. As much as I hated to admit it, the kid was right; the world *was* changing, and little pissed-off Nightmares like him were about to inherit the keys to the kingdom. But not quite yet, and in the meantime, I needed a favor from him. "Listen to me," I said. "I'm sure I'm going to love the world you and your techno-anarchist buddies are building. But right now, the old economy is going to put your spindly little butt in jail if you don't do exactly—and I mean exactly—what I tell you to do."

"Nobody is going to put me in jail over five bucks."

"Michael . . ."

"Nightmare," he corrected.

I sort of leaned on him then. I wasn't angry, I was just in a hurry. If the case was called and we got before Odom, it would be too late. "Okay, Nightfuck, I don't really care what your name is, you need to listen to me now, because I'm old economy, and that's whose house you're in right now." I took out my billfold, pulled out a ten-dollar bill, and pressed it into Nightmare's hand. "Come here," I said, "and do exactly what I tell you for a couple of minutes."

Nightmare shoved the bill into his pocket and followed me across the hallway. The dark-haired man glowered. "That's him," the man said. "That's the little snitch that stole from me."

"You?" Nightmare sneered. "Radio Shack is a multinational corporation that doesn't know you exist. They spend more on toilet paper than your annual salary."

I took Nightmare's arm and squeezed it hard. He winced, which didn't surprise me, since he was about as muscular as a toothpick. I nodded hello to the DA, then turned toward the dark-haired man with a smile. "And you are?" I asked.

"Vincent Bufano," he said. "I'm the manager of the Radio Shack."

"Mr. Bufano," I said, "Mr. Harrod here has something he wants to give you, and something he wants to say."

Bufano looked at Nightmare, who was squirming under my grip. "Give him the money, Michael," I said. He started to speak, but I pressed my middle finger into the center of his bicep so hard he almost wilted. He reached his free hand into his pocket, took out the bill, and handed it over to Bufano. "And now Michael has something he wants to say," I said. "Tell the man you're sorry, Michael."

Nightmare started to pull back, but I had my grip on him. He muttered something under his breath, and the man just sneered. I dug my thumb into the side of Nightmare's arm, getting the nail right in there between the tendons. Then I started to work my thumb back and forth. Nightmare straightened up. "I'm sorry," he said clearly. I pressed harder. "Terribly, terribly sorry."

"And it will never happen again, isn't that right, Michael?" I moved my thumb slowly, filleting the muscle.

"No," he said. "Never again. Not ever."

Bufano looked at Nightmare for a while, eyes peering out above his ample cheeks. He folded the bill, put it in his pocket, and said, "Don't come in my store again, boy." I looked over at the DA, who had watched all this with a bemused smile. She wasn't any more interested than I was in dropping a couple of hours on the case.

"I suppose the state can drop the charges," she said, "if Mr. Bufano has no objection."

Bufano looked at Nightmare, obviously enjoying his penny-ante justice. "He can go," he said. "But like I said, he don't come back in my store."

"So our business here is concluded?" I asked the DA.

She laughed. "Yeah." She looked at Nightmare. "You can go."

I didn't release the grip on Nightmare's arm. "Say thank you to the old economy, Michael," I said.

"Thanks," he muttered. With that, I let him go. He walked back across the hallway, rubbing his arm. I shrugged at the DA, shook Bufano's hand, and walked back over to Nightmare. He looked up at me, grimacing.

"That hurt, dude," he said. "That was uncalled for."

"Let me ask you something," I said. "Which economy is jail in?"

"Nobody was going to jail. Not over five bucks."

"You might be the future, Nightmare, old pal, but you don't know much about the Georgia legislature."

"What does that mean?"

"That means that a lot of good old boys decided that the judges were a little lax around here, and they made sentencing mandatory for petty theft. You would have got a five-hundred-dollar fine, plus court costs."

"I don't have five hundred dollars."

"Plus costs."

"I don't have that, either."

"In that case, you would have got ten days, and served six."

"For five bucks?"

"Ain't the old economy a bitch?"

I could see the wheels turning in Nightmare's head. Gratitude was a relatively new concept for him, so it took a while. "Hey, man," he said after a few moments, "thanks."

"No problem."

"No, really. That would have sucked."

"I agree."

"Look, I don't have the ten bucks."

"You can pay me back another way."

Nightmare's face covered itself in detached indifference. "Payback," he said. "You suck, man."

I got a faraway look in my eye. "I can just picture you in the county lockup, where they sleep in cots, thirty to a room. Young skinny white kid like you would be really popular about two A.M."

Nightmare trembled involuntarily. "All right, what is it?" he said. "But don't make it suck."

"It's right up your alley," I said. "I want you to break into a computer, and I want you to keep your mouth shut about it."

Nightmare's expression transformed itself from insolence, through surprise, and stopped on a crafty, thin smile. "Hell, yeah," he said. "I can do that."

CHAPTER SIX

LIKING DEREK STEPHENS would never have been easy. His particular brand of effete arrogance was never my cup of tea. It's nothing personal; it's just that back in Dothan, we would have kicked his ass a little bit, to give him perspective. Then he could still run off and rule the world, but without feeling quite so entitled. So I didn't really want to see flowers from him on my secretary's desk when I got back to the office around noon. Blu played it off, saying he was just being sweet, and besides, for a guy like him, they cost practically nothing. She probably had no idea how true that was; if he was rich now, it was a safe assumption that he held stock options in Horizn that were about to make him fabulously wealthy. But in my experience, thirty-six roses is a pretty big statement, whether or not they're yellow.

She did look happy, though. Atlanta is full of women living papier-mâché lifestyles, a thin copy of the life they mysteriously expected to become real at any moment. They looked like millionaires, they acted like millionaires, they hung out around millionaires whenever they could, only they didn't actually have any money. To women like that, guys like Derek Stephens had the approximate value of plutonium. He was priceless.

Which was not, frankly speaking, my own current value in that world. Lawyers who have fallen from grace and barely hung onto their licenses trade somewhere in the penny stock range. I watched Blu smell her roses for a while; then I went to lunch with Sammy at The Rectory, the bar where he used to pour drinks but now buys them.

Sammy's life has proved an unlikely theory to be true: if you are miserable, try killing what you want. You'll probably discover you are much happier. It was like that with Sammy. After spending a few years serving drinks to lawyers and eavesdropping on their conversations, he determined to join their ranks. In other words, he started hoping. He got dreams. Unfortunately, the only law school that would accept him met at night in the basement of the YMCA. Considering the academic flotsam and jetsam with whom he studied, he might have taken the fact that he graduated nineteenth out of a class of nineteen as a bad omen. During his first year after law school he failed the bar three times. In desperation, he took a job as the clerk of Judge Thomas Odom in the Fulton County Criminal Court. Within one week he made a startling discovery: all he had really wanted in the first place was to wear a decent suit and have a little power. In other words, he was happy as a clam. See what I mean? It's like my mantra: Strip it down and let it go. Sammy holds in his Seagram's-stained hands the destiny of several hundred actual lawyers, which pleases him greatly.

By the time I showed up at The Rectory, Sammy was a couple of drinks ahead of me. It didn't do his appearance any good. He had the kind of relaxed body that was passable in high school, but which was gradually relocating to less attractive places. He was getting the frat-boy fifteen-years-later look, which was exactly who he was. He still had a quick smile, but you could see a hundred or more drinking nights that had somehow turned into mornings in the widening face, the short brown hair starting to thin, the pale shine in the cheeks. He had partied hard for about as long as the human body can absorb, and unless he took immediate action, he was going to look middle-aged in about six months.

The first thing I did was buy him a drink. He was going to drink anyway, and I try not to make value judgments on what people call recreation. I was going to pump him for information and then ruin his day, so the drink was the least I could do. Sammy, oblivious to the bad news I had for him, was dividing his attention equally between staring at the ice melting in his glass and the waitress who was working the opposite side of the bar.

"Sammy," I said sitting down, "you and your imagination should get a room."

"All I have are dreams, Jackie. Don't take those from me."

"Well, if you'd get out more, maybe get a little exercise."

"Yeah, I'll do that." He took a swallow. This was going to be a three-drink conversation, unless I hurried things along. "You ordering anything?" he asked.

"Yeah, I'm getting the club on rye," I said. "Listen, I need to ask you a couple of things."

"Such as?"

"Such as, who's running McDaniel Glen these days?"

Sammy paused, thinking. "That would be Jamal Pope."

"Pope, huh? I thought he was—"

"Nope. He's at large, as we say. Doing a brisk business, so I hear." He took another sip. "You still got that Doug Townsend thing on your mind?"

"Yeah," I answered. "I want to find out where he got the fentanyl, maybe get a lead on his state of mind."

"I don't believe Mr. Pope is the talkative kind."

"Safe bet. Anything I can use to leverage him?"

Sammy leaned back in his chair. Thankfully, he hadn't had enough Seagram's to cloud his thinking just yet. "Maybe," he said after a while. "You got that scrawny bastard Keshan Washington off a couple of months ago, didn't you?"

"Look, Sammy, it's not my fault a busted taillight doesn't give a cop the right to strip-search a motorist."

"Yeah, and your clients are all just misunderstood. But the

point is, thanks to you Mr. Washington is once again free, walking the streets of Atlanta. Care to guess what he's doing with his time?"

I looked at Sammy. "Working for Jamal Pope?"

"Bingo," Sammy answered. "So the way I see it, the king of the Glen owes you. He'll probably buy you dinner."

"Thanks, Sammy," I said. "Anything I can do for you?"

"Get the Bill of Rights repealed? We got bad people to put away."

"I'll work on it."

Sammy took another big gulp, draining his glass. "Listen, Jack," he said, "if you're going over there, why not have Billy Little send a uniform with you?"

"Sure, Sammy. That'll open up Mr. Pope like a sieve."

"All right, go get yourself killed. See if I care." Sammy flagged the waitress down, and she walked over to our table, all short skirt, long legs, and emphatic breasts. She looked about twenty, in contrast to Sammy's thirty-five. I ordered my sandwich, and Sammy said, "Two more," holding up his fingers like a peace sign. "And one for yourself, sweetheart."

To her credit, the waitress didn't roll her eyes. She just smiled and glided off, probably thinking about her lifeguard boyfriend. But Sammy was about thirty seconds away from forgetting about her, because that's how many seconds it was before I dropped my bomb on him.

"Listen, Sammy," I said, "tell me what you know about Derek Stephens."

Sammy shrugged. "Stephens? Why do you ask?"

"Just tell me."

"Spends his time up in federal court, destroying people for Horizn Pharmaceuticals. It's mostly intellectual property stuff, people encroaching on Horizn patents."

"Yeah, that's getting sticky these days."

"He's not around much, but there's a buzz when he comes in the courthouse. Mostly because everybody hates him."

"Because?"

Sammy raised his eyes. "Classic asshole. Treats everyone like shit, and gets away with it because he's so brilliant. That's the kind of thing that gets annoying after a while. Hits on everything that moves, too."

"So he's not married?"

Sammy shook his head. "He's got a girlfriend, though you'd never know it to watch him operate. But I've seen her three, maybe four times. Real sophisticated. I think she's a college professor or something. Anyway, she walks like she's got a Ph.D. up her ass."

"Uptight?"

"Oh, yeah. Walks on tiptoe, like she doesn't want to get her feet dirty. She's got a ring, too."

"You mean they're engaged?"

"Guess so. But she's high-maintenance, lemme tell ya. That's probably why Stephens likes slumming at the courthouse for secretaries." Sammy took a drink. "Even though they know he's a jerk, they still follow him around like puppy dogs. Then comes the crying."

"Maybe he's a challenge. You know, tame the beast."

"Yeah, and maybe it's because he's rich. Do you know he actually got somebody to give him an underground parking pass so he wouldn't have to expose his damn Ferrari to the elements?"

"He drives a Ferrari?"

"Only on perfect days without a visible cloud. But that's not the point."

"What is the point?"

"The point is that Derek Stephens can basically talk anybody into anything."

I nodded, picturing him putting his powers of persuasion to work on Blu. I shouldn't have interfered. At least I had no specific right to do so. But opportunity so perfectly aligned rarely presents itself. When it does, you almost feel obliged to take advantage of it. Having done my due diligence, I opened the bomb-bay doors. "Sammy boy," I said, "you have a new reason for living."

"That so?"

I nodded. "From this moment forward, there is only one reason for you to get up in the morning, and that is to make the life of Derek Stephens miserable."

"Why the hell would I want to do that?"

I took final aim and released the weapon. "Because the person he's going to make cry next is the woman you love, Blu McClendon."

Sammy Liston's face told me everything I needed to know. There was going to be war.

My secretary deserved to know about Stephens, but that didn't nominate me to perform that task. For one thing, the employer-employee relationship didn't cross that line. Second, she was twenty-eight years old, spectacular to look at, and I had to assume getting hit on by attached men was a natural occurrence in her life. The truth was, I didn't know how seriously to take Stephens. Between chewing up weaker competitors for Horizn and hitting on all the other women in his life, he was probably pretty busy. At any rate, I had just let Sammy loose on him, which would keep him busy for a while.

My own business at that point was to find out what I could about how Doug had died. Working on a case with practically nothing to go on is simplicity itself. All you can do is shake whatever trees you have, and hope to God something falls out. No matter what had happened to Doug, one thing was certain: somehow, he had got his hands on enough fentanyl to end his world. So at two-thirty that afternoon, I took the Ralph Abernathy exit off I-75, turned left on Pollard, and headed toward the McDaniel Glen projects.

Atlanta is a city in the constant throes of simultaneous destruction and reconstruction, and the area around the Glen shows that as clearly as anywhere. While limitless sums of money continue to flow ever northward, everything built in midtown seems to have turned to rust. Some sections—located far away from the suburbs, with their soulless starter mansions and perfectly manicured lawns—are classic ghetto, with buildings that look like they belong in bombed-out Beirut. Then came the Olympics, and a black mayor insisted that the worst of the housing projects be torn down and the residents moved farther south. As a result, a few whites are returning to reclaim and gentrify the largest and most structurally sound of the midtown monstrosities. Old factories are being turned into chic lofts, while rusting cars and condemned houses sit a block away. The result is an odd kind of incoherence as classes of people are crushed together. The Olympic investment skipped McDaniel Glen; it survives, stoic and unchanged, a relic from an uglier time. It is not, generally speaking, a happy place. A breeding ground for hopelessness, crime has settled on it like a plague.

You approach the Glen by turning left at the Pollard Funeral Home— your first sign that all is not well—and drive past Our Lady of Perpetual Help, a retirement and nursing home also with a name made for the area. You cross Pryor Street and drive past the lucky few who grabbed the nouveau-project units built for the Olympics, decent town houses with vinyl siding and reasonable landscaping. But one more turn brings into view the looming, ten-story-tall sign for the defunct Toby Sexton tire factory. The enormous, empty buildings beneath the sign are crumbling, windowless, and covered with graffiti. This is the point where anybody who doesn't live in the Glen silently mouths the words, "No, no, no," and begins looking for an inconspicuous way to turn around. The self-preservation instinct, having been finely tuned by a thousand television shows and news reports, is dropping adrenaline into the bloodstream at its maximum rate. You pull into the first place you can, nice and casual, like you just dropped off some muffins to your cousins. Then you head back toward the well-patrolled, clean parts of Atlanta.

Most of that adrenaline would have been wasted. Everybody knows to be afraid in public housing, but people who never go there are usually afraid of the wrong things. Assuming it's daylight and you aren't driving a four-wheel-drive pickup with Confederate flag license plates, there's not much chance of getting capped. In battered Buicks like mine, people try to sell you drugs for the first ten blocks, then just think you're a social worker and pretty much leave you alone.

The monster of McDaniel Glen is *sameness,* numbing and soul-killing. The place is enormous, over eleven hundred units of identical, reddish-brown brick housing. Block after block, alley after alley, each the same drab, filthy brick, the same rusting cars parked along the streets, the same sad laundry hanging on wires. If you lived there long enough, even dreaming of the outside world would be difficult.

I drove down the Glen's main street looking for Pope, letting the eyes of dealers and bored kids linger on me until I pulled in and parked. I had a pretty good idea where to find him. If by some chance your life should become utterly insupportable and you need public housing, let me give you the rule: every large project has a federal Metropolitan Department of Housing Authority office, and the closer a unit is to it, the better. Those units actually get repaired occasionally and the streetlights mostly work. This is because when the big shots come down from Washington, they like to see the Rainbow Coalition walking around paradise arm in arm. So try to get next door, if you can.

Because of Pope's position in the local drug trade, he is at the top of the food chain in his small, scary world. Jamal is also a government employee, so you can be gratified in the knowledge that you pay his salary. He earns $640 a week as head of maintenance for the Glen, and there is a watermark picture of the Capitol Building of the United States on his twice-monthly check, rendering it impossible to counterfeit. This technological feat is wasted on Jamal Pope, however, because $640 is tip money compared with $30,000 tax-free a month he earns as the CEO of McDaniel Glen Pharmaceuticals.

You might think that there is no job in the world of government housing that you would like to have. But give yourself a second, and look deep into your heart. If you would rather be the king of hell than a slave in heaven, then you should reconsider. The power you would wield as the head of maintenance at an MDHA property is as close to total as available to a person outside certain third world countries. The job requires that you live at the property—a definite negative—but on the plus side, the sad, dilapidated, scary world inside those walls would be your oyster.

The source of your power is a set of keys. Behind the doors they unlock is every lightbulb, every doorknob, every faucet fitting, every gallon of paint, every foot of electrical wire, every toilet bowl gasket, every sheet of drywall—and, since we're in Atlanta, let us not forget every *air conditioner* available to the ever-needy residents over whom you rule. The shine on your ass would be world-class. And this would only be the beginning of your power, because of a second set of keys.

This other set of keys—the nexus of your power—opens the doors to the apartments themselves. You can enter any of the dwellings at will. To disrupt lives—or suddenly make them easier—is at your whim. And yet you have still more power. This is because of the third set of keys, the keys that open the empty apartments.

In the drug business, both supply and demand prefer to be hidden. You, the keeper of the keys, provide the space for each: showroom floor to the left, abandoned crack house to the right. You are wholesale, you are retail, you are middleman. Jamal Pope controlled it all.

I got out of the car and started walking down the street that ran beside the MDHA office. Within twenty steps, Pope, keeper of the keys of the Glen, turned a corner to look at me warily, trying to decide if I was a customer or a problem. He had a solution to each. Jamal didn't look rich. In his late thirties, he wore baggy work pants and a light blue T-shirt that said, *Glock Around the Clock.* We stood about twenty feet apart, staring at each other.

"You hear about Doug Townsend?" I asked.

Pope looked at me awhile, ignoring the question. He wasn't threatening; he was just looking for clues. Then a smile broke over his face. "You that man got Keshan out the joint." It was nice knowing that doing my job well earned me the gratitude of someone like him. But for the moment, he was available, which was what mattered. "Haven't seen my boy Dougie for a while," he said. "Outta circulation."

"Half a gram isn't exactly your kind of transaction," I said. "Maybe you could ask down the chain a ways."

"Point-four-nine," Pope corrected. I nodded; anything under

point-five-oh was considered a misdemeanor citation, with time served. Most deals carefully avoided going over that line. "I'll ask Rabbit," he said. "He'll know."

Rabbit, Pope's chief runner, had gained his job, his nickname, and his renown in the projects for instantly killing a man who tried to usurp Jamal's territory. He earned a thousand dollars a week, and had as many as ten runners working under him at any one time, an interoffice delivery service exchanging money for packages. He was also Pope's fourteen-year-old son.

Pope pulled out a cell phone and punched numbers, apparently to a beeper. About five minutes later Rabbit came from around a corner on a bicycle. "Zup?" he asked. He was a typically eager, hyped-up kid, except that he was dead behind the eyes. In spite of the heat, he wore a black, long-sleeve Oakland Raiders sweatshirt.

"Answer the man's questions, niggah," his father said. "Till I say stop."

The father-son affection was touching. "Listen, Rabbit," I said, "I'm trying to find out what happened to Doug Townsend."

"He dead." Rabbit shrugged. "Been dead a few days now."

"That's right. I need to know if he was clean or not the last few months. Don't worry, it's not about you. I just need the straight answer to find out about Townsend."

Rabbit looked over at Pope, who nodded his head. "He was clean," Rabbit answered. "I hadn't seen his white ass in some time."

"You never saw him try to buy fentanyl, did you?" I asked.

Pope interrupted with a scowl. "I don't move that kinda product," he said. "It don't help to kill your customers."

"I'll tell you one thing," Rabbit said. "My boy Dougie was into some weird shit."

"Weird?"

"Shit I couldn't even pronounce. Real pharmaceuticals. It ain't a buzz, I know that."

"What do you mean?"

"I mean I know everything a motherfucker can take, and I never heard of that shit. Smoke, crack, crank, fine. Otherwise, get off my stoop." In spite of his age, Rabbit was completely comfortable talking product, as though he were a businessman discussing wheat prices in the Ukraine.

"He had fentanyl in his system when he died," I said. "So you don't sell it. But suppose somebody did want to find some. Where would he go?"

Rabbit thought a minute. "Up Dilaudid Avenue, I guess."

I nodded; Seventh Street, nicknamed Dilaudid Avenue because it was where all the prescription business went down, was across town in the Perry Homes projects. "You know anybody over there?" I asked. Rabbit looked at his father again, but this time Pope shook his head. "Somethin' like that pretty tough to find on the street," Rabbit said vaguely. "That prescription shit ain't our line of work."

I thought about the possibility of Townsend selling drugs himself, a theory I could never afford to completely discount with an addict. If Doug had gone that route, it would certainly have taken him into a deeper darkness. I turned toward Pope. "If somebody wanted to get into prescription pharmaceuticals at the wholesale level, where would he go?"

Pope thought a moment. God only knew what kind of experiences and connections were running through his mind. His solution, however, was simplicity itself: "I'd find myself a doctor," he said. "Make a deal, you know, a percentage. Or better, a pharmacist. Depend on how much you want to move. A pharmacist could move more."

I nodded. "I don't suppose you know of any—"

"Time's up," Pope said. He didn't seem angry; it just didn't help business to have a white guy with a battered briefcase standing next to him.

"Last question," I said. "You ever hear of a woman named Michele Sonnier?"

"Sonnier?"

"Yeah. She's a singer. Opera."

Pope grinned. "Hell, yeah. I just love to chill to that shit." He looked at my Buick. "See that, niggah?" he said to Rabbit. "That what the straight life get you." The two of them laughed, and disappeared back into the labyrinth of identical rectangular buildings.

CHAPTER SEVEN

SO IT'S COME TO THIS. *My life is a cautionary tale for a drug dealer's son. Beautiful.* With Pope's words ringing in my ears, I put myself into that detached state of indifference necessary to endure Atlanta's midday traffic. I took the on-ramp back up onto a bloodless, choked artery of concrete built before the word "freeway" became ironic. I was heading south, back toward my office, but I had a stop to make first. I had a shrine to visit. A shrine with a congregation of one.

I trickled south at thirty miles per hour, watching Atlanta change beneath my tires. After ten minutes I turned off on Martin Luther King, a busy urban thoroughfare that takes you deeper into the older, crumbling part of Atlanta. I stopped at a little shop and picked up my usual parcel, my offering. After a few more minutes I climbed the long, gentle hill leading to Oakland Avenue, and saw the entrance to my destination.

Like the street, Oakland Cemetery was named for the trees, and was built long before an acre of untroubled Atlanta grassland cost half a million dollars. To walk onto its serene expanse—dotted with graceful water oaks, hemlocks, and gently bowing willows—is to step out of the clanging noise of messy urban living and into a place where your soul can rest. It is nearly ninety acres of tranquility, and it offers the solitude of a place steeped in history. Whatever noise intrudes from the surrounding city dies in the tremulous leaves of trees as old as Abraham Lincoln.

I parked, got out, and let the peace of the place settle over me. It took a few minutes, but I was in no hurry. I walked out on the green grass, a warm wind on my face. This was familiar ground to me now, and I scanned the names on flat gravestones as I walked. They were a history lesson in southern Anglo heritage: Andrews, Sullivan, Franklin, Peery. Row after row, I passed a hundred and fifty years of southern blood. There was a time when midtown Atlanta was the center of the southern universe, and the rich and connected have been buried at Oakland since before the Civil War.

At a large mausoleum—built by a family wealthy enough to ensconce their dead in a fortress of solitude—I turned left for the short walk to my destination. I counted six gravestones up a short hill, stopped, and looked to my right. Inscribed into a pale marble headstone were these unlikely words: *Ramirez, Violeta. 1977–2001. La flor inocente. Bella como la luna y las estrellas.*

That plot of earth and headstone had cost me nearly every cent I had when I left Carthy, Williams and Douglas. I didn't care. What mattered was that there, surrounded by Atlanta's moneyed elite, lay Violeta Ramirez, innocent flower, as beautiful as the moon and stars.

I laid tulips down across her gravestone, bright red as blood. I closed my eyes and said a prayer for her soul, and another for my own.

Back at the office, Blu had a list of messages waiting for me: one from the DA's office, wanting to set up a deposition; the usual distraught phone calls from clients, some rational, some not; a particularly irate call from the mother of somebody who had been convicted the week before. I had met her son thirty minutes before his trial, so it's theoretically possible he didn't receive everything he deserved in terms of legal representation. But of course, everybody in the room knew he was guilty, so that's academic.

I felt a little guilty about Blu; all that ruminating about ethics made me wonder if unleashing Sammy on her new boyfriend was the right thing. Stephens was cheating on his steady girlfriend, and that made him slime, of course. And God knew he could take care of himself. But Sammy was southern and Stephens wasn't, and that put Stephens at a disadvantage in the game they were about to play. If you ever find yourself the third wheel in a relationship, pray to God the other person is from Wyoming or somewhere. If they're from Georgia—or, God help you, Alabama, like Sammy was—it's time to assume a defensive posture.

I ignored them all and sat down to think. Rabbit's reference to pharmaceuticals was a definite curve. I knew of no reason why Doug would want them, legitimate or otherwise. There was nothing distinctive about Townsend's decline: he had started with ecstasy, which completely fit his personality, and then had become mixed up with coke because of the increasing tendency to blend X with it. That was the insidious thing about playing drug games; people get creative when they should leave things alone. There was smack-ecstasy, coke-ecstasy, speed-ecstasy, and God-knows-what-else ecstasy floating around Atlanta with cartoon names like Daffy Duck and X-Men. One thing led to another, and eventually Townsend decided that what he really liked was the coke, and he could do without the ecstasy. Which probably made him happy for a few months, until his life started to fall apart. At that point, the tragic arithmetic of addiction drove him downmarket. The fact was, Doug Townsend couldn't afford pure coke and he wasn't the type for crack, which is the poor man's alernative. So like a lot of geeks, Doug went for methamphetamine. It was cheap, and for people who like to stay up all night and write computer code, it has magical powers.

None of which cornected him with Dilaudid Avenue and the Perry Homes projects. I seriously didn't want to go down there. For one thing, I didn't have any contacts, and just asking the wrong person the wrong question can dry up an entire segment of society. Word spreads through that kind of place so fast if you blink you miss it. But for now, at least, there was an alternative, and it made sense on a lot of levels to pursue it.

Townsend's computer was set up on a small table in my office. Inside it, I assumed, were a great many answers to my questions. And it occurred to me that the more information I found there, the more unlikely it was that he had killed himself. If he had known in advance the time of his death, he certainly would have deleted anything too horrifying. Even people on death row don't like the idea of being humiliated after the fact.

I picked up the phone and called Michael Harrod. An answering machine answered. Harrod's voice said, "Make it good, you're slowing down my data transfer." Then there was a beep.

"Michael?" I said. "Listen, that favor I needed, it's time to collect." Silence. "I know you're in there, Michael. You never go anywhere when you're not out ripping off Radio Shack." More silence. "Nightmare?"

Harrod picked up. "Yeah," he said. "What up?"

"Remember that little job I had for you?"

"Yeah."

"Well, it would probably go a lot better if you were here."

"Yeah, probably."

"Let me refresh your memory. I saved you from being the pool boy at the Fulton County Country Club. It's time to pay up."

More silence. After a long pause, Nightmare said, "Whose computer is this, anyway?"

"Does it matter?"

"Yeah, because I don't want it to suck."

"A former client of mine. You wouldn't know him."   ·

"What's his name?"

"His name is Doug Townsend."

Dead silence, at least fifteen seconds. Then, "I can see where you're calling from," followed by a dial tone.

*   *   *

I didn't have a chance to figure out what Nightmare's response meant. Before I could put the phone down, I heard Blu rummaging around on the other side of the open door. I hung up the phone and walked in, curious; she was pulling her stuff together, like she was preparing to leave. I looked down at my watch; there was nearly an hour left before closing. For all her faults, she was usually prompt, both coming and going. I walked in, flopping down in one of the waiting room chairs. I watched her push a magazine into her purse, thinking again about how different our lives were. What, I wondered, would it be like to possess such a limited set of assets, but to have those few in such spectacular abundance? What would it be like to be a woman like her, walk into a bar, and have every straight guy in the place check his pulse? And what, I especially wondered, would it be like to know that you had a handful of chances—moments of destiny—when your assets intersected with one of the small number of men with the legitimate power to fulfill all your dreams? Would it matter, strictly speaking, that the guy was an asshole of epic proportions? Blu raised her face to mine, giving me a smile. "Off early today, if that's not a problem," she cooed. Even her voice was like compressed sex.

"It's not actually closing time," I said. "Strictly speaking."

She smiled. "You don't mind, do you, Jack? The phone hasn't rung in an hour." That, I had to admit, was true. "Anyway, I have a date." She pushed a foot into a navy blue, strapped pump. I hadn't noticed she had been barefoot.

"You seeing that guy Stephens?"

Her smile deepened. Time stood still, as I waited for the pronouncement. Four words told me everything I needed to know. "Such a nice man." She picked up her bag and moved toward the door. "If there's nothing else, I'll see you tomorrow, okay? Good-bye, Jack." With that, she floated out the door. I was alone in my office, left with thoughts of Blu being whisked away on the Horizn corporate jet to New York for a no-expenses shopping excursion.

I paced around in my office until Nightmare showed up. He had, against all odds, changed his shirt. The new one had a picture of a surprised-looking sheep, with the logo, *Dolly Lama—Our Spiritual Leader*. His expression was changed, too: I could feel his excitement the moment he walked in the door. "Where is it?" he asked, without saying hello.

I nodded toward my office. "Apparently I said the magic words."

"Yeah."

"Are you saying you knew Doug Townsend?"

"I never met him. But I can give Killah his props."

"Killah?"

"Doug."

"Doug Townsend went by Killah?"

"Look, man, this is an alternative universe. Goin' by Killah doesn't mean he owned a gun. It means *file killer*."

"But you're saying that Townsend had a reputation in the hacker community."

Nightmare smiled. "What hacker community?"

I stared at him a moment, then said, "Computer's this way."

Nightmare followed me into my office, where I had Townsend's computer set up on a small table. Nightmare took a seat, then opened up a valise containing dozens of zip disks. It only took about five minutes for him to discover that the trip inside my former client's computer was no walk in the park. "Shit," Nightmare said.

"Problem?"

"There's hardly anything here. He was working through someone else's mainframe. From the looks of it, Georgia Tech."

"Why them?"

"Because they're huge, and they have a relaxed attitude. The grad students manage the mainframes."

"Are we screwed?"

Nightmare smiled. "All it takes is time."

"Can I get you something?" I asked. "A Coke?"

"Got any spring water?"

"Nope."

"See you when you get back." Apparently, Nightmare was a health nut when it came to beverages. I rose and headed for the little store on the corner near my building. By the time I got back, Nightmare's smirk had faded.

"This is some serious shit," he said.

"Meaning?"

"Meaning this is some serious motherfucking shit."

"That clears things up. Thanks." Nightmare scowled, and I asked, "Are you saying that whoever he was hacking had massive defenses or something?"

"I have no idea who he was hacking," he answered. "But whoever it was, Killah was taking *them* seriously. The defenses are the other way around."

"What do you mean?"

"I mean he definitely didn't want them crawling back up his DSL lines and identifying him. This stuff is protected. It's passwords, which I figured, since Killah wouldn't have had the resources for a hardware lock, like hand or iris recognition. But whatever it is, it's the shit, man. Most passwords are six characters, maybe eight. This one is *twenty*-six. It's just crazed."

"Twenty-six?"

"Yeah. It gets worse, though."

"Great."

"Killah was using the new 4096-bit encryption. So the number of possibilities is like . . . I don't think calculators go that high. Like a billion billion."

"Wonderful."

"Or maybe more. It's so mind-boggling, I can't actually imagine it."

I stared at him, trying to believe in whatever magic guys like him possessed. "So what do we do?"

Nightmare paused, thinking. "I could set up a brute force program," he said, "the kind that just tries everything. But there's a downside."

"Which is?"

"It would take about six hundred years to run."

"How about all that stuff in the movies, where the guy just pushes a few buttons and it's, bam, we're in?"

Nightmare's face showed pure derision. "Pure Hollywood. You work for *weeks* to break something like this down. To get into this we have to aim better, not waste our efforts. I'm running the latest version of Crack right now, but it's probably futile." Nightmare didn't give me a chance to ask. "Automated dictionary attack. It's got every word in the English language in it, so it just hammers away with word combinations. But this encryption is over the top, even with my computer at home working simultaneously."

"You can do that?"

"Yeah, you can spread Crack across multiple platforms, and you get an exponential increase in power. Maybe if I could get the mainframe at Tech working on it, we'd have a shot."

"Can we?"

"Umm, maybe."

"Look, Michael, is this going to work?"

Nightmare shrugged. "You're makin' too much noise, man. Lemme think."

Four hours later, it was almost nine-thirty. Nightmare said he was hungry. I said I would call a pizza delivery company. He said, and I'm quoting him now, "Fuck this shit, I'm going home."

"You're giving up?"

Nightmare stood and began pacing back and forth in front of Townsend's computer. It seemed best not to disturb him, so I just let him do it. "Look," he said after a couple of minutes, "I need to think this out. I'll meet you here in the morning."

"To do what?"

Nightmare looked at me. "Killah was good," he said. "But he ain't Nightmare."

CHAPTER EIGHT

IF YOU WANT TO ROMANTICIZE ATLANTA—and most of us who live here do—see it at sunset. In the dim half-light of dusk—those precious few minutes—it teeters among its various personalities, sublime and untouchable. It is a city built in a forest, its hard edges softened by the tips of hickories, sweetgums, white oaks, and red maples. There is a fragility to the loveliness of it, particularly for those of us who spend our days and nights with the undergrowth that lurks beneath its surface. But as night grows, its sense of history becomes murkier; the tone becomes more urban, less distinctively southern. It is a city caught between sunlight and dark, between history and tomorrow.

The city's past is held captive by the sweet fragrance of magnolia blossoms, which despite the crush of automobiles and skyscrapers, continues somehow to survive. This is a world in which the Confederate flag can be seriously considered a romantic symbol. It is badly fraying along its edges, but its resilience has shut the mouths of a lot of cultural observers, few of them southern. In that world, there are still cotillions for young white girls, as long as they have parents who are sufficiently wealthy and nostalgic. They cling to those conventions because they feel what's coming: Nightmare's new economy. That version of Atlanta is the center of the high-tech South, an essential node in a faceless, soulless world without borders or history. That world will come soon enough. When it does, combining words like "southern" and "gracious" will be as anachronistic as the Sons of the Confederacy. But in between, tenuous and trying desperately not to fall apart, is Atlanta's present, its daylight: urban life in the South of these United States. I have seen its diversity better than most. I grew up in the rural South, so I know the world people come to Atlanta to get away from, which is an important part of their psyche. I went to Emory, so I know what southern children are like who grow up so sheltered and privileged that their idea of a crisis is overspending the limit on their gold cards. I have worked at Carthy, Williams and Douglas, so I know the particular ways the parents of those children screw and reward each other, courtesy of the American legal system. And because my soul failed its most important test, I was now spending my days with the city's refuse, the people whom the combined brilliance of the city's ruling class can't figure out anything to do with except rope off like cattle. For better or worse, I have become an unwanted expert on the damaged southern soul.

In the fifteen miles between my apartment and the Fox Theater, I drove past it all. From south Atlanta you take the loop northwest, into the suburban industrial parks that ring the city, congregating every few miles in glass and steel, twenty stories high; then you hit I-75 and go north, up through the converging railroad lines and truck depots that make Atlanta the largest distribution center in the Southeast; then out over McDaniel Glen, the human cattle pen; and finally, you take the Eighth Street exit, downtown, where the banks and old money do business. From there it's only a few blocks to the Fox.

I was going to the Fox for the same reason I went to the Glen: because it was the only thing I could think of doing. It was the last night of the three-night engagement of *Capulets and Montagues,* and

I knew that for a little while longer, Michele Sonnier would be inside those walls. As I drove by the Fox, I glanced at my watch; it was after eleven. The show had ended a half hour earlier. I pulled into the private parking lot without any problem; the security was long since gone. I parked and got out, walking up toward the stage exit. There was a small crowd there of about twenty people, dressed nicely, but different from the crowd at the Four Seasons. These were the diehard opera fans, mostly college students.

I walked up and asked a young woman if they were waiting for Sonnier, and she brightened and nodded. She didn't know how long it would be; Sonnier took her time, apparently. That was fine by me. I would wait as long as it took.

Every few minutes the door opened and someone stepped out, the crowd deflating over them like a popped champagne bubble when people realized it wasn't the star. I actually felt sorry for a couple of the singers, emerging with smiling faces, only to feel the sudden disappointment over who they weren't. But eventually the door opened again, and the man who had escorted Sonnier through the party at the Four Seasons emerged. I moved into a shadow by the side of the building, content to watch for a while. The man looked bored; he lit a cigarette, absently watching the people in the crowd. A few minutes later Sonnier appeared, wearing a cotton muffler around her neck, in spite of the heat. The crowd applauded when she walked out, and she smiled, but I was surprised by her appearance. She looked very tired, much more so than she had at the party. Apparently doing the opera three nights in a row took a toll.

The little crowd pressed in around her. A couple of people spontaneously embraced her, and the man traveling with her put his hand out, creating a little space for her. She looked like she needed it. She was seriously exhausted. A few people asked her questions about singing; I could see the fatigue behind her eyes as she listened. She had probably heard them all a hundred times. But she answered everybody, and signed autographs. When there were three or four people left, I quietly stepped into the periphery of her vision, although still partially in shadow. Sonnier was looking down, signing an autograph. She felt someone new, and I saw her eyes glance upward. She finished signing her name, and looked up. I was in the half-light, and I don't think she recognized me at that point. She signed another autograph, but I could sense her feeling around for me in the dark, wondering. She had the radar that famous people get, an inner detector for people who want something. A car pulled up, a limo to take her to her hotel. The man went to the car to speak to the driver, and I stepped full into the light, to her left. She turned and saw me clearly, her pen stopping in the middle of her name. Our eyes locked for a second; then she turned her head.

Maybe it was the shock of seeing me again. If there had been the illusion in her mind that I had been deceived the first time we met, that was now over. She was rigid and tense. I stayed to her side, about five feet away, not pressuring her. She kept talking to the last couple of people, but she was rushing now, getting through it. When there was one person left, she called over to the man by the limo. "Bob," she said, "ready to go?"

The man turned to look, and seeing me, walked briskly over to Sonnier. I don't know if he remembered me from the Four Seasons, but he was definitely tuned into Sonnier's tone of voice. Ignoring me, he smiled at the woman Sonnier was with and said, "Walk with us, won't you?" Sonnier was signing her final autograph in midwalk; the limo door was open, and suddenly she was entering the car. I didn't pursue her. There wasn't a point. There was only one question to ask her, and she wasn't going to answer it in the parking lot of the Fox Theater: "Why did you lie about knowing Doug Townsend?"

When Sonnier's door closed, the car pulled out, turning onto Peachtree. I watched the limo's taillights recede into the Atlanta night for a while, then walked across the lot to my car. At the Four Seasons, Sonnier had done a pretty good job of covering, although not good enough. But whether it was fatigue from the show or the shock of seeing me again, she had shown me a lot more in those few seconds behind the Fox. No matter how far apart their worlds were, Doug Townsend had been much more than just a fan.

*   *   *

When my phone rang, it was about one-thirty in the morning. I wasn't blurry, exactly. I was in the dangerous place, drifting in that highly suggestive state between wakefulness and dreams. But that didn't prevent me from recognizing the voice the second I heard it. I'd felt the shiver it sent up my spine once before. "Mr. Hammond?"

My eyes opened. I played the sound over in my mind, just to be sure. "Well," I said quietly, "if it isn't the great Michele Sonnier."

There was silence for a second, then, "Is this Mr. Jack Hammond?"

"Yes."

"I know it's late. I hope you don't mind me calling you at home."

"Not at all." A longer pause, and I asked, "Would it be safe to say you have something you'd like to talk about?"

What happened next in her voice wasn't a crack, exactly, more a kind of low tremor. "Yes," she said. "There is something."

"Maybe it would be easier if I told you what it was."

A small sigh. "Yes, it would. Much easier."

"You want to talk about Doug Townsend."

I could hear her exhale quietly, like a little slump. "That's right. Doug."

"You've called the right person."

"This is all such a horrible thing."

"I agree."

Her next sentence was delivered in kind of a blur, faster than the rest. "Look, Mr. Hammond, this isn't something I really want to talk about on the phone. Can you come up?"

"Up to where?"

"The Four Seasons. The Ansley Suite."

I sat holding the phone, momentarily confused. "Look, no offense, but why aren't you—"

"At home, with my husband?"

"If you don't mind me asking."

"I do mind. Can you come up?"

"Thirty minutes, okay?"

"Yes."

"I'll be there."

It was raining when I pulled under the parking canopy at the Four Seasons. There was no doorman working at that hour, so I parked in an empty spot on my own. I stepped out of the car and reentered a carefully constructed world of magazine living. The fresh flowers alone could have paid my rent.

The Ansley Suite was on the nineteenth floor. I rode up the cherry wood–lined elevator, watched the door slide open, and stepped out. The Ansley was the third door on the left. I knocked. Nothing. I knocked again. A small stirring, then a shadow darkening the viewing lens in the door. Two locks opened, one high, one in the center. Then the door swung open, and I saw the tear-stained face of Michele Sonnier.

She turned back into the room without a word. I followed her in, closing the door behind me. She led me back through a spectacular suite, with two enormous picture windows looking out over the city lights of Atlanta. She sat heavily down on a long, patterned fabric sofa, gently crying. I sat down on the other end, just biding my time.

It took about five minutes, I suppose. It was hard to tell, time was crawling so slowly. For all I knew, Ralston was going to appear at the door at any moment, wanting to know what the hell I was doing with his wife at two o'clock in the morning. When she finally looked up at me, I think she was a little surprised I had just let her cry it out. But I've spent hundreds of hours with people inches away from confession, and I've learned to recognize the moment guilt surfaces. I've watched clients swim as hard against that current as they can, desperate not to be submerged by their own sense of right and wrong. I've learned who to push, and who to watch drown. Confession was on her face, in the slope of her shoulders, the fatigue in her eyes.

Eventually, she brushed her hair back off her face. She wore dark green pants and a tan pullover. "Forgive me," she said. "I'm a little better now."

"It's all right."

"I'm sorry I'm such a mess."

Even through the fatigue, she was still beautiful. Her skin was so smooth and brown, it was almost impossible not to reach out and touch it, if only to be sure it was real. "So you want to talk about Doug."

"Yes. Doug." She stared past me toward the wall. "You knew I lied about him. I thought I was a better actor than that."

I shrugged. "You're a wonderful actor, but I'm a hell of a critic."

Sonnier watched me a moment, then nodded. "People who don't lie are at a premium, and their price is rising." She walked to the bar, the line of her thigh moving through perfectly tailored fabric. "You can't trust anybody these days, from priests to presidents."

"So I noticed."

"It's enough to make a person lose faith, except I never had any to begin with." She poured herself a glass of mineral water. "You're sure you don't want anything?"

"I want you to tell me about Doug."

"What do the police say?"

"They say he's dead. Probably self-inflicted by overdose."

She replaced the bottle and took a sip, delicate and formal. "The police in Atlanta are excellent, Mr. Hammond. I'm sure they know what they're doing."

"That's a very patriotic attitude."

She looked up. "Not every black woman hates the police, Mr. Hammond."

"Not every black woman is a rich opera singer, either."

"What does that mean?"

I shrugged. "It means that race is the eight-hundred-pound gorilla in this town, and I decided a long time ago I wasn't going to play that game. I have nine black clients for every white one, and I'm glad to have them. So if you want to start laying down race cards, I can go home now."

For a second, I thought she might throw me out. But after a tense moment, she relented. "Maybe I misunderstood," she said. "I just get tired of defending myself over being too white."

"I do the same thing to my clients, all day long."

She smiled wanly. "Of course you do. We can drop all that, then."

"Good. And I'm still in your thousand-dollar-a-night hotel suite, waiting for you to tell me what this is about."

She looked away. "Do you know what's always bothered me about lawyers, Jack?"

I felt like laughing. With most people, there's usually a list. "No."

"It's the horrible assumption that it's always best for things to come out into the open. They're always turning over rocks, trying to dig up people's sorrows. There are times when it is better for things to stay in the dark, so people can get on with their lives."

"When somebody dies, you give up the right to privacy," I said. "That's how it works."

"Even when there are innocent victims? When there is someone who has done nothing to anyone, and is simply being dragged through this horrible mess through no fault of her own?"

"Are you talking about yourself?"

She looked genuinely surprised. "Me? Innocent? You really don't understand anything, do you?"

"This is your chance to clear that up."

She looked past me. "I don't know where to begin."

"You can start with how you met Doug."

She nodded, gathering her thoughts. "We didn't exactly *meet*," she said. "He crept up on me, a little bit at a time. I would look out at the audience, and I would see a face. Something would seem familiar, but I'm normally so absorbed in my singing that I can't afford to think about the audience." She focused on the opposite wall. "It took a long time, quite a few performances. But eventually, there was no mistaking it. It was *him*—although I had no idea who *he* was. It was disorienting, at first. Everything would be different—a different town, a different dressing room, different music but he would be the same, just plucked out of one world and set down in another. For a moment, I would wonder what night it was, if I were in the right place."

"Were you afraid?"

"Of Doug?" She shook her head. "No. Opera has its share of obsessive fans, but they're not frightening. They're mostly a little awkward, polite. But no one had ever come close to him. He was *everywhere.*" She exhaled deeply. "He seemed harmless enough. He knew a lot about the music and that set my mind at ease. I mean, seriously. Ax murderers don't hang out at classical music concerts."

"At some point, you began talking."

She nodded. "Yes, just before this current tour. I began to notice him outside the hall, which was a change. He would be smiling this little half-smile, very shy, very diffident. A long ways from frightening."

"Go on."

"I would catch glimpses of him, like tonight, with you. He would hang back, behind the crowds at the stage door. He never asked for an autograph. I don't think he wanted to be considered part of that crowd." She paused, drawn back into a memory. "Finally, he spoke."

"What did he say?"

She smiled softly. " *'L'amore non prevale sempre.'* "

"What's that?"

" 'Love does not always prevail.' It's Italian, from Romeo and Juliet."

"The one you've just finished."

She nodded. "It's my most famous role, the signature. I get asked to do it constantly, but I try to keep it down to a couple of times a year."

"Where was this?"

"San Francisco, I think."

"So what happened?"

"It was charming, in a way. All these people pressing in, and Doug, waiting patiently. I was ready to go, and then, from the side I hear his gentle voice saying, *'L'amore non prevale sempre.'* I looked up, and there he was, looking down at his shoes."

"Did you say anything back to him?"

"The next line, Romeo's line. *'E c'è ancora nessun' altra maniera a vivere.* 'And yet, there is no other way to live.' " She paused. "Look, what he was doing—following me around like that, I mean—if I stopped to think about it, I knew it meant he had some kind of problem."

"I agree."

"But what can you do about it? It's flattering, in a strange way, if you sense the person is safe. You know how he was. He was gentle. We would talk a bit after shows, occasionally before. He said he knew a lot about computers, and that he was starting a small company." She smiled sadly. "I think he wanted me to be proud of him."

"I'm sure he did."

"Yes, he was a child in that way. So I encouraged him. I would listen to his little victories. He was longing for approval. It's all so sad."

Yes, sad. Doug slumped over his couch, dead with an arm full of fentanyl. "But something happened," I said. "Otherwise, I wouldn't be here."

She withdrew again, her body language turning remote. "Doug was brilliant in his way, you know. But he couldn't leave well enough alone. He thought he was helping me, but he put things into motion . . ." She trailed off. She turned her back to me, dropping her voice so low it was barely audible. "One day he came to me, and I could feel something was different. He was still inside. He said he wanted to tell me something. I said fine, but he didn't answer right away. He came close and whispered to me."

"What did he say?"

" '*I would do anything to help you.*' His eyes were boring into me. He didn't even blink. '*To help you with your secret I would do anything at all.*' I had never seen anything like it from him. I honestly believe I could have asked him to jump off a cliff and he would have done it. Or worse."

"Do you have any idea what would make him say something like that?"

She stood silently awhile, gathering courage. "Shall I tell you my story, then, Jack?" she asked. "Shall I give an accounting of my life?" She stared down at the floor, smoothing her pants with the palms of her hands. "It begins in a two-bedroom apartment, with rented furniture, the phone turned off because the bill isn't paid. I'm six years old. I can hear my mother rummaging around in the bathroom."

"She was a teacher, wasn't she? I saw your web page."

She gave a bitter laugh, looked up at the ceiling, and sighed. "A teacher? My mother was a *secretary*. Quite a prize. Mother of the Year material, except for the part about being a drug addict. I think they deduct points for that."

"And your father? The website said he was a doctor."

She closed her eyes. "My father drove a truck. Or so I've been led to believe. I never actually met him."

I stood silently a moment, trying to make sense of what I had just heard. "Maybe I ought to sit down."

"Do that. We're just getting started." I moved to the couch, and she continued. "So mother was a secretary, when she was working. Mostly, she was in love with Valium and Percodan. She didn't start out with any of the really tacky drugs. That came later." She laughed bitterly. "It's surprising how far down a person can go, isn't it? How someone can play with fire for a long time, never noticing the moment that it's too late? One day they're completely lost, and they don't even know it." She looked at me. "Money ran short, of course. She couldn't hold a job after she started showing up stoned during the day. But—" she paused, a look of revulsion passing across her face. "She was resourceful. Men can be quite generous, under the right circumstances."

"How old were you when this was going on?"

"By then? Eight."

"I'm sorry."

"Yeah, well, we're all sorry, Jack. I'm sorry for how my mother stopped caring about anything except how she could get more of the drugs she loved, sorry for how the sight of me made her crazy because it reminded her of what a terrible mother she was. I would say something, and she would look up at me like I was in the wrong house. Having a child around made her choose, and mommy couldn't give up some things. So one day I came home from school and she was just gone. Vanished from the face of the earth."

"You were abandoned?"

"Mommy left with one of her so-called boyfriends. He was a piece of work. The worse she got, the worse the men got. She was finding her level, you see. Drifters who had never worked in their lives. She wasn't exactly pretty anymore, of course. But in a certain light . . ." She turned away. "So to get away from me, she followed him off into the drug world." She choked, as though swallowing down bile.

"What did you do?"

She shrugged. "The great state of Georgia became my new mommy, and she was spectacular."

"Georgia? I thought you were from New York."

"Everyone thinks that."

I paused. "Everyone? You mean—"

"Yes, Jack. Even Charles."

I stared. "That's not good."

"I lived in six homes in four years. I even did time in the Glen."

I looked up, shocked. "The Glen? Are you serious?"

She nodded. "About eighteen months. The foster homes didn't work out. People found me . . . difficult. Which is the understatement of the century. I was a *terror*. And I can't imagine why, since things were going so well. After all, only two of my six foster parents abused me, and only one of those was a woman. So really, it was ungrateful of me."

The image of the cultured diva was shredding before my eyes. More and more, she was sounding like one of my clients. She was recounting the common threads of Atlanta's lost souls: abuse, abandonment, and the sins of one irresponsible generation landing on the next. Yet somehow, the woman before me had managed to end up in another world, surrounded by luxury. "How the hell can anybody handle all that and come out intact on the other side?" I asked.

"Don't be absurd. I'm not intact."

I motioned to the suite. "All right. How did you get here?"

She looked at me pointedly. "I was unloved, Jack. That had nothing to do with the size of my gift. If anything, it's probably the source of it. So I cut my life into two pieces. The first one, I destroyed. Even the memory of it. I carefully constructed a completely new existence, one that started after everything terrible ended. So all that sadness never happened. It wasn't even in shadows. It was simply . . . gone. And that's how I didn't go insane."

"Going back through it must be tough."

She nodded. "Those wounds are deep, and they took time to forget. I had my time of . . . what do the social workers call it? *Acting out.* I got kicked around the foster care system for a while. On the other hand, it was the perfect place to perfect my craft."

"Your singing?"

She shook her head. "*Acting.* You learn how to play nice, to make people believe. Couples would come in, and I would zero in on them, trying to get one of them to want to take me home. Eventually, I became very good at it. I could sit and chat, legs crossed like a nice little girl at a tea party. There were no tragedies, no horrible moments. *Yes, ma'am. I'd love another cookie. No, my mother didn't stagger home under the influence and collapse on the couch for two days. I don't have a mother.* I didn't know it then, but I was practicing for my life. I was learning how to pretend."

Listening to her, I wondered again at the resiliency of some people. I had seen it in my practice; nineteen of twenty are flushed down the system, but one is impossible to kill. For those, you move heaven and earth, because in spite of everything, they have character. "What happened next?" I asked.

"I went home with some people. It was a tryout, a few months together before they made their decision. A nice couple. Nice car, the suburbs. I was thirteen."

"Not many people are willing to adopt a thirteen-year-old girl," I said.

"It's all right, Jack, you can say it. A thirteen-year-old *black* girl."

I nodded. "Either way, it was brave."

"Not exactly."

"What do you mean?"

Her face hardened. "It was the perfect age, considering the husband's intentions. You'll find the percentage of liberals who are pedophiles is about the same as any other group." I sat quietly, adding this sorrow to her litany. There was nothing to say. There are times that tragedy flows like a river, and it takes a strong swimmer not to drown. "I'm not saying he wanted to," she said. "I think he hated himself for it, actually. I know I did. But he couldn't help himself. He just started staring at me, giving me the look. Then one night he came into my room." She stood, beginning to pace a little. "So I fixed things," she said. "I instituted my brilliant plan. It worked perfectly, and he never touched me again."

"What did you do?"

"I got pregnant," she said in a flat voice. There was a long pause. Then she said, "That did the trick. Damaged goods, you see. Not the pretty young thing anymore." She laughed, a sound as near to crying as I've ever heard.

"Was the husband the father?"

She shook her head. "No, no, he hadn't gone that far, not yet. He was more interested in me doing things for him."

"Then who?"

"He was a very *glamorous* boy from the neighborhood. I chose him, which was the point. He was seventeen, and I was thirteen. I would sneak out to be with him." She paused. "I never told the boy about the baby. There wasn't any point. I knew what was going to happen. He had already moved on, anyway. I saw him a few times, and he would try to feel me up."

"What did the foster parents say?"

"The loving couple?" she mocked. "They sent me back, of course. Not what they bargained for. It was a touching goodbye. The husband had to be somewhere else at the time."

"Did you tell anyone what he had been doing?"

"No."

"Why not?"

"Because it didn't matter. He was gone, I was free. I had the baby at the Social Services Center."

"So you have a child," I said. "You're a mother."

Her breathing grew deeper. "She was born. It was a Tuesday. The room was very bright. There was a lot of noise. I never saw her again."

Someone innocent she didn't want dragged through this. Her daughter. I looked up to see the fragile remains of the lost girl's bravado come apart; the hardened veneer stripped away like the dressing of a wound, and her face was left covered in sadness and self-loathing.

"Do you understand?" she said. "I left her, Jack. I abandoned Briah, just like my mother abandoned me." She wiped away tears. "Briah," she said. "My baby's name is Briah."

"It's a beautiful name."

She nodded, her crying subsiding. She walked softly to where I was sitting and stuck out a trembling hand. "T'aniqua Fields," she said. "Nice to meet you."

I stood, taking her hand in mine. "T'aniqua."

"Not exactly opera material, is it?"

I had seen my share of tortured psychology in my time at Judge Odom's court, but this was as dark as any. If people knew how their madness rained down hell on their children, they might have the grace to clean themselves up. "You had the baby," I said quietly. "What happened next?"

"I couldn't go back to foster care with Briah. I had just turned fourteen a few days before. So they took her." She looked at me, pleading in her eyes. "*They took her.*"

"Then you didn't abandon her. She was taken away."

"I did. I didn't fight. I didn't say a word. I just lay in the bed and closed my eyes while they carried her off."

"You were overwhelmed. You were only fourteen."

She turned on me suddenly, her eyes flashing anger. "Don't you get it? I *wanted* them to take her." She turned away and began to sob again. "I hoped it all would disappear, like it never happened. I would have my little girl dreams back. I wanted to be the child I had created. Just a child." She caught her breath, choking on tears. "Two nights later, I escaped. I stole money from one of the social workers and got on a bus. I did certain things—"

She stopped, unwilling to go on. There was a final pause—a silence as the storm gathered strength—and she fell completely apart. Whatever armor she had developed to keep her secret was now utterly, finally in pieces. Or—and I had too much experience to eliminate this as at least a possibility—I was watching a superb performance, even better than what I had seen on stage. I leaped up and steadied her, taking her arm. "Easy now."

"Where is she, Jack? I left her in—"

"I know," I said. *You left her in hell.*

"And suddenly Doug comes to me. He says he will do anything to help me."

"He found out?"

"*Everything,*" she hissed. "How could he do that?"

"There would be records somewhere. It's Social Services. If someone were determined, he could unravel it. Doug was brilliant with computers."

"*Damn him.*"

"He only wanted to help."

"I had this all worked *out,*" she said. "He woke up all the emotions, the regret. I see her body carried away from my bed. I truly think I'm going to lose my mind."

"Take it easy."

"I've made a new life, Jack. It started out as survival, a way to keep from falling apart. But now it's my *real* life."

"I take it," I said softly, "your husband didn't think he was signing up for this?"

She gave a derisive laugh. "My husband went to Groton, Jack. Then to Yale, then Harvard Medical School. He gave money to *Bush,* for God's sake. Charles believes the ghetto is the inevitable consequence of a culture of dependency." She shook her head. "Have you ever been to Horizn's offices?"

"No."

"It gleams, from ceiling to floor. There isn't a speck of dust in the entire building. Even the air is filtered and cleaned. It's perfect." She walked to the bar, putting distance between us. "My husband's world is very orderly," she said. "Mine, unfortunately, is rather a mess." She opened a bottle of Armagnac and poured herself a drink. "Men from Groton don't marry runaways with drug-addicted mothers, Jack. And don't marry women who have had their illegitimate children taken away by Social Services. It hasn't happened once in the history of the world."

I paused, stopped by the logic of her statement. It was patently true. "You're certain he doesn't know?"

She shook her head. "By the time I met Charles, I had been living my new life for more than seven years. God, I believed it myself. I had worked out all the little details of my past, filling in the holes. It was seamless."

I paused, thinking. "How did you meet your husband?"

"Charles came to hear me sing, early in my career. I had only sung some small roles, but it was clear I was being anointed for something bigger. Charles was gorgeous, and clearly ambitious. I fell in love instantly. I was overwhelmed that a man of his distinction would be interested in someone like me. It was the validation that my new life was real. How could he love me if it wasn't? I was home, I was free. I would marry the great Charles Ralston, and the past would never be able to touch me again." She paused. "It took me some time to understand what was actually going on."

"Which was?"

"I had no real experience in the world, and it was inevitable that he would become disappointed in me. But I could sing. That was the one thing that was real. And Charles played it to the hilt. I was like a performing dog, trotted out to do my tricks. For a while, I thought it meant he cared. But eventually, I understood my career has given him some needed social cachet. There are those who aren't impressed with the nouveau riche, particularly in a black man. The arts open those doors." She drained her glass. "Ironic, isn't it? At last, I've become a social asset." She set the glass down on the bar, filling it half-full again. "In exchange for not raising a fuss, I am granted a certain latitude in my life. Charles and I lead separate lives, but we do not disturb each other's world. Especially now."

"You mean the IPO."

She nodded. "The stock offering is the culmination of everything my husband has worked to achieve. You were right when you said he hadn't signed up for this. I feel nothing for him as a wife. But I have no right to destroy him because of my sin. The fact that he is emotionally incapable of anything as a husband isn't his fault. He's simply wired that way."

"Maybe you should wait until it all blows over."

"I'm not going to wait one more minute, Mr. Hammond. My daughter is alive, and she is somewhere in Atlanta."

"What do you mean? Did Doug tell you something?"

"His last email to me. He must have been in a hurry, because it was only a few words. Or maybe he didn't trust the security. *She's here, and we need to move now.* That's all he said." She walked back to the window, taking her drink with her. She peered out into the glimmering night sky of Atlanta. I could feel her searching the darkness, looking for a solitary, unknown girl in a city of millions. "A message like that is impossible to ignore. But where is here? Somewhere. Anywhere."

"You don't think he had her with him, do you?"

"I don't know. I only know I see my daughter in every waking moment now. I can think of nothing else. So I am going to find her, somehow, some way." She turned and looked at me with a pleading expression.

"You want my help," I said.

"When I saw you tonight, I realized I had to take a chance. You said you were Doug's friend, so I'm going to trust you. I have to trust someone. It's impossible for me to search for her without arousing suspicion."

"I want something in return," I said, quietly.

She smiled grimly. "Of course you do. How much will it cost me?"

"Not money. Just your help with Doug. I can't forget what I'm doing here, and that's trying to find out what happened to him."

"What can I do?"

"I'm going to want to know everything that happened between you. Everything."

She nodded in assent, then looked back out into the city. Neither of us spoke for a long moment. At last she quietly asked, "You saw me sing, didn't you?"

"Yes."

"What did you think of it?"

"I thought it was magnificent. You broke the heart of everyone in the room."

The edge of her mouth curled slightly upwards. "That's something, at least. It gives me a reason to live another day." She drained her glass. "I sing to justify my life, Jack. I sing so that God does not condemn me to hell." She turned back to the window and stared listlessly at the city. "I'm tired," she said. "I can't remember being so tired."

"We can talk again tomorrow, if you like."

"Yes," she said, closing her eyes. "That would be better."

After a moment she walked toward me and reached out her hand. I took it, and she led me back through the suite toward the door. She stopped at a small desk and wrote down a number. "This is my cell phone," she said, pressing the slip into my hand. "It's private, and we can speak freely."

"I'll call you tomorrow, when we've both had some sleep."

"I doubt I'll sleep much, not for the time being." She opened the door, but put her hand on my arm as I walked through. "You're carrying a little bomb inside you now, Jack. Be careful it doesn't go off."

I nodded, and stepped into the hall. *The great Michele Sonnier,* I thought, turning away from the sound of a closing door.

CHAPTER NINE

THE NEXT MORNING, I could feel her skin on my fingertips, smell her scent on my clothes. Maybe it was imagination. I looked at the bedstand; there was the crumpled paper, with her number written on it. I sat up in bed, pulling myself together. *My God, Doug never had a chance.* She was fantastic, that was certain. She was beautiful, more beautiful than anyone I'd ever seen. She was exotic, she was sophisticated, she was . . . *Damn it, get a grip. This is about Doug, and that's all.*

No. Not just that, not now. You took on her sorrow, and now you have to deal with it. Somewhere, presumably in Atlanta, there was a fourteen-year-old girl who didn't know her mother. It was an open question whether or not she wanted to know. She could be one more victim of a broken human services system, calloused and indifferent. She could be one of the few success stories. But thoughts of Michele and Doug pulled me back to the beginning, to how Doug died. I tried once again to fit two words together: Doug and suicide. I let them rattle around in my mind awhile, trying them on. I knew why

Billy Little believed they fit: it was easy, and it got Townsend off his desk. Billy was good people, but he was overworked. If Doug killed himself, Billy's load got lighter.

Doug Townsend, for me, was not workload. He was a brave, romantic, and lost man, and at one time, my friend. So when I got to my office the next morning about nine, I was glad to see Nightmare sitting in my waiting room. He was in a funk, because Blu wouldn't let him in my office. The sight of the two of them looking at each other was a collision of cultures, like the model Gisele showing up at your high school prom. A hell of a lot of new economy would have to happen before Nightmare had a shot at Blu. I said hello to Blu and led Nightmare into my office. He had on the same T-shirt, the same black jeans. It was the same everything, actually, but minus the smirk. Hackers might be freaks, but they're among the most persistent people on earth. It's nothing for a hacker to stay awake for two days to crack a particularly secure site. The second I saw Nightmare, I could tell that sometime during the night getting inside Doug Townsend's computer had changed from a payback to me into a passion for him. Late in the night, apparently; he had a worn look that made me think he hadn't slept much, if at all. I was glad to see him, because now I wanted in Doug's computer more than ever.

Nightmare wasn't much for pleasantries. He set a book bag down on the floor and pulled out a zip disk. "This," he said darkly, "was obtained by blood. It's like a code buzzsaw."

"Where did you get it?"

Nightmare didn't smile. "From Satan," he answered.

I decided not to push it; coming from him, I had no idea what that meant. And I didn't care. All I wanted was to get inside that box. Four hours later he kicked me out of my own office, and I couldn't blame him; I was being a pain in the ass. So I gave Nightmare my cell phone number and walked down Poston for a while, the street in front of my office. I got some coffee at a convenience store, paced for a while in front of the body shop across the street, and eventually circled back, just because I couldn't stand to be away. Nightmare wasn't happy.

"What's the problem?" I asked.

Nightmare scowled. "I've run the thing down a million times. Nothing works. What the hell is this?"

I looked at the little asterisks on the screen that stood for something Nightmare couldn't figure out. "And these stand for letters, right?" I asked.

"I was pretty sure, but maybe I'm wrong about the whole idea."

"What made you think that in the first place?"

"It's Killah's style."

"Let me get this straight. Doug was well enough known that you studied his style?"

Nightmare nodded. "It's a small community. But yeah, I knew Killah's thing. He liked that kind of irony, like the time he reset an eBay administrator's password out of the letters for *evilhacker*."

"He hacked eBay?"

Nightmare shrugged. "For about ten minutes, yeah. Killah was the premier cypherpunk in the Southeast, dude. Maybe the whole U.S."

"Cyberpunk?"

"No. *Cypherpunk*. As in code-breaker."

I sat back in my chair. "You must be kidding."

"No way. Killah got major props around the community. But that's what makes this such a bitch. A guy who breaks code is also gonna be pretty good at creating his own. And this ain't my deal."

"What is?"

"Me? Phone phreaking. Cracking phone lines, rerouting, that kind of thing. I'm the greatest the world has ever seen, probably." He stared at the screen. "No word combinations in the English language open this system. Which pretty much leaves us with random combinations, and I'm assuming you don't have a few hundred years to wait." He paused. "What are we looking for, anyway?"

"I'm not sure. Anything that can lead us toward why Doug died."

"Pretty vague."

"There's something else." I hesitated, choosing my words carefully. "We're trying to find someone. A missing person thing."

Nightmare shrugged. "Well, we aren't gonna be finding any-body or anything, unless we can get in this damn computer."

"Nothing fits."

He shook his head. "Nada."

Maybe it was the Spanish for "nothing" that made me think of it. "No word combinations in the *English* language, you said."

"Yeah."

"Not other languages."

Nightmare scowled. "Well, you know, there's only about fifteen major languages in the world, not to mention five thousand dialects, so if you want to start running them down one by one, we can come back in a few months."

"Doug was an opera freak," I said. "Italian, French, that kind of thing."

Nightmare looked up. "Opera? You gotta be kidding me."

"No. Can you run any of those down?"

He shook his head. "Theoretically, if I downloaded dictionaries in those languages. I'd have to reconfigure Crack."

"So what do you think?"

"I think we got shit now, so yeah, let's do it."

I left again, unwilling to stare at Nightmare while he practiced his black art. I came back in an hour, and he was leaning back in my office chair, eyes closed, legs up on my desk. I kicked them off, waking him up. "You got it?" I asked.

He snorted derisively. "Don't be ridiculous. But I got an Italian dictionary in there. And I've got a nice slice of Tech's mainframe slammin' away. I should get a few hours out of it before they dump me."

"Shouldn't you be doing something in the meantime?"

"Like what?"

"I don't know, something." I pointed to the computer. "Is this the glamorous world of hacking? Sitting on your ass for hours while the computer does the work?"

Nightmare grinned. "Go get me some lunch."

"You know, pal, I'm starting to wonder if jail wouldn't have done you some good."

"Portobello mushroom sandwich at Cameli's. With the three-bean salad. I need some protein." He waved me out the door like a Hollywood mogul. I stared a minute, considered the negative implications of picking him up by the scruff of his neck and throwing him out, and started walking out the door. Nightmare called me back. "Dude?"

"Yeah?"

"The spicy mustard, okay? Not the French's."

Blu was already gone for lunch, and I walked back out the door without a word. I went to get Nightmare's sandwich; the traffic was hell, and it was nearly one-thirty before I got back. I tossed the sack of food onto my desk and said, "Well?"

Nightmare ignored the question and rummaged through the sack. He pulled out the sandwich, lifted up one side, and examined the mustard. Satisfied, he raised the sandwich to his mouth and took a bite. "A meat-based diet isn't sustainable anymore," he said, his mouth full. "The amount of grain it takes to feed one cow . . ."

"I'm not in the mood for a PETA lecture, Michael."

Nightmare shrugged and pointed to the screen. "Does that mean anything to you?"

I walked to the computer and looked. The words *L'amore non prevale sempre* flashed on the screen. I reeled. "You've got to be kidding."

"What is it?"

"It's a line from an opera. Doug used to say it."

"It's also the password to his computer."

"You mean you're in?"

"I'm in." Nightmare spun around in his chair and pressed "enter." I heard the hard drive start to run, and we entered the secret world of Doug Townsend.

I believe that loneliness may be the natural state of mankind. We walk from street corner to office building, locked in isolation. I don't know how else to explain what lurked in the files of Doug's computer, his inner chaos turned into binary numbers and infinitesimal voltages. But the unquiet side of his mind was cataloged there, various in its perversity, individual in its bizarre self-expression. In cyberspace, his obsession with Michele was not limited by time or physical dimension. Inside his computer, it flowered into full, demented bloom.

To describe the heart of Doug's experience with Michele causes me pain, because it disturbs the quiet sense of false security that makes normal life possible. I admit that it's false. I know that it is. But I also know that it's essential. It's like ignoring the risks of flying. There is the mathematical possibility that you will crash. There is also no benefit to thinking about it. It's like that in life. If you consider what every apparently nice man or woman around you might be thinking, if only you could peel away their veneer of normalcy, you might never leave the house.

I had spent hours talking to Doug, and not one second was about Michele Sonnier. Many of those hours were enjoyable, the basis of a friendship. Certainly, while we were in college there was no hint of instability, just the lopsided social skills of a geek. Of course, I had to assume that every form of obsession has its beginning. But did this mean every moment between the two of us had been a lie? Even our talks, some as recent as two weeks ago, about his computer business? Had he been, with a titanic act of will, suppressing her name from his lips second by agonizing second? Had he, in the midst of a story about growing up in Kentucky, been longing to speak her name? Or was he split in two, each part of his brain independent, and what I saw was real but only a part of the whole?

There were no answers. Doug was gone. Lost in Michele's persona, he had created bizarre works of art, amalgams of her picture taken to unreal dimensions. Should I remember him by the pages where he had superimposed her face on a photograph of his own body, creating a kind of half-man, half-woman monster? Or what can I make of a church building composed entirely of her eyes?

Having been ushered into his madness, I was forced to admit that my opinions about how Doug died were nothing more than blind theories. It was all a question of which side of his brain was doing the choosing. The Doug Townsend I knew would never have killed himself. The Doug Townsend hidden in that computer was capable of things I couldn't imagine. But I was also convinced that the new, previously hidden, version was unlikely to vanish silently into the night. Surely, that energy would have found expression before its self-inflicted ending.

Nightmare shook his head, obviously shaken. "This stuff is whacked."

I nodded. "I know. But . . . I mean, there's nothing illegal about it."

"If you say so."

"So this is what all that security was about?" I asked.

Nightmare looked up, surprised. "No, dude. *This* is what the security is about." Nightmare hunched over the keyboard; after a few seconds, the logo of Grayton Technical Laboratories appeared, followed by a long list of some kind.

I stared for a long time. I had expected something about Michele's daughter, not this. "Grayton Technical Laboratories?" I asked. "He was hacking them?"

"You could call it that."

"Well, what would you call it?"

"I would call it a total obsession."

"Why do you say that?'

Nightmare punched some keys. "Because there's roughly a terabyte of stuff in here."

"You mean he was collecting a lot of information."

"I mean a fly couldn't take a shit at that company without him knowing about it." Nightmare pushed back from the desk. "Hacking is one thing, dude. It's about getting in. You look around, mess with their heads a little bit. But this . . . he mirrored the entire company. It's just crazed."

"Like an obsessive-compulsive thing?"

"Yeah, the world's biggest obsessive-compulsive was also a great hacker. Not as good as me, though." Nightmare pushed back and stared at the screen. "Dude, this is so beautiful. Considering he was a freak, I mean."

"What?"

"Just admiring the workmanship." He pointed to the screen. "Right here, Killah gets shell access, so he looks local. That's key, because it means he blends into the background, so everybody puts down their guns. From that point on, it's just a matter of escalation."

"Talk English."

Nightmare gave a reverent look. "Killah had the Holy Grail, dude. I'm talking about root access. When you own the root, you can do anything. You can even change other people's passwords. You can set up a hidden entry for immediate access anytime you like. And my personal favorite, a keystroke logger. You hide out on any terminal in the system, and you can print out every stroke that person types. You rule the world."

"And Doug had it."

Nightmare nodded. "He *owned* this place. He could have devastated them. He could have melted them down, and locked their own administrators out, just to be mean. They would have had to watch, like the *Titanic*." He laughed softly and said under his breath, "You freak."

I was thrown; I had expected at a minimum to find out information about Michele's daughter. Instead, I learned that Doug had conducted a massive hack of a company of which I had never heard. "Who's Grayton Labs?"

"Got me."

"Can we look around?" Nightmare shrugged an assent, then punched keys while we took a guided tour of the company. The public pages revealed the thrust of the business was medical research; there were a couple of pages devoted to various drug therapies the company was developing. Within minutes, however, we hit a long list of apparently meaningless letters and numbers. "How far in can we go?" I asked.

"We got the root, man. We can go anywhere, but that doesn't mean we're going to understand what we're looking at. Whatever it is, Killah wanted in there bad. No stone left unturned."

"We already know he could be obsessive. Maybe it was just an expression of that kind of compulsion."

"It's sure as hell some kind of compulsion."

I stared at the screen. "Listen," I said, "guys like you —"

"Hackers?"

"Yeah. I assume people . . . they try to hire you to do things for them? Things they wouldn't want anybody else to know about?"

Nightmare gave me a thin smile. "You mean like what you're doing?"

"I mean corporate types. Businesses."

"It's a boom industry, if you're willing."

"And Killah was good."

"Very, very good."

"Then it's possible Doug was working for someone else. Something off the record." I looked at Nightmare. "New economy, in other words."

"Yeah, that's a definite possibility. A job like that could be worth a lot of money."

"Enough money to buy plane tickets all over the country to see Michele Sonnier."

A look of comprehension spread over Nightmare's face. "Dude, you're on it. That totally clicks."

I looked back at the screen. *So this is just business. He was paying bills. Helping Michele came later.* "Okay. So if Doug was working for somebody, the questions are pretty clear. We need to find out who was paying him, and why they wanted to know so much about Grayton Laboratories."

"Whoever they were, they weren't kidding around. This is one serious hack." Nightmare was sitting quietly, when suddenly I heard him exhale. I looked over at him; he was, if possible, even more pale than usual.

"Killah hacked these guys."

"Right."

"And now he's dead." We both sat in silence, watching the words *Grayton Technical Laboratories* flash on the screen. I tried to think of the right thing to say so I wouldn't rattle Nightmare, but it was too late; the situation had unhinged him enough already. "Dude," he said, "we gotta get off this site."

"Don't panic, Michael."

"Panic? Killah is *dead.*"

"That's right. And that's why what we're doing is so important."

"Are you nuts? I'm cutting this connection right now." Nightmare moved toward the keyboard; I put my hand on his slender wrist, stopping him.

"Look," I said quietly, "I want to find out what this is about. And I need you to help me."

"You don't have enough money to get me to do that."

Nightmare, my ass. "I don't have any money, Michael. But I want you to help me anyway." Nightmare's breathing was shallow, his concave chest moving up and down under his T-shirt. He looked like he'd seen a ghost. "I'm going to piss you off now," I said quietly, "but it's in a good cause."

"Start now, because the sooner you finish, the sooner I can get out of here."

I turned his chair toward mine, facing him down. "You're a talented kid, Michael. Intelligent, resourceful, and in your weird-ass way, ambitious. But I'm going to tell you the unvarnished truth. So far, you haven't done a damn thing with it." Nightmare started to rise; I pushed him back down. "Listen to me, Michael. Hacking a bunch of sites so you can brag to your buddies at some secret meeting where you don't even use your real names—it doesn't mean shit."

"To you."

"To use the vernacular, Michael, you and your hacker buddies spend all day jerking off. I'm offering you the chance to get laid."

"What does that mean?"

"It means you can do something real instead of pretend. You're good at this, Michael."

"Not good. Great."

"All right. You're great. And your life story to date doesn't add up to a thing. For God's sake, I had to get you off a shoplifting charge." Nightmare looked down; he was angry, but for the first time, his bravado couldn't cover his embarrassment. "Do something valuable with it, Michael. Do something important." I shook my head in frustration. "Or just piss it away. Why not? It's what you've done with your life so far."

Michael eyed me warily, but I could see he was still scared. "So helping you makes me a good guy, is that it?"

"Yes, Michael. And helping Doug. They both make you a good guy."

"Killah's past my help. That deal's done."

"Whatever happened to Doug, it has something to do with what's on that screen right now. What did you think we were doing here? Just snooping around about Doug out of curiosity?"

"I didn't care what you were doing, dude. I owed you, and now we're even."

"Come out of the cave, Michael. Do something that matters. Be my partner." Silence, while Nightmare's wheels turned. I could see him trying it on, comparing it against his fear. "Be a man, Michael. Be a man instead of a shadow."

We sat silently for a while. At some point, something clicked in Nightmare. Maybe he was afraid that if he didn't take this chance, he'd never come out into the sunlight. Maybe he saw himself, pale and forty, going slowly insane in front of a flickering computer screen. All I know is that minutes passed, and at last he quietly said, "Okay, we'll be partners. Like in those movies. Like Jackie Chan and that black guy."

I exhaled, relief flooding over me. "More like Abbott and Costello," I said under my breath.

"Who's that?"

I looked at him. "A couple of dead guys."

CHAPTER TEN

THE MUNDANE IS WHAT separates life from the movies. Michael left around two, mostly because I had paperwork for Odom that couldn't wait. If I didn't fill it out, I didn't get paid. This was followed by a meeting with a forty-seven-year old repeat-offending client who proved that drug abuse isn't just for the young. The man had wobbled into my office looking every day of seventy, but apparently, his appetite for chemical destruction had yet to be sated. Taking his case was my contribution to the revolving door that is the American judicial system. It was after three before I could call Michele. She answered immediately. "It's Jack," I said. "Can you talk?"

"It's fine," she answered. She sounded better than when I had left her, nearly restored. "I'm in my car."

"Okay. I wanted to ask you some things. We can talk now, or—"

"Did you find out something?" Her voice was full of anticipation.

"I got in Doug's computer," I said. "I didn't find anything about . . . what we discussed. Not yet."

Her voice deflated. "What did you find?"

Images of Doug's obsession flashed across my memory. Those I would keep to myself, if only to protect Doug's privacy when he could no longer protect it himself. Grayton, on the other hand, was fair game. "A lot of things," I said. "We need to talk."

"I'm on my way to a rehearsal." I could hear the sound of traffic in the background. "It's very tight right now."

"Maybe we can meet later."

"*No*," she said, firmly. "Meet me at the hall around five. I should be finished by then."

"Is it private?"

"There's no one there but my accompanist. You know the Emory campus?"

"Like the back of my hand."

"Good. You remember the little chapel, the one by the Callaway Center?"

"Sure."

"You'll see a sign that says, 'No Admittance.' Ignore it."

"That's fine."

It was too early to drive over to Emory, so I made the fifteen-minute drive home. I checked the news, which was the usual compilation of human misery, so I turned it off. I thought awhile about Michele, and found myself putting up my guard. There is a kind of woman who attracts drama, whether consciously or unconsciously, and the same magnetism can make a man stick to her, metal against metal. That, I reminded myself, I did not need. What I needed was information, and I was willing to help her in exchange for that service. If it reunited mother and daughter, all to the good; unlike her husband, I had spent enough time among the lost of the underclass to understand what had happened, and her determination to make amends now, when it might cost her so much, seemed admirable. But I wanted to keep my focus on Doug.

I rolled over to the rehearsal hall a little early, tired of pacing my apartment. I parked and walked to the front door. I pushed through the entry door, slipped into the darkness at the back, and confronted the power of a perfectly trained vocal instrument in full song. There were only about a hundred seats, and I was less than forty feet away from the edge of the stage. She was in street clothes, in black pants, a blood-red top, and little makeup. Her hair was pulled back in a ponytail. Her voice filled the small hall, the air vibrating with her power. What she was doing was nothing less than astonishing. A middle-aged, balding man was hunched over a piano to accompany her, but he was irrelevant. With effortless, graceful ease, Michele was defying the laws of physics with her voice. There was no strain, no harshness. Just the flow and power of someone three times her size.

I slipped into a chair in the darkness to listen. There was something ravenous in her singing, something desperate and physical. I had seen it in her Romeo—the wrenching despair, the utter commitment to character. Her words came back to me: *I sing to justify my life. I sing so that God does not condemn me to hell.* Those words, then so stark and mysterious, came to life before my eyes. There was no longer any question of the source of her artistry. Why was it impossible to look away when she sang? Because under every note was her indefinable, but utterly real, sadness. She was tortured, and she was turning her pain into something precious.

She sang for twenty minutes or so, starting and stopping a little, occasionally saying something to her accompanist. I could see her looking out into the darkness for me, so at a break I stood. She squinted, caught my face in the dim light, and smiled. That smile, set within the deeply etched sorrow of her performance, seemed as fragile as china.

I had expected her to finish up once she saw me, but instead she paused, turned, and whispered to her accompanist. He gave her a quizzical look, but rummaged through some music. She stepped quietly to the center of the stage and stood, an ebony statuette, eyes closed and motionless. After several seconds she minutely inclined her head. The pianist began to play.

What can a boy from Dothan say about such music? I grew up on my father's recordings of Buck Owens and Waylon, and I kissed my first girl to a worn-out cassette of Guy Clark. That was music built to tear down whatever lies between a human being and his sorrow. I have no use for the stuff coming out of Nashville these days, because it has no heart. But listening to Michele sing that day, I learned that all heartaches are one, and the style is just window dressing. Rich and poor, white or black, none of it matters. Whether it's sung in the celestial tones of an opera or ground out through the gravel voice of a bar singer, the heartache stays the same. It's the common human experience, and when we hear it coming back to us in music, it stops us dead. I stood there listening, knowing that one of the greatest singers on earth was singing for me alone, and I will not pretend to have been immune. I have no doubt that in order to possess a power like the one Michele displayed in that moment, there are those who might even choose to endure her nightmares. If true art comes from pain, then her art ran in stained rivers through her soul.

The collection of consonants she sang could only be Russian, so I understood none of it. It didn't matter. The music alternated between grand sections of strong melody and delicate, soulful phrases. I stood facing her in the dark and let her voice pour over me.

When she finished, she looked down tentatively, as though exposed. She kissed her accompanist on the cheek and stooped to pick up a couple of shoulder bags. She walked gently down the little stairs, stage left. I stepped from my seat into the aisle and moved across another row to meet her. We met with a single row between us, and she leaned across a chair and bussed me, European style, on both cheeks. "Do you mind if we sit in my car to talk?" she asked. "It's more private." She reached into a bag, pulled out some wire-rim glasses with pale green lenses, and put them on. She was wearing the same citrus scent she wore at the Four Seasons.

I nodded, and we started walking toward the door at the back of the hall. "The last thing you sang. What is it?"

She smiled. "I sang it to please you."

"Why would you want to do that?"

"Because you think opera is nothing but stodgy melodrama for rich people, and you're wrong about that."

I opened the back door from the little auditorium, and we

stepped out into the hallway. "Nobody who hears you sing could think that."

She smiled, obviously pleased. "The story is from Pushkin," she said. "Do you know him?"

"Not personally."

"Oh, my God. He's—"

"Yeah, I know him. Patron saint of Russian misery. What do the words mean?"

She stopped walking and paused before answering. "A woman is torn between two lovers," she said. "The first she loves passionately, but he's poor and defeated. He has nothing."

I nodded. "And the other lover?"

"He's a rich and powerful man. He has everything she wants. But she doesn't love him, not like the other."

"Let me guess. The rich guy is evil, and the poor one is good."

She shook her head and started walking again. "It's Pushkin, not some TV show. *Krasoyu, znatnostyu, bogatstvom, Dostoinomu podrugi ni takoi, kak ya.*"

"Which means?"

"It means life is a lot more complicated than we want."

"I agree."

"She doesn't think she's worthy to be the wife of a great prince," she said. "That's what's pushing her towards the poor man. It's the fear of marrying above her station and not living up to it. It's a little bit of a psychodrama."

We reached the exit onto the street, and walked through. "So what happens?"

"She decides to trust the poor man. She risks everything for him." She took a few steps, stopped, and turned toward me. "In return for which the poor man sells her out. He betrays her to win at a lousy game of cards."

"You're kidding."

"So much for your clichés."

"But the prince rides in to save the day, right? It's got a happy ending."

"She throws herself into the Winter Canal. The end." She gave a sad, ironic smile. "It's called *Pikovaya Dama*. The Queen of Spades." She held my eyes a second—just long enough for the irony of the title to sink in—then turned smartly on her heel and started walking down the sidewalk toward her car, leaving me standing. I watched her back, gazing at the gentle swing of her hips. I followed, and when we reached her Lexus she unlocked the doors. We got in and sat, the engine idling. "So tell me what you found out," she said.

That our friend Doug Townsend was broken inside, and that the bending revolved around a titanic, sick adoration of you. "Let me ask you something first," I said. "Do you believe that Doug was capable of loving you? Of something more than just obsession?"

She stared through the windshield. "Who knows? Turandot, Tosca, Romeo. All of them, obsessed. And we call them the greatest lovers in the world. I live in a world of obsession."

"They're characters in stories," I said. "They're not real."

"To Doug they were," she said. "He could live in those worlds. Maybe he was just broken enough to live like he was in a play."

"Then tell me this. Would a character in any of those stories just quietly go off and kill himself without a word to anyone?"

She looked at me. "What do you mean?"

"You say Doug lived in this operatic world. But if I'm going to off myself, I sure as hell would want the woman I loved to know about it."

"The woman you loved?"

"*You*, Michele. Doug was in love with you. You must have recognized that fact. A man doesn't fly all over the United States for a woman unless he loves her." She looked away. "Maybe you think he killed himself because he knew he could never have you, not in the way he wanted."

Her voice grew quiet. "It's not impossible."

"Let it go," I said. "It didn't happen." The gratitude on her face told me I had hit a nerve. "A guy doesn't kill himself over a woman without letting her know," I said. "It's too pathetic. He wants that woman to feel his pain down to her toes."

"He got his wish, if that's what he wanted."

"You're being theatrical," I said gently. I didn't say it to hurt her, but I had seen enough real grief in my life to know that what she was feeling wasn't in that category. She was upset, but she wasn't broken down, not like she was about her daughter.

She started to speak, then checked herself. "All right," she said. "I accept what you're saying. It's better than the alternative."

"Good."

"So where does that leave us?"

"Have you ever heard of a company called Grayton Technical Laboratories?"

She shook her head. "No."

I hid my disappointment. "Then answer me this," I said. "Were you paying Doug for what he was doing for you?"

"He wouldn't accept anything. Not a penny."

"Then I think we have a winner."

"What does that mean?"

"Doug was amassing a huge amount of information about this Grayton Laboratories. I figure a competitor hired Doug to spy on them. It would have been illegal, so the money was probably good."

"Spying? Doug?"

"Our picture of Doug as a simple victim of life was a little off," I said. "He wasn't just good with a computer. He had a serious reputation in the underground hacker world."

She looked shocked. "I thought he was an amateur, like those kids who stay up all night writing emails to each other."

"Those kids, as you call them, can do a lot of damage. Doug was very, very talented. And in my experience, talent goes where it's rewarded, either above ground or below. His skills would be worth a fortune to the right person."

"How did you find all this out?"

"An acquaintance," I said. "Someone from that world. And he says Doug was well known there." I paused. "Listen," I said, "it isn't rocket science to imagine your husband as a possible employer. Horizn is in the same business."

She looked stricken. "Charles? He doesn't know anything about Doug."

"You're sure about that?"

"As sure as I can be. Anyway, Doug would have told me if Charles had approached him." She sighed, suddenly tired. "I have to go out of town tomorrow," she said. "It's what I was rehearsing for. It's in St. Louis."

"Will you be gone long?"

"No. It's a quick turnaround. It's very casual, just one night. We're doing *La Boheme*."

"A casual opera?"

She smiled. "It's a festival. The crowd doesn't dress, not like what you saw. No tuxedos. People come in shorts. Stripped-down staging. Complete chaos backstage." Suddenly, she brightened. "Come with me," she said. "I'm flying alone, and I hate that."

"You're not serious."

"Of course I am. A couple of hours up, the same back. Can you?"

Not for so many reasons. "I don't actually shop in the last-minute-ticket price range," I said. "Sorry."

"Don't be ridiculous. I'm taking the Horizn jet."

"Jesus."

"We can talk about Doug."

"Doug."

"Yes. We'll be . . . friends." She paused. "I need that right now, Jack. You can't imagine what it's like to have someone to talk to who knows everything. It's like air."

I looked away, just to give my eyes somewhere else to land than her extraordinary, caramel skin. "I'm not sure that's such a great idea," I said.

"Come with me, Jack. I'm singing something so beautiful it will break your heart."

"That's the last thing I need." The second I spoke, I knew I had made a mistake. *God help me, she's going to want to know everything. She's not going to rest until she knows what happened to me, how the guilty pain of what happened to Violeta Ramirez makes me understand her so well.*

"I knew there was something," she said. Her eyes were looking into mine, and I prepared for an assault onto my private history. But to my surprise, she released me.

"It doesn't matter," she said quietly. "It always comes to the same thing."

I looked up at her. "And what's that?"

"*L'amore non prevale sempre*. Love does not always prevail." She smiled softly, her mouth warm and glossy. "Think about tomorrow," she said. "I want you to come. We'll be . . . friends."

The merciless traffic of late afternoon Atlanta was in its conspiracy against movement, so there was no point in trying to get home for a while. The area near the university plays host to a variety of cheap, decent restaurants, and I pulled into one for an early dinner. I was three forkfuls into something cheap and forgettable when my cell phone rang; it was Sammy, telling me Odom had let out court early, and asking me to meet him at The Rectory. Thanks to his previous employment there, Sammy has a very tolerable arrangement with the bartender that puts Chivas in Sammy's glass at Seagram's prices. When you drink in sufficient quantities, such niceties add up. By the time I finished my dinner and made the drive over, he was several glasses deep into his special privileges. For Sammy, the perfect night was one in which his credit card limit and his capacity to drink converged in a perfect *x-y* axis. It was early, but at the rate he was going, tonight was going to be a math teacher's dream.

"He took her to Nikolia's Roof," he said, before I sat down.

"Who took who?" I asked, pulling out a chair.

"*He* did," Sammy hissed. "To Nikolia's."

"The one on the top floor of the Hilton?"

"For God's sake, Jack, there's only one Nikolia's. And *he* took her there."

Recognition flickered; Sammy was talking about Blu. "Damn it, Sammy, how did you know that?"

"A guy owed me a favor," Sammy answered. "It's his line of work."

"Don't go over the edge on me, Sammy."

Sammy stared into his drink. "The first rule of revenge is to know your enemy."

"I know, but having the guy tailed . . ." I trailed off, wondering again if I had made the right decision telling Sammy about Stephens's designs on Blu. But it was too late now. "Look, Sammy, Nikolia's is pretty public," I said. "Maybe he'll get busted. Somebody will see him and tell his so-called girlfriend."

"Naw," Sammy said, shaking his head. "I asked around. He had a little private room. He's pals with Nikolia or something."

"Listen, the guy's not married. So technically he's in the market."

"Yeah. He's going to technically get his ass kicked, too."

"Sammy, I'm begging you, don't go psycho on me. Keep it reasonable."

Sammy looked at me, his eyes bleary. "You know what's annoying about you, Jackie old pal?"

"I assume there's a list. You can start with the As." I caught the waitress's eye and ordered a scotch.

"Wrong," Sammy said. "There's only one thing wrong with you. You . . . how's it go? You cast your pearls before swine."

"Do tell."

Sammy set his empty glass down hard on the table. He tried unsuccessfully to make eye contact with the waitress for a refill, then turned back to me. "Look at you, Jackie boy. You're a genius, and you spend all day down in Odom's court."

"Pays the bills," I said.

"I'm down there watching you every day, and I ask myself, what's a guy who talks like a million bucks, looks like a million bucks, knows more about procedure than anybody I ever saw . . . I mean, shit, Jack. You win ninety percent of your cases."

"I plead more than half of them down, Sammy," I said quietly. *Great. Now Sammy is giving me the speech I gave Nightmare. Beautiful.*

"Yeah, but they're all guilty."

"They're not all guilty, Sammy."

"They're *all* fucking guilty, and you know it."

"All right. They're mostly guilty."

"And you get them off, you bastard genius bastard." Sammy looked at me blankly. He was a couple of drinks past fine distinctions in language.

"What is this, harass Jack Hammond night? I got a lot on my plate already."

"My point," Sammy said, gathering his thoughts, "is that compared to you, I'm a moron."

"Sammy—"

"No," Sammy interrupted, "I'm a moron. And even with my limited fucking capabilities, I am going to extract a revenge on Stephens so beautiful it would make a grown man cry." He looked down at his empty glass. "Him, hopefully."

"What are you going to do?" I asked. A worried feeling was growing in my gut. Stephens was way, way out of Sammy's league.

"None of your damn business," Sammy said.

"Sammy—"

"Leave it, Jackie boy," Sammy said. "It's gone beyond you now. All you need to know is this: I see a very bad day coming for Blu's new boyfriend."

CHAPTER ELEVEN

NICOLE FROST WAS NOT aptly named. She was, for a securities broker, remarkably human and warm. She and I had gone to college together, although she hadn't known Doug. She had flown in different skies, the elite group of pretty people who did acceptably academically but even better socially. It was a foregone conclusion she would be successful, and she hadn't disappointed anybody. She had managed my modest investment account in happier days, until I was forced to withdraw every penny just to survive. I called her the next morning after talking to Michele, looking for information about Grayton Laboratories. "Hello, Jack," she said in her unflappably cheerful voice, "great to hear from you. What's new?"

"I've got a big pile of money to invest," I said. "It's all twenties, and you might find a little residue on some of the bills. Hope that's okay."

"Very funny."

"I could take a walk on the dark side. You never know."

"Just defending those people is bad enough, Jack, but that's another story. Since you're not going to make either of us any money, what do you need?"

"A little information."

"You're broke."

"Thanks, I already knew that. Anyway, it's not about me."

"Okey-dokey."

"What do you know about a company called Grayton Technical Laboratories?"

There was a pause, while Nicole riffled through her immense mental Rolodex. "Small biotech company, haven't made a lot of noise. I probably wouldn't know anything about them if they weren't local."

"Nothing spectacular in their pipeline?"

"Maybe," she answered. "I don't follow biotech much."

"Any idea who runs it?"

"Umm, I think the family members are on the board now. Grayton himself is more a figurehead. The stock doesn't do much. Just sits there, mostly."

"All right, next topic. How about Horizn?"

She laughed. "What about them? They're about to make a lot of people a lot of money."

"Going to be big?"

"*Huge.* The hepatitis patent is going to pay off for decades." She paused. "It's the perfect disease, you know. Not to be heartless about it."

"What do you mean?"

"I mean you have to take dear Dr. Ralston's medicine for the rest of your hopefully long life. Fantastic, from an investment point of view. Which is funny, really."

"Why?"

"Don't you know how Ralston made his millions?"

"Not a clue."

"A mere ten years ago, Ralston was a lowly human like you or me. He was heading a research team at Columbia."

"Yeah, I'd heard he was a scientist."

"His team came up with Horizn's treatment of the disease," Nicole said. "Naturally, the university claimed the patent. Ralston was acting as an employee. He had the standard percentage, but he wanted it all."

"He disputed?"

"Right. Nobody gave him a prayer, of course. That kind of contract is usually airtight. But that was before he hooked up with some lawyer—"

"Derek Stephens."

"Yeah, Stephens. Supposedly he's some kind of intellectual property genius or something. Nation's leading authority. He's always getting quoted on *Wall Street Week*. Anyway, thanks to him, Ralston walked out with the patent, and they were both millionaires."

"Both?"

"Ralston didn't have any money, so Stephens got paid with a percent of the patent. So he closed his practice, and they more or less ran off to run the world together."

"Very enterprising."

"Yeah, and now the price of that drug is three times what it would have been."

"Screw the little people, that's what I always say."

"It's a cruel world, darling." Nicole paused. "Listen, Jack, why the sudden interest?"

"Just something I'm working on."

I could hear Nicole's wheels turning. "Jack, you wouldn't be holding out on me, would you?"

"What do you mean?"

"Something brewing on the street that you somehow discovered through your colorful friends."

"Umm, maybe," I said. "Not sure."

"It's not nice to play hard to get when you're asking for favors, Jack. Tell Nicole what you know."

"I can't do that, actually."

"So it must be good," she said, her voice respectfully hushed.

"Nothing would make me happier than to pay you back for all

your kindness with a little insider information. But I'm flying blind at this point."

"Considering your . . . um . . . *professional milieu*," she said, "it would probably be something sordid. You realize that Horizn's offering is in less than two weeks. Bad news would be very, very unwelcome."

"Easy, Nicole. I've got nothing right now. You start passing out unfounded rumors and you'll be selling stocks in outer Siberia."

I could feel the quiet settle on Nicole. "So what are you saying?"

"I'm just asking questions."

"Okay." There was a pause, and her voice suddenly brightened. "Listen, Jack, Ralston's going to be on the Georgia Tech campus next Friday. I just saw a press release on it."

"What for?"

"Because he's brilliant. Check this out. He's in the quiet period, so he can't make any comment on Horizn between now and the IPO."

"SEC regulations."

"Correct. But he's days away from a public offering, and he wants to put Horizn's name in the mind of every investor in the country. So what does he do, darling?"

"Got me."

"He gives away a building. The Charles Ralston School for Biomedical Engineering. It'll cost him four million, and he'll get twenty in publicity. And then he'll write the four million off. I'm telling you, the man's a genius. Anyway, a bunch of us are going. Knowing Ralston, he'll figure out a way to sneak in a comment about Horizn. We can go together."

"You don't mind?"

Nicole laughed. "Of course not. Besides, you make such lovely arm candy."

"Don't kid me, Nicole."

"On the contrary. You have no apparent interest in women, which makes you irresistible. And anyway, there's an adorable guy at Suntrust who's going to be there, and I want to make him miserable."

"Ah. You're using me."

"He needs motivation. So when I hang all over you, don't misunderstand. The ceremony starts at eleven. Meet me out front at ten till?"

"Deal."

"Wear something nice. See you Friday. Ciao, sweetie."

Come to St. Louis, the voice had said. *We'll be friends.*

I spent the rest of that day in court, hearing that voice in my mind. I heard it while Odom gave a pained look during one of my arguments, in which I maintained that, contrary to the arresting officer's opinion, offering to sell marijuana to a stranger who hadn't brought up the subject constituted entrapment. I heard the voice while I blankly stared at a girl who had made the final descent into the hell of prostitution in order to pay for her coke habit. I heard the voice while I worked through lunch, trying to get on top of a DUI on somebody who spoke only Croatian.

Come to St. Louis, she had said. *We'll be friends.*

I looked at my watch; it was two-forty, which would give me just enough time to get to the plane, if I completely lost my mind.

I completely lost my mind.

CHAPTER TWELVE

THE HORIZN JET WAS a polished, black Grumman that looked every penny the seven million or so it cost. The Horizn insignia, a white, artistic *H* on a red background, was emblazoned on the tail. I parked at Brown Field, a private airfield in northwest Atlanta. I locked up—a superfluous act, considering the gated, twenty-four-hour security intended for the luxury cars surrounding my aged Buick—and walked across the street to the reception area. As soon as I opened the door, I saw her.

Michele was sitting in the office alone, dressed down so far only someone fabulously wealthy could pull it off. Her jeans were tattered, and she wore a simple orange cotton shirt, loosely hanging on her trim body. She looked up when I came in, and her smile almost melted me where I stood. She kissed me, her lips soft and warm on my cheek. We walked to the plane together, and boarded.

A private Grumman jet is one way to measure the distance between the merely rich and the seriously rich. People who shop in this price range consider commercial first-class to be an insult to their tastes. They spend hours with the aircraft interior designer, making important decisions like whether they want the bathroom fixtures to be gold or titanium. Thanks to the fortunes of Horizn Industries, this was the world Michele inhabited.

Michele was chatty for the first part of the flight, almost girlish. She smiled and poured us both some champagne, then leaned back to watch the north Georgia mountains flow by underneath us. It was so comfortable, it was as if Charles Ralston didn't exist. But he did exist, no matter what kind of arrangement there was between the two of them. "I've been thinking," I said. "It's a great thing, what you did. You shouldn't play it down. Coming from where you came from, and making something of yourself."

She set down her glass, looking mildly irritated. "You would say that."

"What does that mean?"

She sighed. "It's the black thing."

"Which black thing is that?"

"The one where white people decide which pretty black girl gets to be the house nigger."

I looked at her, surprised. "Maybe you can break that down for me."

"You know I went to New York. I met some people, ended up across the river, in New Jersey. Elizabeth."

"Never been there."

"East hell," she said, her voice flat and detached. "There's a big Portuguese population there. It's not so bad. They take care of their own. But the black areas are something else."

"So what happened?"

"I enrolled in high school. I was lonely, and school is a society."

"Right."

"There was a program that brought orchestras into the schools. Little groups would come a few times a year, like Care packages delivered to Somalia."

"I guess if you're in Somalia you need the food," I said quietly.

"I knew it wouldn't make sense to you."

"I thought we weren't going to get into the white and black thing."

"I know. It's just that . . . why don't we have our own, you know? You get tired of being on the receiving end of all that. We could see them looking around at the school, feeling pity for us. Brave little smiles, like we were hospital patients. It makes you feel worse than before." She looked past me, drawn back into her memory. "But the music. For as long as the music played, it didn't matter where I was. Nothing mattered. Just the notes, the sound. Most of the kids didn't even listen. I crept up to the front, like I was in a trance. I had never seen or heard anything like that in my life."

"Was there singing?"

"Yes. I don't know if she was any good. It's been too long, and I was too easily impressed. But she was beautiful, in a glamorous costume. I watched her for a long time, even before she sang. The way she sat, her legs crossed just so, her back as straight as a ruler. She was smiling at us, and I thought she must know everything in the world. Finally, she stood up and walked to the center of the stage. I was awestruck."

"Like you make people now."

She smiled. "I suppose."

"So what happened?"

"It was only a little chamber group, ten or twelve players. She started singing something in French. *French.* I didn't know much, but I knew I wasn't supposed to like it. It was European. One thing was made clear to me. If things were old and from Europe, they were the enemy." She paused. "Which was a terrible problem, because I thought it was the most beautiful sound I had ever heard."

"So what did you do?"

Her expression darkened. "I started listening to more of it. But not like a student, like a little child. They had everything in the public library. *Everything.* I listened and listened and mimicked. I had no idea if I was any good. I kept it hidden. But it was burning a hole in me."

"How long did this go on?"

"A couple of years. I was singing constantly, learning repertoire, although I didn't even know the words. A few times I sang out loud to my friends. They laughed, or worse. Finally, I couldn't stand it anymore. I had to find people who were like me."

"And?"

"I knew nothing, you understand? All I knew was that people sang at Lincoln Center. One day I worked up my courage, rode a bus there. I don't know what I was thinking. Maybe I expected opera singers to be standing around in costume, singing to each other. But I wandered into the Juilliard School and walked around the halls in a daze. I could hear the music coming from behind the closed doors. I felt like running up and down the halls, just to hear all the different things."

"What happened?"

"I was there a long time, three or four hours. I was afraid I'd get thrown out. I kept ducking away when somebody came by who looked like they wouldn't approve. But finally, a door opened right in front of me, and I couldn't get out of the way. A woman came out of the room and nearly ran over me. I remember looking around her into her studio, which was crammed with books and a piano and little works of art. It looked like heaven."

"What did you do?"

"I froze. She looked at me a second and said, 'Are you lost?'" Michele turned and stared out the Grumman's window, lost in her memory. "I couldn't speak," she said. "The woman was just about to walk off when I managed to say, 'Yes, ma'am. I'm lost.'" Michele looked back at me, brushing off the awkwardness with a smile. "She was kind," she said. "I told her about the singer at my school and about going to the library every day. I told her my favorite arias and that I'd been singing with the recordings. Maybe it was impressive to her, maybe not. After all, she was at Juilliard, and there's no lack of precocious children there. It was something else that made her help me."

"Which was?"

"I said I knew I was supposed to hate her, but I didn't." Michele looked back out the window. "She looked like she wanted to cry."

"Did she agree to teach you?"

Michele drained her glass of champagne. "That's right, Jack. She said I could come up and live in the big house, with the Massah."

"You'll forgive me for calling that attitude a little ungrateful."

"I told you, you can't understand."

"You know, Michele, I can't decide if it's the fact that you get paid a fortune to sing Mozart or the private jet that makes me feel more sorry for you. I'll have to get back to you on that one."

Her eyes flashed. "I've banished men for less than that."

"Tell it to somebody who isn't on a first-name basis with every bail bondsman in midtown Atlanta."

She stared a second, then burst out laughing. "If you aren't going to respond to white guilt, you're really going to piss me off."

I shrugged. "I've heard it all. I'm inoculated. Now tell how you ended up here."

She smiled and leaned over to kiss my cheek. "You don't scare easily. I like that."

She was wrong about that, although she didn't know it. What was scaring me was how much I wanted to kiss her. It was taking an act of will not to cover her impeccable lips with my own.

"I came every Tuesday for a while," she said, "and then we added Thursday, and finally, I was there practically every day. It took a long time for me to figure out what she realized the first time she heard me."

"Which was?"

Her voice dropped. "That no matter what song I'm singing, I'm always singing my own life."

I smiled. "Just like Johnny Cash. That's the secret to his success, I've always thought."

She looked up in horror. "God, Jack."

"If you disrespect the man in black, I'll throw you right off this plane."

She shook her head. "Okay, Jack. It's just like Johnny Cash, only in Italian, in an Elizabethan costume. Fine."

"How did you end up back in Atlanta?"

"That was my husband," she said. "If you're black and ambitious, Atlanta is the center of the universe. It doesn't hurt that the workforce is cheaper." She turned to stare out the window; the mention of Ralston seemed to bring her down. "I need to rest my voice, if that's all right," she said. "I'm going to try and get a little sleep."

We flew on in silence, the plane arrowing its way over Nashville, then turning northwest to St. Louis. Michele closed her eyes, although I didn't know if she was sleeping. Time crept by and I watched her doze, wondering again if I had made the right decision in coming. Her face while sleeping was troubled, as though her dreams were haunted by her awful memories.

We landed at Spirit of St. Louis, a small airfield in suburban St. Louis just off the Missouri River. This was the lowlands, an airstrip dug out of the mud and fecund soil of the delta. The plane taxied up to a limousine already parked out on the tarmac. The man I had seen escorting Michele around at the party and at the Fox Theater got out and stood by the car, watching the plane creep up to a stop about a hundred feet away. The engines spooled down, the whine slowly settling into silence. "Who's that?" I asked.

"Bob Trammel," Michele answered. "He comes early and advances the dates for me. Makes sure everything's ready, that kind of thing."

I peered out the small window of the Grumman. Trammel was early forties, about five-ten, compact build, with coal-black hair combed straight back. Like the last time I saw him, he was smoking. The pilot came back through the seating area, unlocked the door, and pushed the small gangway down toward the pavement. I could see Trammel moving toward the plane, his expression bored. Michele appeared in the doorway first; before she had descended, Trammel spotted me behind her. His face turned unpleasant. While we were still out of earshot I asked, "Been with you long, this guy Trammel?"

She shook her head. "No," she said. "He's Charles's idea. He's been good, though. Very efficient."

We walked down to the pavement, one of the pilots bringing Michele's bag down with him. Michele walked up to Trammel, and whether or not he came from Horizn, she definitely acted in charge.

I don't know anything about opera, but like everybody, I'd heard the word "Diva." In the ten seconds between getting off the plane and walking over to the car, Michele took on the persona in toto. In those few steps, she seemed to stand up taller, back erect, chin a good inch higher. She didn't even bother to introduce me to Trammel. "Get the bags, will you, Bob?" she asked, without looking at him. The car door was open, and she slid in—but only after she took my hand and pulled me in after her. It was a surprise then, feeling her skin against mine. She was utterly in control; I'd never seen a woman exercise that kind of effortless authority. At least in this world, she reigned supreme.

I heard Trammel shut the trunk, and he came around and took the front seat of the Town Car. "Good flight?" he asked. He was watching me in the rearview mirror, trying to make me.

"Have you spoken to Colin?" Michele asked, ignoring his question.

Trammel nodded. "He made the changes. No problem."

I turned toward Michele. "Colin?"

"Colin Timberlake. Artistic director. Such a brilliant man. He uses a baton like a hammer, but there it is." She turned and looked out as an unattractive, industrial part of St. Louis passed by the window. I could feel her withdrawing, preparing inwardly for the performance. If I had imagined some kind of intimate experience on the trip, I had been mistaken; from the second we touched down, Michele was all business. In a few hours she would be taking on a completely different persona, risking her career against another night of brilliance.

Michele stayed within herself for the rest of the drive to Webster University, where the Loretto-Hilton Center was located. We pulled up to the hall, which was quite a bit smaller than the Fox. But it was beautiful, surrounded with extravagant flowers and perfectly manicured greenery. "Nice place," I said, getting out of the car.

"It's small and intimate," Michele said. "Beautiful acoustics." She began walking toward the stage door; I had started in just behind her when I felt a hand on my arm. It was Trammel.

"I know you," he said quietly, pulling me back. "You were at the party in Atlanta. And again, backstage, the last night at the Fox."

"Well, that's the long version. Most people just use my name. It's Jack."

Trammel's eyes were narrow. "There's a great deal to accomplish right now," he said. "I know you won't want to be in the way."

"No," I answered. "I wouldn't."

"The green room's on the other side of the stage. There's Cokes and fruit and things. Wait there."

I walked across the parking lot to the stage door, where Michele had already disappeared. The door opened into a backstage world of faintly organized chaos; people were hurrying across the stage area, putting last-minute touches onto the set. Several raggedly dressed children in stage clothes were huddled together, getting instruction from a woman, probably in how to grovel authentically. Trammel pointed me out of the way, toward a metal door on the other side of the stage. "Green room's over there."

I nodded and walked over to the metal door; behind it was a hallway lined with dressing rooms. None of them was for Michele, so I wandered alone to the green room. It was fairly sparse, just a couple of couches and a lonely spray of flowers haphazardly arranged on a long table. There was a selection of drinks and finger foods; I grabbed a soft drink and popped it. There was a television monitor mounted on the wall, with a camera focused on a wide shot of the stage. Every few minutes different cast members in various stages of dress would walk into the green room and wolf down some fruit or a granola bar, or grab a bottle of water. Nobody spoke, which was fine by me. After about an hour, I glanced up at the monitor; Michele had come back out on stage. There was no sound, but I could see she was talking to a tall, slender man with full, white hair combed back. I guessed he was the director. With or without sound, it was easy enough to see he was doing some kind of pleading. Michele was looking at him with a kind of petulant disinterest. The man began waving his arms around, his cajoling descending into begging. Eventually, Michele put her hand on his shoulder, stopping him cold. She said a few words and walked off the stage. The man continued speaking to her retreating back, then threw up his hands and walked off in the other direction.

The concert was still some time off, so I wandered around campus for a while. About an hour before the concert I drifted back out to the backstage area. I scouted around the dressing rooms and found one with a large star on the door and a sign that read, "Ms. Sonnier." I knocked.

Nothing happened for a second; then it suddenly opened. Michele was standing in front of the door in a half-open robe, her hair pulled back off her face by a barrette. I could see the line of her breast disappearing into the red folds of the fabric of her robe.

"Where's Trammel?" she asked.

"No idea. How's it going?"

"The director is inept, I just banished the costumier, the baritone is tone deaf and sings so loud he makes me sound wrong."

"Glad I came."

She smiled at me and the prima donna vanished. "You're good for me, you know that?" she said.

"Thanks."

"Help me with this?" She turned her back to me and let the robe slide down off her shoulders to her waist. She was wearing a black, sheer bra of lace. Her shoulders tapered down to a narrow waist, and I could see the top of a matching pair of thong panties.

I pulled my eyes upward. "Help you with what?"

"This." She reached out and handed me a drab, brown costume. It was stained, and looked like it had been worn nearly through. She held her hands up, and I pulled it down over her arms. As it reached her waist, she let the robe slip down over her hips. The costume nestled down over her butt, reaching a mid-thigh length.

"I take it you're supposed to be poor."

"Po'." She laughed. "In Paris, though, which helps."

"Yeah, Paris would help."

"You know much about bein' po', Jack?" The smooth, upper-class accent vanished, for the moment. Her voice was suddenly

young and urban, the harsh tone of the inner city. I didn't know if
it was authentic or if she were putting it on, like a suit of clothes.

"I never went hungry. But I know what it feels like to be on the
outside looking in."

"I thought so." She turned, gazing at herself in the mirror.

"I'll go," I said, nodding. "Trammel showed me the green room.
I'll go eat some cheese."

She laughed, her silken voice returned. "You do that," she said.
Her voice was pure music, even when she was talking. She turned
back to me and said, "I'm glad you're here, Jack. Friends is good."

She stood before me in her street urchin's costume—a stun-
ningly appealing combination of innocent waif and worldly seduc-
tress—and I wanted to pull her into my arms and save her from all
the ravages of a bitter Paris winter. "Time to go," I said quietly.

"Yes," she said. Then, she bussed my cheek, soft and chaste. I felt
her lips on my skin all the way backstage to my seat.

Eventually, the crowd started to filter in, a casual mix of students
and older folks, more relaxed than at the Fox. Michele had got me a
fifth-row seat, near the center, and I settled in to watch her sing.

From the beginning, something bothered me. It began as a
vague feeling of discontent, but it grew as the performance continued. It took me about thirty minutes to figure out what was piss-
ing me off. Then, it hit me: if Puccini knew much about being
poor, he didn't put it in *La Boheme*. The program said he started
out broke, but he was famous and rich by the time he wrote the
opera. That screwed up his perspective. It's always the same: once
somebody makes real money, he romanticizes the hell out of what
it was like when he had nothing. He tells stories about how great it
was when he didn't have all the problems of wealth. I know,
because I did it myself. I figure Puccini was about the worst
offender of all time on that score. The picture of Paris in winter
that I saw on stage—a poverty so subtly colorful and charming it
could have come out of a Disney movie—was a long way from the
Atlanta projects. And the bohemians—the painter, the writer, and
all the rest of them—chirped around like Disney birds, too. They

enjoyed the hell out of being poor, mostly. The only one I could get a handle on was Mimi, because she was dying. Not that I think you can't find a moment of happiness in the ghetto. I've seen it, a hundred times. But ghetto humor is tinged with the kind of edgy nervousness that comes from knowing your existence isn't a foregone conclusion. This is what Puccini forgot: When ghetto people laugh, they laugh hard, as a kind of armor against life. The humor isn't charming, it's defiant. The characters in *La Boheme* sang about love and poetry like they didn't have a care in the world. In other words, they acted like rich people who just didn't happen to have any money. The truth is not having any money stinks, and the people who don't have any can tell you how many ways. Johnny Cash sure as hell wouldn't have made that mistake.

Which isn't to say it wasn't beautiful. That, I suppose, is its own statement. It just showed that a thing can be a load of crap on one level, and still work its magic on another. The music was so beautiful it could break you down if you weren't careful. And in the center, lit from within and without, was Michele Sonnier. Jesus, Mary, and Joseph, she sang that night. She was good in Atlanta as Romeo, but this was another level. At times, she sang with the delicacy of a glass figurine, as if her voice would shatter into bright fragments if it were touched. At other times, she sang with a riveting, unashamed sexuality. Believe me, there wasn't a guy in the place who took his eyes off her. She was a miracle.

I suppose it's a gift, because the other people on the stage worked just as hard. Harder, actually. You could see it in their eyes, how they had spent a million hours in dumpy practice rooms, singing scales or whatever singers do. But you could also see fear and a little awe in their eyes whenever Michele sang. It might have even been hatred. Because no amount of effort was going to take any of them to the place that Michele went when she sang. No matter who else was on stage around her, you never looked at any of them. You kept your eyes on Michele, watching her luminous face. It was like she had said: no matter what she was singing, she was singing her life. She had mastered the ability to completely let go, which was why, watching her there in the dark, whatever protections I had erected between the two of us began to come down. I'm not proud of it, but I'm not ashamed of it, either. In view of what eventually happened, its meaning turned out to be so tortured that I'll never completely understand it. But when I look back, I know what it was that bound me to her: we both wanted to disappear into something. It meant different things to each of us, but the essence was the same.

Fall in love. I didn't say the words to myself that night, sitting in the dark, because their time had yet to come. But on some roads, the first step is all you need to decipher the destination. Maybe those words would have come to me that night—premature, but prophetic—but suddenly she was dying again on stage. I had seen her sing twice, and both times she had ended up dead. This time it was from tuberculosis—a gift of the cold Paris air—and I began to wonder if it was some opera thing, all the dying. But whatever it was, this death was completely different from her Romeo. It was a cold, hard struggle for life, and it was chilling to watch. Her voice got smaller and smaller, but it was still beautiful, hanging perilously in the air, the orchestra a whisper beneath her. And then she exhaled her last, tremulous note. You could feel the audience breathing out with her, brought into her world completely. A bit of each one of them was dying, and just like at the Fox, some people around me started to cry. It was exactly like what she had done to me backstage, but she was doing it to a thousand people at once, all of them complete strangers.

And then, as before, it was over. The spell was broken, shattered by applause. Backstage there was another crush of affirmation, dozens of sprays of flowers, scores of well-wishers wanting to touch the star. I lay back, staying at a distance. It wasn't my world, but it was fascinating to watch. I couldn't figure out how she could be lonely with all the people around her telling her how great she was, but she was lonely; I knew that absolutely. She was as lonely as I was, lonely enough to wake us up in the middle of the night with a dull ache in our souls. At one point in the chaos she looked over at me, and I smiled, nodding my head. She smiled back, but it was only a moment's connection. She was quickly pulled back into the throng of admirers.

I walked back out the stage door, looking for relief from the noise, and a little fresh air. Trammel was out there, smoking a cigarette. "Good show," I said. Trammel looked at me as though I had just wrecked his new BMW.

"What are you doing here, Mr. Hammond?" he asked.

"I was just wondering that myself," I answered. "I've decided it comes down to being asked."

His lips formed a kind of sneer. "So you're this season's toy."

"Excuse me?"

"The expression is self-explanatory."

I looked at him: narrow face, intelligent eyes, dark suit not quite put together. "Lemme ask you something," I said, changing the subject. "What's a tour manager do?"

Trammel shrugged. "Collect money, mostly. Say things to people that Michele doesn't want to say herself."

"What kinds of things?"

" 'My dressing room is cold. The bottled water is the wrong kind. The stage manager is incompetent.' And, of course, 'Goodbye.' "

"Goodbye?"

Trammel gave me a leer. "That's right. 'Goodbye.' "

We stood in silence, the smoke wafting up off Trammel's cigarette in the light of an overhead streetlamp. "How often do you say it?" I asked quietly.

Trammel looked over at me. "Whenever necessary."

"She doesn't say it herself?"

Trammel shook his head. "Why should she? She has me."

"But what about Ralston? Surely he doesn't put up with this."

Trammel shrugged. "That's not for me to say. Mr. Ralston can manage his own affairs."

There was some noise behind us; the first few cast members were escaping the auditorium, heading for their cars. Trammel dropped his cigarette onto the pavement and ground it out with his shoe. Before he moved off I said, "One more thing."

"Yeah?"

"Who was last season's toy?"

Trammel's lips formed the sneer once again. His answer was a single word: "Gone."

On the plane, the postperformance exhaustion showed through again. There was a bar, and she asked me to pour her a drink. I set us both up with a scotch, and we settled back for the flight. The plane was a kind of cocoon, the narrow fuselage creating a warm, cozy space. We were sitting side by side, and once airborne she suddenly nestled against me, coming in under my arm. It was a kind of trust, the way she let go, her breathing deep and slow. Her eyes were half-closed, and she seemed perfectly content, her body framed against my own. She was brilliant, an angel, and she was leaning her beautiful, exquisite body against me. She was also married to another man, which is why I needed to blow it up. This was something about which I considered myself an expert. "Trammel said something interesting after the show," I said. "Kind of a stopper."

Michele looked up at me from under my arm. Her skin was so smooth and radiant it was all I could do to keep from touching it. "What was that?"

"He said I was this season's toy."

I admit I didn't expect her to laugh, but she did. "He would say that."

"Why's that?"

"Because he's such a boy."

"What's that mean?"

"He hit on me mercilessly for what, three months?"

"You mean he's just pissed?"

"When he finally got the message, he got sullen. Typical." She looked at me. "Which is why I like you."

"I'm sullen already?"

She smiled. "You don't try."

"To do what?"

"Exactly." She nestled deeper into my side, my arm falling down around her. My fingertips were resting on the upper half of her breast, directly on her lovely, brown skin. It had been two years since I had made love to a woman, and the instant my skin touched hers, I was aware of every day of it.

I sat there without speaking, watching my resolve fall apart. I won't belittle the beauty of fidelity by excusing what happened. I grew up in the church and I know right from wrong. But need speaks its own language. You can turn yourself off inside for only so long, and what lingers inside you will find a way out in the end. For every moment of carefully constructed perfection, there is a loss of control. Or maybe it's finding yourself again, your true self, the one closest to your soul. All I know is that we talked for a while, and I don't remember much about what we said. I know that it felt safe, and that, caught in the womb of our mutual acceptance, it didn't matter that I was a destroyed man locked in a nothing law practice who still owned a few good suits. And it didn't matter that she was in a loveless marriage, and that she was carrying around a horrible guilt I would only later be forced to confront. Damage met damage, in the vain, utterly impossible hope that two wrongs could heal a soul. It's the lie that drives every love story, whether written, sung, or lived.

I'll tell you something, and you can trust this completely: Men act like the idea of being found out is so hateful that they would kill rather than be exposed. But the truth is they are longing to be discovered, and they are desperate to have their weakness accepted. When a woman does that, there's nothing left to say, because she owns him.

What, I remember thinking, *are you so afraid of? Why haven't you started your career over again? Why have you been content to sit in Odom's court, doing penny-ante cases? Why haven't you loved anyone in more than two years? Why is your best friend a failed law student and a drunk? Why haven't you found your level again? Why don't you lean down and kiss this incredible woman, and worry about what it means later?* I could feel myself unraveling, bit by bit. While all those questions were passing through my brain, it wasn't a big deal on the surface, just a deeper breath, a flushing of my face. I got it under control in a few seconds, but it was too late.

She saw through me. She was watching me, her artist's eyes looking into mine with a kind of warm precision, and I was exposed, game, set, and match. I don't know at what point her fingers were touching my face. I don't even remember her leaning up toward my mouth. I just know that at some point my eyes were closed, and her fingertips were tracing under my chin, across my cheek. When her fingers touched my lips, I opened my eyes. Her mouth looked so warm, with her lips slightly parted, that it seemed like the answer to every question was hiding just inside them. I leaned down and I kissed her, and my God, I hadn't been with a woman in such a long time that in the back of my mind I was afraid I had forgotten how to do it.

Now, looking back on it, everything means something different. Not just that kiss—everything, I've come to believe, is like that. Distance changes things. But a part of me hangs on to that kiss, to that moment. I don't know how to lie about it. She was married—loveless or not—and it was wrong. But I had no defense, no armor for it. Touching her lips took me into all my upbringing about white and black and fucked it up, rearranged it, spit it out and I was lost in some earthy bayou, devouring her black skin, going back into time to where there weren't any races and there wasn't McDaniel Glen and the War between the States never happened and Jesus, it was like being kissed by Gaia herself. Some moments we possess for ourselves alone, and they cannot be justified in the minds of others. I only know that no man or woman will ever take those sacred, holy minutes away from me, the minutes the great Michele Sonnier set me free.

CHAPTER THIRTEEN

AFTER THE LOVEMAKING, there is the shock wave. The plane landed and we reentered not just the humid atmosphere of the city, but the realities and concerns that had seemed so remote at forty thousand feet. There was a powerful force to help us reorient to our newly changed circumstances, however, and that was the city of Atlanta herself. She is a willing accomplice to love. Her heavily treed, upper-middle-class neighborhoods are so vast that they invite the illusion that they exist in a state of grace, cocooned from all harm. In that calculated state of denial, the city is susceptible to the soft southern light of late summer afternoons, the same light that fell on antebellum plantations and warmed promenading debutantes. The natural beauty of the place somehow persists: its breezes are still sweet, its pines slender and tall, its honeysuckle fragrant. Cast in that gentle glow, the city willingly accepts its most treasured illusions. And what happens in a city can happen in a pair of human souls. For new lovers, the beauty of Atlanta can be a nightshade to reality. With Michele by my side, there was nowhere else in the world I wanted to be.

We were changed now, a new, complex layer of considerations mingled with an already charged situation. There was married and single. There was black and white. There was rich and tenuously hanging on. There was high culture and low. There were more reasons to run than I could count. And none of them meant half as much as the fact that she had found the lock that opened a door I had successfully held shut since Violeta Ramirez died.

Even illicit love has its codes of conduct, and there was no question that we would meet. If it was too soon to know exactly what it was we were sharing, we both knew it was much more than a moment's loss of control. So we did what every pair of lovers has done, from Romeo and Juliet to this day: we longed for reprieve from the world's concerns, for an uncluttered space in which to simply feel.

We would meet the next day, but not until the afternoon. I sleepwalked through my morning, seeing her naked skin in my mind, the pressure of my fingertips tracing the flushed skin of her body. There was a quick trial for Odom, something which, fortunately, required less than half of my mind to accommodate. I arrived to meet a client determined to fight to the bitter end; unfortunately, being videotaped buying crack from an undercover cop made his approach likely to land him in jail. It was a first offense, and I persuaded him that a guilty plea and a contrite attitude would get him back on the street sooner. It would have been better for my own peace of mind if a lowered, late-eighties Pontiac with rap music blasting out of it hadn't been waiting to pick him up once he was given a suspended sentence and compulsory drug treatment. But I had long ago had to face the fact that I was a better lawyer than savior, and I couldn't change my clients' lives outside the courtroom. I would give them their due diligence, and if they were lucky enough to be free to go afterward, they went with God.

At three I headed to meet Michele at Virginia Highlands, an artsy patch of the city just north of downtown. The Highlands is an essential part of Atlanta's optical illusion, a place that can actually make you believe all the disparate elements of the city are going to fit peaceably together in the end. That day its main street was alive with the rainbow, all God's creatures nodding politely to each other and smiling well-fed smiles: tall Rasta men with their hair pushed up into knit caps; thirty-something women in determined, feminist clothes; young bearded Muslims all in white; lithe, impossibly thin women showing their midriffs and smoking cigarettes. Walking its streets, it was easy to believe that the McDaniel Glens of the world didn't exist.

Michele looked like a rainbow herself, in a loose, flowing skirt of dark purple, orange, and black that made a lovely rustle when she moved. She wore a flimsy, off-white top, and three metal bracelets, all on her left arm. Her hair was pulled back tight and scrunched into a fanning ponytail of cornrows. She hid her eyes behind dark sunglasses, although I doubt there was much danger of opera stars being recognized on North Highland Avenue.

The district specializes in a kind of sanitized, funky edginess that lets people feel progressive without actually risking anything. It's lined with New Age boutiques, vegetarian restaurants, and dimly lit clothing stores that burn incense and have bamboo wind chimes. Michele pulled me into several shops, asking my opinion about this or that; I was out of my depth, since my own taste in clothes is mostly to appreciate the woman wearing them. But she was in her element: here she tried on a pair of Asian earrings, there a belt of indeterminate hide, later, a shirt embroidered with brightly colored rag fragments. It was enough to watch her in her happy extravagances, losing herself in exotic fabrics or watching her show distaste for a pair of preposterous shoes.

I loved every second of it. There, where Buddha, Jesus and Muhammad all seemed to be getting along, we were not black or white. We were free to be man and woman, and that was all we wanted. I remember the hours and the minutes and the seconds of it, the fragile, blessed anonymity we felt. Underneath and intertwined with everything, unspoken but alive, was what we had done the night before. The way she closed her eyes when I pushed my hands down her back, the taste of her shoulder, the crashing moment of oblivion—all of it roamed the edges of our conversation, our fleeting glances, our momentary touches. Each moment had the dizzying rush of our sex on it, and the certain prelude that we would lose ourselves in each other again.

But for now, on that warm afternoon, there was no hurry. We walked the whole district, about fifteen blocks or so, taking our time. Eventually we slipped into the Darkhorse Tavern for an early dinner and a glass of wine. We were ahead of the dinner crowd, and the place was nearly empty. We sat deep in shadows, toward the back. We were giddy, eating off each other's plates. The clock moved, ignored and irrelevant. Gradually, dusk grew outside.

There are times when anticipation is so sweet and exhilarating that it becomes a nearly unbearable pleasure. We moved more slowly as the minutes passed, savoring the unrepeatable moments of new love. We must have been there for some time, because the restaurant had slowly filled around us. We looked up and were surprised to be surrounded by other couples, which pleased us even more. The whole city seemed at peace, and we were comfortably in its center. Over drinks she said, "Your turn."

"What?"

"To tell me your story. I don't know anything about you really, and it's not fair." She smiled. "Except how you kiss, of course."

"How do I kiss?"

"Spectacularly."

"I would think that would about cover things, then."

"I'm being serious. Where did you grow up, for example?"

"Dothan, Alabama. It's pretty much like New York, only more sophisticated."

"I'm being serious, Jack. I really want to know."

"You know all that crap about charming little southern towns?"

"Yes."

"It's crap."

She laughed. "It must have had something good about it."

"Well, they probably wouldn't beat the hell out of us anymore for kissing in public. Maybe."

"That's progress, I guess."

I nodded. "And it had my grandfather, who was as good a man

as ever scratched out what passes for a living in that part of the country."

"What did he do?"

"Tried to turn a few acres of dirt into money," I answered. "Took a shot at ten different things, from chickens to hogs to corn to alpacas."

"Alpacas? The ones they make sweaters out of?"

"I think it's just the hair they make sweaters out of."

"You know what I mean."

"He was no farmer, but I never heard him complain. Maybe he did when I wasn't around. He would walk five miles to help a neighbor, and he would go hungry to make sure you got enough. He was a gunnery sergeant in the Pacific in World War Two. When I think about him, I can't understand what's happened to this damn country. I go into Odom's courtroom, and it's like a whole generation of men just forgot to grow up."

She nodded, staring into her drink. "And your parents?"

"Good people. Alabama dirt farmers, like my grandfather. They're gone now. But they saw me pass the bar."

She smiled. "You're like me."

"What do you mean?"

"You got out."

"I suppose I did."

I paid the bill and we began slowly drifting back toward our cars. In the dusk, our touches became more intentional. Music was drifting out of a passing door; we stopped and listened awhile to a band playing the blues. Michele leaned against me, swaying in time to the music. "Let's go in," she said, pressing against me.

"Didn't figure this as your kind of music."

She leaned back and kissed my cheek. "*Everything* is my kind of music, sweetheart. Except for Johnny Cash, of course."

"What do you have against the man in black? He *loves* you." While we stood talking, the door opened, and a couple walked out. The music poured out into the street, gritty and soulful. We could see the band up on stage, and a small dance floor crammed with joyous, gyrating people.

We entered and blended into the crowd, moving through it happily. No matter where it travels, the blues remains the regional possession of the South for one unalterable reason: it is the only music that contains equal measures of joy and pain, which is the short history lesson of our part of the world. For that reason, it remains an essential element of the southern soul. So we were at home there, no matter what else might separate us. We found a table in the back, and I ordered some drinks. Michele was moving gently in her chair, and I watched her, lost in her graceful motion. She caught me watching, got up out of her seat, and demanded, "Let's dance."

"You gotta be kidding."

She flashed a smile. "Let's see you move your ass, white boy."

I stood and walked her out onto the dance floor. She was free, and she was beautiful, a powerful combination of seductions. She came up next to me, and we started moving together, disappearing into the pulsating music. Our fingers locked together, and we moved together like mirror images.

The mind has the capacity to fix on a thing to the exclusion of other dangers, and we reveled in that state. We were part of a happy crowd of people, listening to the music that will always remind southerners of what we have in common. There are times when to be truly happy you have to deny certain realities, and with the help of the crowd and the music, we willingly did so that night. There was only that moment, and the beat of the song, and the moving crowd, and the sweet sensation of falling in love. I would have been happy for it to last forever.

We left her car in the Highlands and drove to my place. When we got there, we sat in my car outside my walkup. I warned her not to expect much. "It's not exactly the Four Seasons," I said, understating the facts considerably. And then I thought forget it, she's here for me and not the furniture, and I kissed her on the mouth, as hard and passionate as I had in me. She closed her eyes and wrapped her arms around me, and for several long moments, my battered Buick was the most perfect place on earth. I got the door for her, and led her up the steps to my place.

I opened the door, and Michele walked into my nine hundred square feet of heaven, taking it in with a bemused expression: ratty, light gray carpet; a questionable mélange of furnishings, including a tan sofa and recliner, a small television, stark and watchful on a black stand; a five-piece dinette, bought well-used and not great to begin with; and above all, a decided lack of the comfortable details that make a space livable. Seeing it there with her, it looked sad, single, and male.

"It's lovely," she said.

"Oh yeah," I said. "There are days I just can't wait to get home and loll around in all this luxury." I gave her a seat on the couch. "Can I get you anything?"

She shook her head. "No. I'm perfect."

"Yes, you are. Just give me a second, will you?" I left her in the living room, slipping into my bedroom. When I came back, she was staring at a framed document I had received in an earlier life. " 'This is to certify that Jack L. Hammond was admitted to practice in the Georgia Supreme Court,' " I recited. "Signed by the justices."

"It's an honor, Jack. Why isn't this down at your office?"

"I doubt it would make much of an impression on my current clientele."

She stood and walked languorously toward me. "You really need to get over that," she said, wrapping her arms around my waist. "Maybe I can help."

She kissed me then, first softly, then more insistently. "Over what?" I asked.

She pulled back a little, fixing me in her gaze. "Over everything," she whispered, and then we were lost in each other again, and nothing else mattered. The eager, unfettered passion of the airplane was tempered now, and I found my rhythm, happy to take my time in pleasing her, content to learn her crevasses, the precise lines of her hips, her stomach, her backside.

Late in the night I put on a Billy Joe Shaver disc, the one with the song about how love fades. She sat up in bed and listened for about fifteen seconds and said, "It's so awful I can't find words to tell you how awful it is."

"I thought you said everything was your kind of music."

She listened another few seconds, covered her ears, and said, "I was wrong."

"Bullshit," I said. "It's exactly like *La Boheme.*"

"You will never touch my body again."

"Listen, all he's saying is that you take your joy and your pleasure when you can, because you know it isn't going to last."

"*Ain't* gonna last, I believe he said."

"Yeah. Ain't gonna last. Just like Puccini and those damn bohemians. The difference is, the way he says it, I actually believe it."

She was laughing now, flinging herself back down onto the pillows. "All right," she said, "I will make love to that caterwauling if you promise to finish what you were doing a few minutes ago."

"I love my work," I said, moving toward her. I let my tongue trace her exquisite, dark legs from ankle to hip, stopping on a discreet, lettered tattoo high on the inside of her thigh. In the dark crush of the airplane, I hadn't seen it before. The letters spelled *Pikovaya Dama.* Her breathing deepened, and she turned on her side, facing away from me. She reached back for my hand, pulling me up against her until she was wrapped in my arms. She turned her face to me and kissed me over her shoulder. Then she gave me a smile of such surpassing sadness, I could only kiss her again and pull her tighter. "It's not a secret, you know," she said. "You can see it when I wear a bathing suit. But only one in ten thousand knows what it means." She turned her body and pressed herself naked against me, kissing me deep on the mouth. For the next few hours we forgot about the outside world, both willingly intoxicated by the presence of the other. There was the mutual rhapsody of touch and pleasure, leading to the moment of clenched eyelids and the trembling, white light of release.

Sleep followed, sleep like I hadn't felt in years. I was never a man who couldn't sleep with a woman in his bed. On the contrary; Michele's gentle breathing took me down to a place of rest I had nearly forgotten existed. It was dreamless and dark, and past memories, for that time, ceased to exist.

When I opened my eyes the next morning, she was sitting in a chair, watching me silently. I smiled and sat up. "You're dressed," I said. "What time is it?"

"I've already called a cab," she said. "I didn't want to wake you."

"Don't be crazy. I'll take you back to your car."

She shook her head. "It's better this way."

I leaned back, letting the sheets fall down around my hips. "I could take the day off."

She laughed, the airy musicality renewed in her voice. "I have things to do."

And that was the moment when the first ray of reality crept through my blinders: she had another life, a life I couldn't touch. I couldn't ask, *what things?* I couldn't ask because it would have ruined everything. It would be this way or nothing.

There was a car honk outside, and she stood. I got out of bed and stood naked before her, pulling her to me. I didn't ask her when we would see each other again. There are times when questions about the future can wreck the present.

All that morning, taking a shower, getting ready for work, I was saying her name. "The great Michele Sonnier," I said to the bathroom walls, the inside of my refrigerator, the closet where I kept my umbrella. I repeated it in the car, the wipers sweeping a sudden shower off my windshield. I substituted those words for the names of other women in the heartache songs WYAY played. I hummed it walking down the hall to my office. My mood was not to survive long after opening the door.

The first face I saw was that of a uniformed policeman, who was wearing a serious, Sergeant Friday expression. The second was his partner, a round, overweight man stuffed into his clothes. The third was Blu's, who was visibly upset. Her voice cut through the fog of images.

"Jack," she said. "Isn't your cell phone on? I've been trying to call you for twenty minutes."

I looked around numbly. "I don't know. I . . . I guess not. What's going on here?"

The first cop answered. "A robbery," he said in a flat, official voice. "Or at least a break-in. We haven't been able to ascertain what, if anything, was stolen."

"A robbery?" I looked around, momentarily confused. The door between Blu and my office was open; the air felt humid, even though the air conditioner was running. I walked across the waiting area and into my personal office. The window behind my desk was open, letting the morning inside. A few papers were scattered on my desk to let me know that someone had been there.

I walked back over to Blu. "You okay, baby?" I asked. "All your stuff still here?" Blu nodded, but I could tell the idea of somebody going through her things made her queasy.

"Counselor here's got a colorful clientele," the heavyset cop said. "Maybe it's one of them."

"Hang on," I said quietly. A sense that something was wrong was pushing through my initial shock.

"What is it?" Blu asked.

I looked back at the door to my office, my unease growing. I walked back through the door, looking around. Everything seemed normal. I looked at a blank space on the little desk where Nightmare had been working. Doug's computer was gone.

CHAPTER FOURTEEN

DREAD IS INDEFINABLE. If you know what you're afraid of—if you can define it—it loses power. It's the unknown that climbs up your back and attaches itself there, humming ominously like a dangerous electrical current. A robbery and its sense of violation can crank that up to a rattling volume. Guilt plays into your emotional receptors, too; it heightens all your responses, making you hypersensitive. I had the fleeting sense that maybe the robbery was somehow connected to what Michele and I had been doing the night before. Was it coincidence that it had happened while we had been together? Or was it a karmic equalizer, God's way of balancing pain and pleasure?

Guilt. That, for the criminal lawyer, is the operative word. It's no accident that juries don't find defendants innocent. They say they're "not guilty," because somewhere in the collective unconscious roams the knowledge that nobody is truly innocent or unstained. Those words just don't fit the human race. So when you've been experiencing a kind of delirium with someone else's wife—even if you know you're falling in love with her—you start looking for rocks to fall, just to even things out.

So I was feeling the humming, the dread. The first thing I did was give Blu the day off. She was rattled by the break-in, and since I was planning on leaving, I didn't want her to be alone in the office. She looked at me gratefully, picked up her bag, and walked out the door in a near-trot. Next I called Nightmare, just to assess the damage of the loss of Doug's terminal; he didn't answer his phone, which wasn't a surprise. For him, nine in the morning was a time to go to bed, not get up. I left him a message, wondering what cyber-crack of Atlanta he had spent his night visiting. Then I went back in my office, alone, and sat down to think. Someone wanted Doug's computer. My first thought was the most obvious: whoever had hired Doug had stolen it, simply because he didn't want that information public. And it didn't take a genius to put Horizn on the list of potential customers. The theft would be a way to cover their tracks. I liked that theory; it was clean, it worked. But there was another, darker alternative: It was also possible that Doug had been killed *before* he could get the information to his employer, by someone determined to prevent that transaction from taking place. If that was true, there was a third party at work, someone determined and dangerous, willing to commit murder.

Which meant I was going to see Billy Little. If things were going to ratchet up a notch, I wanted him on my side. Industrial espionage was one thing; it was common knowledge companies eavesdropped on each other as a matter of course. If Horizn—or anybody else, for that matter—had been sneaking around Grayton's files, it wouldn't be a big shock to the business world. Even theft of computer equipment wasn't too big a stretch. But killing people was something else. So I drove over to Billy's office in the City Hall East building, a twenty-minute drive.

I practically ran him down in the hall; we both came around the same corner simultaneously. Running into Billy is like running into an impeccably dressed brick. "Listen, Billy," I said, "we need to talk. Can we go into your office for a minute?"

"Lemme get some coffee, and I'll meet you in there."

I walked down the hall, parking myself outside Billy's door. After a couple of minutes he came back around the corner, a cup of coffee in each hand. He handed me one, and I followed him in, closing the door behind us. "What's going on?" he asked.

"I had a break-in," I answered. "Last night."

"Damn, Jack, I'm sorry. Some uniforms come over?"

"Yeah. They filed a report."

"Hell of a neighborhood over there."

"I don't think the neighborhood had much to do with it."

"What makes you say that?"

"Somebody went to a lot of trouble, considering they only bothered to take one thing. Doug Townsend's computer."

Billy raised an eyebrow. "Your dead client?"

"Right. My own computer was sitting five feet away and it didn't get touched."

"Think they got interrupted in the middle of the robbery?"

"That's possible. It looked like they left in a hurry."

"Okay."

"Thing is, I got inside Doug's computer. What I found there was pretty interesting."

Billy took his chair, motioning me to sit down. "Maybe you better start at the beginning."

"Doug wasn't just another drug addict," I said. "He had skills."

"What kind of skills?"

"Computer skills. He was hacking a company called Grayton Technical Laboratories. He had accumulated a massive amount of information about their operations."

Billy's expression clouded over. "Your buddy was a hacker?"

"Yeah. A brilliant one, by all accounts." Billy started to interrupt, but I held up my hand. "Don't get pissed. I didn't know myself until after the fact."

Billy nodded. "Go on."

"Doug had completely penetrated Grayton's network. And suddenly, he shows up dead."

Billy watched me silently awhile. "Addicts die at unpredictable times. But you have my attention."

"And now my office gets broken into, and the only thing stolen is his computer. This wasn't a routine breaking and entering, Billy. Somebody wanted what was in that box."

"This Grayton Technical Laboratories. What are they?"

"Some kind of drug company. Cutting edge stuff, like experimental treatments. I'm looking into it. The point is, it's the same line of work as Horizn."

Billy raised an eyebrow. "Hang on, Counselor. First off, industrial espionage is an FBI matter. Police departments don't even handle it."

"How about burglary? That computer didn't just walk off under its own power."

Billy watched me quietly a moment. "Lemme ask you something, Jack. Why don't you just come out and tell me what's on your mind?"

"What do you mean?"

"I mean you're trying to tell me that Charles Ralston has something to do with this thing, and something to do with your friend, too. It's like a conspiracy theory or something."

"It's a possibility."

"One of about a thousand, though, is my problem. Lemme give you an example. How many drug addicts would you say you've had in your office over the last couple of years?"

"I don't know. All the ones out on bail. Maybe a hundred."

"A hundred. And how many of those, would you say, have ever committed robbery?"

"Damn it, Billy . . ."

"Sixty? Seventy? All I'm saying, your office is a revolving door for people who need money. You've got some nice computer equipment in there. So boom, you're hit." He shrugged. "I'm not saying that's it. I'm just saying that if I had to place a bet, I'd place it on the people who do that kind of thing for a living already."

"It's pretty interesting timing."

"I agree. But before I open a murder case, call the FBI, and implicate one of the most beloved figures in Atlanta in the death of a drug addict, you don't mind if I just take a second and find out, do you?"

I stood. "No."

Billy rose and shook my hand. "I appreciate it. And for the record, I still say you're chasing ghosts."

I stopped at the door, but only for a moment. "Maybe. But they're my ghosts."

I was back at my office by eleven. I called Nightmare again, just to see if Dracula had come out of his coffin. Still no answer. I sat at my desk, knowing I had another call to make, one that I wanted to go away but wouldn't. Michele had a right to know about Doug's PC, as well. It was entirely possible that information about her daughter lurked somewhere on the computer drives, and went out the door with it. Maybe the thief cared about that, maybe not. But if her secret was compromised, her life as she knew it was over.

I punched the buttons on my cell phone. Michele answered, and her voice pulled me back to the night before, and for a few, precious moments, nothing else mattered. I was thrust into the seductive obliteration of our erotic dance, into the falling apart of long-held barriers. Suddenly, I wanted everything to be much simpler. I wanted time to be with this woman, time without the complications of Doug and a hidden daughter and God, there was her husband, too, what the hell was I doing? She was waiting on the phone, but I couldn't pull together a sentence. There was too much noise, all of it internal. "There's been a robbery," I said at last.

Instantly, her voice grew serious. "What happened?"

"Doug's computer," I said. "It's gone. Someone broke into my office. Last night, while we were together."

"My God, Jack," she said. "What if . . ."

"I know," I said. "But don't jump to conclusions. Chances are, if Doug knew something, he would have told you."

"I don't have a good feeling about this, Jack. We have to do something *now*."

"I've got her real name and birth date. That's a start. But you have to give me some time."

"It's not enough, Jack. We have to find her. I'm afraid . . . I'm afraid she's in McDaniel Glen."

"The Glen? What do you mean? Did Doug tell you something?"

"She's here, Doug said. Think about it, Jack. Doug lived just outside the Glen. So *here* could certainly mean that area."

"How did you know where Doug lived?"

"He told me, obviously. *We have to move now,* he said. Like there was some kind of danger. That sounds like the Glen."

"Listen, have you considered the possibility that she's happy somewhere? That she's doing great, and going to school, and has lots of friends, and everything is just wonderful?" I didn't believe that; it's just that in my line of work, sometimes I have had to remind myself that some stories end happily, so I wouldn't go nuts. Michele wasn't buying it.

"I've thought about that a million times. But I know it isn't true."

"Don't let this robbery thing shake you up."

"It does shake me up, Jack. We have to move. Now."

"How do you propose we do that? Go door to door?"

"Why not?"

"Aside from the fact that it's probably futile, you have your own concerns. If you show your face on this, sooner or later, somebody is going to put you together with the girl. You're a well-known figure, Michele. There's no way we could keep your identity out of it. Then you have news cameras and all hell blows up."

"For God's sake, Jack, do you actually think people in the Glen go to the opera?"

"I'm just saying being recognized is a possibility. You must have had your picture in the paper a few times. It's strange what people remember."

There was a moment's silence. "Then I won't be there," she said simply.

"No offense, but the idea of me doing it alone doesn't have a lot of potential. White guy in a Buick trying to find a young girl at the Glen?"

"Will you still be at your office around three?"

"I can be. To do what?"

"Just be there."

*   *   *

I looked out my window at five before three: what looked like Michele's gray Lexus was just pulling into my office parking lot. The car passed directly under my second-story window, so I didn't get a view of who was driving. Whoever it was parked in a space and sat, as though waiting. I went down for a closer look; since the break-in, I was getting cautious about who was in the neighborhood. As I approached, the driver's side window lowered.

"Hello, Jack," the woman said. The voice was unmistakable: it belonged to Michele. But her appearance had been transformed.

"My God, what are you doing?" She was dressed down, not her previous faux poverty look, but the real thing. In her transformation from diva to urban ghetto-dweller, she had systematically stripped away every shred of glamour, replacing it with a nondescript antistyle. Her pants were baggy and dirty, and she wore an oversized, faded University of Miami T-shirt. Her hair was pulled under a ratty hat. There was no makeup, and she wore cheap sunglasses. If she had looked a little more strung out, she would have been perfectly at home in a lineup of my clients. I stared and said, "You look terrible."

"Good. We're taking your car." She rolled up the window, got out, and locked the Lexus. She seemed shorter than I remembered; then I saw the battered sneakers, in place of her usual shoes.

"You're not serious," I said.

"I'm going to the Glen, Jack." She looked at me intently. "You can stay, if you like. I'm going either way."

"There's no way in hell I'm letting you go into McDaniel Glen by yourself."

She stared at me. "I'm probably safer without you."

That stopped me; it was true, I had to admit. With me along, she was a walking billboard as an outsider. "I don't think this is going to work," I said. "Let's slow down and think about it a second."

"I'm going to find my daughter, Jack. It's taken me fourteen years to face this moment. Maybe going to the Glen is futile, but at least it's a start."

I stared. "I'm coming," I said. It had been a long time since I had thought about Professor Spence's principle of magnetic attraction, but I began to get a bad feeling that his words were about to bite us in the ass. When it came to attracting the shit of the criminal class, McDaniel Glen was as near to true north as made any difference. "Dammit, I'm coming."

I was still dressed for work, so we went back by my apartment so I could quickly change. I threw on some jeans and stuffed my cell phone in a pocket. "You ready?"

"Yes. Let's go."

We drove across town, ending up outside the Glen just after four. The traffic on the freeway was already turning into a turgid, drying cement. I rolled to a stop just outside the iron gates of the Glen and turned to face Michele. I was going to ask her something, but her expression stopped me. She was staring at the entrance to a part of her history, her horror. It hadn't hit me until that second what going back inside might mean to her.

"Have you been back?" I asked quietly. She shook her head silently. She was transfixed, the sight of the Glen's iron gates ripping a hole across fourteen years of a past built on a gigantic lie.

"It's like Auschwitz," she said in a whisper. "I was singing in Warsaw, and I went to see it. They call it Oswiecim there. The iron gates looked just like that. I never noticed it before."

I looked up at the entrance; she was right. All that was missing were the words, *Work will make you free.* And then I understood a part of her pain; she had survivor's guilt. She had escaped hell, and like all such escapees, she was tormented about who was left behind. "God knows if this is going to work," I said. "But let's try it."

I pulled the Buick back into the road, heading toward the entrance. There were a surprising number of cars going into the development, testimony that at least some of the residents had jobs. But there was also the ever-present population of teenagers, alternately listless or aggressive, depending on the winds. That was what made the projects so dangerous to outsiders; you had to live there to be able to interpret the weather. A joke could turn ugly in a second, and the warning signs were subtle. A different emphasis on a word, a change in a person's posture, and all hell could break loose. If you knew the system, you could avoid conflicts and manage a relatively safe existence. You might, with luck, actually flourish. I knew it happened, because I saw that life, sublime in its refusal to be daunted, utterly noble in its quiet dignity, could happen anywhere—even Auschwitz, theoretically. Unfortunately, because of my work, I spent all my time with people making different choices. I looked at my watch; it was after four, and we should have several hours of sunlight.

"Just drive slow," she said. "I'll recognize her."

"Be serious."

She shot me a look. "All right, then we can ask. We have her name and her birth date. Maybe somebody will know something."

I nodded, and we cruised down the main street of the Glen, rolling past the MDHA office. I suppose there must be some romantic attachment to everybody's childhood home, but I hadn't considered it possible for the Glen. I was wrong, because I could feel nostalgia filling Michele up with every block we drove. What appeared to me as identical street corners and buildings were, to her, possessed of a thousand unique details. Physically, the Glen was trapped in amber, static as a museum relic. The life that vibrated through it—laughter, tears, babies, friendships, chaos, order—had no apparent effect on the structure, in the same way the exterior of any prison stays the same. The units were like cells, and the individual stories that unfolded within them were largely invisible from the street.

"School bus met here," she said, nodding at a stop sign. "We lined up, like little sheep."

She told me to take a left, and I nodded a yes. "This is my street," she said. She was so intent, she barely blinked. "There!" she said, pointing to the E building. "God, Jack. God."

"Yours?"

I stopped, and she stared at the door a long time. I had no idea what secrets were buried in the brown bricks and rusty steel of that place. "Things happened inside those walls that should never have seen the light of day," she whispered.

"I'm sorry." There was nothing I could do to come to terms with her world, and I knew it. We were too different, separated by cultural chasms as wide as a canyon.

She pointed across the street, to F building. "I knew a girl there. She was nice." She looked back at E building. A group of teenage boys walked out of the main door, laughing and cutting up. "I'm going to ask them what they know."

"Hang on . . ." Before I could stop her, the door was open. She stepped out of the car, and the boys came to halt. They gave her that testosterone-drenched leer that young boys have, especially when traveling in packs.

"Zup, baby?" one of them asked. He oiled up toward her, looking her over, invading her space before she was fully out of the car.

"Back it up," Michele said. Her voice was, in one millisecond, transported to another world. I almost fell out of the car. She was shrill, she was tough, and she was demanding some respect.

The boys laughed. "Bitch don't wan' any from Darius," one of them said. "Bitch got taste, anyway."

The oily one didn't grin. Instead, he moved even closer, nearly touching her. "Come on, baby, why you got to be like that? You gonna like me when you get to know me."

Her voice came back like steel. "Back the fuck up," the woman who sang arias for a living said. I didn't know whether to laugh or cry. It was like the world had turned upside down. Or maybe it was right side up. I wasn't sure. All I know is that looking into Michele's eyes, Darius got the message. There was only way to describe what he did: he backed the fuck up.

Even though I didn't know if it was going to make things better or worse, I opened the car door and got out. Darius nodded to me. "That your chauffeur, baby?"

Michele ignored him. "I'm looking for someone," she said. "I got fifty bucks for whoever tells me where she is."

"All right, baby," Darius said. "What's the name?"

Michele pointedly continued speaking to the group. "She's fourteen," she said. "Her name's Briah. Briah Fields."

"I don't know nobody like that," one of the other boys said.

"Yeah, Briah," Darius said slowly. "I know her."

Michele turned her head toward the boy. "Does anybody else know her?" In the seconds she used to speak that sentence, the other boys copped to the plan.

"Hell, yeah," they started shouting. "I know her. She over on Trenton Street. She in M building. I seen her couple days ago."

Darius moved closer. "Come on baby, I told you I seen her. I'll take you right to her. Gimme the fifty."

Michele didn't flinch. "When I see her, you get the money."

Having discovered that Michele had enough self-respect to despise his presumptions, the boy's mood was deteriorating. I was standing there, trying to figure out if I was going to get us both killed by opening my mouth, when motion to my left caught my eye. I turned to look, and saw a police cruiser turning the corner onto our street. The car was about four long blocks away.

Instantly, the boys fell back a few feet, although Darius kept his eyes on Michele, sending silent threats. The police cruiser pulled slowly by; two officers—one white, the other black—peered out of the window as it passed, their eyes landing questioningly on me. Michele stiffened. The cruiser went up a few car lengths and parked. I looked back at Michele; before I could even speak, she had disappeared into one of the long apartment buildings. But there was no doubt she had been seen.

Shit, shit, shit. The cops walked slowly up to the little crowd. One, a tall, burly sergeant, was definitely in charge. The other, a smaller, beat officer, tailed behind.

"What's up?" the first officer asked.

"Zup?" one of the kids said. Darius, previously the leader of the pack, had fallen back into the crowd. Nobody met the officers' eyes. There's an unwritten rule in the neighborhood, and it works like this: the police demand absolute respect, down to the tone of voice. If you treat them like gods—I'm not exaggerating, I mean gods—

they will give you no trouble, and maybe even cut you a break. But if you give them the slightest bit of lip, they will make your life miserable. It is absolutely imperative for project residents to be respectful. Interactions between police and citizens are therefore mostly one-dimensional, short-answer affairs.

The tall officer walked up to me. "See some ID?"

"Sure, Sergeant," I said, smiling. I pulled out my wallet. He looked at my license, then back at me.

"What brings you to paradise?" he asked, a shit-eating smile on his face.

"I'm a criminal defense lawyer," I said. "I'm getting some information for a client."

The other officer spoke up. "Yeah? Who on? Wonder if we busted him, Bobby?"

"It's a her, and I don't think so."

The first officer sidled up to my car. The kids in the street backed off to let him through. He looked the car over, probably wondering why a lawyer would drive a piece of crap like that. "You wouldn't be here for pharmacological reasons would you, Counselor?"

"No, Officer, I wouldn't."

He stuck his head inside my open window, sniffing. He pulled back out and said, "Got any objection to my looking around in there?"

"Yes, actually, I would object."

"Why's that?" the smaller officer said. "You got somethin' to hide? I think he's hidin' somethin', Bobby."

The kids around were boring holes in me, watching our little circus play out. I was white, and they wanted to see what happened. It was like a science experiment to them, watching a novel chemical reaction unfold before their eyes. I almost wanted to get messed with, just to show them that life wasn't always about race. But I couldn't do that, for the simple reason that I'm a lawyer, and I wasn't about to take the shit being peddled that day by the Atlanta Police. "If you're making a formal request to search my vehicle, I refuse," I said. If it was possible for the oxygen to get sucked out of the air immediately surrounding us, it was. Every kid was staring at the officer, waiting for a withering response. Respect was on the line, and that, along with the Kevlar around his chest, were his most important protections. So I hoped the officer wouldn't force the issue. Predictably, however, he did.

"You're right," he said to his partner. "I think he's down here buying dope." He moved toward the car, sticking his head back inside.

Don't touch the door handle, I thought. *Just puff out your chest a little, and let it go.*

"I'm gonna ask you again," the officer said, pulling out of the car. "Do you give me permission to search this car?"

"I do not."

His hand reached toward the door. The second his fingers touched it, I said, "I'm going to reach inside my pocket now, Officer. I'm telling you this so that you don't misunderstand the action. I'm getting my phone."

The officer stood up, ready to face down a threat. I locked my eyes on his, then moved my hand slowly to my front pants pocket. "Phone," I repeated. I pulled it out and flipped it on. "Here's the deal," I said. "You have two choices. If you think you have just cause, your partner and I can wait here by the car while you go downtown and try to convince a judge that me standing on a street corner gives you the right to a search warrant. Since they all know me by name, that could be a tough sell. But if you want to give it a shot, I've got nothing but time. Or, you can go ahead and open the car door, while I do the play-by-play for Detective Billy Little."

The officer glared. He was pissed and embarrassed. "You know Detective Little?" he asked.

"I saved his life in Iraq," I said, sarcastically. "And unlike you, he's sort of sticky about the Constitution. Like I said, it's up to you. The more I think about it, I don't really care which one you choose. But if you touch the door handle, I'm dialing."

By then, a pretty good crowd of kids had coagulated around the scene, making things worse. You could feel them recording events in their minds, taking notes on how white people handled the police. I wanted to tell them it didn't have anything to do with race, that it was three years of law school, but they would never have believed it. To this day, I don't know who would have been right.

The tall officer backed away from the car, his face a scowl. But I could see he had made his choice. "I still say you were on a buy," he said. "But that's fine. If you're going to fling that constitutional shit around, move your ass along."

"Flinging constitutional shit around is something I never get tired of doing."

"Then move. Or don't, and give me a reason to arrest you."

"I need to find my client."

"We got rules about being inside the Glen, Counselor. If you're not a resident, you have to be visiting one by invitation. Who's your client?"

He was right; McDaniel Glen was a restricted area. I looked across the dirty expanse that passed for grass between the street and the closest building. Somewhere, Michele was inside. She would be left with the crowd of boys to hunt her. "Look . . ."

"That's what I thought. Then move along. Now."

"Officer . . ."

"One more word," the cop said.

I cast a last look back at the building, then moved toward my car. There was nothing else to do. Getting arrested wouldn't help Michele. If she needed saving, I couldn't do it from jail. So I got in, started the car, and slowly drove off, heart in my mouth. About half the crowd dispersed, the rest watching the cops to see what they would do. The officers got in their car and pulled up behind me, trailing me all the way out of the Glen. It was the longest drive I ever took. If I had even stopped to look down a street, they would have busted me. Eventually, I pulled back through the iron gates, leaving Michele still inside. The police cruiser parked outside the Glen, and the officers stared through their windshield, making sure I kept moving. There was no way I could get back inside until the middle of the night, one hell of a prospect. The next shift change for the police wouldn't come until one o'clock in the morning, a time when driving into the Glen had the potential to be a life-and-death decision. I pulled out my cell phone, in the hope Michele was carrying hers. It rang two feet away, in her purse. I hung up and sat in the silence, wondering if I had the stones to go after her, and knowing that I would have to whether I did or not. The last time I had tried to save a woman, things had not gone well. *Damn. Professor Spence's magnetic principle is about to fry my ass.*

CHAPTER FIFTEEN

I'VE HAD DAYS GO by so fast they felt like burning slips of paper, each one turning to ash before my eyes. But sitting in my car two blocks away from the Glen, every minute was an eternity. I couldn't leave. I couldn't go in. I couldn't do shit.

My mind, however, wasn't under those restrictions. It ran at top speed, creating one hellish scenario after another about what was happening at that moment to Michele Sonnier. I shouldn't have been surprised at the way she handled herself before; after all, she had spent a year and a half of her adolescence there, learning to navigate those treacherous waterways. *I'm safer without you,* she had said, and maybe she was right. It was entirely possible my fears were unfounded. It was also possible I was underestimating them. The projects are not a world that easily yields to rational analysis. People live there without incident for a lifetime. Others endure lives of such chronic tragedy they can't imagine a thirtieth birthday. The Glen, I had learned, was a universe unto itself.

After ten or twelve unpleasant situations passed through my

brain, I closed my eyes in frustration. *She can't show her face, because the cops know who belongs there down to the blades of grass. They'd bust her, and society reporters could have a field day imagining why the wife of Charles Ralston—in disguise, no less—had been picked up prowling the streets of Atlanta's worst project.* I had to assume that Michele would do anything before letting that happen. *So it's up to me, and even though it sucks, I am going to go back in.*

One thing I've learned by watching my underachieving clients: sometimes, there is a genuine value to going psycho. If you're in a box, the predictable answers don't apply. You have to rattle the cage, or you're done. So after a couple of hours I did the craziest thing I could think of. I took out my billfold and emptied it of money, stuffing the bills in my glove box. I put on a ball cap, pressing it down on my head as far as it would go. I got out of my car and locked it up. I trotted in the fading sunlight toward the Glen, until I could see the entrance. The cops were still there, sitting on their asses. I trotted a couple of blocks down the street, then slipped down a side street. A few hundred yards down I stopped and took the biggest breath I ever took in my life. I looked right and left, and climbed up over the iron fence that divided McDaniel Glen from the rest of the world. Thirty seconds later, I had dropped off into the other side. The moment my feet touched the ground, I was the whitest man in Atlanta.

Point one: your client gets killed. *Point two*: you find out he was in love with a high-class opera singer. *Point three*: you agree to help that woman find her lost baby. *Point four*: you are walking through the Glen in the growing dark, trying to find her. *Point five*: it is entirely possible that you are not attracting to yourself the shit of others, but rather, things are working in exactly the opposite way. You are the shit, my friend, and you are sticking to everybody you meet.

It was seven or eight blocks to the building where I left Michele, and I started off at a trot. Two blocks later, I no longer had reason to fear what Darius and his pals were doing to Michele. They were coming around a corner and practically ran over me. They turned in my direction and started loping along beside me, smiling. They looked like they could have run for days at that pace. "Hey, moth-erfucker," Darius said, "what you doin'? You trainin' for the Olympics?"

"Yeah," I said, smiling affably. "I'm training for the Olympics."

"You're pretty fuckin' slow," another boy said. They were trolling, engines barely ticking over. Judging by my sudden need for oxygen, I had about another six blocks before I blew a tire. "I don't think you gonna win no motherfuckin' medals," the boy said.

"I'm gonna get my face on the Wheaties box," I said, looking around for Michele. "I'm gonna make a million bucks from en-dorsements."

The second boy—not Darius—laughed. He was genuinely amused. "You a funny motherfucker," he said. I noticed a tattoo on his right forearm; it was homemade, of a six-pointed star. *Not good.*

"I try to be," I said, not breaking stride.

Just then, one of the other boys ran up ahead of me, falling in place about two steps ahead. His right pants leg was rolled up, which, like the star, was a sign of Folks Nation, a national gang with strong membership in the Glen. It would be a point of princi-ple for them to beat the hell out of me, not because I was white, but simply because I was on their turf without permission. Believe me, the Folks Nation were equal opportunity intimidators. *Mayday. Jesus, I am so screwed.* I looked up ahead; if I had my bearings right, I was getting close to where Michele had disappeared. Of course, she might be blocks from there by now. I kept running, all of us mov-ing in close formation, like a fighter group.

"I like that hat," another, shorter boy said.

It's funny how much hell can be contained in such an innocu-ous statement. "I like that hat." Between two casual acquaintances, it's a compliment. In a bar, it's a pickup line. Under the present cir-cumstances, it meant the following: *You are now fucked. If you give me the hat, you're fucked, because you're weak, and we'll make you pay. If you don't give me the hat, you're still fucked, because you disrespected.* I had now entered the full-on Judson Spence rainstorm, and the tide was coming in. I stopped running. Psycho had got me inside the Glen; maybe it would help me find Michele, and get us both out.

The little crowd stopped, the boys circling me. They were lean, scarily alive and virile, carrying within their heads a set of nearly random possibilities that ranged from the magnanimous to the unthinkably violent. There was simple curiosity, too—I could see it in their eyes—at what would make somebody so insane as to tempt the particular fate I was tempting. For a while, I thought that would help, because I was definitely going to play the psycho card. Once you start, you have to keep going. It's all or nothing. "You like oatmeal?" I said to Darius.

He looked surprised. "What?"

"Oatmeal," I repeated. "I was wondering if you liked it." The group laughed, a little nervously. "Personally, I love it. I think it's the food of the gods."

"What you talkin' 'bout?" Darius asked.

"My hat," I said, a little psychotically, I hoped. "Because I eat oatmeal out of it every morning. It's very useful for that."

"That's fucked up," the boy who wanted my hat said.

"Yeah," another boy agreed, "motherfucker's all fucked up."

The kid who wanted my hat was determined. "I don't care if he is crazy, I still like his hat."

"I need it," I said. "I need it because I eat oatmeal out of it every morning." The kid who wanted my hat gave me a quizzical look, then fell back a few feet. For one beautiful, shining moment, I was free. They were going to buy it. They were going to leave the poor crazy white guy alone, and I was going to find Michele, and we were going to walk in the moonlight back to my Buick. It was probably the fact that I was thinking such happy thoughts that I didn't notice the roundhouse left coming at me until it was too late. Then, everything disappeared.

CHAPTER SIXTEEN

"THE STAR-SPANGLED BANNER" was playing, badly and out of tune. Fireworks were going off, impossibly close. Sparks were raining down on top of me, burning my skin. I could feel them individually, searing into me. I opened my eyes. Light flooded into my pupils like razor blades. I shut them again, moaning.

"Wake up. You all right, now."

Tentatively, I partially opened one eye again. That's when I realized I was on my back. "Whfff."

"Just lie still. You was just out awhile."

I moaned again, gurgling something unintelligible. I felt a warm wetness in my mouth. Then I felt a shooting pain up my back, crackling through my neck, drilling a hole through the roof of my skull. The last few minutes came back to me, in spite of how much I didn't want them to be true. I had just had the living hell beat out of me. I tried to sit up, managed it halfway, and let it go at that. "All right, now," the voice said. "Take it easy."

I managed to pry both eyes open, letting myself acclimate to the light. I looked around; I was inside, sitting on a sofa in a clean, small room. I didn't see where the voice was coming from. "I would've taken you to the hospital," the voice said, "but they would have made you sit in the emergency room for five hours before they saw you. You not bad enough to rush."

"Could have fooled me," I said, managing my first coherent sentence. I looked left, following the voice. There, smiling affably at me, was Jamal Pope.

Time to go, every synapse in my brain sang in chorus. My body, however, was singing a different tune. My limbs felt like crushed ice, only colder. "How did I get here?"

Pope laughed. "Nothin' happen on my stoop without me knowin'," he said. "Rabbit brought you in."

"Remind me to send him a card," I said. "But I really have to get going." I kept sending messages to my legs, but they weren't picking up.

"Take it easy," Pope said. "Don't rush. You need a second." He stood and walked to the kitchen, which was in sight of where I lay. I looked around; apparently, he didn't spend his money on furnishings. Things were decent, but not that different from any other apartment. It made me wonder what the point of making all that money was. Then another shooting pain made me forget about everything else for a while.

Pope walked over with a glass of water and handed it to me. "Drink this," he said. "You need it after a beating."

I took the glass, drinking a few swallows. "Thanks. What time is it?"

"'Bout twelve." He looked at me. "You shouldn't oughta fuck with Folks Nation. They don't like white people."

"They've made that clear, thanks."

Pope laughed. "Word is you was with a woman," he said. "Word is she fine."

"Yeah," I said cautiously. "I was doing research on a case."

"Word is she not from around here."

"She's from Bowen Homes," I said. "She's helping me on something."

"Bowen? So I guess I wouldn't know her."

"No, probably not." Pope looked at me, a shallow smile on his lips. It was obvious he knew I was lying. Unfortunately, it was impossible to tell what else he knew. What I needed to do was get the hell out before he could ask me any more questions.

"What her name?"

Damn. Lemme go, Pope. And let her go. Let all of us go, you merciless bastard. Let us all just live our lives without all this shit. "T'aniqua," I said. "T'aniqua Fields."

Pope's face was implacable. "Well, I guess you right," he said. "I don't know her." He walked over and put his hands underneath me. "Tell you what," he said. "I'll help you find her."

"Uh . . ." Words were forming, but the pain of straightening out my body turned them into a low moan.

"Easy," Pope said. "You all right. Stand up, now. Get yourself together."

I leaned on Pope, reorienting myself to an upright world. When the spinning stopped, I felt better. My head was clearing. I took a step, then another. "I can make it," I said. "Thanks."

"Yeah," Pope said. He picked up some keys. "Let's go find T'aniqua. I hear she fine."

"Really, Pope, I don't want—"

Pope's grip on my shoulder, which had, until that second, been friendly and supportive, turned subtly painful. The change wasn't dramatic, but it was exquisitely communicative. The message was clear: *You are completely in my world. I have ways for you to lose this argument you can't imagine.* I looked up at Pope, whose smile hadn't wavered. "Yeah," I said. "Maybe she's still around."

"I wouldn't want anything to happen to her," he said. "It gets dangerous around here at night." Then more pressure, moving me inexorably toward the door. We walked outside, me limping but finding my balance again. A couple of boys appeared from out of nowhere; one of them was Rabbit, Pope's son. "What up?" Pope asked.

Unlike the first time I had seen him, Rabbit was living up to his nickname. He was a lean bundle of nervous energy. "I ain't seen her," he said. "Word's out."

Pope turned toward me. "Looks like your friend's playing hide-go-seek. We better go help her out."

Pope led me toward his car. Here, at last, was an expression of his real income. A beautiful black Mercedes sat waiting on the street. He had resisted any tacky moves toward the pimp world; it was bone stock and exquisitely polished. Even in the streetlights, it glowed. A boy materialized out of the ether around me; first Pope's door was opened, then mine. I sat down on expensive leather, feeling my bones ache with the impact. Pope took his seat and lowered the windows. "We find her," he said. "We just gotta ask around."

"I'm sure she would have walked out hours ago," I said. "She's got no reason to hide."

Pope started the car and we glided down the main street of the Glen. Within blocks, I learned what respect meant in the projects. It's not an exaggeration to say that Pope was treated like a head of state. We couldn't get thirty yards without someone glad-handing him, kissing his ass. Some were storing up favors against an unknown future offense; others were angling for work or a break on product. He greeted them all by name, receiving them into his royal court for a moment's blessing.

McDaniel Glen at midnight was alive. There were even small children sitting on stoops, playing and laughing. Nobody looked scared. They were having fun, mostly. Sticking close to their stoop, playing by the rules, but having a hell of a time. There it was, in all its glory: society. People just being people, chatting and laughing. It almost made me smile, except that threading its way through all that goodwill was a black Mercedes paid for with human misery. No one, it appeared, had seen Michele. Pope's questions got more pointed as we drove, and I could feel his wheels turning, wondering who this T'aniqua Fields was, and what she and the white lawyer were doing in his world.

It took about twenty minutes to cover all of the Glen. As we pulled back up to his apartment, he got a phone call. Pope grunted into the phone a couple of times, then looked at me. "She ain't here," he said. "Somebody thinks she left couple hours ago."

"Figures," I said nonchalantly. Bullshitting Pope was essentially a waste of time, but I was hoping that if I didn't grind my lying in his face he'd give me a break. It was, like everything else in his world, merely a question of respect. And to my eternal gratitude, Pope pulled out an umbrella for the shit storm.

"You better get goin'," he said, looking at me. "She probably lookin' for you."

There was a moment's recognition between us, and I was gone.

CHAPTER SEVENTEEN

SO SHE MADE IT OUT, *probably hours ago. She's safe.* Pope believed it, and one thing was certain: nothing happened in the Glen without him knowing about it. That assurance, however—and I knew, at least intellectually, that it was absolute—failed to stop me from driving every block around the edges of the Glen for at least an hour, looking for her. But eventually, there was no way around it: Michele had vanished. I turned my car toward my house, and by the time I got there, it was nearly two. There was no way to check on Michele; the only number I had was her cell phone, which was now resting on my dining table. I considered calling the police—even though to do so would have revealed her identity— but discarded the idea. I had been overreacting, which was pretty understandable, considering my last few hours. It had been less than fifteen blocks from where I left Michele to the edge of the Glen, and she had certainly made that walk often enough as a young girl. There was no reason to believe she couldn't have simply vanished under the gates into Atlanta.

Which was all bullshit, because for the next five hours I slept about ten minutes. Saturday morning came, and the weekend loomed like an eternity. I prowled my apartment for most of the day, frustrated at the impossibility of reaching Michele. I stared at my phone, thinking that at least she would call me. I paced. I slept in fits and starts, feeling the nervous energy that comes from exhaustion. I looked at myself in the mirror, watching the topography of my face pass through an inflated black and blue, until by Sunday afternoon, the swelling was beginning to recede. But two days to imagine everything bad that could have happened to her was at least one day too many; by early Monday morning, I couldn't take it anymore. I had to do something, so I called Nightmare. At least it was better than staring at myself in a mirror.

Once again, I was speaking to the beep on Nightmare's answering machine. "Wake up, Michael. We've got to move." Nothing. I was not in the mood. "Dammit, it's Jack," I said. "They've stolen Doug's computer."

Nightmare picked up the phone. I could hear him breathing, slowly coming to consciousness. "What?" he mumbled.

"Doug's computer. It was stolen out of my office a few nights ago."

Nightmare's voice cleared. "Who stole it?"

"Whoever doesn't want us to find out what's going on."

There was silence, as Nightmare thought over the preceding few sentences. Apparently, he didn't like their meaning. "That is not good." Then, a dial tone.

It took me a moment to realize what had happened: I had been ditched. I called back. Nightmare picked up, but he didn't speak. "Don't lose your nerve, partner," I said quietly. "I need you." More silence, but I could feel the tension climbing up Nightmare's skull. "You and me. Jackie Chan."

"They stole Killah's desktop?"

"Yes, Michael." I didn't mention the trouble with Michele and my getting thrashed by emissaries of Folks Nation; more tension was the last thing Michael needed.

Nightmare's voice dropped to a whisper, as though someone

was in the next room, eavesdropping. "Dude, you are so completely busted."

"Probably."

"It means they know we were on the site. They know where the hack came from."

"The call came from my office. There's no connection to you."

"I'm pretty sure I want to keep it that way."

"Explain this to me, Michael. I thought you said all the data was on Georgia Tech's mainframe."

"It is. But the access was on Doug's. I figured if they sent a ping out, it would stop at Tech. But they got to the other side and located you."

"How could they do that?"

Another long silence. "I don't know," he said quietly.

"What do you mean, you don't know? I thought you were king cyber god or something."

"You are dead shit, dude. Seriously."

"Don't overreact, Michael. If somebody wanted to kill me, I'm an easy enough target. What they wanted was the computer, and they got it. They probably wanted to make sure we can't get back on."

"In that case, they're screwed, because I can get back on anytime I want."

I shook my head in disbelief. "Are you serious? You can get back on?"

"Sure, no problem. If I were nuts, that is."

"Michael, we have to get back on the site."

"Yeah, dude, we'll just hack right back on there, and then sit and wait for them to come kill us. Gotta go now."

"Just tell me how we can get on."

"I can emulate Doug's access."

"Wouldn't they know that?"

"Duh."

"So what good was taking Doug's computer?"

"Like you said, they don't know about me. At this point, they probably just want to find out how you got in."

"Will they be able to?"

"Just because they have Doug's PC, that doesn't mean they can get through his security. If you hadn't come up with that Italian stuff, we'd still be staring at the screen."

"You're certain of that?"

"Reasonably."

"Okay. Then we have to get back on, and we have to do it without getting detected. There has to be a way. Think about it, Michael. Come up with something."

Silence, another long stretch of it. I half expected him to hang up again, in which case I was prepared to drive over to his apartment, bang on his door, and wring his neck until he agreed to help me. "Where is this Grayton Laboratories, anyway?" he finally asked. "What's the address?"

"I don't know. Hang on." I looked Grayton up in the phone book. "It's on Mountain Industrial Avenue. I know where that is. It's off 285. It's two exits past Stone Mountain."

Another pause. "All right," he said. "Meet me at the Sandy Spring branch of the public library. You can find the address in the phone book. Be there at eleven."

"The library?"

"Yeah."

"Why?"

"I'm not telling you on the phone. Just be there."

The Sandy Spring branch of the library was in north Atlanta, about forty-five minutes away. By the time I got there Nightmare was pacing outside of the building, looking hunted. When he saw my face, he practically folded up on the pavement.

"You look like shit," he said.

"A minor disagreement," I said. "The swelling will go down in a few days." Nightmare looked at me for about five seconds, then started walking toward his car. "Stop right there," I said.

Nightmare turned. "Whatever happened to you needs to stay far away from me, dude."

"Listen to me, dammit," I said. I was getting exasperated, and I wasn't in the mood for Nightmare's waffling. "I have just had a lousy couple of days. I have had the hell beat out of me trying to protect somebody. I have had my office broken into and been burgled. Not to mention the fact that I've been falling in love with the wrong woman. The least you can do is turn on a damn computer and type some commands. Now haul your ass in there and help me out, or I am going to go completely nuts."

Nightmare stared, eyes wide. "You're losing it," he said.

"Probably."

"Falling in love with the wrong woman?" he repeated.

"That's right. And it puts me in a bad mood. Now do what I tell you, before I take out my frustrations on you."

Nightmare reluctantly turned toward the library. "I hope you left some marks on whoever did this to you."

"None that I can remember. Now get a move on."

I followed Nightmare into the library, a nondescript, single-story brick affair tucked into a woody neighborhood. The place was relatively empty, except for the staff of four or five. Nightmare led me to a row of computers in the back of the building. "They've got broadband here," he said. "And it's unregulated. In a few minutes you'll see some geezers in here downloading porn."

"Our tax dollars at work," I said. "Our rather mine, since you probably don't pay any."

"Damn right," Nightmare said. He sat at the last computer, took out a small plastic gadget no bigger than a key chain, and pushed one end of it into a port on the front fascia of the computer. "Flash memory," he said, beginning to type. "Just keep an eye out for anything weird," he said. "Other than you. Have I told you that you look like shit?"

"Yeah. Now tell me what you're doing."

"I'm going to Tech from here. The library system has its own routers, and it's impossible to locate one computer on it. If they ping back, they'll figure out it's coming from the library, but they can't pinpoint which one. There's about thirty branches, spread out all over town. And anyway, this branch is as far away from them as possible. Just in case."

"Nightmare, you're a genius."

"I know. Now watch for creeps. This could take a while."

I sat a few tables away, letting Nightmare work. The morning edition of the *Atlanta Journal-Constitution* was lying on a table near me, and I searched through the business section for any news about the Horizn IPO. A couple of pages in I saw a picture of Charles Ralston with the headline, TAKING HIS WINNINGS TO THE STREET. I skimmed the article; the consensus was, a week from now a lot of people were going to get rich, with Ralston and Stephens richest of all. The initial offering price was thirty-one dollars a share, but expectations were that price would last about fifteen seconds. If you weren't an institutional trader or a part of the firm, you had no chance. The reporter thought it would close the first day over forty, with a one-year target price of fifty. The SEC paperwork said Ralston and Stephens held five and a half million shares each. While I was doing some staggering math, Nightmare came over to my table. He looked rattled, but he was holding it together. "You okay?" I asked.

"Yeah. We're on. What am I looking for?"

I paused. "Briah," I said. "Briah Fields."

Nightmare worked for about five minutes, then came back shaking his head. "Nothing," he said.

"You're sure?"

He shrugged. "Yeah. I mean, pretty sure. So that's what this was all about? I can go home now?'

"One more thing," I said. "LAX."

"Like the airport?"

"Just the letters. LAX. It was on a notebook in Doug's apartment."

Nightmare shook his head in disbelief. "You gotta be kidding me."

"No. Just look for it."

"I'll give us twenty minutes," he said. "Then I'm cutting the connection." I followed him back to the terminal. Nightmare began searching files, coming up with nothing.

"What are the big sections?" I asked. "Is the site partitioned in any way?"

"Yeah," Nightmare said. "There's financials, communications, clinical trials—"

"Clinical trials," I said. "Try that."

Nightmare shrugged and started his search. For a long time there was nothing, but suddenly Michael said, "Damn."

"What?"

"Here it is."

The screen revealed two columns, each with four names. Each name was coupled with an address and phone number. At the top of the page the heading read: *Test 38, LAX: a double blind clinical trial of Lipitran AX. A treatment for the cure of Hepatitis C. CRO: Atlanta Mercy Hospital. Supervising researcher: Dr. Thomas Robinson.* I stared at the screen. "LAX. It's got nothing to do with the airport. It's some drug. Lipitran AX. These names must be the people on the trial." I ran down the list, looking for anything familiar. At that moment, the world stopped. Third down the right column was Doug Townsend's name, with his phone number. I blinked, thinking the name would go away.

Nightmare broke the spell. "Killah," he said. "He was takin' this drug?"

Lights went on all over my brain. *Hepatitis, source of all things profitable for Charles Ralston. Maybe Grayton is trying to cut in on Horizn's action.* "Hepatitis? I don't think Doug had that."

"Maybe he did and never told you."

"Maybe," I said hesitantly. "But surely with him dead, the people doing the test would want to know what the hell was going on. He would have just disappeared off the study." We sat thinking for a moment, when it suddenly hit me. "There's one way to find out what's going on," I said. I looked around; there weren't any people near us. I pulled out my cell phone and called the first number on list. A subdued female voice answered. "Is Brian there?" I asked.

The only answer was a low moan. "Brian Louden?" I asked. "May I speak with him?"

"Brian's dead," the voice said, choking. "My sweet baby died a week ago last Thursday."

I felt my stomach tighten. "I'm very, very sorry," I said. "Honestly. I'm so sorry to have bothered you." I hung up.

"What did they say?" Nightmare asked.

"Give me the second name." *Chantelle Weiss, 4239 Avenue D.* I called the number. A man answered. "May I speak with Chantelle?" I asked.

"Who is this?" the man said.

"This is Dr. Robinson."

"The hell it is."

"Excuse me?"

"Is this some kind of sick joke? Ain't you the man who killed her? Why you calling here and asking for her? You sick in the head?"

"I'm sorry," I said quickly. "I've called the wrong number." I clicked off the phone and sat back, stunned.

"Well?" Nightmare said. He was sweating, in spite of the air-conditioning. A sick feeling was crawling all over me.

"Give me the third name." *Jonathan Mills, 225 Trenton Street.* I dialed the number. A man answered. "I hate to bother you. This is Henry Chastain, from Mercy General."

The voice answered, "Yes?"

"This is very awkward, and I apologize for inconveniencing you."

"It's all right. What do you want?"

"I'm conducting some research for the hospital, and I've misplaced Jonathan's file. I'm terribly sorry to ask you this, but could you tell me for what Jonathan was being treated?"

"Hepatitis C."

"Jonathan was a participant in Dr. Robinson's clinical trials, is that correct?"

"Yes. Who is this again?"

"It's Henry Chastain, with Mercy Hospital."

There was a pause. "Can you tell me what this is about?"

"I'm doing research about fatality rates for different diseases." I was feeling worse and worse about the ruse, but there wasn't any other way. "If you'd prefer not to speak about this," I said, "I certainly understand."

Another pause. "Jonathan didn't die from the hepatitis," he said. "He died from the treatment."

"I see. I'm very sorry. Can you tell me what happened?"

"I just told you. He took the treatment, and he died a week later." The voice was silent a moment. "Can I call you back?"

"That won't be necessary," I said. "You've been a great help." I hung up the phone.

"What is it?" Nightmare said. "What's with all these names?"

I stared at the list, dread and sorrow crawling up my spine. "Dead," I said, looking at Nightmare. "All dead."

It took a good twenty minutes to talk Nightmare down off the ceiling of the Atlanta public library. After a great deal of whispered profanity, I finally walked him out to his car, a Toyota Corolla in worse shape than my Buick. I put my hands on his shoulders. "You gonna bail on me?" I asked, watching him carefully. "Just when it gets thick?"

He stared at me, caught between his fear and an adrenaline buzz ten times bigger than anything his pathetic on-line world had ever served up. "Look, all I'm saying is this is getting serious," he said. "Like cops kind of serious. What are you gonna do about all this?"

Good question. You keep turning over rocks, sooner or later somebody really nasty is going to show up. "When I started this thing, all I thought I was doing was picking up some stuff for an unlucky client," I said. "I don't like how things have spiraled out of control any more than you do."

"Then I don't have to explain why I'm out of here."

"You aren't out of here, and I'll tell you why."

"This ought to be good."

I took a breath and let him have it. I don't know if I was making it up or if it was the truest thing I ever said. I only know it was enough for me, and it had to be enough for him. "Because this is what we have to do," I said. "We have to. It's the kind of twisted destiny that drives you crazy but you know it's real."

Nightmare stared. "What the hell are you talking about?"

"You and me," I said. "Who else is going to figure this thing out? You think this Jackie Chan thing was just comic relief? I need you, dammit. And you need me. Because we're talented in different ways, and that makes us dangerous. Look, Michael, Doug Townsend was my friend. And there's seven other names on this list, all of them dead. So I'm not here just to connect some tawdry little dots between some drug companies. I'm here to take whoever is behind this down."

Nightmare watched me for a while, then actually laughed. "You are one crazy motherfucker," he said.

"Whatever it takes."

"This is about the girl."

"The girl."

"The *girl*, dude. You said it yourself. You're falling in love with the wrong woman."

I stared. "I know, dammit. I know."

I sent Nightmare home, watching his battered Toyota turn out of the library parking lot and disappear into the traffic. I stood alone in the parking lot awhile, listing badly to the side. My face hurt. My ribs hurt. My right leg hurt—somehow, I had banged the knee while getting the hell beat out of me, and hadn't noticed it until all the other pain subsided a little—and all I could do was play Nightmare's words back to myself. *The girl.* There are times when life is trying to tell you something. Doug was dead. Now, seven more. It was a bad time to go deaf.

Practicing low-rent law teaches you a lot about the psychology of perpetrator as victim. You can actually begin to spot the identifying characteristics in a crowd: the detached eyes of a boy who is about to go off on his girlfriend, leaving her bruised and crying; the resentment faintly radiating off a girl looking for someone's billfold or purse to lift. After two years of watching the parade of misery that is Judge Odom's court, I had developed a kind of unwanted radar. There were times when walking down a busy street was like seeing ghosts. There, that ironic slump of contempt in a man's posture; and over there, the glassy, zoned-out vibe of an addict. Policemen get the radar, too, and for them, it's an asset. It's like a tool. But for a defense lawyer who specializes in the disadvantaged, the radar can make the worst parts of a city seem like a trauma ward.

Standing there outside the library with bruises all over my body, I had to admit something that pissed me off greatly: no matter how hard I put the radar on Michele, she resisted analysis. She was impenetrable. I was making decisions on the basis that she was a legitimate victim, the innocent recipient of undeserved pain. For that version of her, you moved heaven and earth. It's the little dream that hums in every lawyer's optimistic brain, right until life starts to strangle it out of him: *Make the bad thing right.* She had made a bad mistake as a mere child, and now was trapped in a world that would be utterly unforgiving of that kind of indiscretion. But it was also possible that she was a trauma magnet, a woman who lived at a high pitch of anxiety and who sucked everyone near her into her suffering. The diva. These were the clients Judson Spence taught us to avoid at all costs. The truth was, I still didn't know in which category Michele belonged. Which was slowly driving me crazy, because making the wrong choice about that could have serious repercussions. You could spend your life fixing people who weren't going to deserve it and weren't going to appreciate it, and, in the end, were going to get you covered up in their special neuroses to the point that you couldn't breathe. I knew that because I had defended scores of them. They were the ones who—having received my best legal defense on my best days—had copped their old attitudes before they made it out the courtroom door.

I got in my car and looked at myself in the mirror. It wasn't the bruises that stopped me. It was the indecision. If I was going to the wall for her, I needed to know the reason. *Why,* it was time to wonder, *did I feel myself falling in love with her?* Was it the power of her artistry, the ineffable quality that made you feel she was baring her soul every time she sang? Or was it—and I didn't want this to be true—the beautiful wound she carried, so vulnerable, so needing of mercy? Because if that was it, then I could just rename her Violeta Ramirez, and drive my car off a cliff.

I stared at my swollen face in the mirror, ground to a halt. *No, I thought, before I drove off the cliff I would have to extend my deepest, most sincere condolences to Mr. Charles Ralston: first, for screwing his wife, and second, for the exasperated hell he had gotten himself into. Yes, he was sophisticated and well-educated, and by reputation, something of a snob—which wasn't a crime, after all—but maybe he had fallen for her, just like Doug. Maybe he had seen her performing at Juilliard, and his little scientist's heart had been pierced and now he was attached to a beautiful, talented crisis. Hell, they don't call them divas for nothing. Maybe if there was one day in his life he could undo it would be that day, the day he wandered into Lincoln Center and poked his head inside the auditorium door and saw her: young, brilliant, and lethally high-maintenance.*

Maybe, given enough time, I could have come to a conclusion. If I had only been given ten or fifteen minutes of silent contemplation, I might even have made choices with different endings. But I didn't get those minutes, because my phone, snug inside my coat pocket, went off, shocking me back into reality. I flipped it open and found out that the next several hours of my life were going to be anything but contemplative. While Nightmare and I had been breaking into the electronic ether of Grayton Labs, Sammy had been exacting his very personal, very efficient revenge on Derek Stephens. As usual, the story begins with a woman crying.

CHAPTER EIGHTEEN

BLU WAS TRYING TO TALK through gasps of air, and it wasn't working too well. "Mr. Stephens . . . Derek . . . very upset . . . Sammy . . ."

"All right, baby. Just sit down." I had driven hard over to my office, wringing out whatever performance was left in the Buick's engine on my way across town. When I walked in, I saw my secretary sitting in my office chair, her mascara ruined, her eyes puffy and red. "What's this all about?"

"He just called," she said. "Derek. He called and he was yelling."

"About what?"

"I don't know. It was something about Sammy, and somehow he was upset at me, and I don't know why."

"But what happened with Sammy?"

She sniffled. "I don't know. But he did something to make Mr. Stephens angry."

"Why would Stephens connect that to you?"

"Because he knows Sammy has a crush on me."

"How does he know that?"

"I told him."

"Why on earth did you do that?"

"I met Mr. Stephens down at the courthouse, and Sammy walked by us. He gave Mr. Stephens a look, and a couple of minutes later we could see Sammy spying on us from behind a column."

"God."

"So I told Mr. Stephens about how Sammy had this crush on me, and we laughed about it. I think Sammy might have seen us laughing."

"Not good."

"And now something terrible happened, but I don't know what."

"All right. Stay here, baby. I'm going over to the courthouse to find Sammy, if Stephens hasn't killed him yet."

The drive toward the courthouse gave me plenty of opportunity to imagine hellish scenarios where Sammy—overweight, lungs exploding from years of aerobic underutilization, reflexes slowed by several emboldening shots of Seagram's—suddenly discovers that Stephens, in addition to being a brilliant lawyer, is, unfortunately, a black belt in Tae Kwon Do. I pictured Sammy flat on his back on the highly polished linoleum of the courthouse floor, careening in surprise and humiliation, his body in a nearly frictionless recoil from a perfectly executed karate kick to his solar plexus.

These concerns, it turned out, were a waste of my already depleted supply of adrenaline. I didn't have to wait long to find out exactly how Sammy had extracted a pound of Stephens's flesh for having the temerity to be rich, handsome, and in possession of the affections of Blu McClendon. The courthouse was humming with it like a shorted electrical circuit.

I like to think the elegance of what Sammy did emanated from deep within his southern soul, but maybe that's romanticizing things a bit. Probably spending all day in the Fulton County Criminal Court system had taught him a newly devious way of thinking. Wherever it came from, it was a textbook example of everything revenge should be: simple, effective, and scrupulously legal.

Ever since I told Sammy about Stephens, Sammy had juggled the case of a certain Burton Randall, getting the timing exactly

right. Burton was a courthouse legend, a true object-specific klep-
tomaniac, and Atlanta's most prodigious car thief. The consensus
was that Burton couldn't help himself. He loved to steal cars, he
needed to steal cars, he lived to steal cars. And he had, like the true
connoisseur, exquisite taste. The better the car, the more desperately he wanted it. He would walk right by a beater with the keys
sitting in it, but he would take ungodly risks for something he
really wanted. Burton had been ready for his court date for days,
but Sammy—the scheduling power of the clerk of the court being
absolute—kept blocking the legal arteries, keeping him in limbo.
His lawyer was getting pissed, but, since taking an antagonistic
attitude toward the clerk is certain to have unpleasant repercussions, Sammy had his way. Sammy was waiting for two very specific
planets to align: first, for Derek Stephens to be in court doing damage for Horizn Pharmaceuticals, and secondly, for the weather to
be absolutely perfect. Stephens had been in court all week, but the
weather hadn't cooperated. This morning, however, had dawned so
bright you could cut diamonds with it, and Sammy made sure that
Judge Odom's early schedule was magically cleared for the long-
delayed case of *Georgia v. Randall*. Simultaneously, Sammy just happened to make it clear down in the basement that the good judge
was not pleased at the preferential treatment a certain lawyer was
receiving regarding parking privileges. The car would be moved
upstairs, or Odom would see that it was towed.

So it was that the bright red Ferrari 360 Modena of Derek
Stephens was sitting, exposed and unprotected, in the side parking
lot of the Fulton County Courthouse when Burton Randall was,
having been bound over for the seventh and far from final time,
released under his own recognizance, pending a future court date.
The fact that Sammy had pointedly mentioned to no one in particular the car's type and exact location as Burton walked out of
the courtroom was, it's fair to say, intentional.

When Derek Stephens's Ferrari was found three hours later, it
had around two hundred very fast, very hard miles on it. But the
mileage hardly mattered. The extensive body work it now
required—the result of a short but spectacular contretemps with

the Atlanta Police, continuing to an exit-ramp guardrail, and finally and most conclusively, a large, heavily bolstered street sign—meant that Stephens would never, ever be able to advertise the car as a "Ferrari 360 Modena, mint condition." More appropriate would be, "Ferrari 360 Modena, parts car."

I looked for Sammy for the next few hours, but it wasn't until five that evening I found him, holed up at Captain's, a bar about fifth down our list of hangouts. He was sitting, smiling pleasantly to himself, a row of empty glasses arrayed triumphantly before him. I walked up to his table, and he tilted his head up at me. "Jackie boy," he said, his smile widening. "You've come to share in my hour of triumph."

I looked him over, checking for signs of insanity. His suit coat was draped on the chair opposite him, as though he had a friend coming back from the bathroom. But I knew he was alone. He was always alone, when he wasn't with me. His tie was loosened, and his top shirt button was undone. "Come to save your ass," I said, sitting down. "You've pissed off a very powerful man."

Sammy's response was sublime in its precision. "Fuck him," he said, and then he smiled, sitting heavily and contentedly in his chair. After a moment, he grew thoughtful, and amended his comment. "Fuck him," he added, "all the way to hell."

"Sammy," I said, "you are disturbing the elemental forces of the universe. Derek Stephens is going to crush you."

"How?" Sammy demanded. "I did nothing, Jackie boy. *Nothing*. I scheduled a court date. So let him sue me over that."

For a moment, it seemed possible that Sammy might get away with it. That feeling only lasted a few seconds. "But listen, Sammy, Stephens isn't the kind of guy who necessarily plays by the rules. He's going to take this personally."

"Let him," Sammy retorted. "He knows where I work. I'll smash his face in."

"I'm not talking about a fistfight."

"Jackie," he said, "you have me confused with somebody with something to lose."

I looked at him warily. "What does that mean?"

"It means I have nothing, Jackie boy. I rent an apartment. My car's got a lien on it. I've got a decent stereo, and five suits. I earn thirty-six thousand dollars a year. And for one beautiful moment, I kicked the ass of one of the richest and most powerful men in the South. Do you think for one minute that I care what he thinks he's going to do about it?"

I sat watching Sammy, feeling a moment of illumination. Just when I needed it, he was reminding me where I had gone wrong. Sammy had arrived at the place of perfect, existential freedom, namely, not giving a damn. I felt watched over, as though the universe were looking out for me and mine. Me, Nightmare, and Sammy. The Father, Son and Holy Spirit. We were all on a collision course with something, and we all had our individual lessons to learn. A kind and benevolent universe had just made sure I didn't miss a thing. It was true I didn't know whom to believe. It was true that I wasn't even completely sure I wanted to find out the truth about Michele Sonnier. But Sammy had once again proved the validity of the one pure philosophy of living: *strip it down, and let it go*. Once you get that free, you become as dangerous and unpredictable as a daisy cutter bomb.

Sammy, moved by the profound philosophical lesson he had found at the bottom of a bottle of Seagram's, looked at me, smiling. "So leave it, Jackie boy," he said. "I stood up to Derek Stephens and I did it for the woman I love. I'm happy."

In that moment I decided that whatever else happened in this mess, Sammy was going to survive. He might be an ineffectual drunk, but he knew what the hell he was doing when it came to a catfight. I almost felt like praying. Instead, I decided to buy Sammy a drink. "Sammy," I said, " tonight is your night."

"Damn right."

I paused. "He's probably going to kill you for it."

Sammy nodded. "Probably."

I held up my hand, and the waitress came over to take our order. "Whatever he's having," I said, "and bring the bottle."

CHAPTER NINETEEN

TUESDAY DAWNED BRIGHT and unwelcome, birds and traffic and human activity unpleasantly clanging through a well-deserved hangover. I opened an eye and looked at the clock: a quarter till nine. I called Blu, just to see how she was holding up. "You okay, baby?" I asked. "What kind of torture has Stephens been dreaming up for Sammy?"

There was a slight pause before she answered. "I haven't spoken to Derek since yesterday," she said.

"As in, 'He's not taking my calls,' or as in, 'We just haven't had the chance to talk'?"

Another pause. "The first one," she answered, a catch in her voice.

"Baby, it's going to be okay. You realize he's scum."

"Don't say that, Jack. You don't know him."

"Hope it stays that way," I said. "But right now I want to know how you are."

"I'm fine. Michele Sonnier called."

She said her name casually, as though I hadn't been thinking of it every second since the last time I saw her. "She called? What did she say?"

"She said, 'Tell Mr. Hammond I'm fine, and that I'll be in touch.'"

"That's it? She's fine and she'll be in touch?"

"Yes."

"You're sure?"

"Yes. Are you coming in?"

I sat back in bed. *She's fine. She'll be in touch.* Relief flooded through me, combined with desire, combined with a sudden annoyance at myself for feeling either of them. *This,* I decided, *is a test. The universe, amused that only hours ago I decided I didn't give a damn, is calling my marker.*

"Jack?" It was Blu, getting impatient on the phone. "Did you hear me?"

"Yeah, sure. What was the question?"

"Are you coming in, or what?"

"Not right away," I said. "I'm looking for somebody."

"Who?"

"Don't worry about it," I said. "I'll call you later this morning."

I hung up and got dressed. In fact, I did not call that morning, because it took most of the day to find the man I needed. He wasn't at his office. He wasn't at his home. As soon as I mentioned his name to anybody who knew him, they wanted to change the subject as soon as possible. Apparently, the guy was radioactive. I had just about given up, when his secretary called my cell phone around three. She was worried about him. She was also whispering, as though she was afraid somebody was going to overhear. *What do you mean, worried?* I asked. *Worried,* she said. *That's all I want to say.* But if I went to Orme Park, I might find him there. He was a small man, brown hair, and he might be a little the worse for wear. It was the best she could do.

"Thomas? Thomas Robinson?" The man was in sweatpants, a light pullover, and hadn't shaved in a few days. He looked like hell. *At least he fits the description.* "Dr. Robinson? I was wondering if we could talk for a minute."

The man looked up at me, indifference on his face. "Nothing's stopping you," he said. Then he leaned forward on his park bench, scanning the grass for birds. He held in his hand a little bag of seeds, but so far, there weren't any takers. Even the birds were keeping their distance.

"Nice day," I said, sitting down beside him. "You hang out here much?"

"Lately I do," Robinson said. He was smallish, maybe five-eight, and slightly built. His hair was cut short and conservatively, but it was mussed, and looked like it hadn't been washed in a while. He fingered the seeds, absently scanning the park for birds.

"You're a little tough to track down," I said. "Your secretary said you're not keeping regular office hours."

"Not lately," he said quietly. He turned away, as though he was willing to sit there silently as long as it took for me to go away.

"Look, I'll just get right to this. I've got some questions about Lipitran AX."

There was a pause, and his voice lowered even further. "What are you? A lawyer?"

"How did you know?"

Robinson laughed quietly. "Because after the tragedy come the carrion birds." He looked up into the trees. "You're wasting your time."

"Why is that?"

"There won't be any lawsuits, not this time."

Even though that hadn't been my intention, I decided to play along. "How can you be so sure?"

"Over what? The treatment didn't work. So what?" He looked down, twisting the top of his paper bag of seeds tightly. "So what?" he repeated quietly. "They signed waivers. Airtight. Drawn up by people like you. So see you around. There's no corpse here for you to feed on."

I scanned his face. He looked shattered, broken down. We sat in silence for a while, until he looked up at me. "Still here?" he said. "I told you. There's no pot of gold. Go chase ambulances or something." He looked away. "Don't mind me," he said. "I just killed seven people."

"Seven? I thought there were eight."

Robinson looked up at me. He was wrecked, full of the sarcastic bile that comes with guilt. "Seven," he said. "One lived. Lacayo's his name." He paused thoughtfully. "Not dead, not exactly. I mean, he's not what I would call well. He's sort of mostly dead. Down at Grady Memorial, clinging to the tiny little bit of life he has left."

"Why don't you tell me what happened?" I asked quietly.

"Yeah," he answered. "It'll do me good to go over it all one more time."

"I'm sorry. It's important or I wouldn't still be here."

Robinson closed his eyes. "Lipitran AX was supposed to be the silver bullet for hepatitis C," he said. "That would have been a great thing." He opened his eyes, looking at me. "It's spreading like wildfire, you know."

"So I hear."

"Did you know we're up to E?"

"Hepatitis E? I didn't know that."

Robinson nodded. "People keep fucking and taking drugs, is the reason why," he said darkly.

"How dangerous is C? Sorry, I'm not an expert on it."

"Lucky you," Robinson said. "Hep A and B, they're the common ones. For most people, they aren't fatal. They can make your life miserable, if things get out of control, but they don't kill. D and E we're just learning about. But hep C is dangerous as hell, although a lot of people don't know it."

"Dangerous how?"

"In about twenty percent of people infected, the carrier develops liver cancer. And that cancer is completely immune to any treatment on earth. It progresses quickly and fatally. If you get it, you are going to die." He looked out across the park. "Having hep C is like Russian roulette. Every time you go to the doctor, you spin the chamber. You've got a one in five shot of finding out you're dying. It's highly motivational."

"So a treatment to cure hepatitis C would be immensely profitable."

"It would also save a lot of people's lives."

"Listen, I'm not sure how to ask this, but how often does a meltdown like this happen?" I asked. "Where everybody—"

"Dies?" Robinson finished. "We don't do that too often. Usually we're satisfied with not helping people." He looked out at the park. "Most of what we try doesn't work, you know."

"I didn't, actually."

He nodded. "Of course you don't. We don't let people know, because if we did, we couldn't get anybody to sign up for our next brilliant idea." He looked down. "But this time not helping them wasn't enough. This time we had to kill them." He looked over at me, confusion and anguish on his face. "They blew up," he said. "Every orifice. Massive bleeding from the eyes, the nose, ear, everywhere. It looked like . . . Jesus, it looked like Ebola. They started coming in after the second treatment. They were screaming, bodies blowing up in agony."

"My God."

Robinson hacked up a gob of phlegm, then spit it onto the grass. He was past any niceties of conversation. His voice was brittle. "The science looked so good," he said. "Perfect, right from the beginning. Put the stuff in a test tube, watch it eat hepatitis like crazy. Stick it in a mouse, it's like magic. We actually thought we could cure this stuff in a handful of treatments. That's why there weren't any primate trials. It looked so right, the FDA fast-tracked us straight to humans." He looked up at me. "Which just goes to show you."

"What?"

"A human being isn't a mouse." A bird finally circled, landing about fifteen feet away. Robinson perked up, and began entreating the sparrow. "Come on, sweetie," he said. He was cuckooing, like a child. "Come on, have a little seed." The bird turned his head, then hopped closer. Robinson gently tossed a couple of seeds on the ground. The bird skittered forward in a flash, picked up the seeds, and flew off. Robinson followed it with his eyes until it disappeared in a flush of trees. Suddenly, he looked up at me. "Every one of them," he said. "I told every one of them how great it was going to be."

"They must have known there were risks."

Robinson stared at me, anguish coming off him like waves. "For a long time we couldn't get people to go along," he answered. "We posted signs, ran ads. Nothing."

"Why?"

Robinson shrugged. "I-V drug abusers aren't exactly health nuts. Anyway, they don't trust the health care system. They're all convinced we'll turn them in." He paused. "Then a few people showed up, all of a sudden. Just a few, real nervous."

"Because they thought you were going to bust them?"

"Yeah, maybe. But it was just a twenty, twenty-five percent chance to get the cancer, see. So people had a hell of a decision to make. But I worked on them. In my scientific arrogance, I *told* them I would cure them."

"And something went wrong."

Robinson's face was set in stone. "You could say that." He stood, beginning a slow amble across the grass. I followed, a couple of feet apart. After a few steps, Robinson muttered something under his breath.

"What's that?" I asked.

"My glittering career," he said. "It's just something I say. 'My glittering career.'" He laughed, a short burst of bitterness. "Just when you think it can't get any worse," he said, "it does." He stopped and looked at me. "Take a look, pal. I'm a member of the two-time losers' club."

"Two-time?"

"Not just anybody can screw up on this level twice in a lifetime. It's like a gift. I've got a Ph.D. in fuckup."

"What was the first one?"

Robinson stopped. "I'm not really in the mood to open a vein, so maybe you ought to come to the point. I've got some suffering to get back to."

"I need your help."

"Help a lawyer? Why would I do that?"

"Because I don't believe that what happened to your test happened by itself. I think you got a push."

Robinson's eyes narrowed. "What the hell are you talking about?"

"I think there's someone influencing events. Someone behind the scenes."

Robinson's face hardened. "Then that somebody would have to be the most unscrupulous bastard who ever walked the earth. You better have a reason for what you're saying, okay? Those people are *dead*."

"Were you aware that your company's network security had been compromised?" The blood drained from Robinson's face. "It was a massive hack," I said. "Everything from operations to trials to email. The smallest details of Grayton Labs have been downloaded to an outside computer."

Robinson reached out and grabbed my wrist like a vise. "Who?" he demanded. "Tell me who."

"My client."

"I'm going to kill him."

"Too late, actually."

Robinson released me. "He's dead?"

"Yes. His name is Doug Townsend."

Robinson stared. He started trembling. "I remember him. Tall, pasty skin. He was your client?"

"That's right. So you don't need to hate him. Anyway, I'm certain he was working for someone else."

Robinson swayed a little, disoriented. "I killed him? I killed the guy who was stealing our secrets?"

I shook my head. "He died of an overdose of fentanyl."

Robinson looked up. "Fentanyl? Was he in the hospital?"

"He was in his apartment. He had apparently injected himself with something like a truckload of it. Nobody seems to know why."

Robinson shook his head. "Not likely," he said. "He practically had to be tied down to get the shots we gave him."

"He told me he was paranoid about needles."

"Terrified. The idea that he could pull himself together and find a vein . . . maybe, if there were about twenty holes in his arm."

"That's what I thought. But the point is that killing himself with fentanyl would have been redundant. He was going to die from Lipitran anyway."

Robinson stared at me. "So what else do you know?"

"That Doug was a pawn. But over the last few months he had been paid quite a bit of cash. It was obviously money paid to hack your company. And I think I know who he was working for." I paused, weighing my words. "If I'm right, it's almost certainly the same person who is behind what happened to your clinical trial."

"Who?"

"The name that keeps running through my mind is Charles Ralston."

Robinson swayed for a moment, as though struck with a blow. He looked up in anguish and began speaking to the sky. "You're not satisfied just destroying me," he said. "You have to grind what's left into dust."

"I take it you know him?"

Robinson brought his gaze down to me. "Yeah, I know him," he answered, as though spitting out poison. "And in a world of chaos, him doing this would make perfect sense. He's already crushed me once, so this is just more of the same."

"You've gone up against Ralston before?" Robinson nodded, the pain evident on his face. "Then there's only one question left to ask," I said. "Will you help me?"

For the first time, Robinson's expression wasn't tinged with the acrid scent of death. He actually smiled, revealing a raptorlike joy of revenge. "To get Ralston? To do that, you can have my blood."

Pulling Robinson out of his anger enough to make sense was like sobering up a drunk. He was deep into a binge, and he needed time to shake it off. I took him over to Trent's, a watering hole near the park where I found him. He was actually trembling a little as he sat, fingers gripping a cup of Sumatra. Whatever he had with Ralston, it went deep. All I had to do was wind him up and he went off on a barely controlled burn.

"Let's get something straight right off," Robinson said. "Ralston's no great scientist. He loves to play that. But the truth is, he's average. His real gift is theft."

"Explain."

Robinson set down his cup. "I was on a research team at Emory. This was what, eighty-six? The hepatitis thing was exploding over urban centers, and I was determined to do something. I worked my ass off and got an R01 grant . . ."

"R01?"

"The big NIH grants, the ones for millions. Four point one million, in this case."

"That's a lot of money."

"Yeah. I had sixteen grad students under me, spinning hepatitis-infected blood like crazy. The university was committed, the resources were there, and we were making progress. The key was isolating a particular enzyme in the blood that had an affinity for hepatitis."

"An affinity?"

"It's lab talk. When cells bind together, we say they have an affinity for each other." I nodded. "But obviously this wasn't happening in nature. If it had been, T cells would bind to it and hepatitis would be like a cold. We would just get over it."

"So what did you do?"

Robinson shrugged. "Ideally, you find an enzyme that occurs naturally you can work with. You tinker with it, engineer it. If you can get it to bind, you're halfway there. Then you try to combine the agent that kills the virus with the enzyme that binds to it, and you have a guided missile to the disease."

"The silver bullet."

"Silver bullet, miracle drug, whatever. That's the dream the scientific community uses to get the public to come up with the funding. *Give us this money, and we'll cure your cancer with one shot.* Only one problem: we're just two guys sitting in a restaurant talking about it. To get this enzyme to bind to this virus, whatever, sounds easy. But it's actually incredibly hard to do. A lot depends on starting with the right enzyme in the first place, and then modifying it. But there are hundreds to choose from."

"So what happened?"

Robinson leaned forward. "We did it, and it was nothing but hard work. We worked around the clock for so long I had students quit the program. I was a *bastard*. But finally, we made a huge breakthrough. The fact is, there is already an enzyme in the body which is very close to ideal, called P137. Nobody had considered it because it occurs in almost undetectably low levels. It hides in the blood stream, just taking up space. As far as anybody knows, it doesn't do anything. It's a holdover from our genetic past, something that we might have needed a hundred thousand years ago. So it's there, buried deep in the molecular shadows, a trace of a trace."

"And then?"

"We needed to have more of it. A lot more. For a while, I tried to stimulate natural production in the body, but it didn't go anywhere. The breakthrough was in figuring out how to synthesize it. And once we did that, we didn't need to worry about how much the body made. We would make as much as we wanted, and we could manipulate it any way we chose."

"I see."

Robinson looked at me. "I hope you do. We were in a race with death at that point, and suddenly, we can see the finish line." He paused. "You have to realize, we were just seeing the real numbers from urban centers. The AIDS thing was getting a lot of people tested. And we were beginning to grasp that hep C was going to ultimately be just as damaging. It didn't have the clout in the public's mind, because AIDS seemed so much scarier. But the truth was, at least in North America, hep C had the potential to kill more people. There are already three million people with it, you know."

"I didn't."

"Right. So there we are, just on the verge of the thing. But we can feel it. Like there's a little fog, and in just a few seconds exactly the right wisp is going to move to the left and there it's going to be, what we've worked years to discover." Robinson's eyes were wide. He was high on the pure ecstasy of science, drawn back into his love of his work. "Then," he said, "I made my fatal error."

"Which was?"

Robinson looked out the window, suddenly listless. There was fatigue in his eyes, the long suffering of a terrible defeat. "Ralston," he said. "Charles Ralston, king of thieves."

"Tell me how it happened."

"Hubris. Ego. Stupidity. All mine, as it turned out." He looked down into the coffee, retreating into the past. "I was at a seminar up at Columbia."

"Where Ralston was working."

"Right. Look, I was excited, okay? I mean . . . We were going to save a lot of people from dying. It's pretty hard to keep that to yourself."

"My God. You mean you—"

"Not much," Robinson interrupted. He rubbed his temples, deep in regret. "Just the slightest little bit. But I lost my head. I remember my words exactly. 'P137 has suddenly become very important in my life.' I think I even smiled when I said it. I thought it was wonderfully cryptic."

"It is, actually."

Robinson shook his head. "Not to Ralston. I didn't know it, but he had been working on the same thing at Columbia. And they were getting nowhere. He was headed in the wrong direction, naturally. I told you he's mediocre."

"So you said."

"Mediocre, but not an idiot. I had given him the keys to the kingdom. He knew a lot about enzyme synthesis, but nothing about where to take that knowledge. Once he knew where to look, it was only a matter of weeks before he had it wired."

"Wasn't your research patented?"

Robinson shook his head. "The disclosure form was sitting on my desk. And I had made an enabling statement."

I reached back into my law school memory. "A public utterance, which, to a person of reasonable expertise, allows them to duplicate your technology." I shook my head, stunned. "You voided your patent before you even got it filed."

Robinson nodded. "Ralston got on the phone to Stephens, who was living in New York. He was already famous for patent expertise, especially in the area of pharmaceuticals. On Stephens's advice, Ralston resigned from Columbia the next day."

"So Ralston beat you to it?"

"By the time I knew what happened, Stephens had a beautiful, airtight package." He shrugged. "The rest, including my career, is history."

"I take it Emory wasn't amused."

"It was the single greatest humiliation in their history. Those grad students had slaved, and I'm talking twenty-four-seven, for months. They were going to be a part of something historic. And boom, one stupid statement from me and it's up in smoke. I couldn't show my face." Robinson picked up his cup, drank a sip. "I vanished for a while. I was mud in the academic world, and no labs would take a risk on me. It got so bad I took a job as a rep, calling on doctors."

"I'm sorry."

"Yeah. That was hell. Horizn was making a fortune on my research, and there was nothing anybody could do about it. Stephens didn't make my mistakes, obviously. Their patents were untouchable."

"What kind of fortune are we talking about?"

Robinson shrugged. "There's an exploding patient population, reaching epidemic proportions in the third world. Ralston has a treatment that every one of those people needs to take for the rest of their lives. So you can call it billions."

"So let me get this straight. Your career is in tatters. Ralston is riding high. And somehow, you get resurrected. How did you get connected to Grayton?"

"Look, I like to heal people, okay? It means everything to me. But this is an ego game. You say Ralston was riding high? Don't forget it was on *my* research. So I went to Grayton. I told him that what Ralston was doing was fine, as far as it went. But there was a way to beat him."

"Which was?"

"Go deeper. Forget treating the disease as a chronic condition. Mount a serious attempt at a cure."

"And Grayton bought that?"

Robinson nodded. "You have to be willing to take chances or you lose. Grayton was trying to hang on, but it's hard to compete with the multinationals. And I knew more about hepatitis than anybody, including Ralston and his team. For all its beauty, Horizn's drug is one generation removed from the most cutting-edge proteomics. I ought to know, since I invented it. So I told Grayton that if he wanted to try, I could take years off his start time. Somebody like Eli Lilly wouldn't bite on me, not with my past. But Grayton has to take different risks. So we made a deal." Robinson looked past me, his eyes focusing on an unknown place in his mind. "And it was beautiful. The old man lined up everything I needed. People, equipment, every resource. It was going to be my resurrection." His voice dropped to a whisper. "And then everything went to hell."

"Do you have any idea what happened?"

Robinson shook his head. "I've gone over it a thousand times. I've checked our data and rechecked. And I'm telling you, those people should be walking around right now without a hepatitis molecule in their bodies. Instead, they're in morgues."

I sat thinking quietly awhile. "Let's assume Ralston is behind the hack into your system," I said after a moment. "What's behind that? Is he just trying to steal your drug, like he did the last time?"

Robinson looked up in surprise. "Steal it? Robinson wouldn't want Lipitran if I gave it to him."

"I don't follow."

"Lipitran is a *cure*, not a chronic treatment. Who wants to cure people when you can just treat them forever?"

"So what is it, then?"

"If we come to market, his company is worth zip. If Lipitran goes wrong, he gets to keep selling his drug for the next twenty years." He looked down into his coffee. "Seven dead people takes care of that, don't you think? Lipitran is as dead as those patients."

Robinson was fading back into his depression. "So here's what we have," I said, forcing his attention back on me. "We've got your computer, downloaded for Ralston. He knows exactly what you're doing. He desperately wants to stop you."

"Okay."

"But we have no idea how."

Robinson shook his head. "Which is where the air comes out of your idea," he said bitterly. "Believe me, I want you to be right. But we're just throwing around theories in a coffee shop. I was there, in the lab. There are only two ways for this to go wrong. He'd either have to alter the compound itself or change the dosage to toxic levels. And he couldn't have done either."

"Start with the compound."

"Strike one, pal. There is no place—and I mean *no* place—where Ralston could have compromised the purity of that compound. It was made completely in-house. I checked its purity myself, repeatedly. It was continuously monitored until the moment it was given to patients."

"All right. Then how about the dosage?"

Robinson shook his head. "Strike two. I supervised every treatment. Nothing went wrong, and there were no adverse reactions at the time."

I nodded. "That still leaves us one strike."

Robinson smiled grimly. "Wrong. Strike three is that maybe this is just fate. Maybe those eight people were just unlucky enough to have the worst doctor on earth. Me." He stared at me, anger and disappointment etched on his face. Then he pounded his fist on the table. A few people around us glanced over, and I motioned for him to calm down.

"No," he hissed. "No. I'm telling you, the science on this is perfect. The compound was right. The dosages were on the money. There must be some other way for him to have screwed me."

"You mean screwed them, don't you, Doctor?" I said quietly.

Robinson looked down. "Yeah, them," he said. "Screwed them."

"Look," I said, "my agenda is a little different. I want justice for one person, and that's Doug Townsend."

Robinson looked at me. "You've got a problem there," he said. "I can understand that Ralston might have hired him to break into Grayton's computers. And I can follow that after he outlived his usefulness, they would want him dead. But if all that is true, they would have known Doug was in the clinical trial. And if they knew that, they would never have bothered to shoot him full of fentanyl."

"Because they would have known he was dead already."

"Who screws up the perfect crime? Killing him again is pointless."

"Agreed. And murder involves the police, the last thing they would want."

"Okay, then. Maybe you ought to start considering the possibility that somebody else killed your friend."

"I'm taking this one day at a time. But we're fighting the same war. If you really have a cure for hep C, you have to fight. You can still save all those lives." I paused. "And get the man who destroyed your life for the second time."

Robinson looked at me. "I'll do anything I can, but I've given you what I know. If these people figured out how to screw with that test, they're operating on a level so high it's unprecedented." He stood, picking up his bag of seeds. "Right now, we got nothing," he said.

"We?"

Robinson looked down at me, wary optimism struggling through a mass of defeat. He wanted to believe in what I was telling him down into his fibers. But he also knew he couldn't take another shock. If he let himself connect with me and we went down in flames, whatever was left of him was going to land in a psychiatric ward. He was dangerously close to there already. But he pulled himself together enough to say what I needed to hear: "When you get more, you know where to find me."

*   *   *

I don't know what the price of a human being is. I grew up believing in the infinite price tag, the one set by God. We all had the dignity of the Creator, and anybody who tried to lower the price with a bullet or a knife had to pay the difference with his own. In those days, human dignity was a zero-sum game. Nobody had the right to mess with the totals, because we all were affected. But it gets harder and harder to cling to that idea. Lately, in the court of Judge Thomas Odom, I've seen a human life go for as little as twenty bucks—the small, sad collection of paper and metal an unlucky victim got capped over by a hyped-up, needy addict. And I've seen the same murder buried on page ten of the newspaper, while the whole town went nuts saving a squirrel who got caught in a drainpipe. So, in the absence of a consensus, you have to choose whom to believe. Either we're all connected to each other by some common soul, in which case, killing is wrong, wrong, wrong. Or we aren't, and the strong eat the weak. The answers couldn't be more different.

The thing is, you don't expect people who sell medicine for a living to be confused on that subject. You expect them to be firmly on the side of the living, without any ambiguities. You can almost believe that, until you realize how much money is at stake, and then all the old battles over human nature come back to haunt you. Because history shows that once a few billion dollars are on the table, nobody is what I would call safe.

That was the moment I started to hear the clock ticking in my mind. *Tic, tic, tic:* It was Tuesday, and the next Monday morning Charles Ralston and Derek Stephens were going to be the recipients of an unfathomable transfer of wealth when tens of thousands of people bought into the future of Horizn's hepatitis treatment. *Tic, tic, tic:* According to Robinson, a successful test of Lipitran would have put every penny of that into jeopardy, and even the future of Horizn itself. *Tic, tic, tic:* To be fair, Robinson was badly damaged, crushed by guilt and defeat. It was theoretically possible his hatred for Ralston stemmed from that, and that he was deluding himself about the rest. Too much failure doesn't just make the world look terrible—it makes the world look pissed off at you specifically, custom-designed to make your life miserable.

Robinson was pretty far down that road. Which led me to this: I had six days to find out what price tag Ralston and Stephens would put on eight people, most of whom were drug addicts and down-and-outers. I needed to find out if they believed in the zero-sum of mankind. I needed to find out if they were monsters.

Everything was clear. I knew exactly who the bad guys were, and I knew exactly who I wanted to save. I understood everything, and I cherished that clarity. It was beautiful, and it lasted about fifteen minutes.

CHAPTER TWENTY

"JACK? WHEN ARE YOU coming to the office?"

"First things first, baby. How are you? Did Stephens freak out or what?"

"There's someone here, Jack. Someone to see you."

I looked at my watch. It was nearly five. "Yeah? Did I miss something on my schedule?"

"It's Mr. Stephens."

I snapped to attention. "He's there? Now?"

"Um hmm."

"In my office?"

"Um hmm."

"Tell him not to move."

"I don't think he's going anywhere."

"I'm on my way."

Derek Stephens didn't look pissed off. He didn't look like he was holding his sense of calm together with a titanic effort, either. He looked like it was just another day, and he had never even thought of combining the words Sammy, Liston, and Ferrari. He rose—smiling, inexplicably—from one of my waiting chairs with so much casual insouciance it was as if he was welcoming me into *his* office. I'm telling you, it's like a gift. He even spoke first. "Jack," he said, "I'm glad you're here. I was hoping you had a few minutes."

I looked at Blu. "You okay, baby?" She nodded, her face blank. "Tell you what," I said. "Why don't you go out and get a little coffee?"

"There's coffee here, Jack," she said. Her voice was unsteady.

"That's all right, baby," I said. "Take a little time. I'll see you here in a few minutes." Blu looked at Stephens a second, then picked up her purse. "Sure thing," I said to Stephens. "Right in here."

I walked into my office, tossed my sunglasses on my desk, and motioned to a wing chair opposite my desk. Stephens looked around, probably trying to figure out how I practiced law in the same square footage as his executive bathroom. But even though I've been known to sling my share of bullshit in court, inside my office I take none. Zero. Zip. After my talk with Robinson, I was prepared to take even less than that. It was entirely possible that I was in the room with an unprincipled murderer. It was also possible I was dead wrong about that, so I took as neutral a tone as possible. I sat down, let him stare at my still-swollen left eye and said, "What's on your mind?"

Stephens sat there looking at me, a slight smile playing on his lips. After a while he said, "I've got an idea, Jack. Let's you and I be friends."

I returned the smile. "Gee, I don't know, Derek. Why would I want to do that?"

"Because that way, I can give you friendly advice, as opposed to the other kind."

"I wasn't aware I needed either."

Stephens shrugged. "The people who need it the most usually aren't. But I have the feeling we got off to a bad start. Let's try it again."

I decided to give him some rope, just to find out what he wanted. "I'm all ears, Derek old pal," I said.

"You've been poking your nose where it doesn't belong, Jack. Specifically, up the skirt of the wife of Charles Ralston."

Okay, so this is going to be ugly. That's fine, I can go there, no problem. "You'll forgive me for not wanting to hear that from somebody with a pathological need to screw secretaries."

Stevens smiled, as though he were thinking, *Good. You have spunk. That makes this so much more interesting.* "Not that this is the topic, but you don't approve of my relationship with Blu?"

"I'm afraid my answer wouldn't be entirely complimentary."

Stephens waved his hand magnanimously. "Not a problem."

"The thing is, Derek, Blu's really a very sweet kind of girl. Heart of gold, but not very sophisticated. You, by contrast, are an effete snob who thinks that because you've read a few books you're better than other people. But that's a matter of taste, so that's not what's really bothering me."

"And what is?"

"The fact that you'll date my secretary for a while, and you'll definitely take her to bed. You'll enjoy her very considerable charms for as long as you find them interesting. But doing anything that means regarding her as a complete, living human being—like marrying her, for example—isn't something you'd do in a million years. Not that I want you to marry her, naturally, but that isn't the point. The point is, you wouldn't marry Blu because then you'd have to introduce her to your Fortune 500 buddies as representative of your taste in women. You'd be afraid she'd embarrass you at a dinner party, like maybe lean over and ask you which fork to use or who the poet Dante was or what's the big deal with Kandinsky's paintings, anyway? Or maybe she'd say something sweet and simple like she was thinking of having your bedroom painted cornflower blue, and all your New York tight-ass friends would roll their eyes, and that would *kill* a guy like you. No, Derek old pal, you aren't going to marry Blu McClendon. But you'll definitely use her for a while, and you'll drop her when you're done. She doesn't know how to recognize your particular kind of slime because it's not in her nature to think along your lines of evil. I, on the other hand, am a man who knows a bastard when he sees one coming. And the more I think about you, the more I despise my own gender."

Stephens sat listening, leaning back in his chair, his eyes half-closed. The smile playing on his lips flickered, and he looked at me. "It's a tragedy you lost your compass, Jack. Sincerely. You would have been marvelous." He leaned forward. "I've been checking up on you, naturally. I can't have you snooping through Michele's underthings without doing that." He pressed his fingertips together thoughtfully. "Short version, since I'm a little pressed for time. You were talented, you were bright, and once upon a time, you were ambitious. But you yielded to the wrong temptation, and here"—he looked around my office disparagingly—"you are." At that second, I made a silent vow: *If he says her holy name, I'm going to punch his face.* Stephens kept on talking, his voice as steady as a contractor's level. "What was it, two years ago? Just a few years out of law school. You were up at Carthy, Williams and Douglas. Good firm, and you had good prospects. Then came your little indiscretion, and you fell off the rails. The point is, you've already blown yourself up once on the altar of a beautiful woman. Do you really want to make the same mistake again?"

I was fully aware of how many lifetimes of financial servitude I would be rendering myself by breaking Stephens's legs, but at that moment, it seemed like a bargain. "You're sitting on top of the world right now, aren't you, Derek old pal?"

He smiled. "It would appear so."

"You've got a girlfriend—probably some Connecticut hardass who majored in gender studies, given the fact that you can't keep your hands off southern women—but at any rate, you've got one. Meanwhile, your 'little something on the side' happens to be one of the most beautiful women on earth. And to top everything, you're less than a week away from becoming incredibly rich."

"And your point is?"

"You got nothing."

Stephens seemed amused. "Nothing?"

"That's right, nothing. And you know why? The whole thing

lacks nobility." I leaned forward. "You didn't do the *work*, Derek. You know, the part where you and Ralston earn what you have? You stole that hepatitis treatment, and that kind of takes the shine off things."

Stephens fixed me in his clear, untroubled eyes. "There's only one man who says that," he said. "How very interesting that you've been speaking to him."

"He's a real fan of your boss."

"Tom Robinson is a fine scientist. He did some good work, although not as good as he imagines. But he made an error, and he can't live with himself. Do you want me to feel sorry for him? I won't. Business is war, and everybody who succeeds knows it." He paused, looking around my office with a slight smile. "Look at this place, Jack. Is this why you went to law school?"

"At least I didn't steal it."

Stephens shrugged. "All right, Jack. You don't like me. Fine. You think I'm unscrupulous. Fine, again. But I'm not going to ask for your trust. I'm going to earn it."

"That would be a neat trick."

"Watch." Stephens paused, looked straight at me, and casually said, "Has Michele told you about Briah yet?"

With those words, the world listed badly to the side. It was the big secret, the one Michele had begged me to keep private at all costs. Stephens had said her name with so much ease he might have been talking about the weather. "Briah?" I whispered.

"Yes, Jack. It's all right. I know all about Briah, and so does Charles."

"She said . . ."

"I know, Jack. She lies."

"She doesn't know that you know."

"Of course she does. All you have to do is ask her. When you see her face, you'll know I'm telling you the truth."

I closed my eyes. The implications of what he was saying were too vast to contemplate. I had gone to the wall, and if I had done it for somebody who was using me, it was going to change the way I felt about the world. Stephens sat waiting, patiently letting me gather myself together. "Did you know Michele has a criminal record?" he asked.

"No." A wave of nausea began forming in my gut. "What was her crime?"

"*Crimes,*" Stephens said. "T'aniqua was a very unhappy little girl."

"T'aniqua."

"Yes, Jack. We know all about that, too."

My breathing was getting labored. It was hard to find air. "She said Ralston could never know. She said he would never accept it."

"He *does* know, Jack. So there's no point in arguing about whether or not he could accept the fact."

The logic was irrefutable. But it didn't answer the question burning a hole through my humiliation. "Tell me why," I said. "Why make all this up? If Ralston knows, then why beg me to help her find her daughter?"

"Because she can't reach her by any legal means," Stephens said. "So she uses her considerable skills of manipulation to get people to help her." He paused. "No doubt she told you that Social Services took the baby away at birth."

"Yes."

"One of her favorites. She's also maintained that the child was taken from her in a shopping mall, or that the father stole her from her." He smiled sadly. "If it makes you feel any better, you aren't the first. You're . . . fifth, I believe. Which makes your friend Doug Townsend the fourth."

I stared. "You know about Doug?"

"What you need to understand is that I know everything about Michele, Jack." He looked at me levelly. "*Everything.*" The vision of what happened on the Horizn jet came flashing back through my mind. "It's all right," Stephens said, as though reading my mind. His eyes gleamed. "She is luminous, isn't she? When she opens her mouth, you're convinced she's a goddess. So much beauty, it's breathtaking. But it's an illusion. She's a deeply troubled woman."

He paused. "Michele was a wild child. When Briah came along, it shouldn't have surprised anyone she failed to accept her responsibility regarding the baby."

I felt like I was turning to stone inside. "What happened?"

"There was an accident. The baby was nearly drowned while Michele was partying with friends in another room."

"I see." Only I didn't see. I was more confused and broken every moment.

"She was bathing the little girl, and got distracted. By marijuana and alcohol, as it happens. The baby was saved by police who had gotten a tip on the party. A neighbor heard the noise and was concerned the child wasn't getting proper attention. The police busted the place, and found Michele and her friends in the living room. Stoned." I couldn't speak. "The police searched the house, and they found Briah on her back in a bathtub. The water was inches from her mouth. If she had even turned her head, she would have drowned." Stephens grimaced. "So yes, Jack. Social Services removed the child. Anything else would have been irresponsible. But they did it to save the little girl's life."

"Where is she now?" I asked. "Where is Briah?"

"What makes you think I know that?"

"Because you seem to know everything else."

Stephens watched me, considering. "Fair enough," he said, after a moment. "I do know. But it isn't any of your concern. It's enough to say that Charles has seen to it that the child has everything she needs." He sighed. "Every once in a while, Michele gets regret. She decides she has to find her daughter and explain everything. After all these years, she wants to be a mother. It's understandable, I suppose. But Briah is in a far better place, and nothing good can come from that meeting."

I sat in silence awhile, trying to make sense of things. The world was upside down. The woman I had been falling in love with was turning out to be someone who had mercilessly used me, and my so-called enemy was trusting me with his deepest secrets. Suddenly, a thought flashed through my brain. "Listen," I said, "Sammy isn't the smartest guy in the world. Have some mercy on him. He's just . . . frustrated at who he isn't."

"I'm not going to do anything to your friend," Stephens said.

"He trashed your Ferrari," I said. "Or he had it trashed."

"I'm aware of that."

"And you're going to do nothing."

"That's right."

"Blu said you were upset."

"Wouldn't you be?"

"I'd be nuclear. So why aren't you going to do anything about it?"

"Because although your friend is a pathetic worm, he is chronologically extremely lucky. If I am going to get my name in the paper six days before Horizn goes public, it is not going to be over a lover's spat with a disgruntled court employee."

"And after?"

"Horizn's stock price will be fragile a long time, Jack. It's going to run up fast, and that will make people nervous. Stability is everything. And frankly, when I go on MSNBC, I don't want the first question to be about some southern-fried, redneck argument about a car."

I stared. Nothing—I mean nothing—about this conversation had gone the way I thought it would. "He gets away with it," I said.

"He does." He leaned back in his chair. "Which brings us to you."

Suddenly, I understood what the hell Stephens was doing in my office, and why he was risking giving me so much unvarnished information about the secret life of Charles Ralston's wife. *Damn right, he's not wasting his expensive time. He's here to make a deal.* "I'm something of a loose end, aren't I?" I said.

Stephens shrugged. "If you like."

"You want me to stop nosing around about Doug's death. You don't want any cages rattled."

"A billion dollars are at stake, Jack. Every penny of it rests on the spotless reputation of Horizn."

"Not really my problem."

"No, but what if all your questions were answered? And you do have questions, Jack. Questions about your friend."

"I'd like nothing better than answers."

Stephens reached in his pocket and set a card down on my desk. "Tomorrow morning, at Horizn offices. Give that to the guard at the gate."

I raised an eyebrow in surprise. "To do what?"

"You have an appointment with Charles Ralston."

"Is that a fact?"

"You have your suspicions, and time with Robinson made them worse. But Robinson's latest tragedy is his own, and Horizn had nothing to do with it. In the interest of peace, Charles has agreed to meet with you personally and discuss these matters. In my opinion, he shouldn't give you the time of day. But of course, I wouldn't put up with his philandering wife, either. So he's a better man than I am about some things." He rose. "In the meantime, I'm also going to assume that you'll be reasonable about Michele."

"You mean keep away from her."

"This is a sensitive time, and she's a volatile woman. When she falls apart, nobody wins." He rose and began walking toward the door. Before he reached it, he paused and turned back around. "And I have a message for Tom Robinson. One inflammatory word from him that gets into the media, and there won't be anything left of him or Grayton Labs to bury. He has nothing to prove, and I take the libel laws in this country seriously. Understood?"

"I'll pass it along."

"You do that."

Stephens left, and I sat alone in my office. Alcohol, for so long my sweet blanket of anesthesia, beckoned like a lover. I was wearing my guilt and stupidity like a sunburn. After the heat, comes the pain. And after Derek Stephens, came the personal recriminations.

I had backed the wrong horse. I had got my ass kicked. I had— and this was the hardest to swallow—opened up to the beauty, elegance, and talent of a woman I supposed to be so far beyond me that even to be near her was like a dream. And I had just learned that for her it had been an illusion, another role.

Love, I was being reminded, can be a bitch. The mere possibility of it made people act like idiots, and everything that had happened since Doug Townsend died convinced me of it more. Doug was doomed by trying to do something for Michele. Without that fatal obsession, he would still be alive, off drugs, and turning his life around. Sammy had risked his own existence losing his mind over Blu. *And I've just had my hat handed to me by Derek Stephens. Who, it should be noted, is presently breaking the heart of my secretary.* I opened my bottom drawer, pulled out a bottle and a glass. I poured a drink and sat looking at it, watching the light flicker in its amber, liquid depths.

I heard some soft talking in the outer office, and then the door closed, meaning Stephens had left. I looked at the glass of whiskey, thinking about Blu. I'd heard it said many times that being beautiful can be a pain in the ass. But I hadn't really understood it, not until now. But Blu's most persuasive assets were also her most dangerous trapdoors. On the one hand, a guy like Sammy—who, in spite of being a little deranged about her, was actually quite chivalrous in his lecherous heart—was always lurking around to make life complicated. Smile at him, and he's likely to show up with flowers and a bottle of champagne. On the other, a guy like Stephens—who held in his hands the power to grant her every wish—was only going to use and discard her. I downed the drink, refilled the glass, and stared at the second just like the first. I don't know how long I stared. I just know that at some point the door to my office opened, and Blu, walking a little unsteadily, came in. "How you doing?" I asked quietly. "You okay?"

"Sure," she said. "You had some messages on your desk."

"Listen, Blu, if you want to talk about anything . . ."

"No, that's fine." She ran a hand through her TV commercial hair. "I'm fine, really." She crossed the room to my desk and pushed a piece of paper across it. "I'm resigning," she said. "I'm giving my notice."

I stared at the paper, then back up at her. "What are you talking about? I don't accept."

She blinked a few times, and I wondered if she had been crying. "It doesn't matter, Jack. I'm leaving either way. I'm just trying to be professional."

"But why?"

"Just because."

"Is this about Stephens? Dammit, Blu, if he's pressuring you . . ."

"No," she blurted, her face reddening.

"Then what? You can't just leave without telling me what's going on."

She turned, and suddenly, there wasn't any doubt about whether she was crying. She was leaking all over the office. "Don't make me spell it out, Jack. Just let me do it."

I stood up, walked to her, and put a hand under her chin, tipping her face up to mine. "You can do what you want. But just tell me why."

She stood in front of me, spectacular even in her pain, her perfect face scrunched into anguish, tears coming from her flawless, cerulean eyes. And then she said something so human, so generous, so completely noble that it went like an arrow through my heart. "I'm doing it for you, Jack," she sobbed. "Because as long as I'm here, Sammy isn't going to call here anymore."

I let go and sat back on my desk, stunned. She was right, of course. She had lived through enough idiotic, outsized declarations of love like Sammy's to know what came next. Sammy wasn't going to come within ten miles of her, although he was still going to love her so much it drove him a little insane. Once a man lays it out that hard and gets turned down—not that Sammy had expected anything else, he wasn't *that* insane—he can't just pick up the phone and make small talk. The male ego simply doesn't accommodate it. It would simply be impossible for him to dial my phone number knowing that her voice was going to be on the other end. But being right didn't mean I was going to just let her walk out the door. I was fully prepared to pretend I didn't know what she was talking about, in the hope that we could both just lie to each other a little bit and get on with things. "Don't be ridiculous," I said. "Of course he's going to call."

She wasn't buying it. "He's not going to call, Jack. God, men are so—"

"Look—"

"You can't stay afloat without Sammy," she interrupted flatly. "And he's not going to call with me here. He's been humiliated, and he won't be able to face me. So it's simple. I have to go."

"But listen—"

"And anyway, he's your best friend, Jack. I'm not going to ask you to give that up."

"So Stephens didn't ask you to leave?"

"No."

I thought about it a minute, then ripped her resignation paper into pieces. "Then there's no way I can accept this. You're staying."

"You'll go broke."

"But you want to work here."

"Of course I want to work here. You're . . . yes, I want to work here."

"Then you're going to keep working here."

She looked at me awhile, her tears subsiding. Her breath was still coming in painfully alluring gasps of lucky oxygen. "Why?" she asked. "Why do that for me?"

"Because at this moment I'm embarrassed for the male segment of the human race, and I am going to make amends. I am going to do something unprecedented. I am going to do you a favor, and I am not going to use it to get in your pants."

It took a couple of minutes, but she pulled herself together. She smoothed down her top, adjusted her skirt, and pushed her hair back off her face and behind her ears. Then she walked straight up to me and kissed me gently on the cheek. "Thank you," she said, a tiny smile escaping her lips. "Thank you very much."

"You're welcome."

"You really will go broke."

"Probably."

"Well, then, if there's nothing else." She wiped her tears again, turned, and walked out the door.

CHAPTER TWENTY-ONE

WEDNESDAY CAME TO ATLANTA like a whisper, a faint, golden luminescence spreading upward in the east. I sat in my apartment and watched my small fragment of the city come to life, light by solitary light. Newspapers were getting thrown onto porches, while alarm clocks for the early risers—the ones with the brutal hour and a half commutes—were shocking people out of the last, most precious, hour of sleep. A lone car, headlights gleaming in the fading darkness, rolled under my third-story window. I had not slept. Instead, I had spent the last few hours alone in my apartment, my only company a bottle of scotch and a list of eight names.

There are people who, when drunk, float into the black emptiness of nearly comatose sleep. I am not one of them. I can drink all night, although it's invariably a lousy idea. It's lousy because with alcohol, I become eerily attuned to the misery of the world, which is a heavy enough load to carry sober. So my bottle of scotch and I spent the night in too-familiar territory, ruminating on priests who preyed on children and overpaid CEOs and Clinton getting blow jobs in the Oval Office—in other words, the collapse of decency in this once-proud country. Before me—grist for my angry mill—were seven names of the formerly living: Jonathan Mills. Chantelle Weiss. Brian Louden. Keisha Setter. Najeh Richardson. Lavaar Scott. Michele Lashonda Lyles. Doug Townsend. To which I could probably soon add Roberto Lacayo, clinging to life in the hospital.

As the sun rose, I stared at the list, holding each name in my mind. Of their number, only Doug was a complete person to me, full of the details that make life meaningful. But it wasn't hard to imagine the common ground of the other lamented lives. Somewhere they had all gone off the tracks, finding themselves infected with a dangerous disease and willing to take a chance to get help. If they died in the crossfire of a corporate battle, they were nothing but sacrificial pawns. And just because the whole world was falling apart didn't make that acceptable.

I sat there in silence for another half an hour, sipping whiskey. I don't know what I expected; maybe I thought God was going to appear in my crap apartment and explain how everything works. All I know is I finished the bottle at about six-thirty, which was the moment I got free. I put down the glass, realizing that I had wondered enough about things that have no answer. The reason for the way things were was: there was no reason. None at all. They just were. *L'amore non prevale sempre*, baby, and that was the truth of things. To survive, you got to strip things down and let them go. Only then can a man get free enough to find his way through this mess. *There is no God*, I thought, *and I am His prophet*. I got up feeling triumphantly atheistic and made myself some coffee. I looked at the empty bottle of scotch, and made a vow: I would no longer drown my so-called sorrows. I would stay in touch with my pain, letting it burn into my cells the importance of detachment. The world was too big a place for me to make right, and I wasn't exactly driven snow, myself. But if I could figure out what happened to the men and women who got murdered trying to rid themselves of hepatitis, I would do it. I would do it because that was the kind of man I was, and it didn't need any explaining. So at eight-thirty I took a shower, letting the warm water wash away a lifetime of mistakes. At nine I put on a sport coat, got in my car, and drove to Horizn Pharmaceuticals.

The Horizn campus was set north of Atlanta in Dunwoody, a quiet, heavily forested area that serves as home to several midsize corporate offices. As soon as I pulled into the headquarters, I saw the imprint of Ralston's internal psychology on the physical plant. Ralston, having built his company on dubiously acquired technology, was making damn sure nobody made him a victim of the same thing. He had made Horizn a fortress of high-tech security. The chances of entering the premises surreptitiously were zero.

The main buildings were hidden far from the entrance, which was secured by a guardhouse. The road in was barred by a long, substantial-looking mechanical arm. Behind it, reverse spikes threatened the tires of any vehicle capable of breaking through. Cameras mounted high on both sides of the gate stared down. I rolled to a stop, and a uniformed guard wearing an earpiece slid open his window. His voice was polite. "Can I help you?"

I handed him Ralston's card. "Jack Hammond," I said. "Here to see Charles Ralston."

"Please wait." The guard spoke softly into something hidden in his lapel. Nothing happened for a long moment. After a while he said, "Please turn your face toward me, Mr. Hammond. The camera's having a hard time picking you up." Curious, I turned toward him. After several seconds the guard pointed ahead and said, "Just follow the road." The arm moved upward, and I drove through.

Now on Horizn property, I followed a winding, black asphalt road into dense woods. At intervals, surveillance cameras mounted on tall poles marked my progress. After about a quarter mile I came around a gentle curve and saw the main complex: a six-story rectangle of bronzed glass and steel, connected by a covered walkway to a smaller, curved building two stories high. I headed toward the taller building and parked in the lot in front.

I walked through the lot toward the building, disembodied

security recording my every move. I quickly ascended the low stairs to the front door; before I could touch it, it slid open. I walked forward, only to meet another glass door ahead. As I waited, the door behind me slid closed; I was now trapped between the two doors. Cameras glared down from above. A voice came through a hidden loudspeaker: "Please look to your left." There was another wait of several moments; then the front door silently slid open. I walked out into a large atrium that was open to the top of the building. Enormous, well-manicured tropical plants reached upward to the bronze-filtered sun. An attractive brunette was standing several feet away from the door. "Hello, Mr. Hammond," she said. "Please follow me."

The woman walked me toward an elevator across the lobby. She pressed her hand on a flat metallic surface integrated into the wall by the elevator door. The door opened, and she motioned for me to enter. I stepped in alone, and the door closed. I looked around; there were no buttons; apparently, the elevator was an express to Ralston's office. A video camera stared down at me from above. The elevator began to move briskly toward the top of the building.

After the ride, I stepped out into a small reception area of dark paneling and upholstered chairs. The room evoked a kind of English drawing-room elegance that seemed out of place in such a high-tech palace. Rows of plaques, community service awards, and photographs of Ralston with the glitterati lined the walls. There were framed thank-you notes from the White House, from the governor, from the mayor. The Harvard and Yale degrees were displayed as well, lit from above by a hidden beam. But the place of honor was reserved for a photograph from the *Atlanta Journal-Constitution*, showing Ralston defiant in a city council meeting, arm raised, finger pointing accusingly. The caption below the picture read, *Charles Ralston champions needle-exchange program for city's underclass.* A middle-aged, studious-looking woman met me. "Can I get you anything, Mr. Hammond? Tea? Coffee?" I shook my head. "Then if there's nothing else, you can go in." She pressed her hand on another identification device, and the lock on a door to my right clicked. She pushed it open and motioned me forward.

If Ralston's reception area was a paean to his civic accomplishments, his office was the opposite: it was the most pristine, uncluttered eight hundred square feet I had ever seen. There was virtually nothing in it, its starkness amplifying its size. Apparently, Ralston's definition of luxury was untroubled space, with nothing to interrupt his mind. The room occupied a corner of the building, giving it two exterior walls, each of bronzed glass. Light passing through gave the room a golden, sepulchral, glow. The other two walls were painted a dark green, with large, abstract works of art mounted on them. Toward the far end of the room was a desk—a gleaming, silver surface mounted on a thin, polished metal pedestal—again, with nothing on it. Ralston's office chair was black leather stretched across a chrome frame. There were no other chairs. Apparently, visitors stood. It was a monk's cell built for a millionaire.

Ralston didn't turn when I entered. He was standing at the far end of his office, arms by his side, eyes level, staring into the woods surrounding Horizn. He wore a dark, exquisitely tailored suit. For a while, neither of us spoke. Eventually, he turned and looked at me. His features were as precise as a ruler, with a straight, narrow face, and thin, determined lips. But he wasn't menacing; instead, there seemed to be a weary sadness around him, a grayness hovering over him like an aura. He didn't look like a man a few days away from winning the biggest victory of his professional life. When he finally spoke, his voice was so low I had to strain to hear it. "Why does business have to be war, Mr. Hammond?"

The room was stark and quiet; I hesitated to break its silence with my own voice. "I don't know," I answered softly.

He made a small motion with his hand. "Come here."

I walked across yards of immaculate gray carpet to a spot a few feet away from him. He motioned out through the glass walls. "It's beautiful, isn't it?"

The woods below shimmered with a golden, surreal glow. "Yes, it is."

Side by side, we looked out into the wooded expanse surrounding Horizn. "I'm not a businessman, Jack. I trained as a scientist.

Did you know that?" Ralston stared out through the glass, unblinking. "Have you ever wanted to turn back the clock, Jack? Go to a
point in time when everything was perfect?"

"Yes."

He turned and looked at me, his eyes level, inquiring. After a
moment he nodded, as though he approved. "I loved research as a
young man. Pure research, not chasing government grants around.
Just observing, and asking why." He smiled. "That's a beautiful
question, isn't it, Jack?"

"The question why?"

He nodded. "You trypsonize a protein and discover there are fifteen fragment peptides. Why just fifteen, and not sixteen? The
answer has nothing to do with business. It's a question for a scientist." He paused, looking past me, as though reminiscing. "You
start out in business with ideals. You want to help people, maybe
make a dollar or two along the way. And somehow, without actually noticing it, it turns into war." He fell silent again, lost in his
own thoughts. "I'm sorry about the delay at the gate," he said, after
a moment. "Bugs in the facial recognition program. It's nothing
personal. Everyone who enters the building is put in the database."
He looked up at me ruefully. "Even my wife's lovers." A terrible
silence followed, the kind that swallows you up. I started to speak,
but Ralston waved me off. "It doesn't matter," he said. "Once she
chose you, there was nothing you could do."

"I was under the impression we were choosing each other."

Ralston gave a wan, vaguely sympathetic, smile. He walked to
his desk and touched its surface; the spot under his finger lit, and
the glass walls gradually darkened several shades. Eventually we
were standing in a somber, gold cocoon. Ralston touched another
place on the desk, and the wall behind him flickered into life,
revealing a gigantic plasma screen six feet across. The wall of light
showed an enormous double helix.

"This is my life's work, Jack," Ralston said. He stared at the
image, mesmerized. "Magnificent, isn't it?" He touched another
button, and the strand of DNA began to replicate, the double

helixes folding back on themselves, the splines splintering and recombining, until finally it had created a precise copy of itself. Ralston watched, rapt. "My wife finds me cold, Jack."

"I know."

"I'm a scientist, you see. Not a philosopher, or an artist. But here . . ." He pointed to the screen. "Here is my philosophy, if you like. Here is my art." The duplication continued, two becoming four, four into eight, eight into sixteen. "It's life, Jack. Omniscient. Omnipresent. Omnivorous." He pointed to the screen. "*That* is my philosophy, and I have all of nature on my side."

I stood watching the screen, thinking about Ralston's words. "There are no choices to make in that world," I said. "No genuine intelligence. No morality."

Ralston smiled."You believe in a certain kind of world. The romantic vision. Good guys and bad guys. Clint Eastwood getting the girl."

"I like clarity."

"I would, too, if it existed." He pointed to the screen. "Can I tell you something that the rest of the world is only now finding out?"

"Yes."

"There is no such thing as ethics, Jack. They don't exist. Chemistry *is* theology."

"Hell of a world you're building."

"All right, Jack. You want to moralize with me. Does the fact that you feel guilty about sleeping with my wife give me a reason to hate you any less for it?"

"I was given to believe it didn't matter to you one way or the other."

Ralston gave me a look of reproach, but didn't respond immediately. After a moment, he asked, "What did you come here for, Jack?"

"I was invited."

"You were invited because you wanted to come and because it would have been impossible to see me any other way."

I paused, thinking. "All right," I said. "I wanted to look you in the face. You're the big mystery, the man behind the scenes.

Stephens, I understand. He puts on a big front, but lawyers don't make things. They're like suckerfish. They need a shark to latch on to. You're the shark."

Ralston's smile flickered. "You're a very smart man, Jack."

"So I'm here to try to figure you out, man to man. You caught hell for the needle-exchange program, and it was a brave thing for somebody in your position to do. It cost you money, and points with the political machine around here. So maybe you're just a tough businessman, and it's really Robinson's ineptitude that killed those people. If so, no hard feelings, and I'm sorry I slept with your wife." I paused. " It's also possible you're an unscrupulous bastard who's willing to trade the lives of eight innocent people for a huge sum of money. Considering the way things are in the world these days, I'm not going to be shocked if that's the way it turns out."

"And what would you do if you decided I was guilty of such a sin?"

"I would take you down." I paused a moment, then added, "I would also make sure you never got close to Michele again."

Ralston watched me intently a moment. "Have you made up your mind?"

"It would be pretty easy, if Robinson wasn't such a basket case. So no, not quite."

Ralston nodded thoughtfully. "You realize I can't have a man like you running around making noise right now, don't you, Jack?"

"Sorry."

"I want to make you a proposition."

"I'm listening."

"You say you want the truth. I will give you five minutes to ask me anything you like. If I know the answer, I'll tell you. I promise you in advance that I will not lie. But in exchange, I want something from you."

"Which is?"

"Peace. A cessation of hostilities. Rumors have power, and the kind you're carrying around are very unwelcome."

"It puts me in an interesting position."

Ralston shrugged. "My offer is on the table."

"I suppose my agreement would depend on your answers."

Ralston looked at me a moment, then quietly said, "Fair enough. You may begin."

"Was Doug Townsend working for you?"

"Yes."

So he means what he said, and the next few minutes are going to be unvarnished. "Did he hack Grayton for you?"

"For the purposes of this conversation, yes."

"What does that mean?"

"It means that this is not a court of law. We're just having a friendly conversation."

I nodded. "How did you find him?"

"Corporate security department came to me. They told me that someone had breached our network. Someone very talented."

"An expert in cypher technology."

"The best they had ever seen. He was penetrating deeper and deeper with every attempt."

"Why didn't you have him arrested?"

"Because locking up a mind like his behind bars would be an idiotic waste of talent. Did the Americans lock up Wernher von Braun just because he worked for the Nazis? On the contrary, they put him to work. The important question was to identify this intruder, find out what he wanted. Was he a competitor? Domestic or international? Or was he an independent, a rogue who was simply amusing himself with the challenge?"

"So you find Doug."

"Yes. We controlled his access, but he was allowed free rein within those limits. I didn't want to spook him. He had to be handled carefully." Ralston got a faraway look in his eyes. "There were things about him that were predictable. Genius IQ, already on the outskirts of society. Deeply flawed, with no observable social life. The standard details of a hacker." He paused. "Of course, that was before we learned what he really wanted, his true purpose for violating Horizn."

"Michele."

Ralston smiled wanly. "Such a troubled young man."

"He was looking for a way to get close to her."

Ralston nodded. "Horizn meant nothing to him. Michele was the true obsession. The company was connected to her, so he explored it in the same way he explored everything about her life. He had only one real talent, and he used it." Ralston looked at me. "But what to do with this tragic little figure? Too talented to destroy, too dangerous to ignore. So we did the logical thing. We made him one of us."

"You forced him to hack Grayton for you in exchange for access to Michele?"

"Force wasn't necessary, Mr. Hammond. In exchange for five minutes with my wife, he would gladly have cut off one of his own fingers."

I winced. "It's repellent."

"Ah. The romantic point of view again."

"You used your own wife."

"She knew nothing about it. As far as Michele was concerned, Doug was as he appeared, nothing more. You have three minutes left."

"Did you have anything to do with what happened to Lipitran AX?"

"Your question is vague."

"Did you kill the eight patients on the Lipitran test?"

"No. You should think of us as passionately interested observers."

"Now you're being vague."

Ralston smiled. "All right, Jack. Let me put it this way: with the help of your friend, we were able to learn how far along Grayton was in their process. Not very, as it turned out."

"Then you knew the test was going to fail."

"Yes."

The next sentence calculated the difference between the two of us as clearly as anything could. "If you knew that, then you knew those people were going to die."

He shrugged. "You see the dilemma. There was no way to come

forward without revealing how we obtained the information. To intervene was impossible."

"Not impossible," I said. "Just difficult."

Ralston's face was implacable. "Do you know what I despise, Jack? What I abhor above all things?"

"No."

"A lack of thoroughness. Imprecision. Shoddy work." He glared, for the first time showing real passion. "You want to find a way to blame me for those tragic deaths. But I did not kill those people. The truth is that if Thomas Robinson was a competent doctor, those people would be alive today. To observe a death is not to cause it. You have one minute."

If there was a confession hidden in his words, it was impenetrable. I was running out of time, and I changed tack. "Do you know how Doug Townsend died?"

"I'm told he died of a drug overdose."

"Are you saying you had nothing to do with that?"

"I not only wouldn't have killed Doug Townsend, I would have gladly paid for a security detail to protect him. Grayton is only one of our competitors, Jack. Your friend's talents were of immense value. I would gladly have extended our relationship indefinitely."

"Then who did kill him?"

"I have no idea. But I'd give a million dollars to find out. Time's up." We stood facing each other in the silence. The only sound was the faint whir of the air conditioning system. "So tell me, Jack. Am I the beast you feared?"

I stood watching him a moment, not moving. "One more question," I said.

Ralston let a thin smile form on his lips. "You're time's up, Jack. But all right. One more."

"You say Doug Townsend was valuable to you."

"Immensely."

"So if you knew those patients were going to die, why did you let him participate in the Lipitran test?"

There was a moment's stilted silence, and Ralston's face drained. The implacable serenity on his face began to disintegrate, decomposing into what looked like anxious, barely contained fear. He took a few moments to compose himself, but he wasn't successful. He spoke in a dry whisper. "What did you say?"

"I said that Doug was taking Lipitran AX. He had completed two courses."

Ralston walked woodenly to his desk and pushed a button. *He didn't know. My God, he didn't know.* The door behind me slid quietly open. Ralston looked up at me with unblinking eyes. "Goodbye, Mr. Hammond."

I walked rapidly across the Horizn parking lot, thinking about what Ralston's bombshell meant. *He didn't know. Charles Ralston may run his little world, but at least one thing happened that he didn't control. And it scared the crap out of him.* I was dialing Robinson as soon as I cleared Horizn security. If there was one man on earth who could tell me what Ralston's fear meant, it was he. I got his machine, the predisaster, cheerful message, now dripping with irony. I left a terse message on his phone, telling him to call me back as soon as possible. I drove south down Highway 400 toward I- 285, heading back toward town. I tried Robinson again about four miles later, hoping to connect. And got his jaunty machine again. I nearly pitched the phone out of the window in frustration. Which is why I nearly missed my turn onto 285. Which is why I had to rip across three lanes of traffic to make the on-ramp. Which is why, worried about what kind of chaos my last-minute move had caused, I glanced back in my rearview mirror. Which is why I saw a white Econoline van leaning hard on its tall tires, trying to make the same sudden move. Which is the moment I realized I was being tailed.

I slowed as I pulled up onto I-285, just to be sure; the van dropped back and pulled over a lane, trying to stay inconspicuous. I sped up to about I-80, and the van picked up speed, matching my pace. I could make out a driver and passenger, although it was possible there were others in the cargo area. *Mayday. Not good.* I tried to calm myself with the fact that even if they were from Horizn, that didn't mean I was in danger. Ralston might be a criminal, but I doubted he had special-ops killers hanging out in the parking lot just in case he suddenly needed somebody capped. More likely, they were sent to observe me, keep tabs on my activities. They probably didn't even know why.

Fine. Then I'll keep things simple. Life as usual, until I figure out who these clowns are. I continued toward my office, letting the van shadow me all the way down I-285 and onto my exit without problems. They kept their distance, staying back about sixty yards. I pulled onto Cleveland, the mostly residential street leading to my office, the van following. *Unless,* I thought, *they were the guys who broke into my office and stole Doug's computer. Which meant they know exactly what they're doing.* I looked in my mirror; the van was six inches from my rear bumper. *Shit.*

I floored the gas pedal, the old V-8 pulling hard. I hammered down Cleveland, trying to look several blocks ahead. The street was mostly empty of traffic, although there were a variety of parked cars looming like an obstacle course. I tried for my phone, only to watch it slide off my passenger seat onto the floorboard. Which probably saved my life, because it's impossible to drive flat out down a city street while making a phone call anyway.

The heavy van was handicapped compared with my sedan, and I was able to put some distance between us. But any turn that took me toward a crowded intersection, or even a car pulling out ahead of me, would end the chase. I looked back again; the van was about three blocks behind, following hard. I only had seconds before I would run out of road. Then a late-model Chevy Caprice pulled out in front of me from two blocks ahead. He was gunning it down the middle of the road, making it impossible to pass. *Damn, there's two of them. I missed this guy watching the van.* The Chevy ahead of me started slowing; apparently, the plan was to trap me in between the two cars. The Chevy's brake lights were glowing, and I was coming up fast. I had no ideas, and no time to think. I slammed on the brakes, bracing myself for impact from behind. The van was racing toward me, filling my rearview mirror. The Chevy locked tires, sliding right a couple of feet under heavy braking. On impulse, I whipped my car hard to the left and floored it, ripping off my outside mirror against the Chevy's. The van was farther back, but was too wide for the same maneuver. He touched the Chevy on the left tip of the bumper, spinning it out of control. I accelerated toward the end of the street, slammed on the brakes, turned left, hauled ass one block to Pine, turned left again—going the wrong way on a one-way street—turned right again a block later, and ran hard away from the two cars. After several blocks I turned left, putting more distance between us. I looked around; both the van and the Chevy were gone, for the moment. I pulled onto Fairburn, turned right, and floored it.

Okay. I'm okay. A good five miles away, I pulled into a grocery store parking lot to catch my breath and calm down. *Shit, this is getting serious.* I sat for a minute, breathing heavily. I leaned down to the floorboard to get my phone, sat back up, and saw the van screech to a stop parallel to me in a cloud of gravel dust, two feet from my driver's door. The man in the passenger seat was calmly aiming a gun through his open window at my head.

Guns clarify the mind. In the face of their compact, efficient ability to hurl death, nothing else matters. The man motioned for me to lower my window. I complied, and he spoke. "Don't move. Is your door unlocked?"

"Yes."

"Turn off the ignition. Then stay still. Don't even blink."

The driver of the van got out and opened my door. "Scoot over," he said. He entered the car, the gun barrel pointed at my torso. As soon as he was seated, he pushed the gun into my crotch. "We're gonna take a ride," he said gruffly. "Stay quiet, and keep your head facing forward."

The man in the van moved across to the driver's seat and drove slowly away. When it was about twenty yards off, the man in my car pressed the barrel down hard, making me wince. "Just take it easy. Don't try to be a hero."

We followed. We drove north about ten minutes, eventually turning west on I-20 toward Birmingham. We drove another twenty minutes or so, the man not speaking. Eventually, the van pulled into an underground parking garage, on top of which was a fairly run-down, six-story office building. The man in the van punched in a code for the lot, and a mechanical arm raised. We followed in before the gate closed.

We pulled into the garage and parked by a fire door. My driver took my arm in a vise grip and said, "I'm going to follow you out your door. Move slowly, and don't make any noise. Do as you're told, and you live." I nodded, and we moved together across the bench seat through the passenger door. Once outside, the man pressed the gun into my back. "Nice and easy."

We walked the short distance to the fire escape door. The other man opened it, and we began to ascend the metal stairway. Three floors up, the man opened the door to the floor. He motioned for us to follow. By the time we exited the fire escape, he had unlocked the door of an office directly across the hall. The man behind me pushed me through, and closed the door behind me.

"What's this all about?" I asked. The men said nothing, but one of them pushed me through the first room into another room located behind it. The room was nearly empty, with just a couple of metal chairs huddled alone in a corner. One of the men crossed the room and opened a closet door. He went inside and brought out a roll of gray duct tape. He walked to me and growled, "Stay still. Do not move." He pulled off a large swath, and cut it off with his teeth. He pulled it tightly around me head, covering my mouth. He pulled off another swath and circled my head again, this time covering my eyes. Then he roughly pulled my hands behind my back. He taped my hands together so tight the pain was like scalding water. Then he rolled me onto my stomach and pulled my legs backward and up, forcing my spine into an agonizing arc. He taped my ankles to my wrists, sealing me in a contortionist's pose. Then—still, without saying a word—he pushed me into the closet. I rolled onto my face against the back wall. I heard the door close. There was a click, and the door locked.

CHAPTER TWENTY-TWO

THE SHAPE OF PAIN changes over time. In the beginning, it's all jagged edges and serrated knives. After a while—hours, in my case—it gives way to great, encircling waves, crushing you under its weight. Then the nausea begins, pushing you out to sea, farther, farther, with no chance of swimming against its angry tide. Eventually—God knows how long later, because by now time has lost its meaning—it shifts again, turning into towering, unscalable mountains of ice. But all the shapes are angry. For the first few hours, the mind tries running from the pain, seeking relief in distant corners of semiconsciousness. For a few precious moments, the mind can detach, going to a Zen place beyond the moment. Ground to anguish by the relentless, searing agony, you long for shock, where the mind detaches. It becomes a heavenly vision, a drop of water in a desert. *Just let me pass out. I'm begging you, just let me go away.* But this particular pain—the agony of arms and legs made bloodless by a backward supine position and torture-tight binding—did not evaporate into a dreamless coma. Instead, it simply grew, and grew, and grew, until it was a monster demanding my every thought. I could feel every agonized sinew, every stretched connective tissue, every muscle screaming for release. I played my mind games, trying to find a hollow place in my mind to run to, only to be thrust back by a body pushed into positions it simply does not go.

To fight pain like that, your weapons must be of equal terror. And I learned that day the only thing on earth that can definitively conquer pain is its hungry cousin: *fear*. Because even in the greatest agony, fear can still be felt, separate and distinct. In the blinding light of pain there came a black dot, at first small, then growing, finally finding its name. I was afraid that if I did fall unconscious—which I greatly desired—I would lose my hands, or at least several fingers, to necrosis, or even that I could stay in the closet so long I would die of thirst.

So I started pressing back against the tape, which, to my horror, hurt even more. It wasn't going to work that way, not unless I pushed with everything I had, in which case I might dislocate both my arms, and still be in the tape, only now in a darker agony. So I waited a while longer, maybe an hour, playing fear against pain, listening to each, wondering if I could survive a moment of exponential increase, and then I said fine, I'm even going to let go of this, letting go is the only thing that has ever worked, and I prayed to the prophet Sammy Liston—he who had taught me the value of stripping everything down and acting as if there was nothing left to lose—and I pushed my legs and arms out as hard as I could.

A bright wave of anguish engulfed me, and I passed out. There was an indeterminate time of blackness, and I finally came around. I tentatively moved my legs. With a bit more struggling, they were free. In that moment, everything changed. Inch by painful inch, I worked my way into a sitting position. Then, with infinite care, I pulled my hands underneath my buttocks and underneath my legs. I lifted my hands to my eyes and pulled off the tape around my eyes and mouth.

It was pitch-dark in the closet; no light came underneath the door. I sat for a while, grateful to be able to breathe. Blood began to flow into my limbs. But my hands were still brutally bound, and it took a good twenty minutes of pushing and biting to get them free.

Finally unbound, I attempted to stand up. I failed, collapsing to all fours, breathing heavily. Every muscle, joint, and bone in my body ached. I was dizzy, and I leaned against the wall for support. I tried again to rise, leveraging myself against the wall. Gradually, with effort, I stood. Blood rushed downward, pushing open closed veins. I stood unsteadily for several minutes, carefully moving wrists, bending elbows, gently bending knees. I tried the door; it was locked, as expected. There was nothing for it, so I lunged with my good shoulder against it. It hurt, but in comparison with what I had already experienced, it was tolerable. After three more tries, the cheap lock pulled apart from its plywood anchor, and the door flung open. I walked carefully out, expecting an assault at any moment. I tried the door from the small office to the main reception area; again, it was locked. Here I made a mistake; I began kicking it with a vengeance, and with the first impact on my foot, I nearly fainted with pain. I resorted to the shoulder again, which, I was sure, was rapidly turning black-and-blue. Eventually the lock gave way, and the door flung open. I stepped through. The place was deserted.

I limped through the office to the front door and walked out into the hall. Apparently, the entire floor was unoccupied, because in spite of my banging, there was no activity. I looked at my watch; it was 5:30. The light was fading outside. I had been in the closet for more than five hours.

Cautiously, I took the elevator down to the parking garage. I pushed the door open a couple of inches, wincing at the screaming noise the metal door made as it moved. I opened the door, half expecting to see my captors. But the place was empty. My car was sitting in its place, undisturbed. I opened the door; the keys were still sitting in the ignition. I fell into the seat, unable and unwilling to use my arms to lower myself. Everything hurt, but everything also worked, which was a relief. With the blood flowing again, the pain was subsiding.

I started the motor. I sat awhile, listening to the engine, getting my bearings. I looked into the rearview mirror. There were fragments of gray adhesive clinging to my skin. The line of the tape was visible, the skin reddened from irritation. I backed the car out of the spot, drove out of the garage, and, swiveling my head painfully to make sure nobody was following me, drove back toward Atlanta. Instead of the crush of rush hour traffic I had expected, there was almost none. It took a few minutes to realize what had happened. The sun, so low in its arc, was not setting. It was rising. It was five-thirty in the morning, not the evening, and I hadn't been in the closet for five hours. I had been there for more than seventeen.

CHAPTER TWENTY-THREE

THERE WAS THE DRIVE HOME, still hurting. Then crawling into bed fully clothed, falling thankfully into real sleep. I woke up some hours later and realized I was ravenous. Walking was still painful, so I hobbled to the kitchen and made something to eat. I slept some more, and finally, at about one in the afternoon, took a hot shower. I let the water run over me, exhausting the water heater. I dried off, walked naked to my bedroom, and looked at myself in the mirror. There were wicked, dark purple and blue marks on my wrists and ankles, and it hurt to move around too fast, but other than that, I was okay. *So you were kidnapped, taped, and put into a closet. They didn't rob you. They didn't steal the car. They didn't say a thing, and they didn't ask you any questions. They just stuffed you into a room and walked off.*

I dressed, but the next few hours were on again, off again; I slept, and ate, and drank more water than I'd ever imagined possible. There was some cramping, sudden contractions that would jar me up out of bed like a hot iron inserted into my flesh. But they subsided, and I came back to myself for real about seven that evening.

I tried Robinson again, and predictably, got his machine. I walked back toward the bed, thinking about falling back into it. I sat down, closing my eyes, letting my limbs relax. I must have drifted a little, because I wasn't sure when the quiet knocking on my door began. I stood up and listened; there was more knocking, gentle, almost cautious. I stood, reaching quietly into the night-stand by my bed. I pulled away a stack of magazines and pulled out my disused revolver, a relic from teenage target practice in Dothan. It wasn't particularly threatening-looking, but it was all I had. I wasn't actually sure it would even fire. I moved through the apartment to the front door, which, frustratingly, had no peep hole. The wavy hardwood floor creaked as I approached, and the knocking stopped. I moved to the side of the door, my cover blown. "Who is it?" I asked, grasping the gun.

"Jack, oh, Jack," a voice said. "For God's sake, let me in."

Only one woman on earth had a voice like that. I unlocked the door, pulled it open, and Michele, crying, pushed into my apartment.

She flung her arms around me, holding me tightly. She buried her face into my shoulder, pressing against skin still raw from my capture. I winced, and she pulled back. She pulled down my collar, seeing the red marks from the stretched tape. "My God, Jack, what happened to you?"

"Some guys," I said.

She reached out and gently touched my face just underneath my right cheekbone. In addition to my soreness from being tied up, I was still a little the worse for wear from my time with Folks Nation. "There's swelling here," she said. "Oh, darling, I'm so sorry."

"I went back into the Glen to find you, and ran into our friend Darius and his pals. The kidnapping came later."

She looked up. "Kidnapping? What are you talking about? Who did this to you?"

"I'm thinking your husband, actually."

She turned rigid. "Charles?"

"I've been to see him."

Her eyes widened in shock. "Why did you do that?"

"He invited me. Well, he used Stephens to do it."

"God, Jack."

I looked away. "Stephens has a little different version of events than you do. It wasn't pleasant listening."

She grabbed my arms, pulling me close. "Before you say another word, I'm sorry I lied to you. I did it to protect someone."

"If it was me, I'd have to say it was a total failure."

"I lied to protect Briah."

I disengaged from her and walked away, leaving her in the doorway. The truth was, I wasn't sure I wanted to have the conversation. It was time to get off the roller coaster. "I tell you what, Michele," I said, "maybe you should find another guy to help you work through your problems. Somebody with more tolerance for dishonesty."

She looked at me imploringly. "Explain how that works to me, Jack. My whole life is a lie, and you want me to find the right moment to stop. It doesn't get easier, you know. It gets harder. There are layers. . ." She stopped, unwilling to continue. She was trapped between the residue of fourteen years of illusion and the growing realization that the game was over. But whatever sympathy I might have had for her difficulty, I knew I had reached my own limits for the way she handled her life. I wanted clarity, and if I didn't get it, I was going to walk away and not look back.

"This is how it works, Michele," I said. "You've taken the lie as far as it stretches. Maybe it made sense in the beginning. But you can either watch things slowly unravel and take you down, or you can take control of your life and declare your independence."

She was breathing heavily, obviously frightened. "I'll lose everything," she said. "Even Briah."

"You'll lose her anyway, if you don't start telling the truth."

She looked at me, frustrated. "Don't you understand what's

going on here? Of course Charles knows about Briah. He knows everything about everyone. But the only thing that keeps her safe is keeping her existence secret."

I watched her, not wanting to be taken in again. "Talk to me. But if you so much as whisper something that isn't true, I'm gone."

"Charles and I were a terrible match, right from the beginning. He knew all the best people from his days at Groton and Yale. From the beginning, it meant everything to him to fit in. God, Jack, he even picked out my clothes. *This* dress, *these* shoes, no, not *that* brooch, you can't be serious, darling. Down to the fingernail polish."

"You seem to have moved past that."

"Yes, the street look is my little rebellion. Charles despises it, but he realizes it has a professional use. I was younger, then. I had no feelings of my own. Charles told me what to feel, even how to think. I believed him, for a while. He was born to the life I was living as an impostor. I assumed what he did was right. He gave money, joined charitable causes. But there was an ulterior motive for every penny. He had a chart of all the best people, and when we were invited anywhere by them socially, he checked them off his list."

"I don't see what this has to do with you lying to me about Briah."

"It has everything to do with her. Years passed, but I couldn't get Briah completely out of my mind. I decided to look for her, just to see if she was all right. At least that's what I told myself. I don't know what would have happened if I had actually found her. But I was clumsy, and Charles found out. He was more angry than I've ever seen him. I actually thought he was going to hit me." She looked away. "It wasn't that I had a baby, although that was bad enough. It was that his wife was a lying little ghetto girl with an illegitimate child. It didn't help that the father was a gang member. You simply cannot imagine what the thought of that did to him. He said he didn't get his Ph.D. to pick up some welfare boy's trash." She grew still. "That day was like a death," she said quietly. "It was the day I learned what kind of man my husband really was. My husband *despises* the ghetto, Jack. It took me years to find out why, but when I finally understood it, it was like a bolt of lightning. Everything about him—his whole life—suddenly made sense."

"Why is it?"

She looked at me, her face like stone. "My husband is ashamed to be black," she said. "He is bitterly ashamed that he is *negro*. And every time he looks at me, he is reminded of that fact."

There was a long, bitter silence in the room. At last I said, "You could leave him, you know."

She shook her head. "I can do no such thing, not as long as there is a Derek Stephens," she answered. "People think Charles runs Horizn. That's a joke. Derek Stephens is in charge of every major decision."

"You're saying your husband is just a puppet?"

"In the beginning, Charles was merely distant, but not evil. He was more of a machine, I guess. But since he began working with Derek, he's changed. Derek is a very bad man, Jack. He's poisoned whatever was good about Charles. They spend hours together, talking and scheming."

"So why does Stephens care if you divorce your husband?"

"Because I'm an asset to Charles, and therefore an asset to Horizn. Maybe when the IPO is over, he'll find some way to get rid of me and make Charles look like a martyr. But I have no doubt that he would sooner see Briah killed than have the CEO of Horizn ridiculed by her existence."

I looked at her warily. "Stephens says Social Services took Briah away from you because you were negligent."

She shook her head. "How could I be a negligent mother, Jack? I never even left the hospital room with her." She walked to me quietly, crossing the room to where I stood. She took my hands in hers and lifted them to her face, gently pressing my fingers against her mouth. "I'm sorry, Jack. I lied to protect Briah. It will never happen again."

"I want to believe that."

"Forgive me. I'm trying to do too many things at once." She put her arms around me, and I stepped a little awkwardly, off balance.

I limped with pain, and she apologized, taking me by the hand. We walked through the apartment to my bedroom, where I sat on the bed. She gently pulled off my shirt, running her smooth, beautiful fingers over my skin. "Do you have something for that?" she asked. "Any antiseptic or anything?"

"In the kitchen," I said. "Under the sink."

She nodded, kissed my shoulder, and went to see what she could find. There was a rustling and she came back, holding a white tube. "This will help," she said. "It'll soothe you." She walked to me, pressing me down on my stomach. "Lie still," she said, sitting beside me. She rubbed the cool ointment into my skin, gently kneading my muscles. "I'm so sorry they did this to you." I closed my eyes and let her rub my muscles, gently kneading the sore, overextended joints. I relaxed, and life flowed back into me. She turned me over, and she fumbled with my pants, pulling them down over my hips. I lay in my underwear, bare-chested, and she gently kissed my chest, my stomach, moving her hands over my legs, inside my thighs. I was tired, not just physically, but in my soul. With every moment, I relaxed more deeply, until I was fluttering just above sleep. I heard her voice, soft in my ear. "Get some rest, sweetheart."

I fell back on the pillow and closed my eyes. She climbed under my arm, laying her head on my shoulder. Sometime deep in the night—the dark outside was moonless and pitch—I awoke, and, finding her sleeping peacefully beside me, I pulled off the covers, leaving her body stark and beautiful on the white sheet. I watched her sleeping awhile, her chest moving rhythmically up and down. *Do you believe her?* The question came to me, a whisper in my mind. I watched her face, looking for traces of guilt. Somehow, she became aware of me, because after a few minutes her eyes fluttered open. She came to herself, looked at me, and smiled. "You look better," she whispered. "I'm glad."

"I am better," I said. "Much better." In that dark, moonless night, I let my fingertips answer my questions, tracing her stomach, moving up toward her breast. She moaned, letting herself fall under my control, giving in to the motion of my hands, my kiss.

What came next was an exquisite blur, a time out of time. Minutes passed, and when we finally joined our bodies she was transformed. She was strong—she demanded everything I had—and ravenous. Everything I had seen on stage—the complete abandon, the giving over to the moment—was present in her lovemaking. There was a wildness to her that night, a desperate, breathless passion. When her moment came, she raised her head, biting her lip, reveling in the pressure, the grip, the friction. I followed just after, and when I opened my eyes, she was looking up at me, smiling, driving her hips into me as hard as she could. And then it was over, and she pulled me down again, deep, into dark, dreamless sleep.

CHAPTER TWENTY-FOUR

THE NEXT MORNING, Friday, I rose to find Michele dressed again, just as the last time we had spent the night together. She was rumbling around in the kitchen, and I walked up behind her, my bathrobe open. She leaned back against me, letting me kiss her neck. "Hungry?" I asked. She didn't answer, and I turned her around to face me. "You okay?"

She looked down. "I have to go," she said. "Charles has a speech at Georgia Tech. I have to be there."

"He still insists you go through the charade?"

She nodded, clearly miserable. "I hate the thought of one more second with him. It's unspeakable."

"I'm going, too."

She turned to face me. "Jack, that's not a good idea. If he saw you, it could turn into a confrontation."

"Nothing's going to happen. I'm going to see what I can find out."

She looked at me a moment, but saw my resolve. "All right," she said. "I have to go. The speech is at eleven, and it's already after eight. I have to change clothes, make myself presentable for the circus." She sighed, anxiety etched into her face. "It doesn't matter," she said. "We're all going to do what we do, now." She looked up, kissed me quickly on the cheek, and turned to go. She stopped herself, looked back, and said, "I love you, you know that, right?" She smiled, but there was sadness in her expression. "Don't say it back," she said. "It's easier."

I walked to her, kissed her forehead, then on the mouth. "Be safe." I picked up her purse, which she had left in my car when we went into the Glen together. "Your phone's in here," I said. "Charge it up. I might need to find you."

She accepted the bag, and kissed me on the mouth. "Don't let Charles see you, Jack."

"Don't worry."

Michele left, and I started to get ready. I gave Robinson a final call; once again, I got his cheery, unintentionally ironic message. I left another message, and hung up. A little after ten, the phone rang. I answered, hoping it was Robinson, and heard Blu's voice. "Jack? Where are you? Where have you been? Aren't you coming in?" Having so recently talked her out of resigning, I decided it wasn't the right time to tell Blu I had just escaped a kidnapping. "Yeah, I'm sorry." I glanced over at my answering machine; its red light blinked insistently. "What have I missed?"

"Nicole Frost just called. She wants to make sure you're still going to meet her at Georgia Tech."

"I'm going."

"She wanted to remind you about meeting her out front ten minutes early."

"No problem."

"Are you sure you're all right?"

"I'm sure. Anything else?"

"I've got a list, actually. Oh, and Billy Little called. Twice."

"What did Billy want?"

"Just for you to call back. He said it was important."

"Look," I said, "I've got to get moving. Call Nicole back and tell her I'm coming, okay?" It would be better to call Billy later. He would want to know everything, and I wasn't ready for him to weigh in. If he took things over—and he almost certainly would, given his penchant for doing things by the book—I would be knocked out of the loop. I had nothing against the police, but I'd already decided that if anybody was going to figure out what had happened to Doug and the others on the Lipitran test, it would take somebody under the radar, determined enough to break a few rules. I hung up and dressed, grateful for the time my body had to pull itself back together. Thanks to eighteen hours' rest and Michele's ministrations, I felt something like normal as I made the drive downtown to Tech.

Georgia Tech's campus is nobody's idea of an idyllic college campus. Distinctively urban, it crouches in the shadow of Atlanta's skyscrapers, symbolically dominated by the economic power that looms over it. The buildings are antiseptic, more like office parks than comfortable, ivy-covered bastions of learning. I wedged my car into three-quarters of a space and labored up a steep hill toward the Ferst Center, where Ralston was going to give his speech.

The usual collection of Tech students—the T-shirted, shorts-wearing future of America—was milling around between classes. The steps to the Ferst were alive with them, a mélange of denim, bare midriffs, and backpacks serving as background to a much smaller group of freshly scrubbed, impeccably dressed money managers, like Nicole. The brokers, smiling at each other with anxious, toothy grins, stood out among the students like architectural relief. Having themselves been recently released from the hallowed halls of learning, they already looked a million miles apart, from a different planet. They were still young—at least they clung to a healthy residue of youth—but unlike the students, the unwritten message tattooed across every forehead was this: *sleep later.* To the left of the hall, there was a collection of local news vans, satellite dishes perched on their roofs. The upcoming IPO for Horizn was attracting the business media like flies.

Nicole was on the stairs of the hall, chatting brightly to a handsome, prosperous-looking man in his late twenties. She was smiling, her shoulder-length black hair pulled back. She wore a pale blue dress, hemmed just above the knees, and matching, toeless heels. She had always been thin, but now, she was absolutely waifish. It made sense, considering she probably hadn't taken a lunch break in three years. But the glossy mouth and bright, intelligent eyes that had kept many an underclassman up at night dreaming were still intact. When she saw me, she brightened, if possible, a few more watts. She walked over, stopped, squinted at my face, then reached up to pluck off my sunglasses.

"Jack?" she asked. "My God, what happened to you?" I started to answer, but she waved me off. "You don't have to say a word, Jack. It's those clients of yours. They're horrible. Honestly, I don't see how you can do it."

"Yeah, I guess thieving CEOs don't usually have much of a left hook."

"Jack, how awful of you." Carefully, she put my sunglasses back on my face. Then she straightened my collar with her free hand. The friction on my neck—still sore from the taping—wasn't pleasant. "Look at you, darling. Have you lost all your ties?"

"Burned them for fuel," I said. Nicole and I went back a long ways, but I wasn't going to open up the last couple of days to her. "Let's go get some seats."

Nicole grimaced. "You pain me, Jack. You really do."

We climbed the stairs and entered the building, which was an angular redbrick affair with an Italian marble sculpture out front. A crowd was filing through the open atrium into the auditorium, and we followed in, taking seats two-thirds of the way back, stage left. Two video screens were integrated high up on the stage proscenium, one on each side. "Full house," Nicole said. "And there are the cameras." A gaggle of reporters were standing around just off stage at the front of the hall, their cameramen perching video equipment on their shoulders.

"There he is," Nicole said, pointing to the front of the hall. There, stage right, was Ralston. He was standing with his back to the crowd, talking to a tall, gangly man in an ill-fitting suit. I watched Ralston for a while, thinking about being with his wife, quieting the pangs of guilt with the realization that their relationship had been a sham for a long time. The nature of their mismatch went deeper than the fact that she had lied about her background. They were from different eras as much as from different classes. Ralston might be chronologically older, but he was far more modern. Michele was emotionally a romantic, attached by her art to a time when love felt like destiny instead of Ralston's dry chemistry. Ralston was the new man, and so his brand of evil was new, far removed from the barbarism of Atlanta's mean streets. He didn't have the sullen, dispossessed anger of Folks Nation. He was simply tired of morality, as if, in his carefully and scientifically considered opinion, the whole idea of it had worn itself out and ceased to be relevant. His was a flat hate, without passionate chasms and valleys. Ghetto hate was alive, unpredictable, and, therefore, something that could be changed and healed. Ralston had become a simple machine for consumption, like the virus he had staked his fortune on treating. Sitting there surrounded by his ideological children, I felt distinctly out of place. *You believe in a certain kind of world, Jack. Good guys and bad guys.* Maybe that was it. Maybe there were no good guys and bad guys anymore. Maybe there was just deciding what you could tolerate in yourself, and then doing it. Maybe I was a dinosaur and the Nightmares and Ralstons and Stephenses and smart, attention-span-impaired kids from Georgia Tech were going to leave the rest of us in their hermetically clean, genetically engineered, dust.

"And there *she* is," Nicole whispered. I turned my head, saw her, and was sucked back into the human. She was seated in the front row about fifty feet to my right, so I had an angle to see her profile. She wore simple gold earrings, and her hair was up, like it had been at the Four Seasons. She was so beautiful it hurt. The sight of her rocked me with lust, desire, passion, even love—antiquated ideas from another era, maybe, but still powerful enough to walk me into a beating by Folks Nation. Maybe we were both dinosaurs, both twisting in a new, brittle wind, uncomfortable as hell in the decade in which we found ourselves, and looking for comfort. Being the son of a beaten-down failure of a man who scratched dirt for a living in Dothan, Alabama, had taught me enough about desperation that her world wasn't as alien as it seemed. And there was the ineluctable chemistry of her messiness, the antiquarian character of how badly she needed saving that drew me to her. I wanted to be her knight in shining armor, and it was the wrong fucking century.

Nicole leaned toward me and whispered, "I wonder if he was rich when they got married."

"Because?"

"*Look* at her, darling. Women like that don't marry college professors." She paused. "He must have been at least a little rich. Just not stinking rich, like he's going to be."

"The IPO."

Nicole nodded. "He's going to make a lot of people a lot of money, me included. So be nice."

Ralston motioned to Michele, who stood and walked to her husband. He put his arm around her and they stood together, talking with the man wearing the bad suit. Ralston whispered something in Michele's ear, and she smiled wanly. It was hard to watch, knowing what even that moment of theater cost her. She hated him, but she feared him and Stephens more. But as long as they held in their hands the life of her daughter, she would do what they asked.

A couple of minutes later the lights dimmed, and the noisy hall quieted. Ralston took his seat beside his wife, but they didn't speak. I could just make them out in the half-light coming off the stage. Michele was staring straight ahead, a blank, dead stare on her face. The tall man Ralston had been speaking to appeared on stage to scattered, halfhearted applause. House lights from above lit the dais, leaving the crowd in relative darkness. "Good afternoon," he said. "Welcome to the campus of Georgia Tech. I'm Dr. Barnard Taylor, Dean of the School of Biotechnology. This is a very exciting day for us." As he spoke, a black-and-white image of a young Charles Ralston materialized on the video screens to each side of the stage. Nicole leaned over and whispered, "Show time."

The picture showed a youthful, eager Ralston in a laboratory, wearing a white smock. For a simple photograph, it was remarkably communicative: Ralston's face was alive with ambition. He looked intense and happy, thoroughly in his element. "Charles Ralston began his career at something near and dear to our hearts," the speaker said. "Doing research." Scattered chuckles filtered upward from the crowd. "The work of Dr. Ralston has extended the lives of many thousands of people. Antiomyacin is, to this day, the only drug proven to manage the effects of hepatitis C, thus greatly diminishing the incidence of liver cancer for those infected. It has given hope to those who eagerly wait for the day of a cure."

My conversation with Robinson flashed through my memory; Robinson had convinced Grayton to ante up millions to cure hepatitis C. There wasn't any question who had to lose if they were successful: Ralston, and Horizn. The picture on the screens changed to show an exterior of Horizn's current offices. "In the last fifteen years, Charles Ralston has taken Horizn into new areas of pharmacological research, making impressive gains in the treatment of nephritis and other renal diseases. In the process, he has become a fixture of Atlanta business, employing over fourteen hundred people." Dr. Taylor smiled. "Some of them are even graduates of Georgia Tech."

That comment drew the first genuine applause; a few hoops and hollers were heard in the hall. "But I want to talk about the personal side of Charles Ralston, something that gets too little attention in the climate of today's business." The video screens dissolved to show a black-and-white video shot panning slowly across the wrecked world of the Atlanta projects. Located only a few miles away from where we were sitting, the contrasts were staggering. The chairs we were sitting on—about which we hadn't given a thought—were more luxurious than anything inside those gates. "*This* is the public health scandal of America," the speaker said. "While politicians pander for votes on tax breaks for the rich, they do nothing to stop the poverty, racism, and hopelessness that is killing our poorest citizens. If African Americans were considered a separate population group in the world, their infant mortality rate would rank number forty. And when I look out at the business landscape, I don't see many people reaching inside that world to effect change. We have among us today one shining exception to that indifference."

The screens changed, now showing a moody, Annie Leibowitz-style black-and-white photograph of an adult Ralston. He stared into the camera like a sphinx, inscrutable and—ironically—undeniably romantic. "The Horizn needle-exchange program is everything right about American business, and a challenge to other pharmaceutical companies," Taylor said. "Instead of merely profiting from the treatment of disease, Charles Ralston does something to prevent it. Horizn holds the patent for the most effective drug in the world for treating hepatitis C. And yet, at considerable political and financial cost, the company does all in its power to protect the citizens of Atlanta from needing the drug in the first place. There are people in this city who don't believe in the needle exchange, and thankfully, Charles Ralston doesn't bother listening to them. Instead, he just chooses to save the lives of his people. I celebrate that courage and generosity, ladies and gentlemen. And today, that generosity is extending to our community in a new and exiting way. I'm going to give you the chance to celebrate this extraordinary man with me. Ladies and gentlemen, I want to introduce you to the best friend the Georgia Tech research community ever had. Please welcome Dr. Charles Ralston."

Ralston rose from his chair, and he got the love. He began his walk up the stairs to the stage, a phalanx of media in step with him, their lights basking him in harsh illumination. For twenty-first-century Atlanta, this was the complete package: the brilliantly educated, ultra-successful black man who reaches back into the projects to give a brother a hand. Although the audience was overwhelmingly white and Asian, the applause was sincere, wildly enthusiastic, and prolonged. I have no doubt Ralston could have announced he was running for governor, and most of the people in the place would have signed up to help on the spot. Ralston took the stage and reached his hand out to the dean, who ignored it and emotionally embraced him. Ralston, momentarily startled, seemed nonplussed; he patted the dean's shoulders gently, like a parent who doesn't want a child to muss his clothes. The oblivious Taylor hugged Ralston's neck awhile, then released Ralston to the microphone.

Ralston stood calmly in his exquisitely tailored suit, motioning for the applause to die down. "Thank you, honestly. Thank you so much." Eventually, Ralston got the crowd quieted. "It's a great pleasure to be here among my fellow scientists. I return to the academic world from time to time, just to remind myself of what I fell in love with as a young man. I look out and see your faces and I feel great envy. Envy at what you will see in your lifetimes. Envy at the world you will create. Envy at the power you will one day hold in your hands."

As Ralston spoke, the auditorium grew still. They were soaking up his words like acolytes listening to a religious leader. "There are those who will fight you on your journey into the future. They will throw their gods up at you and try to limit your research. You must fight them. Always remember two things: first, they are nothing new. Pope Pius forced Galileo to get on his knees and beg forgiveness for having the temerity to suggest that the earth revolved around the sun. Those who oppose your research are descendants of that ignorance. Second, remember that you will certainly prevail. Not possibly. Not even probably. Certainly. Those who fear the forward progress of science will one day take their place on the ash heap of history, alongside those who believed the earth was flat and that black men"—here, Ralston stopped a moment, choking back emotion—"That black men were possessions, something to be bought and sold." He looked back out into the audience. "All such ignorance will one day be defeated. Horizn has made a commitment to genetic research at Georgia Tech for the same reason we are committed to research everywhere: because of the incalculable benefits to mankind it promises. I believe in that world, the world of the future. I believe in a world where people don't have to travel to Bombay to buy a desperately needed organ on the black market. That might be fine for a rich white man from Europe, but it doesn't help my people here. I believe in a world where the whooping crane is brought back from the edge of extinction through the science of cloning. And above all, I believe in a cure for the great diseases we face, diseases that confront my people disproportionately. I will never stop pushing—whether it's through research or the needle-exchange program—to save their lives."

Applause spontaneously erupted through the hall. Ralston stood in its wake, waiting a long time for it to subside. "I leave you with this thought," he said. "There are those who think a scientist lives in an ivory tower, that science doesn't involve normal concerns. To them I say that science is life. Nothing exists outside its influence. And today, the need for scientific understanding in public policy is unprecedented. We stand at the portal of a new Eden. For every Eden, there must be an Adam and an Eve. We are witnessing the next step of human evolution, the creation of the transgenic human. Everyone in this room is incredibly fortunate to be alive at this moment, our moment of triumph. For half a million years mankind has been crawling toward the instant we release ourselves from the shackles of our genetic destiny and begin the process of choosing our own. It is nothing less than an emancipation from gene-slavery. It is the most important event in the history of mankind. By comparison, the inventions of the wheel and fire are mere trivialities. And you"—he gestured with open, outstretched hands, like a sign of the cross—"will be its masters."

There was another, even greater, outpouring of applause. Ralston nodded offstage, and a man and woman walked out, carrying one of those large, phony checks they give to lottery winners. The check was facing away from the audience, so the amount was hidden. "This is the cheapest money I've ever spent," Ralston said. "The Charles Ralston School of Biomedical Engineering will do important work for the benefit of mankind. And if some of you studying there should need employment when you graduate, well, I think we might arrange something." More applause, followed by a cheer as the oversized check was turned over. The amount was four million dollars.

The crowd rose, and Ralston motioned to Michele, waving to

her to come on stage with him. She inflated upward out of her chair, lifeless but obedient. Her capacity for matrimonial theater finally exhausted, she walked woodenly toward the stage, incrementally gaining momentum. When she reached her husband, she turned and faced the cameras, her face expressionless. Even an attempt at a smile was beyond her. The cameras flashed light across their faces.

Nicole pulled on my arm. "I think I'm in love," she said, cooing. "He's magnificent."

"You sure you want him as the new Messiah?" I asked quietly.

Nicole look surprised. "You're missing the point, Jack. It's all going to happen either way. The only question left is who is going to profit."

There were a few last moments of camera flashes, a final stiff smile, and Ralston released Michele. Free of his touch she deflated again, turning away and walking off stage. Before she could manage more than a few steps, however, a face I hadn't expected came into view: Bob Trammel, the man with her in St. Louis and at the Four Seasons. She stopped when she saw him, but Trammel advanced with the same pleasant, utterly fraudulent smile I had witnessed before in St. Louis. She started to walk around him, but he placed his hand on her arm as she passed, steering her toward the wings of the stage. Together, they disappeared into the enormous black curtains.

"Hang on a second, will you?" I asked Nicole.

"I'm running, darling," she said. "Call me later?"

"Yeah. I'll do that."

Nicole waved down some people she knew from Shearson, and I made my way against the flow of the crowd toward the stage. By the time I arrived the media had dispersed, and no one noticed when I slipped up the side stairs. Ralston had already left the stage, escorted by the dean to whatever was next on the agenda. It was only three or four steps to the curtains, and I slipped into the darkness, looking for Michele. I pushed through, and in the dim light on the other side I could see Trammel from behind, about fifteen feet away. He was holding Michele firmly by the arm, his face very near hers. Suddenly, Michele wrenched her arm free. She looked terrified, as though Trammel had just threatened her with something. Trammel started speaking again, but I had seen enough. I sprinted—a little painfully, but reasonably quickly—the fifteen feet or so between us, and Michele saw me first.

"Jack!" she said, stepping quickly out from Trammel's grasp. "Jack, it's too late. You've got to get out of here."

When Trammel spun to face me, he gave me an evil smile, the kind that black belts turn on unsuspecting people unfortunate enough to wander into their plans. For a second, I thought I was due for my third beating of the week. I was just about to retreat into that glassy state required to not care what was going to happen next—the essential ingredient in a street fight—when the stage door opposite us opened, and a large group of noisy students began pouring into the space around us. A bespectacled woman of about forty was saying, "Come on, class, we only have the stage for an hour," and holding the door for a throng two and three deep.

Trammel dropped the attitude, but I barely noticed. What I did notice was Michele slipping through the crowd and out the door. Trammel—his face wrenched into an unsuccessful attempt at calm—took a step to push through the students, then checked himself. Even in his elevated state, he realized that two amped-up men chasing after a woman on a university campus isn't exactly low-key, especially with ten television trucks loading up outside. The seemingly endless class filtered through. The teacher, who was holding the door, eyed us suspiciously, like she had a pretty good idea who belonged in the area at that moment, and we weren't on the list. When the last student finally passed, she walked directly up to the two of us and said, "May I help you?"

Trammel stared, apparently unable to speak. I smiled at her and said, "Yes, you certainly can. We're lost. Can you point us toward the Couch Building?"

"Certainly," she said in a schoolmarm's voice. She pointed past us, out the doors at the opposite side of the backstage area. "Straight *that* way. You'll run into doors to the outside when you pass through. It's all the way across campus."

"Thanks," I said, nodding. I looked at Trammel. "Come on, Bob, old pal," I said. "We don't want to get in the way of the nice lady's class." Trammel shot me a wicked look, then turned and followed me across the stage. I could feel him right behind me, the teacher watching us.

There are times when waiting around for what happens next is a sucker's bet. Bob Trammel—having recently been interrupted in the process of manhandling a woman—was not, I decided, a reasonable man. So when I opened the stage door and walked through, I didn't wait to hear what he had on his mind. Instead, the moment we were both in the landing with the door safely closed behind us, I pasted him with the hardest punch I've ever thrown in my life. It connected somewhere between his left cheek and eye, sending splinters of pain through my fist. But it also knocked Trammel down the landing stairs, collapsing him into a heap at the bottom. I didn't bother asking how he was. Instead, I bolted through the doors leading to the hallway, out through the exterior doors, and into the sunshine of Georgia Tech.

I can hardly express the exquisite pleasure that I received from rearranging the soft tissues of Bob Trammel's face. Locked somewhere in the genetic information that Ralston and his friends were so determined to manipulate, there still roamed a pleasure center undiminished by time, connected directly to the primordial joy of wiping a self-satisfied smile off the face of a bully. It was all I could do not to turn around, go back inside, and do it again.

I trotted around to the other side of the building, but there was no trace of Michele. Once I got to my car I got in, started it up, and pulled out into a messy coagulation of noontime traffic. Cars were barely moving in any direction. It would have been quicker to walk.

I had crawled a couple of blocks toward I-75 when I saw Michele's silver Lexus several cars ahead and one lane over. She was going to turn right onto 75, toward south Atlanta. I pushed my way into line behind her, and pulled out into traffic a hundred yards or so after she did.

It would have been easy to get her attention, but I didn't. I kept her car in sight but hung back, playing a hunch. If she was in danger, I wanted to be close enough to protect her; on the other hand, I wanted to know what that danger was, so I decided to let her drive on. At one point I crept up adjacent to her left quarter-panel, several lanes away. Her expression was rigid, the blank stare of a mannequin. I dropped back a few car lengths behind and continued to follow. It was a few minutes later when our destination began to occur to me, although I resisted the thought as long as possible. But when we missed the Crane Street flyover and turned off the freeway, I had no doubt where we were going. Michele was headed back to McDaniel Glen.

I watched her car glide under the iron gates, rolling past her as she did. A block later I turned around and followed inside. I could see her car about a hundred yards ahead. Tracking her undetected inside the gates would be difficult; the streets were as straight as boards, and normally saw very little traffic. I slowed, watching the Lexus move down the street. Eventually, it stopped a few feet away from the curb; I pulled in behind another car, watching through the glass of the car ahead. It was a good place from which to observe; my own car was completely obscured, but I had a clear view of what was happening ahead. I put the car in park and took a look around; nobody was in sight.

After a moment a man came out of the building opposite Michele's car. He walked toward her, motioning for her to lower her window. My heart froze. It was Pope. He leaned forward, resting his arm on the door. He and Michele talked, but I couldn't hear a word. What was definite was the tone of the conversation: unpleasant. Both sides quickly grew agitated, and after a couple of minutes, Pope backed off from the car. I slipped my transmission into drive, holding it still with the brake. If anything went down, I wanted to be able to get to Michele as quickly as possible. My options against somebody like Pope would be limited. I was unarmed and he was as deadly as a jungle cat. Unless I drove him over, a fight wouldn't last long. But driving him over wasn't something that I was unalterably opposed to doing.

The argument seemed to flare a moment longer, then subsided. Eventually, Pope moved back toward the car, a thin, shit-eating smile on his face. He reached a hand inside the open window, and I could see him stroke Michele's hair. I almost retched with nausea. *My God, Michele and Pope? Not possible.* She said something, and her car started slowly rolling forward. Pope pulled back, watching her car pick up speed away from his building. She turned right a few yards down the street, then headed back toward the entrance to the Glen.

I opened my car door, which was enough to get Pope's attention. He turned toward me, peering down the street. I got out and stood. Pope watched me quietly, but his normal affability was gone. I walked away from my car, hands clearly visible to my side. When I was about fifteen feet away from him, he said, "You healed up pretty good."

"I need some answers," I said. "About the woman you were talking to just now."

Pope shook his head. "This ain't a lucky time for you. You got to quit while you ahead."

"Listen to me, Pope," I said. "You're in charge here, right? Not the police. I mean, nothing goes down in the Glen without your say-so."

He shrugged. "That's right."

"So it's up to you to enforce some decency around here. You can't let all hell break loose."

Pope tilted his head. "What you drivin' at?"

"You're extorting Michele over her own daughter, aren't you?" Pope's demeanor darkened, but I pressed on. "Kill me after I finish, Pope. Just let me say this. It's too much. You have to rein it in. It can't actually be hell in here, can it? It can look like it, sure. I mean, people can destroy themselves and there can be poverty and despair and all the rest of it but Jesus, Pope. There have to be some kind of limits, don't there?"

Pope watched me silently awhile. Like Ralston—his counterpart in the legitimate drug trade—he proved that being a completely amoral killer who made his living dealing death didn't mean he couldn't be thoughtful, even philosophical. But his morality was carefully cordoned off, restricted to the nonbusiness areas. Eventually he said, "You and this girl. That ain't such a good idea."

"Yeah, I know. Thanks."

Pope pointed to my Buick. "How much gas you got in that piece of shit car?" he asked.

"I don't know."

Pope shrugged. "The thing for you to do is get back in and drive away from here till you run out," he said. "Just drive as far away from here as you can, so I don't have to fuck you up."

"For the love of God, Pope. Do something for your own people."

Pope's eyes narrowed. "You did a good thing for my boy Keshan a while back," he said. "But you seriously pushin' your luck."

"But listen to me, Pope. Look around. Seriously."

Pope looked around, taking in the Glen halfheartedly. Then he shook his head. "Naw, see, you got this all wrong. I didn't make this world. I just got to survive in it. Now this here is just business. Your girl tryin' to find somebody. I told her I'd take care of it for her. It's like a service. Like a finder's fee."

"Is her daughter in the Glen or isn't she?"

"For fifty thousand dollars she will be. That's all that matters."

"It's a human being, Pope. For God's sake, Pope, you're black. Don't you see the irony?" I was growing exasperated. "I'm sure she'll pay you anything you want."

"That's pretty much how we left things."

"Look, you did a good thing for me once. You let me walk even though I was talking bullshit." Pope watched me quietly, saying nothing. "So I'll return you the favor. You're making a mistake. You're getting involved with things you don't understand. Michele has powerful people who don't want her to find her daughter. Helping her will seriously piss them off."

Pope laughed. "Like who?"

"People from the outside. I'm not talking about a little inconvenience, Pope. There are people who fly around in private jets and have serious money. They're powerful, and they've already killed seven people."

I could feel Pope leaning in, listening intensely. "Maybe the price goes up."

"For the love of God, Pope, don't be a fool. It's going to end like shit."

Pope laughed, although his usual bravado was scaled back. "Let them come into my world and try it out for a while," he said.

Pope's intransigent ignorance was grinding my patience to dust. "Derek Stephens doesn't give a damn about your world," I muttered, under my breath.

Pope shrugged. "Derek Stephens is about the only white man I ever saw who *did* give a damn about my people."

I stopped, momentarily startled. "You know Stephens? Derek Stephens? Chief operating officer of Horizn Pharmaceuticals?"

Pope nodded. "Hell, yeah."

"You mean to tell me Derek Stephens has set foot in McDaniel Glen?"

"Naw. I meet him outside, with the needles."

"What are you talking about?"

"For the program. I give him the needles."

"The needle-exchange program? You mean he picks up the used needles personally?"

"Yeah, he my boy. Rabbit collects the needles with the names and addresses of all the people who turn 'em in. Stephens showed him how to do it, real organized. You get the needle, have the user put the cap on it. Don't want to get stuck with that shit. Then you mark down who gave you the needle, his address and all that."

I stared at him. "There's a record that matches individual needles to people?"

"That's what I'm sayin', white boy. So don't go talkin' shit about Derek Stephens, 'cause he my boy."

One thing had repeatedly been made clear during all the political debates about the needle-exchange program: it was scrupulously anonymous. Now I was finding out the opposite, and stranger yet, that none other than Derek Stephens was picking up the used needles. Something was wrong, although I had no idea what. All I knew was that if anybody could tell me, it was Thomas Robinson. I was already heading for my car. "I gotta go," I said.

"Don't come back," Pope said, and I could hear in his voice that he meant it.

It was a half hour to get home, which made it pretty close to three by the time I arrived. I went to my briefcase and found the list of the people on the Lipitran test. Then, I got a city map and pressed it flat on my dining table. I found the first name: *Chantelle Weiss, 4329 Avenue D. Avenue D. That was familiar.* I found it on the map and marked it with a black felt-tip pen with a small x. It was in the heart of McDaniel Glen. *Jonathan Mills, 225 Trenton Street.* I found it, a few streets over from Weiss. *Najeh Richardson.* Not inside the Glen, but right outside. It was the same with the others. Every person on Robinson's experimental trial either lived in the Glen or was on the border. *Okay. So they lived in the Glen, and they were drug addicts. Which means there's a good chance they were participating in the needle-exchange program. If they were, that connects them to Horizn. But what the hell does it mean?* Suddenly, something flashed all over my brain like Christmas. *He was poisoning these people with the needles. He hid something in the cartridges, and when they shot up, they killed themselves. That's got to be it.* I didn't even bother calling Robinson again. *I'm going to that damn park to drag Robinson out of his stupor.*

I stashed the papers in my desk, went downstairs, and got in my car. I made the forty-minute drive over to the park where I had met Robinson before. He was sitting motionless on his park bench. I parked and trotted across the street. He heard me coming, turning toward the noise. When he recognized me, he looked away.

I skipped all the pleasantries. "Where the hell have you been?" I demanded. "I've called you twenty times."

Robinson looked like he hadn't slept in a while. He gazed over impassively and said, "Blah, blah, blah."

"Great. You're back in your depression."

"Yeah. And you want to know why?"

"Not really."

"It's because we're not going to get the son of a bitch, that's why. Because he's"—Robinson paused, then spat—"better than me. He's better, damn it."

"I know how Ralston and Stephens killed your patients."

Robinson stared. "What are you talking about?"

"They used the clean-needle program to poison them."

Robinson shook his head dubiously. "That'd be a hell of a trick."

"Listen to me. It looks like all your patients participated in Horizn's needle-exchange program. And if that's true, they all got needles from Ralston. So they showed up for clean needles, and somehow he used the needles to poison them."

Robinson's reaction wasn't what I had expected. If anything, he looked bored. "That's it? That's your theory?"

"Yeah. There's more. Stephens—"

"Save it."

"Save it? I'm telling you, this has to be it!"

Robinson looked up, annoyed. "Except for the part about how it's impossible."

"What do you mean?"

"Look, this is a federally regulated clinical trial, Jack. We don't allow our patients to continue taking intravenous drugs while they're on the test. For God's sake, they'd just be reinfecting themselves. Think it through."

"But if they're addicts, maybe they—"

"No, Jack. We don't take pixie dust and assume they just go along with our request. We put every one of them on oral methadone the day they sign up. Which means that from that day forward, the only needles they get are from us, when we give them the Lipitran. Okay, Einstein? *No needles from Horizn.* Maybe they participated in Ralston's bleeding heart program before they signed up, but not after. And even if somebody did slip through the cracks, it couldn't have been all of them. It's impossible."

I stood, watching my theory blow up into tiny pieces. "Damn it! I was positive I had them."

"Yeah, well, get used to disappointment. *I told you.* If Ralston scuttled the Lipitran test, it means he was operating on a completely unprecedented level."

"I remember."

"Then don't come to me with idiotic stories about poisoning people with needles. This is world-class science. *If* we're right about the whole thing in the first place."

"But . . ."

Robinson stood and looked at me skeptically. "What gave you this crazy idea anyway?"

"I went to see Ralston."

Robinson's look darkened. "You saw him?"

"Yeah. And then I went to McDaniel Glen. I found out Derek Stephens personally picks up the used needles. Stephens, not some flunky. The C-O-O of the company." At Stephens's name, Robinson began to listen in earnest. "That's not all," I said. "The used needles are matched to individual users, names, addresses, the whole thing. So the program isn't really anonymous. They match specific needles to individuals."

Robinson was focused on me completely now, his eyes an unblinking stare. He began pacing, grating out words between his teeth, like he was arguing with himself. After several minutes, it was all I could do not to grab him by the neck and force him to tell me what he was thinking. He ground to a halt, turned toward me, and whispered, "Oh, my God."

"What?"

"How could a person even think of something like this? What kind of mind would it take?"

"*What*, damn it?"

"He used the needle-exchange program to kill my patients."

I almost hit him in frustration. "That's what I've been trying to tell you!"

"No, Jack. Nobody got poisoned. I knew that was impossible. For God's sake, there would be residue around the puncture marks. It's *infinitely* more elegant than that."

"Then tell me."

Robinson stood quietly, his face ashen. After a second he said,

"Be quiet and listen to how a psychopath thinks." He began pacing in front of me, as though he was beginning a lecture. "The human body has a way of handling toxins. It's called the cytochrome P-450 system. Ever hear of it?"

"No."

Robinson stared at me. "Yeah. Well, you ever wonder what happens when you take an aspirin?"

"You lose your headache."

"No, I mean what happens to the aspirin itself. Four hours later, it's gone from your system. What happened to it?"

"I just figured it wears off."

"It's metabolized by the cytochrome P-450 enzyme system."

"Aspirin's a toxin?"

"What happens if you take a bottle of it?"

"It messes you up."

Robinson shrugged. "Toxin."

"Okay, I get that."

"Good. So a toxin enters the body, and the P-450 system analyzes its chemical structure. Then it turns on a few genes—two or three out of thirty thousand or so—and tells the body to manufacture the correct enzymes necessary to metabolize the intruding compound. Pretty impressive, considering you don't even know it's doing it. You're sitting on your butt eating Cheetos."

"Okay, but what does this have to do with Ralston killing your patients?"

Robinson gave me a haunted look. "Remember thalidomide?"

"Yeah," I said slowly. "All those babies born with deformed limbs."

Robinson nodded. "That's the P-450 system running into something new and giving up. See, the system has been honed for millennia to handle what happens in nature. But we're inventing things and putting them into bodies, things that have never existed before. All that fine-tuning doesn't add up to shit when you're talking about synthetics."

"Okay."

"Lawyers gave the manufacturer a hard time over what happened on that, but the truth is, there wasn't any way to see it coming. They tested, sure. And for ninety-nine percent of the people, it was fine. Only one problem. If you happened to be pregnant, your baby didn't have arms." He paused, giving me a dark look. "Look, Jack, what do you think a clinical trial is, anyway? We *give* it to people. That's the test."

Robinson's stark admission hung in the air. "I thought things were more predictable."

"Yeah, well, that's important because if people didn't think that, we'd never get anybody to let us try things on them."

"But what does Ralston have to do with this?"

"It's not just thalidomide, Jack. *Every* drug has a tiny universe of people who can't metabolize it. Maybe it's only one percent, maybe less. The more powerful a drug is, the higher the number. Lipitran packs a hell of a wallop. So it's inevitable that some small percentage of people are going to lack whatever enzymes are necessary to metabolize it. If they take it, bad things are going to happen."

"What's your point?"

Robinson turned away from me, confronting something he didn't want to face. He stared across the park, his body still. "What if you could find those people in advance?" he asked quietly. "What if you knew enough about genetics that you could actually figure out who a drug was going to kill before they even took it and make sure they got on a clinical trial?"

"Is something like that possible?"

Robinson turned back to me. The blood had drained from his face. "Ralston could do it. He would need two things, and I'm just realizing he had them both."

"Which are?"

"First, he would need Lipitran. Thanks to Townsend's hack of Grayton, Ralston had all the information he needed to manufacture a small batch."

"And second?"

"He would need the DNA of hundreds of addicts. Maybe even a thousand."

"The needle-exchange program."

"Yeah. The big, I'm a hero to my people needle-exchange program." Robinson retched back a wave of nausea. "He wasn't helping those people. He was using them as cannon fodder."

"Tell me how it worked."

"Like everything, it's simple once you figure it out. Ralston makes a batch of Lipitran and gives a dosage to one of the addicts. It would only take one, and the guy wouldn't even have to know he was getting it. The victim's P-450 system starts grinding out the enzymes a normal person produces to metabolize the drug. Then the addict comes back a few days later for a clean needle. He gives Stephens the old one. Ralston washes it out with physiological saline, and swimming around in the blood components left in the syringe is the precise human enzymatic response to Lipitran. The rest is just screening."

"He uses the turned-in needles."

Robinson nodded. "Every one of them contains the DNA of the addict who used it. And inside that DNA is everything Ralston needs to know. He spins it out, looks at the proteomics, and sooner or later, he finds a small universe of people who don't have the enzymes they need."

"It would take a long time, wouldn't it?"

"Yeah. How long has the clean-needle program been going on?"

"Couple of years, I think."

Robinson laughed grimly. "Just as long as our program for Lipitran." He closed his eyes. "Once he isolates these poor bastards, he knows that the second they take Lipitran, they are going to die like dogs."

"He told me he didn't kill those patients. He said they died from Lipitran."

"He was right," Robinson said, shaking his head. "He didn't touch the compound, and he didn't touch them. We could have given those patients armed guards and it wouldn't have made any difference."

"But how could he get them on the test?"

Robinson shrugged. "They're drug addicts, and he controls

their clean needles. Ralston could even promise them pharmaceutical heroin after the test, which would be like gold to a junkie."

I stood by Robinson in the silence of the park, thinking about how sometimes being gifted and talented doesn't have a damn thing to do with virtue. "But we have him now, right?" I said. "I mean, what you just said. He's busted. He's going down."

Robinson spat into the grass. "He walks."

I stared at him, badly wanting off the roller coaster of ups and downs. "What?"

"He walks, Jack. It's just theory. I can't prove a word of it."

"Because?"

"Because no one survived. All I would need is one. By surviving, that patient would, by definition, have the enzymes the dead patients lacked. Then you could compare the survivor to the others, and demonstrate that the test had to have been manipulated. But with all of them dead, it's impossible."

"Lacayo!" I retorted. " 'Mostly dead,' you said. He's still alive."

Robinson gave a dry, brittle laugh. "Died two days ago," he said. "Blew up, like the others."

"God, that's unbelievable. How did you find out?"

Robinson looked down. "Went down there," he whispered. "Went to see old Lacayo. His mother saw me hanging around. She hit me."

So that's why I haven't been able to find you. You've been here, nursing another wound over a final dead patient. A hot, brittle breeze whipped across the park. Robinson looked across the empty expanse of grass, his face a map of defeat.

"He's better than I am," he said. "He's better."

"You could give Lipitran to someone else," I said cautiously. "Make a new survivor."

Robinson looked at me. "You want to know the definition of genius? Ralston's protected by law, now. Once the FDA withdraws their sanction, I can't give Lipitran to anyone else without committing a felony. Medical malpractice. Reckless endangerment, probably even attempted murder." He grimaced. "And whose life do you want me to risk, anyway? It's theory, Jack. Do you want to stand up in a court of law and say you gave Lipitran to another person after eight people died horribly from it?"

I shook my head. "No."

"Even if the patient lived, I'd still go to jail for the rest of my life." Robinson looked up at the sky. "Don't you get it? It's the perfect crime. It's unprecedented. He killed eight people by using their own bodies against them. He became a hero while he did it. And to top it all, he ended up with the entire federal government protecting him from anybody ever finding out."

We stood beside each other in silence, partly in awe over Ralston's genius, and partly in revulsion over the ends to which it was put. After a while Robinson asked, "Where did that ridiculous idea about poison needles come from, anyway?"

"I'm sorry about that. I thought we had them."

"Yeah, well, we didn't."

"The whole thing started when I found out Ralston didn't know Doug was taking Lipitran."

There was a moment's pause, and Robinson slowly swiveled his head around toward me. "Say that again, please."

"Ralston. He didn't know Doug was on your test. I told him when I saw him."

"What did he do?"

"He fell apart. Seriously rattled."

"Rattled?"

"Yeah."

Robinson lunged at me, grabbing me by the collar. "Listen to me now, Jack. You have to get me Doug Townsend's body, and there's not one second to lose."

"His body? That's a hell of a request."

"If Ralston didn't know Townsend was on the test, it means Doug wasn't screened. Doug must have put himself on the test without Ralston knowing it."

"Which means?"

"Which means he's a *survivor*."

"He's dead, Doctor."

"From *fentanyl*, Jack. Not from Lipitran. Do you understand what I'm saying? Everything we need to nail Ralston is inside Doug Townsend's body this moment."

"Hang on a second. If Doug was on the test, don't you already have a sample of his blood?"

"Of course I do. *Before* he took the Lipitran. Then he vanished off the program."

"Murdered because he would have been cured."

"Exactly. Now tell me you know where his body is."

"He's on ice, at the police pathology lab."

"Okay. But listen to me, Jack If I can figure this out, Ralston can, too. In fact, he must have, the second you told him Doug had taken Lipitran."

"So why didn't he kill me when he had the chance?"

"What?"

I suddenly realized in my haste I hadn't said anything about Ralston's thugs. "Ralston arranged a little detour for me after I left Horizn. I got tied up and thrown in a closet."

Robinson stared. "How'd you get out?"

"Force of will. At any rate, if they were trying to kill me, they were pretty bad at it."

"They won't make that mistake again."

"So what about you?" I asked. "You need to get out of sight."

"I'll go to Grayton until you call me. It's built like a fortress."

"Okay. I'll get back to you in a couple of hours."

"Stay healthy, Jack. The mind that figured out how to kill those patients is capable of anything."

Robinson's urgent demand to get Doug's body would require more than a phone call to Billy Little; a request that big had to be face-to-face. I looked at my watch; it was ten before five. Billy never left before six, so I knew I could find him. When I walked into his office, he looked at me in surprise. "So there you are. What'd you do, fall off the earth?"

"Sorry, Billy. Blu told me you called."

I slid a piece of paper across his desk. He stared down at it. "Grayton Technical Laboratories? What's this?"

"It's the company Doug was hacking. I told you about them."

Billy nodded. "Yeah, that's right."

"They want Doug's body. Not they, exactly. The lead scientist, Thomas Robinson."

Billy raised an eyebrow. "That a fact?"

"Robinson was conducting a clinical trial, and Doug was on it. He thinks he can learn something about the test from Doug's body."

"What kind of clinical trial?"

"Hepatitis C."

Billy watched me a moment, then said, "You know what I'm wondering right now?"

"How it is you didn't know Doug had hepatitis? None of us did."

"No. I'm wondering why all of a sudden Doug Townsend has the most popular corpse in town."

"What do you mean?"

"I just mean they're late. Grayton Labs. Thomas Robinson. Whoever."

"Late?"

"Late, as in we don't have the body anymore. It was released yesterday." Billy stood and walked over to a gray filing cabinet. He opened it, pulled a paper out of a folder, and handed it over to me. "Lucy Buckner, Phoenix, Arizona."

I stared at the paper. "Doug's cousin? She won't even return my calls."

"Yeah, well, she returned Ron Evans's calls."

"Who's Ron Evans?"

"The guy who showed up with her notarized power of attorney to take possession of Doug Townsend's body." He looked at me sympathetically. "I couldn't send it to the DA, Jack. There was nothing to *send*. The victimology report closed a couple of days ago, confirming the suicide. This guy Evans shows up to claim the body, and there wasn't a legitimate reason to say no." I stared at Billy for a second, too stunned to respond. *Seamless. No body, no proof. That was why they didn't kill me. They just needed me to be somewhere else for a while. Just long enough to take care of Doug's body, and close the deal.* "We go back, Jack," Billy said. "So why don't you tell me what's really going on here? This guy Townsend. What was his real story?"

I was tired, more tired than I could ever remember. "It's okay, Billy. There's nothing you or anybody else can do, now."

"Don't be a hero, Jack. If you're getting into something over your head, I can help."

I closed my eyes. "It doesn't matter. It's over."

There was only one piece left to put into the puzzle, and later that night I did so listlessly, only to complete the circle. I found Doug's cousin's number and called her. A female voice with a southern accent came across the line. "Who's this?"

I forced myself to speak. "This is Jack Hammond. I was Doug's lawyer. I left you a couple of messages after Doug's death."

She sounded irritated. "I already told Mr. Evans, they can do whatever they like with his body. Help science, or whatever."

"What man was that?"

"I've been over this before. If Doug's death is going to help science or research or whatever, then, fine, they can have him. Well, for the three thousand dollars, like we said."

Three thousand dollars. Pocket money. "Someone offered you three thousand dollars for Doug's body?"

"Look, if Doug was in any more trouble, I didn't know nothing about it. I told that boy a hundred times to stay off those damn drugs."

"I'm not accusing you of anything, Ms. Buckner. I'm just trying to get some information about the man who paid you for Doug's body."

"Well, like I told you. He just said medical schools would pay money for his body for science."

"Did he say what school?"

"No. He said if I signed the papers and faxed them back, he would give me the money. I said that was fine by me, except I wasn't faxin' nothin' until *after* I had the money."

"Did you get it?"

"Money order, three thousand dollars. Went down to Western Union and picked it up. I faxed him from there, too. I ain't got a fax."

"Do you still have the fax number, Ms. Buckner?"

"Yep. I got it right here. It's 404.555.1610."

I wrote down the number. "Did he leave you any other way to get in touch with him?"

"No. Doesn't surprise me there's some kind of mess, though. That boy was nothing but problems, right from the beginning."

I clicked off without saying goodbye and dialed the fax number. I got a recording for a movie theater in Cobb County. *Seamless, as usual. Take over a number for a while. They'd never even know they were used.* I hung up and fell back into a chair, limp. *This time, it really is over.*

I closed my eyes. *So close I could taste it.* I had missed getting justice for Doug Townsend and seven other victims by what—hours? Eight people were dead, their endings invisible and untraceable.

And so the world spins, I thought. Ralston and Stephens would make their billion. The projects would lose a few more souls, which the greater city of Atlanta, never having cared much about them in the first place, wouldn't even need to forget.

Sometime deep in the night, I awoke, stark and alert. I stared at the ceiling a second, wondering if I had lost my mind. But I hadn't. There was a flaw, and it had nothing to do with cells and genes and science and other impenetrable things I could barely understand. It was beautifully human, and the fact that I was still alive meant Ralston and Stephens hadn't figured it out yet. If things stayed that way long enough, I had the bastards.

CHAPTER
TWENTY-FIVE

AT EIGHT O'CLOCK the next morning, I climbed into the Buick. It was limping after the high-speed chase; the alignment had suffered, and the transmission—God knows how long it had been since the fluid had been changed—was showing signs of trauma. But it held together, and I pulled into the Atlanta morgue about an hour later. It was Saturday, but since crime never rests, neither does the facility. The morgue is conveniently attached to the police pathology lab, with which it shares an entrance.

I don't like crime labs. They remind me of hospitals, and the crime pathology lab of the Atlanta Police Department is as much like a hospital as I want to get. It's spotless, smells distinctly of chemicals, and is lit with an angry, defiant light. What it doesn't have in common with a hospital it shares with jail: it bristles with electronic security. It's located in south Atlanta, in an industrial park, far from police headquarters. There is no identifying sign on the building, and because the loading dock is in the back, I doubt that many of the other tenants in the park even know its purpose. It is kept clandestine for very good reasons: first, because the value of the immaculately pure testing materials inside it is immense, and second, because a great deal of highly sensitive evidence is stored there. Upon arrival, cameras record your every move. Before you can leave the reception area, you're issued a temporary ID, which must be worn at all times. I showed my driver's license, signed in, and told the secretary I wanted to see Dr. Raimi Hrawani, the pathologist in charge of the lab. As Doug's lawyer, I had a right to his file. I looked up at the cameras, and felt like praying.

After a few minutes, a woman in a white smock came through the large double doors opposite my chair. She was in her mid-thirties, olive-skinned, with brown hair cut short, pulled behind her ears. I'd never met her, but I had seen her name on several cases. Hrawani had a stellar reputation, and had given testimony on several high-profile murders. "Hello, Mr. Hammond," she said in an East Indian accent. "I understand you want to talk about Doug Townsend. I don't have a lot of time. We had some unpleasantness in south Atlanta last night, so we're heavily booked."

"Detective Little says his body was released."

"That's right. All the papers were filled out correctly."

"When was this?"

"About four-thirty yesterday afternoon."

"Was there an autopsy?"

She shook her head. "We were basically just a holding place."

"So there are no tissues or blood samples?"

"A Valtox test was administered on the scene, but the test consumes the sample. I believe a photograph was taken, however."

"Can I see the photograph?"

She handed me a plastic badge. "Clip this on your shirt and follow me."

"To where the dead people are?"

"That's right." I followed Hrawani through heavy metal doors into the secure part of the Altanta P.D. crime lab. The tone is industrial, a place for work and nothing else. There isn't a single image in the place to soften the view. The lab is built in a square, with a large, open work area in the center, with four autopsy tables. The tables are perforated, stainless steel, and they shine spotless in the harsh hospital light. Surrounding the tables are some medieval-looking tools, including saws, drills, and pliers. This central work area is ringed by offices along the sides. I followed Hrawani into her office, a square, spartan space with gunmetal-gray metal filing cabinets, metal desk, and a padded chair on wheels. There was a faded picture of a man and a woman arm in arm, in front of an ornate, colorful building. She noticed me looking and said, "My parents, forty years ago. Before I was born."

"Where was the picture taken?"

"Pakistan. Islamabad. They say it was beautiful then." She motioned for me to take a seat, and she did the same. She pulled out a large manila folder. "So. Do you use drugs, Mr. Hammond?"

"No."

"If you ever feel like starting, just give me a call. I can provide a marvelous bit of perspective."

"Hell on the body?"

"If people saw it from my point of view, they'd do nothing but eat Grape-Nuts." She took a seat, motioning for me to do the same. Then she reached under her desk, grabbed a metal trash can, and kicked it over beside me. It was lined with a plastic bag. "Just in case," she said.

"I'll be fine."

She shrugged. "It's usually the men who lose it." She reached into the folder and pulled out two photographs, spreading them across her desk. I spent the next several seconds swallowing back bile, trying to acclimate to the stark, relentless images of a naked, merciless death. Doug was lying on a metal table, his shirt off, his body obviously lifeless.

"Your client was somewhat emaciated, which is fairly normal with extended drug use. They get appetite suppression and can't keep weight on. You see the sunken cheekbones, the dark, hollow eyes? There are the discolored burn marks on the fingertips. Although your friend was more careful than most." She looked at me. "But there aren't any track marks, so it's also clear he wasn't an IV drug abuser."

"Doug told me several times he was terrified of needles."

Hrawani flipped over another picture which showed a close-up of Doug's left shoulder. I stared, disbelieving: the words *Pikovaya Dama* were tattooed in the same style of lettering I had seen on Michele, although the image was less exquisitely made. The letters on Michele's thigh were delicate, obviously made by an artist. Doug's had a crudeness of execution, lacking finesse. But there was no doubt about it. He had a copy of her tattoo cut into his skin.

"So the hepatitis was from the tattoo," I whispered.

"It certainly could be. Do you know what the writing means?" Hrawani asked.

"It's Russian," I said. " 'The Queen of Spades.' "

Hrawani raised an eyebrow. "Apparently, your client overcame his needle phobia."

Ralston's words came back to me: *I have no doubt that for five minutes with my wife he would have cut off one of his own fingers.* "He had a powerful motivation."

Hrawani gathered the photographs together and replaced them in the folder. "That's all I have," she said. "It's not much, unfortunately."

"This Ron Evans, the one who picked up the body. Did you personally see him?"

"No. But we can ask Charlie, the deinur."

"Deinur?"

"The man who handles the bodies."

I nodded. "Thanks, I'd appreciate it."

I followed Hrawani out of her office into the work area. She called out to a large, muscular black man in his late thirties. His shoulders and arms were massive, like a weightlifter's. "Charlie, can you come here for a second?"

The man looked over, nodded, and walked toward us. Hrawani introduced us and I asked him if he remembered anything unusual about how Doug's body was picked up.

He paused, thinking. "Not what you'd call weird," he said. "But I expected a service, like a funeral home. I see the same six, seven companies in here all the time. But this was different."

"Was it an ambulance or a hearse?"

"Hearse, I think. But no markings on it. No company."

"Did he sign for the body?"

"It would be in the log, up at the front desk."

Hrawani, Charlie, and I went back to the reception area. While Charlie was rummaging for the logbook, I pointed to a closed-circuit TV monitor showing the rear exterior of the building. "Is this always recording?" I asked.

Charlie nodded. "Runs twenty-four-seven. Inside and outside."

"So you would have a tape of the man picking up the body."

"Not tapes. We're on hard drives, now. But yeah, we would have a record."

"Can I see it?"

Hrawani glanced at me doubtfully. "We're getting into an iffy area here, Mr. Hammond," she said.

"What the man did outside the building is public," I said. "That's all I'm asking about."

Hrawani considered a moment, then nodded to the deinur. He shrugged, found the time in the log, and punched some numbers on a nearby terminal. The screen showed a Ford Econoline van parked in the loading area. "That's it," he said. "That's the truck."

"Can you move ahead to show Evans?"

Charlie punched an arrow on the terminal, advancing the picture in one-minute increments. After several punches, the screen showed Charlie and another man wheeling a body on a gurney through the back doors. He looked to be in his mid-fifties, with a slight build, and balding. When it came time to transfer the body into the truck, he let Charlie do most of the work. So far, there hadn't been a clear picture of his face. But just before he pulled out, he gave Charlie a perfunctory handshake. That was the single moment he faced the camera head on. "Can you freeze that?"

"Sure."

"Is there any way you can print out that frame?"

Charlie gave Hrawani another look, and she paused again. "My client's off the police radar screen," I said quietly. "Before he slips away entirely, I'd like to run down some things. It would mean a lot to me." Hrawani nodded to the deinur, and Charlie punched a couple of buttons. A nearby laser printer whirred into life. After a few minutes, he pulled out an enlarged, fairly pixelated photograph of the man's face. "Not perfect, but you can definitely make out the features," he said. "Best I can do."

I carefully put the picture in my coat pocket. "Thanks, it's fine."

I turned to Hrawani. "I appreciate your help. I'll be in touch."

I turned in my badge, walked out to the car, and got inside. I felt the picture in my pocket. Now, all I needed was Nightmare.

This time I didn't even bother phoning. I headed directly to the West End, where Nightmare lived. By now it was after ten, the city traffic finally light. The West End is a low-rent area, working-class, full of older apartments with low ceilings and iffy maintenance. I parked and walked up to his door. I could hear dark, brooding rock music emanating from the apartment. I knocked; there was no answer. I knocked again, louder. The music abated; I caught a shadow of someone passing across some closed blinds. "It's Jack. We need to talk." Nothing. "I'm not leaving, Michael. Come out of the cave." There was the sound of opening locks, and the door opened. Nightmare peered out of his apartment.

"I'd invite you in, but the place is kind of a mess." He stood in boxer shorts and a T-shirt. He looked frayed, as though he hadn't slept in a couple of days.

"You okay? You don't look too hot."

"Unless you wanna ask me for a date, I don't see what difference it makes."

"That won't be a problem," I said, pushing past him. "This won't take long." I walked into Nightmare's apartment. It smelled like laundry hadn't been on Nightmare's agenda for at least a month. There was some nondescript furniture, and a small stereo, the cheap, all-in-one kind with attached speakers. Beside it was strewn a collection of hand-labeled CDs. But no computers. "Where's all the gear?" I asked.

"In the back," he said. "I keep stuff away from the windows. Bad neighborhood."

"Go put on some pants, Michael."

"We going somewhere?"

"Yeah, but that's not the point. I don't feel like looking at you in your underwear." Nightmare shrugged and walked to a bedroom. After a couple of minutes, he came out wearing some dirty blue jeans and a wrinkled shirt. I stood there staring at him, trying to ignore the fact that justice for eight murdered people was about to depend on him. "So here's the thing, Michael. I need you to help me one more time."

Nightmare looked down and stuffed his hands into his jeans pockets. "Look, dude, I've been thinking this thing over. If you're going to keep hitting me up, I'm going to need some bank for it."

"You're kidding. You're holding me up for money?"

"No, all I'm saying, I'm like an independent contractor. I got no ax to grind either way on this deal."

"Whatever happened to partners? Jackie Chan?"

"I'm just saying, dude."

"Yeah. You're just saying." I walked up to him—he flinched, as usual—and I grabbed him by the collar. "Do you know how these people died, Michael?" He shook his head. "They died by exploding inside themselves. They died by bleeding from every orifice of their bodies simultaneously. They died like dogs, in agony. So you and I are going to Grayton Labs now. You're going to help me solve the hideous murders of eight people. I was hoping you'd do it because you were a decent kid underneath your ridiculous, posturing exterior. But if you don't do it for that, you'll do it because if you don't, I'm going to beat the living hell out of you."

"Grayton Labs?"

"That's right."

He peeled back my hands, and I set him down. "Yeah, that's cool," he said.

"Just like that? I say Grayton Labs, and all of a sudden you're all smiles?"

"Look, I said I'd do it."

There wasn't time to argue. Robinson was waiting. "All right. You need anything?"

He picked up the same shoulder bag he had used at my office. "Let's go."

If Horizn was a high-tech palace, Grayton was a blue-collar work space built for efficiency. The lab was located in a long, brick building of three stories. The structure was obviously a couple of decades old, and little had been done to modernize its look. Landscaping was nonexistent. That, combined with the security surrounding it, made it look more like a prison dormitory than a player in the brave new world of genetic research.

Grayton security lacked the technology of Horizn—no doubt for economic reasons—but made up for it in human intimidation. Robinson had called the guard, so we were let through the entrance to the parking area. Nightmare and I walked through the front door and stopped before a surveillance station displaying a dozen television monitors. Two armed guards were seated behind the bank of screens sweeping the exterior and interior of the building. As we approached, one rose. We signed in and were directed to a couple of straight-backed chairs several feet away.

Five minutes later Robinson appeared. His face showed a fragile hopefulness, but fear lurked around the edges. I stood. "This is Michael Harrod."

"Call me Nightmare."

Robinson stared at Michael silently a moment, then turned and headed toward a hallway. "Come with me."

Walking through Grayton's mostly empty hallways, Robinson might as well have had the black plague. The few people around ducked into offices when we appeared, or simply stared, giving Robinson unabashed, malevolent looks. Robinson was not immune. By the time we got to his laboratory, he was practically limping with shame. I stopped him at the door. "We're going to fix this, okay?"

"I risked the whole company and lost."

"Why don't they just fire you?"

"They can't. I have a contract."

"Can't they buy it out?"

"I don't want the money. I want my revenge. And for the next four months, I have access to the lab."

"What about support staff?"

Robinson looked down, grappling with his humiliation. "Nobody here is to lift a finger to help me. I'm anathema."

Before we walked in, Nightmare pointed to the ceiling at what looked like a large shower head. "What's that?" he asked.

"Emergency bath," Robinson said. "You'll see them scattered around on all the floors. We use a lot of harsh chemicals around here. The idea is that nobody is ever more than thirty feet from a blast of water to get something off them. Just pull the lever."

Nightmare stared. "Ever see it used?"

"Once." Robinson nodded but didn't elaborate. He pushed open two large double doors, and we walked into a large, rectangular room about fifty feet long and thirty-five wide. Robinson flipped some switches and the lights above flickered on. The space was crammed with machines of staggering complexity. A labyrinth of computer monitors were scattered around the room. But everywhere were empty chairs. It was apparent that until recently, this was a place of concentrated activity, with accommodations for at least ten assistants. Now—in the face of Robinson's failure—the place was as melancholy as a tomb. Two machines, humming quietly, dominated the center of the room. Nightmare made an audible sound of lust.

"Nice, huh?" Robinson said.

Nightmare looked around wistfully. "What I could do with this much computing power—"

"The body," Robinson interrupted. "When can we get it?"

Here we go. "We can't," I said. "It's gone." Robinson stared a second, then began to tremble. "Don't panic. I know where it is."

"What happened? You said you had a guy."

"They beat us to it. While I was tied up—"

Nightmare interrupted. "Dude, you got tied up?"

I waved my hand, shutting him up. "While I was tied up, somebody got the body released. It was picked up late yesterday afternoon."

Robinson, already on his last legs emotionally, spoke with a cracked voice. "Who has it?"

I laid the picture from the pathology lab down on a work table. "This guy," I answered. "He's got Doug."

"That's it?" Robinson exclaimed. "That's all you've got? A photograph?"

I pointed to Nightmare. "We've also got him."

"I don't know the guy," Nightmare said, looking surprised.

"Of course you don't know him. But I know somebody who does, and you're going to ask him."

"How you figure that?"

"When I went to see Ralston, I had to check into a facial recognition program."

Nightmare raised an eyebrow. "Biometrics. Damn, man, that is thorough."

"Everybody who comes through the door." I pointed to the picture. "This guy is working for Ralston. Which means he's in the database, too."

Nightmare's vaguely interested expression vanished. "Dude, you have finally completely come unhinged. Grayton was one thing, but I am not going to hack Horizn."

"If you can get access to their database, you can not only identify this guy, you can probably tell us his favorite color."

"Look, I got nothing against hacking Horizn. As far as I'm concerned, they're *choice*. But not for you, and not this way. You are out of your mind."

"You will hack them, Michael, because this is too important for you to crap out on us."

"Even if I agreed, I would need weeks, and that is no lie."

"Tell me what's involved, because we don't have anywhere near that kind of time."

"To do it right? First, I'd get on EDGAR, the SEC site, take a look at their filing. See if they have any affiliates, if they operate under any other names. Maybe there's a back door from a subsidiary."

"No way. It would take far too long. Next?"

"Assuming they're smarter than that, because they are? I'd take a couple of days and search all the security message boards and blogs, see if there's anything posted. Sometimes people talk about their problems. If there was nothing there, I'd start mapping them, real patient. See which domain names they operate under, which ports are listening. You got to be careful, not get in a hurry. You map the whole network, one DNS at a time. Then—and only then—do I start nibbling away at them. I show patience, dude. I do not blow up like an amateur."

"Just keep going. What happens next?"

"What do you care? I'm already at a week."

"Just tell me, Michael."

Nightmare shrugged. "How many employees do they have?"

Robinson answered. "About fourteen hundred," he said.

Nightmare nodded thoughtfully. "Fourteen hundred. Okay. So I'd probably look for a Joe."

"What's a Joe?" I asked.

"Hacker term. Somebody lazy enough to use his own name as his password. Almost every company has one, and one is all it takes."

"Then what are we waiting for?" I demanded. "We can get a list of the employees, can't we?"

Michael looked stricken. "They're not idiots, you know. They got protections. Maybe Joe is the janitor, dude. And the janitor can't exactly access the human resources database without setting off flares. One wrong move and I'm toast. Or in the case of these guys, more like dead."

"All right, all right," I said. "There has to be another way."

"There isn't." Nightmare sat down, sulking. "They've probably done away with the body by now, anyway."

"All the labs have incinerators," Robinson said, nodding. "We use them for the laboratory animals."

"Nice," Nightmare muttered. "I'm here with a bunch of monkey killers."

"It doesn't matter," I interrupted. "I can guarantee you Doug isn't at Horizn. It would bring murder evidence right into the offices. I don't see that happening."

"You might be right," Robinson agreed. "Bringing a body bag

into a place like that is no walk in the park. Everything gets signed in and out. Unless a ton of people were in on it, there'd be no way to ensure security. There would be tapes to erase, a log at the guardhouse, people to bribe, potential physical evidence left behind. And a big random factor, like somebody just walking in the wrong room at the wrong time. It would be easier to handle it somewhere else."

I turned back to Nightmare. "So it's up to you."

"Then you're out of luck," Nightmare said flatly.

We stood in silence for a minute, when I suddenly pointed at Nightmare, who flinched involuntarily in his usual, paranoid way. "What he was saying earlier. About finding somebody they do business with. How does that work?"

Nightmare shrugged. "Evil trick. You find somebody they do a lot of business with, which means there's a lot of data flow between them. And maybe this other company has lousy security, so you hack them instead. Then it's just a matter of waiting for them to communicate with each other. Once they do, you run a remote procedure call. Lets you crawl back from the second company to the actual target. Of course, you can only stay on as long as the first company is connected. When they go, you go with them. But by that time you probably figured out how to sign back on as them in the first place."

I stared. "For God's sake, Michael, why don't you just get a normal job? With brains like yours—"

"Yeah, whatever," Nightmare interrupted. He gave me a doubtful look. "Are you saying you know of some company like that?"

I turned toward Robinson. "Not a company," I said. "The United States government."

"My God, you're right," Robinson said. "The National Institutes of Health. Horizn would be online with them every day, sometimes for hours. I've seen departments just keep an open connection, because it's easier."

I turned toward Nightmare. "That's it, Michael. NIH. Can you do it?"

Nightmare sidestepped away from me, gaining a little space.

But I could feel him torn between his familiar anxiety and the tantalizing prospect of a new victim. His ego was pushing him into uncharted territory. "We'd have to know the names of the guys who access NIH—"

"I know *all* their names," Robinson interrupted. "I can make a list in two minutes."

"Okay," Nightmare said. "*If* one of them turned out to be a Joe, then maybe. If you had all that, I mean."

I looked at Nightmare. "Let's do it."

Nightmare was wary. "I'd still have to sign on at NIH, and I don't have credentials there." He pointed at Robinson. "So if this is going to work, I have to go on as him."

Robinson looked up from his list. "What?"

"There's no point in me hacking NIH if he has credentials. It would be a waste of time. So I go on as him, or it's nothing."

I started to protest, but Robinson reached out and put his hand on my arm. "It's okay. Let's do it."

"You sure?" I asked.

"I'm dead already, unless this works. We're just talking about formalities."

"Is that where you normally log on?" Nightmare asked, pointing to a terminal.

"Yes."

"Fifty grand."

"Michael—"

"Fifty grand, dude. This is serious high-tech work, and it costs."

"So do hospital bills."

To this day, I don't know if I was serious or not. But Michael must have seen something in my eyes, because he sat down and said, "Well, at least go get me some damn mineral water."

After a couple of hours of pacing, I finally went to a vending machine and bought fifteen dollars' worth of prefab sandwiches, some chips, and soft drinks. I handed out a couple of sandwiches, storing the rest in a fridge. Nightmare wolfed his down, but Robinson refused to eat. I planted myself in an office chair at the far end of the laboratory, hating every minute that passed. A laboratory full of incomprehensible equipment is a lousy place to spend the day. I tried to talk to Robinson a couple of times, but he wouldn't have it; he kept pestering Michael to see how his hack was coming, and eventually Michael told him to stay out of his hair. More hours passed, and eventually, the facility started to close down around us. At some point—after alternating bouts of equally ineffectual sitting and pacing—I must have drifted off a little. I felt my legs get kicked, jerked my head up, and saw Michael leering down at me. "I got it," he said. "I'm great, you know. The greatest who ever lived, probably."

"And?"

Nightmare held out a printed page. "Dude works for Horizn. His name isn't Ron Evans, either. It's Raymond Chudzinski."

"Nightmare, you're a genius. What time is it?"

"I know I am. Maybe, like, six-thirty or something."

"Has Robinson seen this?"

"Not yet. He's in his office."

"Let's go get him." I took two steps toward Robinson and pulled up short. I felt ice in my blood. "Michael, I never mentioned Ron Evans's name to you."

"Huh? Yeah, you told me."

"I didn't, Michael."

"Well, I guess Robinson did."

"I didn't tell him the name, either." I put my hand around Nightmare's throat and pushed him up against the wall. Nightmare squirmed under my grip like a spider, all arms and legs. "You sold us out, you piece of shit. There's only one way in hell for you to know who Ron Evans is, and that is for you to have helped Ralston get Doug's body." Disgusted, I released him. He fell back against the wall, limp. "I've already talked to Doug's cousin. She faxed paperwork to an Atlanta number. That number turned out to be a movie theater in Fulton County."

"What about it?"

"You're a phone phreak, Michael. You reroute phones. That's your deal. You *told* me."

Nightmare started trembling. He backed away, trying to put some distance between us. "That's bullshit," he said, and it was so obvious he was lying that he dropped it. He looked up at me with a terrified grimace. "They came to my apartment. They were serious, okay? Like guns kind of serious."

"Who did? Tell me, you piece of shit."

"We didn't exactly trade business cards," Nightmare said, bitterly. "They said they tracked me when we were on Grayton. But they let me on, to find out who I was."

I described the men who had bound me into a closet, and Nightmare confirmed they were the same. "Look," he said, "these guys have their thing wired, you know? I'm talking serious technology. They tracked me on *Grayton,* dude. We never stood a chance."

"They paid you, you little vermin. That was what mattered."

Nightmare looked at me, his bravado broken down. "Okay, I'm not a superhero like you. Yeah, I took the money. But it wasn't about that." He looked up, his eyes watering. "I was scared, okay? I never wanted to get into a thing like this. This Nightmare stuff is all bullshit, you know? Mess with people's heads a little. Free long-distance. Break into a site and post some stuff, talk shit in some chat rooms. And I meet you, and all of a sudden I'm doing industrial espionage and eight people are dead and *shit,* man. Those guys were going to break my neck. They looked like they'd had a lot of practice." And then, to my absolute horror, he actually did start to cry. Having played the role of Nightmare for God knows how long, he revealed himself to be nothing more than Michael Harrod, scared kid. I knew from personal experience the men he had met were no picnic. For somebody like Michael, they would be terrifying, an irresistible force. I reached down and grabbed his shoulder, but he shook off my hand, burning with humiliation and guilt.

"So why do this?" I asked, holding out the paper. "They're not going to be happy if they find out you helped us."

"All you guys think you know me," Nightmare said, sniffling. "Ralston or whoever those freaks were, even you, with your father-figure speeches. But I got principles of my own." He pointed to the picture. "I did that for Killah," he said, anger creeping into his voice. "He was one of the community. A little messed up, that's all."

"They didn't need you to pull this off, Michael. They can handle this level of technology themselves."

"Yeah."

"They wanted to get you involved, because they knew you were working with me." I stared. "They paid you to keep an eye on us, didn't they? So that you would keep us from finding out any more."

Nightmare looked down. "Yeah."

"So does this mean you sold us out or not? Do they know we were inside their site?"

Nightmare wiped away his tears. "Everybody's always pushed me around, you know? Everybody in school, whatever. As long as I went, anyway. So I went underground. Nobody pushes me around in that world. And I got to thinking about Killah, and how these guys wasted him. Killah was just like me, you know? He didn't fit into polite society. So I thought maybe instead of being a jerk, I could get these guys for him. That would be something, you know? To actually get these guys."

I watched him teeter between his brilliant, alienated adolescence and something like adulthood. It was like seeing a foal try to stand on its spindly legs. But if he was telling the truth—a serious question, but that was all I had—he had finally done something decent in his life. It was a start. "Let's go," I said.

Nightmare wiped his red eyes. "Where to?"

"To get Robinson."

"So what are you gonna do to me?"

"You were in over your head. I know the guys you're talking about, and they were too much for you. And since I can't wait any longer to find out if you're a liar or not, I'm choosing to believe you. So move it."

Nightmare stood, trying to compose himself. He limped behind me, still blinking back tears. We walked into Robinson's office, who took a look at Michael and stood up, concerned. "What happened?"

I held out the picture. "Michael came through," I said. "We've got the guy. Raymond Chudzinski. We find him, and we find the body."

A voice behind me muttered something unintelligible. "What's that?" I said, spinning around.

"I know where they took Killah," Nightmare said quietly.

I stared. "Where?"

"Funeral home in Walnut Grove. He's being cremated under a different name. Something like Harrison, I think."

"You knew? Damn it, Michael, why didn't you tell us?"

"I might have been scared, but I didn't turn into an idiot. I was waiting to see if I could pull off the hack. If they're going down, I'm a free man."

I looked at my watch. It was 6:45. "They'll be closed. But it's a bad idea to wait. For all we know, they actually dispose of the bodies after hours. I say we drive."

"Are you guys nuts?" Nightmare asked. "The guy's been dead for days. He'd be decomposed."

"He could have been dead a year and it wouldn't change his DNA," Robinson said. "But pulling genetic information out of necrotic flesh is no picnic. If we can get blood it'll go faster."

Nightmare winced. "Shit, dude."

"Shut up, Michael," I said.

"If Townsend was kept refrigerated, I don't care how long it's been," Robinson said. "Anyway, I only need a minute quantity."

"And if he hasn't been refrigerated?" I asked.

Robinson paused. "We'd have about twelve hours, I'd say. Not that the DNA would degrade. It's just that the blood would become so coagulated it would be almost impossible to get out."

"There's nothing we can do now," I said. "We know the body was refrigerated until it was picked up. If the body hasn't been cremated, we can get what we need. If it has"— I turned to Robinson— "they walk, right?"

"This is our last chance, Jack. If there's no body, they walk."

"It'll take nearly an hour to get out there. Let's roll."

CHAPTER TWENTY-SIX

THE FUNERAL HOME was located several miles east of town, deep in the exurbs that flow outward from Atlanta like a many-armed Shiva. Nightmare rode in back, Robinson shotgun. We rolled out I-20 to highway 138, turned northeast and began the trek to highway 81. The rising moon was a thin sliver, and in its dim, silver light we watched deeply wooded hills begin to flatten out, and the terrain turn more rural. About ten miles past the county line, I saw the place. It was twenty minutes past eight.

I pulled into the lot, which had only one car, a black, older model Mercedes sedan. "Stay here, Michael," I said. "This shouldn't take too long." I turned to Robinson. "You ready?"

Robinson fingered a syringe kit, then slid it into his breast pocket. "Yeah."

We left the car and walked to the front door of the funeral home. There were no lights on, and it looked deserted. I tried the door, and it was locked. I tried the buzzer; nothing. I tried again. After a while, there was a rustle, and the door opened. A small man of Mediterranean extraction appeared, dressed in street clothes. "We're closed," he said. "Can I help you?"

"I'm hoping we're not too late," I said.

"Too late?"

"This is . . ." *Here goes nothing.* "Mr. Harrison," I finished, mumbling the name a little. "He was held up in Charlotte. He insisted I drive him out here for a moment with his dear brother."

"Mr. Harrison," the man repeated, looking confused.

"Brought in yesterday," I said. "For cremation."

"Harriman," the man said, brightening. "For a moment, I thought you said Harrison. My hearing's not the best."

"That's right," I said. "Mr. Harriman."

"Well, like I say, we're not open. But you've driven all the way out here. I'm not going to send you away, under the circumstances. Come on in."

The man stood away from the door; Robinson and I entered the funeral home. We walked down a long, dingy hallway decorated in cheap, generic melancholy. The lighting was subdued, the carpet worn, and the walls covered in a crimson wallpaper. "Gene D'Anofrio," the man said, shaking hands. He gave Robinson a sympathetic look. "So sorry about your brother. I didn't receive any details."

Robinson was smart enough to nod somberly and keep his mouth shut. "Mr. Harriman's just hoping to have a moment alone to pay his respects," I said. "They were very close."

"Of course."

We turned a corner, and D'Anofrio led us toward a large double door. "I was worried we might have been too late," I said.

"No, your brother is right here," D'Anofrio answered. "Plenty of time."

D'Anofrio opened the door, and we followed him into a small, paneled room. There were a handful of plush, upright chairs upholstered in dark red. "Well, if you two gentlemen will hold on a moment, I'll bring Mr. Harriman on in."

"Thanks," I said. "We appreciate it." D'Anofrio disappeared through a side door. Once we were alone, I said, "Is he just going to wheel him in here on a gurney?"

"I don't care if he carries him on his back, I just need two minutes alone with him. Can you keep D'Anofrio busy?"

"No problem." We sat silently for several minutes, until the quiet was broken by a recording of organ music coming through mounted speakers. "God," Robinson said, "he's pouring it on."

"He's just being decent," I said. "And in a couple of minutes, you're going to redeem all this madness with a few cc's of Townsend's blood."

Robinson nodded. We stayed still until the door opened again. There was no gurney. There was no body. D'Anofrio entered carrying a small, bronze-colored urn, which he placed on a felt-covered stand. He nodded somberly, backed out of the room, and closed the door behind him.

Robinson and I sat alone, staring at what contained the charred, microbiotically clean dust that had been Doug Townsend. His priceless DNA, once hidden in the proteins of his cell structure, was now obliterated. "Fuck," Robinson said. "With no disrespect to the dead, but fuck." He stood, repeated his sentiments, and walked out of the room.

With Robinson gone, I sat alone in a dimly lit room with Doug Townsend, college friend with the big heart and the out-of-bounds love for an opera singer. I had not protected him in life, and I had not avenged his death. And I had to answer for my own weakness toward Michele, the middle spoke of the entire wheel. She had opened me up in a way that I had feared would never happen again. And then used me for her own tortured purposes.

I walked to the bronze urn, put my hands on it, and bowed my head. "God, in Whom I do not believe, I present exhibit A, proof that there is no clarity in this world. There is only mess, and more mess. The evil flourish. The good—who, I freely admit, are pretty screwed up themselves—die young. You do not intervene in these atrocities, and therefore, You are null and void. Wherever You are and whatever You are doing, it would not appear to be anywhere near the city of Atlanta, Georgia."

I turned and walked out the door. Robinson and Nightmare were waiting. It was going to be a long drive home.

No one spoke for at least twenty minutes. The miles slipped past silently, a dead pall on the three of us. Around ten we hit the city's unremitting traffic—ever churning, no matter the hour—turning the trip into fits and starts of progress. "God, I hate this town," Robinson said, breaking the silence. "I'm thinking I'll move. Maybe out west."

Nobody answered, which seemed about right. Fifteen minutes later, I looked over at Robinson. Something had happened; he was sweating like a dog. "You okay?" I asked. Robinson glanced over at me, then back at the road. He looked like he'd seen a ghost. "Seriously," I said, "you don't look too good. You want me to pull over or something?"

"We didn't get them," he said. "They got away."

"It's all right," I said. "They have no reason to bother any of us, now."

"We have to get them, Jack."

"We can't. You got to let it go, now. They played better than we did, and it's over."

Robinson nodded an assent, but he continued to unravel right before my eyes. Disturbingly, he started the same grating conversation with himself he had when I'd been telling him about my meeting with Ralston. Nightmare leaned forward from the backseat and got a look at Robinson. "What's up with him?" he asked. "He's going bat-shit."

"Shut up, Michael." But he was right. Robinson was melting down. *I should have seen this coming. He had too much at stake to lose.* "Hang on," I said. "I'll have you back to your car at Grayton in a few minutes."

Robinson grabbed my arm and squeezed. "Listen to me, Jack. We have to get them. There's still a way."

"What are you talking about?" I said. "You told me this was it. No Doug and they walk, right? You have to have the blood of a survivor. No survivor, no case."

"Yeah," Robinson said, nodding his head. "But I can make a new survivor."

I looked up ahead; there was an exit a few hundred yards away. I took it, rolled down to the stop sign at the bottom, and pulled off the road. I jammed the car into park. "We've been through this," I said. "You're not going to give that drug to anybody, Doctor. You'd go to jail for the rest of your life. Reckless endangerment. Medical malpractice. Even attempted murder."

"Me," Robinson said. "I can give myself Lipitran. The drug will generate the enzymatic response, and I can do the spectrometry on my own blood."

"Calm down. You're getting too excited."

"Me, Jack. I can give it to myself."

"But this is all theory," I said. "If you're wrong . . ."

"Dead," Robinson said. "Blow up from the inside out. Blood everywhere. Boom."

"He's right," Nightmare said. "We can still get them."

I turned to Michael. "Shut up, I'm telling you." I looked at Robinson. "You're not in a great frame of mind right now," I said. "You've had a bad few weeks. It's not a good time for you to start giving yourself experimental drugs."

"There's nobody else," Robinson said. He was clenching the armrest. "I can't give the drug to anybody else. FDA pulled it. Felony to administer it after that, Jack. So nobody else. I can give it to me."

"It's a felony even to give it to yourself," I said.

"Nobody else, Jack. I know I'm right. Take the drug, watch those enzymes come to life. Then we'll get the bastards. It's simple proteomics, see? Take my blood. Run it through the mass spectrometer. *Boom. Boom, boom, boom.*"

"There is no conceivable way I'm letting you do this."

"Doesn't matter," Robinson said. His eyes were staring out, unblinking. He was out on the edge, dancing with madness, holding himself together with a supreme act of will. "I'm doing it. You can't stop me, can't stop. So go fuck yourself, because I'm doing it."

"I can take you to a hospital for psychiatric evaluation."

Robinson laughed edgily. "I'm a doctor, you idiot. I'll tell them *you're* insane."

"Damn it, this is crazy."

"Says you. I'm doing it."

I looked out the windshield. Cars were flashing by our left, accelerating from the stop sign. Life was going on all over Atlanta. Good guys and bad guys and everything in between. And sitting beside me was a guy willing to stake what was left of his barely sustainable life on the chance to redeem himself and the deaths of eight mostly innocent people. I'll tell you why I didn't stop him. First, because it wasn't my decision to make. But second, because he had just taken Sammy's philosophy and armed it with a nuclear warhead. He had let *everything* go, even his own life. There may never have been anybody so dangerous in the history of Atlanta. If anybody was going to get Ralston, it would take that kind of commitment. "How long will it take?" I asked quietly.

Robinson's left eye was developing a tic. "Don't know," he said, "Longer is better, more pronounced response. Bigger dose, too. Bigger, longer. Eight hours. Twelve hours, maybe."

"Shit," I whispered to the sky, and we disappeared back onto the freeway, a miscreant, an unhinged scientist, and a lawyer with no faith left. The three fucking musketeers.

CHAPTER TWENTY-SEVEN

IT WAS ANOTHER THIRTY MINUTES to Grayton Labs. During the drive, Robinson calmed down; having made his choice, he shored himself up. It was nearly ten when we dragged back into the parking lot. Robinson walked us past security. The rest of the place was deserted.

I fell into an office chair on wheels, rolling to a stop after a few feet. Nightmare stood, hands in pockets, looking like Dracula caught in sunshine. Robinson was talking to himself, muttering something inaudible. "Look, you don't have to do this," I said quietly. "Killing yourself won't bring those people back to life."

Robinson jerked his head around. "What about the rest?" he asked. The tic had come back, but his voice was still level. He was making peace with his risk. "All the people who Lipitran was supposed to save? The liver transplants that won't be necessary? The deaths from cancer? The chronic fatigue, the loss of quality of life? What about them?"

"I can't answer that."

"I'm a doctor," Robinson said. "I *heal*. And if the only way to do it is to inject myself with Lipitran AX, then so be it." He walked over to the far side of the lab, dropped to his haunches, and opened a small refrigerator. He pulled out a small glass vial, and closed the door. He brought the vial over to us, and pulled out the syringe he had taken to the funeral home. "Two years' work, and thirty-five million dollars." He held it up, and the overhead light glinted through the clear liquid. "All a huge waste, unless this works." He prepared the syringe and pressed the needle through the rubber top of the vial. He withdrew 5 cc's, then hesitated. He pulled back the stopper a little further, going to 7 cc's, then 10. I started to protest, but he shook his head. "Don't," he said. "It doesn't matter, now. Either I bring them down, or I couldn't care less."

Robinson sat at a table. He was sweating, beads of perspiration forming on his forehead. He wiped them off, then picked up a rubber ball. He pumped the ball with his hand, filling his forearm with blood. He pulled out a brown strip of elastic, tied off his bicep, and started flicking his wrist to get a vein to rise.

Nightmare and I stared. Nobody spoke. I didn't know if what he was doing was brave or crazy, but it wasn't my decision to make. Robinson had cast his die. If he was wrong about Ralston, he would die in agony like his patients. There was nothing more. Robinson looked up at me, our eyes locking in a sudden, terrible moment. He pressed the needle into his arm, his eyes widening slightly at the puncture. Then, he slowly, methodically, pressed the stopper down, emptying 10 cc's of Lipitran AX into his body.

Time became an enemy. If it had been difficult waiting while the lab was full of people, doing it in a deserted building was like dragging ourselves through setting concrete. The minutes passed like hours.

Robinson tried to send me home; he needed several hours before it was worth doing a test. The work would be tedious, and screwing it up would make the awful risk he had taken meaningless. I was an automaton, not having had any real sleep in more than twenty-four hours, but I couldn't leave him. Maybe the drug would kill him, maybe not. But at least I could stand watch.

Robinson, now in a cold sweat, staggered into his office. He fell down into his chair and closed the door. Nightmare started after him, but I caught him by the arm. "Leave him," I said. "He needs some time alone. He might fall asleep, which would be a blessing. You should do the same."

"Me? I'm all right. You look like shit, though."

I smiled. "Yeah."

"You can trust me, you know. I mean, if you're worried about leaving me alone with the doc."

"I'm not worried, Michael," I said, and I wasn't. But he was right; without sleep, I was in no position to help Robinson with any tests. I turned off the lab lights, went back to my chair at the far end of the lab, and fell into it. For the next couple of hours, I drifted in and out. Nobody came into the lab, not even security. Robinson's banishment was total. We were untouchable, lepers in a world designed to cure the sick.

Around two in the morning, I went to check on Robinson. I opened the door cautiously, unsure of what I would find. But when I looked in, he was sitting up, staring straight ahead. I was certain he hadn't slept. He had been feeling every sensation in his body, terrified he was moments away from an internal breakdown of horrifying consequences. "You okay?" I asked.

He looked at me, his eyes hollow. "Yeah. Thanks."

"How do you feel?"

"I don't know. Some nausea. Nothing too bad. As predicted."

"So we're okay."

Robinson gave a weak smile, then looked back at the wall. I closed the door behind myself, then woke up Nightmare, who had been dozing in a chair. "You hungry?"

Nightmare looked up and asked, "How's the doc?"

"He's okay. Scared, I guess."

Nightmare nodded, closing his eyes again. I pulled up a chair, rolled it next to Robinson's office door, and fell into it.

The night passed in fits and starts; at one point, Robinson walked out of his office, eyes still staring, and grabbed my arm. "Seven hours," he said. "I'm not dead."

"No."

"Couple more. We'll wait a little longer."

A few hours later, the sun began coming up. A little before nine, I knocked softly on his office door. There was no response, and I opened the door; Robinson was slumped over his desk. I quickly moved toward him; as I approached he sighed, and I realized he was sleeping. It had been more than nine hours, in the range he had said necessary for the enzymatic response to be easily measurable. I gently nudged his shoulder, and he started awake.

"It's okay," I said, quietly. "You're fine. You were sleeping."

Robinson sat up in his chair, preternaturally alert. He sat breathing, taking stock of himself. He reached over, pulled out a wastebasket, and vomited into it violently. It was a terrible moment, until he straightened back up, coughed, and said, "Thank God. I've needed to do that for hours."

"You mean you're okay?"

"Yeah. Like I said, the nausea was a part of things. I feel better." He stood. "I'm . . . I'm all right. What did you do, just sit up all night?"

"I was in and out. In, mostly."

"I appreciate it."

"So you're alive. Tell me how this thing works."

Robinson nodded and said, "Meet me in the lab. I've got to clean up."

I went out into the main lab area, woke up Nightmare, and together we waited for Robinson to return. He opened the big doors a few minutes later, carrying a paper cup of water. He set his cup down and pointed to a large, rectangular machine shaped like a casket, six feet long and two across. It was humming quietly. "QTOF tandem mass spectrometer," he said. "With the electrospray ionization source, they're four hundred thousand each. We have two of them."

I pointed to the machine. "So what's this thing do?"

Robinson brightened incrementally—it was a small change, but noticeable. I could see it then, the spark I had first witnessed at the park when we met. He was a junkie, and research was his drug.

"What this thing does," he said, "is truly beautiful. Measures the mass of blood components. That lets you isolate the likely possibilities for enzymes. Everything has a specific mass, and you don't want to waste time on nonproductive elements." Robinson led us to a long table filled with instruments. "The point is to find the enzymes that are in a survivor's blood that are lacking in the dead patients. I'm the survivor . . ." He looked at us meaningfully. "So far, anyway. I'm using Najeh Richardson, one of the dead patients, for the other blood specimen. I want to isolate the metabolizing enzyme I have he lacks."

"How?"

Robinson smiled. "You won't believe me."

"Why not?"

"Because you won't believe how elegant and simple and beautiful it all is. You'll think it's magic, only it isn't; it's just beautiful, lovely science." Robinson looked at us. "What's red and blue make? Think back, school days. Red and blue. Mix them together. What do they make?"

"I don't know. Purple, I guess."

"Purple!" Robinson's energy spiked upward, his fatigue receding. "Damn right, purple." Now come here," he said. "Look at these."

Nightmare and I followed Robinson to the end of the table. "You extract the blood of both subjects, me and Richardson. Remember, you want to find out what's in mine that isn't in his."

"Right."

"You spin out the red blood cells, some other things that don't matter to you. The point is, you're left with the protein extracts. A few thousand proteins from each sample." He picked up two small, rectangular slides of glass. "You use a voltage to spread my proteins out on one slide, the ones from Richardson on the other. You with me?"

"Yeah," I said, doubtfully.

"Next, you dye my samples red, and Richardson's blue. Then you combine them on a 2-D gel."

"Which means?"

"You overlay them on top of each other, until they're completely mixed together." He looked at us. "So what does red and blue make?"

"Purple," I said.

"Yeah." Robinson opened his arms, as though he had just said something profound. He saw my blank look and said, "Think, damn it. So what happens?"

"I got no idea."

Nightmare came to life. "Red and blue, on top of each other. Any components that are in both samples turn purple. A red part *and* a blue part. Any components that are only in one sample stay their original color. Red *or* blue. The unique ones would stand out like crazy."

Robinson's smile was so genuine, I wanted to cry. If he went down over this, it was going to be a loss for humanity. But he was still vibrating on pure science. "Exactly."

"How long does all that take?" I asked.

"There's a lot of prep time. When I finish the gels, there are likely to be quite a few unique proteins, and most of them have nothing to do with Lipitran. They're just unique qualities to each person. I can narrow them down, leaving a handful of likely candidates. I'll trypsonize the protein extract of those to get their amino acid sequences. Then I can go onto the NIH site, compare them with the human genome, and identify the precise enzyme." He paused. "For one person working alone, at least two full days. But with help . . ." He pointed to Nightmare. "You want a job?"

Nightmare looked around, as though Robinson must have been talking to someone else.

"Hell, yeah," he said. "What do you want?"

"Every second of your life until this is over." Nightmare smiled, possibly the first smile of his life not tinged with sarcasm and irony. Robinson turned to me. "You should go home," he said. "Change clothes. Take a shower, for God's sake."

"Are you going to live?"

"Apparently. The point is, you can't help here. What are you going to do, baby-sit for a day and half? And as far as Ralston's concerned, Doug's body is cremated and we're no threat to him. We're working free."

I sighed, deep with fatigue. "Yeah, I'll go change, take a shower. I'll call you."

Robinson shook his head. "Get some sleep, Jack. I'll call you when we get closer to any results."

I motioned for Nightmare, and he followed me out into the hallway. "You did good, Michael," I said. "How's it feel?"

Nightmare smiled. "Weird."

"I have a reward."

"What's that?"

"Do you have any money?"

"Guess you forgot how we met."

"Yeah. But seriously, can you get any? From your parents, or anybody?"

He paused for a while, considering. "My parents," he said. "They're stinking rich."

I paused a second, then burst out laughing. "You little counter-culture shit," I said. "The only reason you turned into an anarchist is your parents could afford to pay your rent."

"Don't make me laugh."

"I'll laugh for both of us. Of all the hypocritical—"

"Hey, it's not easy growing up like that."

"Yeah. But there is a trust fund, isn't there?"

Nightmare's pasty face turned red. "Yeah, whatever," he said.

"Millions?"

"A few," he said. "But not till I'm thirty-five. They don't trust me, the little—"

"Save it," I said, interrupting him. "Beg them for a few thousand. Whatever you can get. Steal it from Radio Shack, I don't care. Imagine somebody is going to kill you if you don't get it. That's how serious I am. And tell Robinson to do the same thing."

"What are you driving at, dude?"

"There's more than one kind of revenge, Michael. Wait and see."

*　　　*　　　*

I dragged myself home, nearly asleep by the time I got there. Robinson was safe behind the guarded gates of Grayton, and I was hoping for a few hours sleep. I walked in the apartment, looking around suspiciously for signs of disturbance. But everything was in its place. I locked the door behind me, pulled off my pants, and fell onto the bed. I slept about four hours, which I badly needed. When I woke, it was nearly three in the afternoon. I took a shower and changed clothes, both of which gave me a burst of energy. My first impulse was to call Robinson. I knew he would only have just started his test, but I just wanted to hear his voice and make sure he wasn't turning to chaos inside himself. I walked back to the living room and stared at the answering machine, which was still blinking. Reluctantly, I pushed play. The messages spilled out into the dead air of my apartment. There were a couple from Blu, wondering where I was. The original message from Billy, asking me to call back. And then my world turned upside down again, because the last message on the machine was playing, and the voice was Michele's. She had called only a few hours ago.

Jack, it's me. Can we meet? We need to talk. Things have gotten . . .I'm sorry about the way things got. I told you not to show yourself at the speech, darling. Can we meet tonight? I wish you were here. I need to see you. So much has happened, so much madness. About nine, tonight, at your office? Can you? I love you.

I sat back against my couch, listening to her voice. In the last seventy-two hours, I had been lectured by Derek Stephens, had my secretary resign, had my car run off the road, been kidnapped, wrapped with duct tape and thrown in a closet, escaped, gone through a pointless exercise at a funeral home, and watched Thomas Robinson risk his life trying to find some reason for his life's work. I had done these things because I wanted justice, and because I was in love with a woman who I believed was married to a murderer.

I was not immune to the fact that she had lied to me about her husband knowing the truth about her. Hearing her—disembodied for once, absent her intoxicating presence—I admitted that I didn't actually know how deep the lies went. What had she said? *Maybe you can tell me how that works, Jack. How a woman whose entire life is a lie finds the right moment to stop.*

It wasn't that discovering she'd lied to me meant I couldn't love her. Trust is rigid—it snaps like a dry twig—but love is elastic. When a woman you care about is drowning, you don't give her a personality test, you throw her a rope. But there was still an open question about what happened afterward. Loving a woman like Michele was a high-stakes enterprise, and I had already paid one hell of a price. I was wondering how high it would go, and who would end up paying. But sitting there listening to her voice, I suddenly realized that there was a way—final, and indisputable—to bring trust and love together again or to separate them forever. The real story of Michele Sonnier was buried in the court records at the Fulton County Courthouse, and my best friend had the keys. If I hurried, I could catch Sammy before he left.

CHAPTER TWENTY-EIGHT

AT LEAST I COULD BEGIN with good news. "You don't die, Sammy," I said. "You live."

I had managed to catch Sammy before he left, at about four-thirty. I pulled him into his small office, sat him down, and closed and locked the door. After I laid out for him what Stephens had told me about the car, Sammy looked up warily; it was obvious that the initial endorphin rush that had come with his declaration of independence had run out about forty-eight hours ago, and he was stoically expecting his beating. "But he's going to have my taxes audited or something, right?"

I shook my head. "Derek Stephens can't have you audited, Sammy."

"Yeah, but you know. I mean, something bad."

"You walk, Sammy. It's the timing. You're lucky."

That last comment was an utterly new concept for Sammy, so it took some time to enter his list of realistic possibilities. "Lucky," he repeated, as though speaking a foreign language. "Me."

"Yeah. He isn't doing anything about the car."

Sammy looked up from his desk. "Because of the quiet period."

"That's right. He can't afford any bad publicity right now. What you did to his car would be on Letterman by tomorrow."

"Right."

"So if you can just lay low for a while, you'll be fine." I paused. "By the time the dust settles, maybe you can have moved to Siberia or something."

"Yeah," Sammy said, gradually coming to terms with his extraordinary good fortune. "I can lay low." His smile, although still tentative, was finally beginning to gain strength. "I can lay low, Jackie boy. I can definitely lay low."

"Except for one thing, I mean," I said.

Sammy's face froze in mid-smile. "I knew it," he said sullenly. "He's going to have my knees broken, isn't he?"

"No, no, Sammy. I mean lay low except for one thing."

Sammy's face clung uncertainly to the vestiges of hope. "What are you talking about, Jackie boy?"

"You've got access to all the court records, right?"

Sammy nodded cautiously. "Yeah."

"Even the juvenile ones."

Sammy stood and pointed to the door. "Nice knowing you, Jackie boy," he said, his smile vanished. "I got things I gotta do."

"Hear me out, Sammy."

Sammy sat back down and fixed me in his clerk's gaze. "They're *sealed*, Jack. Which means that the only person who can combine the words 'Sammy,' 'access,' and 'juvenile records,' is His Honor, Judge Thomas Odom."

"But all I'm saying, Sammy, is that you do have access. You go down there all the time."

"That's right. For *Odom*."

I tried to keep it light. "Because he needs to know what the little beasties were up to before they showed up in his court. And what I'm saying is, it wouldn't be that big of a deal for you to make a request for one more person while you were down there."

"You're dreaming."

"Sammy, I need this."

"And I need my job."

"It's not going to cost you your job." Those were words I definitely needed to believe, because Sammy's job was the single connection between him and a meaningful life. It was his reason for being, his entrance into that part of society that wore decent suits and said please and brought him drinks in clean glasses.

"Why," Sammy said, "should I do this for you?"

"Because I am on the precipice, Sammy. I am being asked to help a very disturbed woman."

Sammy stared. "It's that girl. Ralston's wife."

"Yeah."

Sammy whistled. "Damn, Jackie. She is seriously under your skin."

"This, from a man who risked all for—"

"I know," Sammy interrupted. "But that was a hell of a statement. You gotta admit."

I nodded. "Listen, Sammy, Stephens didn't just talk about you. He had quite a bit to say about Michele, too."

"So?"

"So he says . . ." I paused, hating the idea of finishing the sentence. "He says she's nothing but a talented liar. He says I'm confused by this voodoo chemistry she has. He says she's the special kind of sick who gets her jollies by manipulating a man to get what she wants. And the thing is, Sammy, is that even though I love her, I am not fool enough to believe that what Stephens is saying is outside the realm of possibility." I felt nauseous, but I was determined to face things head-on. "The truth is lying somewhere in the basement of the building we're in right now. And you have access to the records. Five minutes with that file, and I find out who's lying."

"She is."

"How do you know?"

"I don't. It's just easier that way. You get to walk off."

"I'd like nothing better. But it turns out she's married to a murderer."

Sammy exhaled. "I wouldn't throw that kind of statement around, Counselor, not unless you can prove it."

"I'm working on that. What matters right now is that eight people are dead, and Ralston killed them. Well, Ralston and Stephens."

"Jesus, Jack. Are you sure about that?"

"Reasonably."

"Because seriously, Jackie, this is my ass."

"I know. But there's no other way. I've got to know, one way or another."

Sammy looked at me a second, then stood. "You're going to have to buy me a bar to pay me back for this. You realize that."

"Yeah. I know. Look, she had a different name back then. It's Fields, T'aniqua." I picked up a pen and scribbled the name on a piece of paper.

Sammy looked at the paper awhile, then looked up. "All right, God damn it. Anything for love."

"Thanks, Sammy."

Sammy picked up his briefcase. "Shut up and wait here. Don't talk to anybody, don't answer the phone, and don't open the door unless it's me. I'll be back in few minutes."

I don't claim to have known for sure that Sammy would help me, but I was hopeful, simply because I understood him so well. On the one hand, Sammy Liston was damaged goods. His mood alternated between a poignant bitterness over his underachievement and an unrequited lechery for unavailable women. But on the other hand, when it comes to stripping things down and letting them go, he is a Jedi master. Underestimating him in that department is a serious mistake. After about fifteen minutes Sammy walked in, sweating nervously.

"You didn't look like that while you were doing it, did you?"

"Like what?"

"Like you were robbing a bank."

Sammy closed the door behind him, went behind his desk, and opened the briefcase. He tossed out an old, faded manila folder. "You got ten minutes."

"It's an inch thick."

"Then you better get started."

I nodded and opened the folder. There were at least a fifty pages of material, some of it twenty years old. There wasn't time to go page by page, so I scanned sections at a time, piecing together her life history. *Born: Atlanta, Georgia, Fulton County Hospital. May 17, 1974. Mother: Tina Kristen Fields. Father: unknown.*

The pages revealed the litany of foster parents, six in all. It was, to put it mildly, the kind of horrifying childhood shuttling between miseries that inspired Dickens. Whatever pain Michele Sonnier carried on stage with her, she had earned it. But unlike what Stephens had said, there was no record of any criminal activity. I flipped to the end of the file, searching for records of the birth of her daughter. Near the back, I found the juvenile court's decision. I scanned through the legalese until I found these words:

> *Although Miss Fields may well desire to remain with the child once she is delivered, the court must act in the interest of the infant. In this case, these interests are enormously complicated by the status of the mother. She is herself dependent on foster care, and therefore, may not reasonably assume the obligations of motherhood herself. Likewise, her foster parents have made clear they cannot take on the responsibilities of a newborn, nor are they inclined to attempt to teach Miss Fields to be a mother. The court sees no viable means of keeping mother and daughter together in the same home. Placing them together in another home would be extremely difficult, time-consuming, and not without its own risks. At this point, the court feels the only possible course of action is to place the child in protective custody.*

I looked up at Sammy. "Is this everything? Stephens said she had several run-ins with the police."

"If it's not in there, it doesn't exist."

I flipped through the pages again. "The court took her away, but there's nothing about any drug flap. They didn't drag the kid out of her house. She never got home with the baby." I stood and shook Sammy's hand. "You're my hero."

Sammy smiled and picked up the folder. "Get out of here before you ask me any other favors."

I left Sammy's office, got in my car, and called the direct line to Robinson's lab. Nightmare answered. "It's me," I said. "Tell me what's happening."

"Everything's okay. Robinson threw up again awhile back, but he said it was normal."

"Has he drawn the blood?"

"Yeah. He waited as long as he could stand it, because we won't have time to do the testing twice. We've been at it a couple of hours. He figures maybe twelve more with both of us working to get a result."

"You hanging in okay?"

"I guess. Every time he coughs, I think he's going to explode."

"You're both going to have to sleep before you can finish," I said. "There's no way you can run straight through and not make mistakes."

"Naw, it's not like that. Robinson says the last five or six hours are just waiting on NIH to match the enzyme to the human genome. We'll crash then."

"Okay. Just relax, Michael. I'll be there later tonight. If anything changes, call me."

"Yeah, no problem." The phone clicked off.

Judging by Robinson's estimates, there wouldn't be a result until tomorrow morning, at the earliest. I was staring at three hours before I met Michele. The truth was, I needed the time. Given Ralston's merciless worldview of people as nothing but chemistry, it didn't bother me that we might be hours away from bringing his house down around him. But it wasn't just Ralston and Stephens who were about to have their world turned upside down. Michele would be caught in the crossfire of their destruction, and that was a different matter entirely.

The world is too big a mess to believe in unstained lovers, and I had come to terms with how she had handled her life. Born into hell, she had used her tools of survival in earnest. But she wasn't like her husband. Whatever precious there is about the human soul remained and even thrived, in spite of what she had been through.

And that made her more than valuable. When she sang, it made her spectacular.

If Robinson's theory checked out, there would be lawsuits that engulfed Horizn, certain to require her deposition. There would be publicity-hungry tabloids, anxious to expose her colorful past. But in spite of everything, I believed she would survive. There are some people who remind us of what it means to be human, even in their flaws. That was the first moment when my mind truly settled, when I knew how much I wanted to see her again. Loving Michele wasn't a replay of Violeta Ramirez. Loving Michele was something I was going to do with my soul.

I got to my office a little early, looking around. Michele's car wasn't there yet. I got out and walked across the lot, going upstairs to wait. I took the stairs to my second-floor office, opened the door, and hit the lights. The door to my private office was open, and a small light was on. I walked over, pushed the door open, and saw a figure sitting in my chair, facing away from me. The chair slowly turned, revealing Derek Stephens. He wasn't smiling. He also had a gun.

"Close the door," he said. He looked at me calmly. "So Robinson got his head out of his ass long enough to figure things out."

"Where's Michele? I swear to God, if you hurt her, I'll rip your head off."

Stephens ignored my question. "Pretty smart of you, hacking into our photo recognition software." *Please, God, tell me Nightmare didn't sell us out again.* "Trying to help Robinson was a bad idea," Stephens said. "Everything was tidy. And now, more people have to die." Stephens looked annoyed. "Let me ask you something, Jack. Why do you continue to believe in your failed values when they're so clearly not working? Your idiotic insistence on justice is now going to cost you everything."

"You'll lose. Don't ask me how. But somehow, someday, you'll lose."

Stephens shrugged. "I don't like wasting such valuable commodities, but I can't make your choices for you."

"You'll probably get over it. Now tell me where Michele is."

"I'm a human being, Jack. I don't like killing. Especially when people of quality are involved."

"There are eight people in McDaniel Glen who would like to talk to you about that, only they can't, because they're dead."

Stephens shook his head dismissively. "I'm not talking about them. I mean people like you."

"What do you mean, 'like me'?"

"People with something to offer."

"White people, you mean."

Stephens shrugged. "Doug sealed his own fate by getting on the Lipitran program. Looking back on it, I should have anticipated that possibility. Nobody on earth knew more about how effective Lipitran was going to be. After all, he provided the information to us."

"So he took the initiative and put himself on the test."

Stephens nodded. "I didn't tell Charles about it. Cleaning up messes like that is my job."

"Here's an antiquated idea for you, Derek. You're a bastard. Doug had no idea what you were going to do. If he had, he would never have helped you."

"I regretted having to kill him. I couldn't care less about the others."

"I wonder how Ralston would take your particular brand of racism."

"He would agree completely."

"Oh yeah, I forgot. He hates his own people."

Stephens laughed derisively. "His people?" he jeered. " His people are vacations in St. Bart's and courtside seats to the Hawks. It's art openings and investment banking. Race has nothing to do with skin color, Jack. It hasn't for at least a decade."

"Where does Michele fit in?" I asked.

His expression darkened. "She's too well known to disappear, but we can't let her continue to blow up all the time. We've tried to manage her, but it's become too dangerous. It was an almost intractable problem, to be honest. I was deeply concerned. And then, she was kind enough to solve it herself."

"Which means?"

Stephen shrugged. "How do you kill a famous person? It's almost impossible, unless she's accommodating enough to go of her own volition to one of the most dangerous places in America."

I felt like ice. "She's in the Glen."

"Of course she's in the Glen. And I find this a great irony, Jack. She's there to buy back her conscience." He looked at me. "Sorry she couldn't make her appointment with you. But Jamal Pope called to say he had her daughter waiting, and that in exchange for a great deal of money, she can have her. She was to call no one, and come alone. That is an invitation she found irresistible."

"You're paying Pope to kill her."

"Apparently he's very good at that kind of thing. Tomorrow's papers will show that Michele Sonnier, driven by an unreported drug addiction, foolishly went into the bowels of McDaniel Glen in search for what she wanted. Unfortunately, she happened upon some members of a gang who had plans for her seventy-thousand-dollar car. There was an argument, and she lost."

"And that's the end of her life? A frame-up about a drug deal gone bad?"

Stephens looked unconcerned. "It's the kind of mundane thing that actually happens, which makes it perfect."

"And me?"

Stephens got his faraway look again, the one he used when he wanted to detach from certain details. "You, Sir Gawain? You finally get your wish. What you've wanted from the first is to die for a lady."

I stiffened. "Where did you get that idea?"

"I told you, Jack. I checked up on you. Didn't that girl two years ago die because of your indiscretion? And haven't you believed that your life was not really worth living from that moment on?" He smiled. "I'm giving you the opportunity to make amends for Violeta Ramirez, Jack. You get to go out in a blaze of chauvinistic glory. For God's sake, I'm doing you a favor."

"You said her name."

"Who? Violeta Ramirez?"

I lunged across the desk for him, determined to break his neck. I tackled him chest high, driving the chair back against the wall. He looked up in surprise and anger, and I hit him hard in the gut, forcing his breath out in a gasp. Stephens brought the gun down hard on the back of my neck, and I went down to a knee. Stephens stuck the barrel of the gun into my face. I ground to a halt, the pistol instantly clarifying my mind. Dying without laying another finger on him wouldn't wipe the self-satisfied smile off his face, and it wouldn't do anything to keep Michele alive. The gun's barrel shone in the dim light, shiny and lethal. I backed down, moving away a couple of feet. "Don't misunderstand me, Jack," Stephens said. "Just because I would prefer Pope to do this doesn't mean I can't do it myself. There's too much at stake not to do whatever's necessary."

I kept my eyes locked on the gun, which was a foot from my face. "So what happens now?"

Stephens stood. "It's time to go." He pulled me up, pressing the gun barrel into my ribs. "Story time is over. Move." We walked back through the office and out into the hall. Stephens kept the gun glued to my back as we went down the stairs to street level. Once outside, the street was deserted. He pressed the gun between my shoulder blades and said, "Over there. The gray Ford."

"A Taurus? Kind of low rent for a guy like you."

Stephens kept moving. "It's nondescript." He opened the driver's door and shoved me in. He came in after me, pushing me across the bench seat. He shut his door and pushed the gun into my stomach. A strong bump in the road would probably discharge it. "Here's the rules. If you so much as move, I'll kill you. Then it's just a matter of dropping off your body to Pope and letting him take it from there. You follow?"

"Yeah."

"Good. Now let's go find your girlfriend."

He pulled the Ford out into the abandoned street, making his way toward McDaniel Glen at a steady, unobtrusive pace. We stopped at all the lights, Stephens driving conservatively. Halfway there I said, "You still have Robinson to think about."

Stephens kept his eyes fixed straight ahead. "The doctor is distraught after a second humiliation. He's destroyed yet another employer's fortunes. His life is no longer worth living."

"Think the cops will buy that?"

"Robinson's personal journal is kept on his computer at Grayton. It's been thoughtfully rewritten, impeccably backdated in the computer code for the last month. Investigators will find his mood turns increasingly dour, his faith in himself shaken. He is friendless, ashamed to show his face. He becomes despondent. Eventually, he decides to put a stop to his life. It's all there, line after painful line. The chronology will withstand any level of scrutiny."

"And Michael?"

Stephens laughed. "He is Doug's successor, in every sense of the word. So troubled, so easily controlled." He turned and looked at me. "Who do you think handled Robinson's diary?"

I stared, growing cold inside. The truth was, at that moment I had no idea if Nightmare was helping Robinson or making sure the tests were scuttled. And if Stephens had anything to do with it, I would never know.

It was about a twenty-minute drive to the Glen. The streets were relatively clear, and we moved down the freeway anonymously, just another of the scattered cars on the road. When Pryor Street approached, he pushed the gun harder into my stomach. "Don't get any ideas. Pope has the back of the Glen cleared for the next hour."

We pulled off Pryor and slowed for the entrance to the Glen. Stephens turned left into the project, rolling down A Street toward the back of the subdivision. There were a few people around, but apparently the word had got out to mind your own business. Nobody even glanced as we rolled past.

We drove slowly through the Glen, turning left again at the far end of the project. These units were the most isolated, their backs butting up against the iron gates that surrounded the city within a city. Stephens brought the car to a stop and unlocked the door. "If you make a wrong move, I'll kill you on the spot." He opened his car door and slid out, keeping his gun on me. "Move," he said. I slid out after him, and he grabbed me by the arm, pushing me in front of him. We moved together down the dark sidewalk a few feet, and I felt the gun barrel pushing left to go around a corner. I obeyed, walked behind a building, and saw the one thing I most did not want to see: Michele and Pope. A second, younger girl was firmly in Pope's grasp. I had no doubt it was Briah. Stephens, seeing the young girl, cursed and pushed me along faster.

"Something wrong?" I asked.

Stephens jabbed the gun barrel into my ribs. "Shut up and walk."

Michele, hearing Stephens's voice, whirled to face us. Her face was contorted with pain. "Jack! God, help me, Jack."

Briah stood beside Pope, leaning slightly. Her eyes were glassy; there was no doubt she was high. She was watching us, rocking a little from side to side. Physically, she was a startling image of her mother, only younger. This was Michele before she had reinvented herself, the girl she had left behind fourteen years ago. For Michele, it would have been like looking in a childhood mirror.

"What the hell is this?" Stephens said. "The girl's not supposed to be here for this."

Pope looked annoyed. "You're early. Ain't you got a watch?"

Stephens went off on a tirade. "Hammond showed up early. But have you lost your mind? The Briah thing was only a setup, you fool. You weren't supposed to actually try to do a trade."

Pope's voice turned threatening. "Nobody calls me fool."

"You're bringing another person into the equation. It's messy. You don't know what you're doing."

Instinctively, I started looking for cover. I knew what Stephens, apparently, did not: disrespecting Pope in his world was a life-and-death decision. This was no boardroom, this was the Glen, and in the Glen Pope wasn't just a CEO, he was his own enforcing militia. Pope, as if on cue, calmly reached behind his back and pulled out a Glock 20, one of the highest-powered handguns on earth. Its bullets explode on impact, carving a hole of flesh in the victim's interior twelve inches across. By comparison, Stephens's gun was a toy. Pope waved the pistol in the air, not directly at Stephens, but there wasn't any doubt it was a threat. "Let me explain somethin', *bitch*," he said. "You don't own me. If we need some motherfuckin' clarity on that point, let's get onto it."

With the word "bitch," the air instantly turned malignant. A shudder shook through Stephens's body. He was white, he was unfathomably rich and privileged, and a black man who looked like he hadn't showered in two days had just insulted him. "What did you just call me?" he said.

Pope acted bored, which was also bad news. Both men were seriously underestimating the other, and that was a dangerous combination. I tried to make eye contact with Michele, but she was focused entirely on her daughter. "Turn up your hearing aid, *bitch*," Pope said, leaning on the word. "That way I don't have to repeat myself to your sorry ass. If you'd have waited a few minutes, I would have had this shit over with."

Stephens was trembling with anger and frustration. For a second, I thought there was going to be a shoot-out right then. But Stephens hadn't risen to his position of power by being undisciplined. He had too much to lose, and with considerable effort he mastered himself. "You don't complicate billion-dollar deals with this kind of crap," he said. "It's bush league."

"That's *your* money," Pope shot back. He shook Briah, who hung limply in his hand. She looked like she would fall to the pavement if he let go. "This right here is *my* money."

Stephens shook his head. "You don't need to show the girl to get the money."

"She's *from* here, bitch. She ain't a fool, like you. She had to see the girl first."

While Pope and Stephens were arguing, Michele had been inching toward Briah. She was oblivious to anything but her daughter. "Baby," she murmured, her voice catching. She began to weep again, her pain escaping in little sobs. Briah stared at her mother, peering through a chemical haze.

"This is getting out of hand," Stephens said. He pointed at Briah. "Now she's seen me. You follow? She's *seen* me. This was not the deal." He put the gun in my back and pushed me toward Michele. I put my arm around her, steadying her. Michele stayed focused on her daughter. "Baby," she whispered again. "Baby, I'm so sorry."

Pope looked at Michele and put his arm around Briah. "Don't you worry none about her," he told Michele. "She all right. She livin' good."

Strictly speaking, it wasn't smart to open my mouth. But seeing Pope—a man who had made his living off the misery of his own people—act like Briah's sacred protector got a response before I could calculate the results. "With you?" I demanded. "Kept stoned all day? Is that what you call good?"

Before Pope could respond, Michele collapsed back against me. The complex, massive regret was crashing down on her. Even though it was through no fault of her own—or maybe it was, it was such a mess, it was impossible to be sure—she had lost her child. And now she was face-to-face with a living memory of everything she had tried to escape. She fell against me, falling apart in frustration, guilt, and tears. Stephens pulled her away from me, forcing her to stand up. "She's losing it," Stephens said, angrily. "You may run this place, but sooner or later, people are going to get curious."

Michele began to make a high, painful wail of despair. Pope, finally seeing Stephens's point, grabbed Briah by the arm and said, "All right, let's do this bullshit. But not here. Back behind the building."

Seeing Pope manhandle Briah was enough to turn me to killing. I don't mean that in any abstract sense. I mean that I ached for his literal and final demise. But first I wanted to tie him to a chair and force him to watch the loathsome parade of human tragedy he had promulgated. My mind flashed with acts of revenge, knowing that they were futile. If I could have killed Pope where he stood, he would have experienced no deathbed conversion, no sudden regret. His evil was ingrained now, a part of his actual fabric. He would have lost consciousness angry that his plans were screwed up. Still, to kill him would have been something. It would have been a statement of outrage and a valuable public service. The legitimate forces of society had so utterly failed to control him that I was, in that moment, willing to trade several years of my own freedom in exchange for the justice killing him would represent. Pope was already walking away, Briah at his side. Stephens had his hands full with the collapsing Michele, and for a brief moment, I was free. I took a step, and the hard barrel of a gun was once again pressed against the back of my head. "Move," a young, nervous voice said in my ear, shockingly close. It was Rabbit, Pope's son.

At the moment of impending death, things go into slow motion. I remember walking toward the dark back of the alley, my vision narrowed, my senses distorted. My mind was filled with unrelated things: the crunch of my feet on crumbling gravel, unnaturally loud in my ears; a sudden, unexpected puff of wind banging a paper cup against a wall; a single, naked bulb shining in a distant window. I tried to gather my thoughts for some defense, but all I could think about was the gun against my skull, and how the slightest move would make Rabbit impulsively pull the trigger. Judging by his history, he would have even less compunction about killing me than his father would. We marched as a little group down the alley behind the last building of the Glen, until we reached the bricked-off dead end. It stank of urine and sweat and everything horrible about hopelessness and generations of poverty. Michele and I were pushed into a corner of the dead end. She was stiff and unresponsive now, wooden with the truth of failing her daughter a second time. She was murmuring, barely audible, "My baby, my baby." We stood side to side, facing Pope, Stephens, Rabbit, and Briah. The world got smaller and smaller. There was nothing outside these few feet of brick. I pulled Michele into my arms, futilely attempting to shield her. "I'm sorry, darling," I said, and pulled her close against me. She looked up into my face, and we held each other, ready to die.

From out of the darkness, I heard Pope's voice. "Rabbit's gonna do it. He's still a juvenile."

Stephens's voice answered. "I don't give a damn which one of you does it. I just know I paid for it, and I want it done as soon as I'm out of here." There was a dangerous, horrifying silence. Then Stephens said, "You'll have to kill the girl, too."

"I ain't killin' no girl," Pope complained.

"It's your mess, damn it," Stephens said. His voice was getting shrill. What was about to happen wasn't going to get him three years' minimum security and an SEC fine; he was treading into twenty-five years to life. The energy level between the two of them was elevating rapidly. "She shouldn't have been here," he said. "She could have gone right on living her pathetic little life and never known her mother. But now she does know, thanks to you and your greedy little side deal. So you have to take care of her."

"That's bullshit. It ain't my fault you ain't got a watch."

"Dammit, Pope, clean up your mess."

"You didn't pay me no money for her."

I cautiously raised my head and peered into the darkness at the two men arguing. They had turned to face each other, ignoring us for the moment. Pope still had Briah by the arm, and Rabbit held his gun on us. Pope and Stephens were standing about ten feet apart from each other. "I'm not going to argue with you," Stephens said, angrily. "Take care of the girl."

Pope raised his Glock and pointed it at Stephens. The threat, however vague before, had just landed on its target. Pope was seriously angry. "White people all the same," he said bitterly. "You come in here, act like folks in the project ain't worth shit. Kill this one, kill that one. Like black folk ain't nothin' but slaves." He shook Briah, who had come to life enough to realize something bad was happening. She was futilely trying to extricate herself from his iron grip. She had both her hands clawing on his fingers, but Pope barely noticed. "You think I kill people 'cause you snap your fingers?" he said. "Like we breeding stock? That's disrespect."

Stephens was vibrating with frustration. "For God's sake, Pope, what do you want?"

"The price is the same as the other two. Twenty-five thousand dollars."

Stephens stared at Pope's gun. He was on Pope's turf, and he was running out of both time and options. "All right, dammit," he said, at last. "Just do it. The police are going to come through here at some point."

"Don't worry about no police."

"All right. Give me five minutes to get out of here." Stephens whirled and started back toward his car. After several seconds I heard the car door, and he pulled out, heading out of the Glen.

Pope turned to me. He still held Briah by the arm in his iron grip, but she had finally become aware that she needed to get away from Pope as soon as possible. She was clawing at him, and Pope was trying to get her calmed down. He didn't want to have to shoot her in the back if he let her go. "Dammit, girl, settle down a second." Briah was crying, trying to kick him. Finally, she pulled his hand up to her mouth and bit down hard on his hand. The teeth sank down into his flesh with brutal force. He pulled back in surprise and pain. "Dammit girl, what you do that for?" He reached out and backhanded her across the face, knocking her down with a vicious blow. She staggered, fell to her knees, and collapsed onto her side.

There was a wail beside me, as the voice that had made the most beautiful music on earth turned into a shriek of outrage and horror. Michele hurled herself onto Pope like a hurricane. She was a blur of arms and legs and teeth and screaming anger from hell. The sheer frenzy of her attack was breathtaking. She had finally reached the state of pure chaos, of unrestricted freedom where everything she loved had been stripped away and let go. She didn't give a damn what happened next, she just knew she was going to stop Pope from hurting her little girl. She started punching him, pulling his hair and kicking him with total, blind fury.

Rabbit stepped in front of me, the gun at my head. If I even moved, I would be dead. I was forced to watch something horrible. All of Michele's anguished, delayed love for her daughter had surfaced, but Pope was far stronger. Gradually, he began to subdue her. He took some vicious shots, but eventually he got her arm behind her and clamped it down backward with terrific force, forcing her to cry out in pain. She continued to try to hit him with her other arm, but I could see it would be over soon. It took thirty or forty painful seconds for the evil in Pope to overcome the good in Michele. I was trembling with rage, but there wasn't a thing I could do.

And then something terrible and wonderful happened, something that I couldn't have predicted in a million years. A moment of grace flickered tenuously in hell. Briah, for the moment forgotten, cried out, "Mama?" in a desperate, little girl's voice. It was probably the first time she had ever said the word. But she had put together that Pope was about to kill her mother, and whatever chemicals coursed through her body weren't enough to block that out. With that realization, she threw herself at Pope. It was ugly and not particularly forceful, but it did the job. Pope buckled forward, barely holding his balance. His gun skittered across the pavement, stopping about six feet beyond my grasp.

That was the moment I had waited for, the moment I saw it all clearly. I didn't give a damn anymore. Ignoring Rabbit, I lunged low and dove for the gun on the ground. The moment my fingers touched metal there was a loud pop, and a pain like I'd never felt before stabbed through my leg like electric fire. Rabbit had caught me with a bullet in the left thigh. My fingers closed on the gun. I gasped and rolled away, clutching the Glock in my outstretched hand. For once, Pope's jungle reflexes did me a favor; he had shed Michele and was on me in less than a second, preventing Rabbit from finishing me with a second shot. We clutched each other, fighting for control of the gun into a half-standing position. Michele, her fury unabated, jumped on Pope's back and began slamming her fist into his head and neck.

The three of us were in a terrible dance, whirling and moving in a tight group. I got the gun pointed straight up, where at least nobody was going to get accidentally shot. Michele kept pummeling him from below. Pope was immensely strong, but the odds were turning against him. In another few seconds, we would overwhelm him, and the situation would be completely different. "Shoot, dammit!" he yelled to Rabbit. "Shoot the motherfuckers!"

Rabbit didn't need his father's encouragement. He had been trying to get a clear shot, but it was impossible. The mass of bodies was in constant motion, and at this range, a bullet from a gun like his could easily pass through its intended victim and into Pope as well. "Which one?" he cried.

"Either one, dammit!" Pope yelled. I spun Pope around, forcing his back to Rabbit. But Briah wasn't finished. She clambered to her feet and stood, swaying and crying. "Mama, mama," she wept, and began moving unsteadily back toward the three of us. She was a wild card, not quite in control, but a force. If she reached us we would all tumble to the ground, and what would happen next was impossible to predict. Pope saw the movement out of the corner of his eye and said, "Her, damn it! Take her out!"

Rabbit turned to Briah, and the moment of grace flickered again. I don't know if it was because she was a young girl, no older than himself, but he hesitated. He stood woodenly, the gun pointed vaguely in Briah's direction. Suddenly, they were two teenagers, caught up in a horrible, adult world, and they had no business being there. They should have been out on a field, playing catch, or falling in love. They should have been a million places but in the dim light of the Southeast's most desperate housing project. They should have been doing anything else with their lives but playing out a young American tragedy with death in the air. Standing there looking at each other, they were *children*.

For a moment, I thought Rabbit might throw the gun down and walk off. You could feel it; human decency was raising its quiet voice, telling a teenage boy that something was terribly wrong, and even though he was too young to understand how he found himself in this godforsaken back alley of hell, this was a moment when the evil in the world could and should be silenced. Everything froze and the night turned horribly quiet. Briah stood unsteadily in the dangerous air, a human target caught up in a game she had no more chance of understanding than Rabbit. It was the whole universe contained in one second, governments and futile poverty programs and black and white and the collapse of the family, all compressed into one boy whose anger had turned back into sadness and confusion before our eyes. I swear to God, it was the whole history of the world. Rabbit turned and looked at his father, his face covered in sudden confusion. It was in his eyes, like a kind of pleading: *What have you done to me here? How have I turned into this in so few years? Why is the world so unbelievably hard?* But Pope's cold breath blew out the flame. His voice cut across the night air, killing hope; the moment passed, and the world spun once again on its familiar axis. "Shoot her!" he screamed. "Shoot the bitch!"

Rabbit turned to Briah, closed his eyes, and pulled the trigger. But in that awful moment between father and son, Pope had loosened his grip. Michele wrenched free and lunged in front of Briah, taking the bullet full in her own chest. The bullet exploded through her, knocking her backward and collapsing her against the filthy wall. She slammed hard against the brick, her breath forced outward in a great sigh. She looked straight ahead in a frightened, surprised stare, and slid downward toward the pavement. Briah, in shock to have met and lost her mother in a terrible handful of moments, stumbled and fell to the concrete, trembling and sighing in a heap.

Rabbit stared at Michele and Briah, then dropped the gun. He turned woodenly back to his father, his expression blank. He had shut down, his conscience and mind seared into silence. Pope didn't hesitate. He made a lightning-quick move toward the gun. The world turned horrible again, when defending myself meant killing a man in front of his own son. And in spite of the chaos unfolding that night, I knew that inside the fourteen-year-old, budding sociopath called Rabbit, there was still a living, breathing, confused child who desperately wanted to live something like an ordinary life. The question that I had milliseconds to decide was whether or not I was willing to die for that vision.

There was a tremble in my soul, a crack of sound, and my bullet sent Jamal Pope to hell.

The sirens were coming. Rabbit was long gone, and I had no ability to follow. My leg was bleeding profusely, and I couldn't walk anymore. I made my way to Michele, pulling her halfway into my lap. I held her, stroking her hair. Her eyes fluttered open and settled on me. She smiled, reached up, and touched my face. I took her hand, kissed it, and replaced it by her side. I had finally made peace with loving her, and I was losing her the same day. It was unbearable.

"You're going to be okay," I said, pressing her fingers inside mine. "You're going to be fine."

"My baby? I saw . . ."

"She's all right," I said. "Nothing happened to her."

She squeezed my hand. "Can she see me? Jack, darling, I don't want her to see me like this."

I looked across the dark alley to where Briah lay unconscious about fifteen yards away. "No. She's . . . she can't see us. She's fine."

Michele closed her eyes. Her breathing became labored, her chest rising and falling with the effort. She grimaced as pain shot through her body, then let her go. Her eyes opened again, more slowly this time. "I'm back in the Glen, Jack," she said. Her voice was getting whispery now, thinning out as her life ebbed. "Back where I started. It's like nothing happened. I did nothing with my life."

I reached down and held her face in my hand. The pain in my leg was like a hot iron. "You made the most beautiful sound in the world," I said. "You made music for the angels." She smiled then, and my own resolve to be strong crumbled. I began to weep. "I wanted to protect you," I said. "I wanted to protect you so much."

She squeezed my hand weakly and said, "It's all right, darling. It's all right." The sirens had come closer, and a crowd had tentatively begun to gather. With the police arriving, even Pope's threats wouldn't keep people away. I held Michele closer, shielding her from view. She whispered something I couldn't quite make out. I leaned down, and she breathed into my ear, "You'll take care of her, won't you, Jack? You'll take care of my baby?"

"Yes, sweetheart. I promise." With those words, another woman entered my life.

Michele's hand relaxed. She coughed, her body convulsing gently with the exhalation. A thin line of blood appeared at her mouth. I reached down and dabbed it away with my shirt. I couldn't bear the sight of her life draining away. It was like a wound on my own body, a rent across my own soul. I heard car tires screech; it would all be over soon, just a few more seconds. A harsh light flooded the scene, forcing me to squint. In the glare, I saw that Michele's blood had moved beyond her soaked clothing, gathering in an awful pool beside her body. She spoke again, her voice barely audible. "The bullet was Briah's," she said. "It was for Briah."

I kissed her forehead. "That's right, sweetheart. You saved her life. She's going to be fine."

"I was a good mother then, wasn't I, Jack? A good mother?"

I pulled her closer. "Yes, sweetheart. You were a very good mother."

A flashlight forced my hand up to shield my eyes. "Police," a hard, masculine voice said from behind the light. "Let her go and lay down on your stomach."

"It's time to go," Michele said. "Time to let go."

I ignored the police, rocking her gently. "That day, at my apartment. You told me you loved me."

"I remember."

"You said not to say it back. You said it was easier."

"Yes." Her voice was a whisper.

"I do. I want you to know. I do, more than anything." She looked into my eyes, and I knew she understood. "You're going to be fine, sweetheart," I said. "The ambulance is on the way."

I held her gently, my heart breaking into pieces. I wanted to go back in time, to our day in Virginia Highlands, the day when we were perfectly happy and nothing else existed but the sweet exhilaration of each other's presence. I wanted to change everything that happened from that point on, to walk together out of Atlanta and vanish into some quiet, safe world where we could love each other. But it was too late for that. I gently moved the hair from Michele's face, and she looked up at me, her eyes dimming. I watched the light in her go out, the muscles relaxing, her head gently falling back against my chest. Her breathing slowed, and then, with a great sigh, she let go. I reached out and gently closed her eyes, still rocking her in my arms. I felt the cop's hand on my shoulder. It wasn't rough; he realized he had stepped into something finally, ultimately, personal. I could hear the second siren, the ambulance that would be far too late.

"I'm sorry, baby," I whispered to her. "I'm sorry."

There was some confusion, the shock of unknown people pushing near us. The police were in force now, four or five officers rapidly cordoning off the area. The cop knelt down beside me. "You're hit. The ambulance is on the way. Two minutes." I nodded. "The lady," the cop said. "Who is it?"

I looked up at the cop, who was asking a question it would take a book to answer. Michele had spent twenty-eight years trying to answer it, remaking herself into a magnificent woman. Now she had come home, one more victim of the world she had risked everything to leave behind. *She's the Queen,* I thought. *The Queen of McDaniel Glen.* But in the end, I gave the answer that would protect her memory the longest."Fields," I answered. "T'aniqua Fields." There was another shooting pain through my leg, and darkness overtook me. The cop caught Michele in his hands, and I fell unconscious onto the pavement.

CHAPTER TWENTY-NINE

A DIM GLOW became brighter, its light beginning on the outside of my vision, gently penetrating and illuminating inward, growing, until I could feel the brightness through closed eyelids. I fluttered my eyes open, squinting in the harsh, fluorescent lights of a hospital emergency room. Billy Little, his face concerned, was staring into my face. He peered at me a moment, then said, "Yeah, he's coming around. Come take a look." A young, Arab-looking man, no more than twenty-five, appeared over Billy's shoulder. "That's fine, then," he said, in a thick British accent. "The wound drew a lot of blood, but it wasn't that deep. Another half unit, and he'll be fine."

I looked at the doctor, trying to figure out how I had got there. I felt a throbbing in my leg, and the pain brought everything back to me; there was the grapple with Pope, the awful, frozen moment when Rabbit fired his gun. And above all, there was the crushing memory of Michele in my arms, her life ebbing out of her in an unstoppable stream.

Billy took the doctor's place in my field of vision. He touched my shoulder. "You haven't been acting very sensibly lately, Counselor," he said. "I don't expect to be making hospital visits to lawyers."

"Sorry." The word came out in a slur. "What are you doing here?"

"When the doctor says you're able, we're going to have a long talk about why I'm not going to charge you with murdering Jamal Pope," he said. "Not that I mind him being dead."

"It was self-defense," I said, a little clearer.

"Of that, I have no doubt. Get some rest." The doctor told Billy that was enough, and I slipped back into sleep. It was dark, and full of angry dreams. When I awoke, there was early-morning sunlight coming in my room; apparently, I had slept through the night. A new doctor came in shortly after I awoke to check on me. He examined me briefly, and told a nurse to unhook my IV. "You're a lucky man, Mr. Hammond," he said, looking at my chart. "The bullet passed through your lower left thigh, leaving two nice clean holes. We've repaired the vein and replaced your plasma. You're going to be fine."

"When can I leave?"

"In a few hours. Although I'd say your marathon days are over for a while."

I nodded, and he left. My head was clearing, as evidenced by the throbbing in my leg. I didn't ask for any painkillers; I was willing to trade the discomfort for awareness. A few minutes after the doctor finished, Robinson's face appeared. He looked pale and anxious.

"My God, Jack," he said. "What happened to you?"

"You first," I said. "How are you?"

"Me? Between throwing up and running tests, it was one hell of a night. But I'm okay."

"And?"

Robinson smiled with the innocent pleasure of a child. "We got the results from NIH an hour ago. It's just like I said. Those patients were screened, and Ralston and Stephens are going down."

I closed my eyes, letting myself relax into the hospital bed pillow. *They're going down.* I let that news settle on my wounds, both external and internal. It would be enough to ease the pain in my leg. It would fall far short of erasing the ache in my soul. Suddenly, I opened my eyes. "Where's Michael?"

Robinson put his hand on my shoulder. "I know about the calendar," he said quietly. "He confessed, about halfway through the night."

"And you're okay with that?"

"He was scared, and I couldn't have done what had to be done without him. Yeah. We're okay."

Nightmare appeared from behind Robinson, the frazzled look of an all-nighter on him. "Hey," he said. "You look even worse than usual, dude. And that's saying a lot."

"You didn't sell us out, Michael. I'm grateful."

Michael flushed, his pale skin reddening. "Maybe I'll go straight for a while," he said. "See how I like it." He smiled. "But don't get used to it, dude. The dark side is strong."

I sat up cautiously, relieved that all my parts moved as ordered. "What time is it?"

"About seven in the morning," Robinson said. "They'll probably want to keep you a few more hours, just to be safe."

"Get my stuff, because we're leaving now."

Robinson looked surprised. "Not likely," he said. "You don't want to end up back here with your leg bleeding again."

"Then tell them to get in here and wrap it." I said. "We've got two hours to get to Nicole Frost's office at Shearson Lehman. All of us do." I looked at Michael. "Did you get the money together, like I told you?"

Michael nodded. "Thirty-eight hundred bucks. It's all I could get."

"It'll have to do." I turned to Robinson. "Did Michael tell you?"

"Yeah. What's this all about?"

"Did you get it?"

"I don't have any real money, Jack. I've mostly been getting paid in Grayton stock. It seemed like a good idea at the time, when it was selling at about thirty."

"What's it at now?"

"About five."

"How many shares do you have?"

Robinson shrugged. "There was the signing bonus, and everything since then . . . about a hundred and sixty-eight thousand shares, all together."

I was too tired to do the math, but I knew it would be enough. "It's okay," I said. "I'll have to explain while we travel."

"It's all I have," Robinson said. "It's my retirement."

"You gotta do what you gotta do. But if you can trust me, you're going to be glad you did."

Robinson watched me thoughtfully a moment, then nodded. "When I met you I was finished. The only thing left was the funeral. Thanks to you, I've got my life back. So yeah, I can trust you."

"Good. Get me wrapped up, and get Detective Little over here. In exchange for us delivering him on a silver platter the case that makes him a lieutenant, he's going to do us a little favor. And that favor is going to pay you both back for helping me."

The next few hours were lived in spite of a broken heart. There would be time for grief, I knew that. And it would take the shape and form that it took. But for a few hours, I had no choice but to cordon off a seared part of my heart and stay focused. Because I was going to play one final card, and the timing had to be exactly right.

At nine o'clock, Nightmare, Robinson, and I—leg tightly wrapped, and helped by a cane—stood in the lobby of Atlanta's Shearson Lehman offices, looking like hell. We had arrived with not a minute to spare, so no one had cleaned up from the night before. My leg was in a tight bandage, throbbing like crazy; Robinson, managing under the effects of sleep deprivation and a powerful antiviral drug, looked like walking death; Nightmare, meanwhile, was disturbing the ambience of one of Atlanta's most conservative business environments with his previous day's choice of army fatigue pants and a sleeveless, orange-and-black T-shirt for the band System of a Down. Predictably, he was nervous as hell. "Explain this to me again," he said, vibrating slightly.

"I've gone over it the whole way over here," I said.

"I know. But there was something about how we might get crushed."

"Or go to jail," Robinson said. "He said that, too."

I turned and faced them both. "You don't have to do this. We can walk back out the door. I just wanted to pay you back for what you did. If this doesn't work for you, I understand. It's all I've got." After a moment Robinson nodded, and eventually Nightmare did the same. "Okay," I said. "Horizn is going public today. We're going to buy it as high as we can, and sell it short. We're betting the stock will go down."

"And we're buying it on margin, which lets us control way more stock than we can actually afford," Nightmare said slowly.

I nodded. "We buy at a set price, and for every dollar it goes down after that, we win."

"And if it doesn't go down?" Nightmare asked.

"We're crushed," I said, wincing. My leg was hurting like hell. "They don't play nice around here."

"And it's not going to be insider trading." Robinson said, doubtfully.

"That's right."

"Because of the timing."

"Correct."

Robinson looked dubious. "Are you sure they won't cancel the IPO after everything that's happened?"

I shook my head. "You don't stop an IPO a few hours before it's scheduled. Anyway, as far as Stephens knows, everything went as planned. He may have tried to reach Pope, but he isn't going to pull the plug based on not getting a phone call returned. He's millions into investment banker fees, and pulling the plug would put a light on them that there's no way they could survive. Trust me. This IPO is going off, without a doubt."

The large doors behind us opened, and Nicole walked in with her usual cheery impeccability. She saw us and stopped cold. "Jack?" She looked at the bandage. "Oh, my God. What happened to you?"

There wasn't time for a long explanation, so I skipped it. "We want to open a margin account." Nicole laughed nervously, as though she'd decided I had lost my mind. "We're serious," I said. "And we're in kind of a hurry."

The laughter stopped. "Have you looked at yourselves?"

"For the sum of two million, five hundred and thirty-one thousand, four hundred dollars, please."

There was a hushed silence, then she grabbed my arm and whispered, "Are you crazy, Jack? I know things have been bad, but playing the market on margin isn't the answer." She pointed to Nightmare and Robinson. "Who are these people, and what are they doing here?"

"There's collateral," I said. "One hundred and sixty-eight thousand shares of Grayton Pharmaceutical. It's trading at about five." Nicole's mouth, then in the process of reloading, snapped shut. "We also have a cashier's check for thirty-eight hundred dollars, courtesy of my business associate, Mr. Michael Harrod. Michael, shake hands with your new broker."

Michael stuck out his hand like a Rockefeller. Nicole regarded it warily, shook it, and looked like she wanted a washrag. The doors behind us opened again, and several impeccably dressed executives spilled out into the lobby. "You'd better come upstairs, Jack," she said. "You and your friends aren't doing my image any good."

Nicole bundled us onto the elevator, which we rode up to the second floor. The doors opened, and we walked into the catwalk overlooking the Atlanta trading room at Shearson Lehman, a place that makes NASA look old-fashioned. It's a spotless world in which row after row of gleaming plasma screens monitor the continuous transfer of the world's wealth from one set of hands to another, mostly in an upward direction. The executive offices, including Nicole's, look down on the traders' area like Romans on gladiators. And as at the Coliseum, at the end of every trading day there would be the dead, the wounded, and the privileged winners. It was Nicole's job to make sure her clients stayed firmly in the latter group.

Nightmare, Robinson, and I followed Nicole out of the elevator toward her office. There were a lot of suits walking around, even more than usual, according to Nicole. Some of the higher-ups had gathered, ready to watch the fireworks when Horizn opened. One office we passed had a bucket with a bottle of Cristal Roederer cooling expensively in ice. Four or five people were in the room, chatting with the high, anxious voices of children on Christmas morning.

Nightmare walked in a haze, probably imagining the damage he could do if he ever got access to their computer system. We filed into Nicole's office, a comfortable space containing a modern-looking desk, a coffee table, a leather couch and some fabric-covered wing chairs. A LeRoy Neiman painting hung on one wall. I pointed and gave her a questioning look.

"I loathe it, but it makes my male clients feel better," she said. "Before I ask them to give me all their money." She motioned for us to take a seat and pulled up a chair herself. "Now, why don't you tell me what this is all about? This is a busy morning."

I set the briefcase on her coffee table and flipped it open. "These," I said, "are certificates of Grayton Technical Laboratories stock. Together with our cashier's check, their current value is eight hundred forty-three thousand, eight hundred dollars. I trust they're self-explanatory."

Nicole stared at the briefcase. "I see." She pulled out a calculator and punched some buttons. "It's not enough, Jack. Margin accounts can't exceed fifty percent."

"We intend to sell short. It's seventy-five percent for that, right?"

"Intend to sell what short?"

"It's seventy-five percent, right?"

She watched me a moment, then said, "Yes, Jack. It's seventy-five percent for selling short. Technically."

"So that's two million, five hundred thirty-one thousand, four hundred dollars." I pulled out a piece of paper and put it on her desk. "This is my life insurance," I said. "It has a cash value of twenty-one thousand dollars. I've made Shearson Lehman the assignee. You can cash it at your leisure."

A longer pause, as Nicole—who, although an absolute minx

socially, handled her business affairs like a nun—considered. "It's hardly conventional."

"It is legal, though. That's the point."

"You gentlemen realize that if this stock goes down you are going to suffer huge losses." ·

"We do."

"Which means you are going to get called."

"Right."

"There's no grace on a margin this big, Jack. You'll have to cover at the close of every business day. No exceptions. You could lose everything before you know what hit you." I nodded silently. "You do understand the commissions on margin are higher."

"I do."

Nicole watched me levelly a moment, then said, "If you gentlemen will wait here a minute, I'll have some paperwork for you to sign."

I had set my grief aside for a few disciplined hours, because I was burning inside. It wasn't a righteous flame, exactly. I had made too many of my own mistakes for that. But it was white hot, and it had a well-earned target. After we signed, I stood pacing as Nicole started her trading software on her desktop computer. The side wall facing the trading area was glass, and Nightmare and Robinson pressed up against it, noses against the window. The traders were already at their places, chatting between themselves, beginning the morning's caffeine assault on generic fatigue.

In the four or five minutes between that moment and the opening of trading, we were like a little band of brothers, three unlikely *compadres* thrown together by circumstance. And we were about to go to war. You could feel the energy between us, part hope, part anxious fear. I walked over to the glass, and we stood there, mesmerized, thinking about what was about to happen. At ten o'clock, Nicole's voice pulled me back into reality. "Boom," she said, smiling. "Off to the races. Now tell me what we're doing."

"Put Horizn on the screen," I said.

"Horizn." She looked paler, if that was possible, than usual.

I walked back over to Nicole, looking over her shoulder. My entire body went tense as I watched the numbers. Horizn's stock symbol, HZN, flickered an instant at the starting price of 31, but that lasted seconds. Quickly, it rose to 32.50, then 33.17. Nicole looked at me. "Tell me what you're doing. It's going to get expensive."

"Not yet," I said levelly. Thirty minutes later, Horizn was at 38.12. Nicole was growing anxious.

"Jack, this is crazy."

I shook my head. By eleven-fifteen, Horizn had exploded to forty-six dollars, well on its way toward its anticipated one-year level. Buying was frantic, as traders made bids only to see the price vanish before the order was filled. I glanced at Robinson, who was giving me a nervous look. "When it hits fifty," I said.

Nightmare was trembling. "I hope you know what you're doing," he said.

"You can get off the train anytime you like," I said. "It's your decision."

Nightmare turned back to stare at the trading floor, but shut his mouth. At about eleven-thirty, the buying pace slowed. Over the next ten minutes, the price glimmered in the mid-49s, flirting with but not hitting the magic number.

"It's running out of steam," Nicole said. "There's some day traders taking quick money."

I looked at my watch; it was twenty minutes until twelve. "Buy five thousand shares," I said. "At market."

Nicole looked stricken. "C'mon, Jack. It's flagging. Go a quarter under and wait."

"Market," I said, eyes fixed on the screen.

"It's your money," Nicole said, typing on the screen.

I watched my order flash a moment, then get devoured. That reenergized things for a while, but the magic 50 hadn't been broken. "Buy another five thousand," Robinson said. Nicole looked up.

I nodded at Robinson, who was wide-eyed, but otherwise calm. "He's right," I said. "Another five thousand, at market." Nicole typed, and within seconds, we had our buyer. A few seconds after that, the price started back up—nothing dramatic, but with renewed energy. A few minutes later, HZN crossed the magic fifty-dollar mark. With that psychological barrier passed, another round of buying took over, pushing the stock even higher.

"Blessed Virgin," Robinson said.

"Yeah," I said. "Blessed Virgin, come to us in our hour of need." I looked at my watch one last time, turned to Nicole and said, "Turn on the TV. You can leave the sound off. Tune to Channel Five."

Nicole looked at me, her expression blank. By now, she was in a dream state, just along for the ride. She picked up a remote control and turned on a TV across the room. It was a soap commercial. I looked back at the trading numbers. Horizn had just crossed 53.

The commercial ended, and a "Breaking News" banner popped up at the bottom of the screen. The picture changed to the PR room the Atlanta Police Department used for press briefings. Billy Little was standing behind a group of microphones. The room was silent as we watched Billy Little make a short announcement. Nightmare watched from across Nicole's office, his face white. Robinson, on the other hand, went calm. His eyes were fixed on Little, waiting for the detective to say the words that would make his life make sense again. "I'm going to sell some Horizn shares short, Nicole," I said. "I want you to get it on your screen, ready to send."

"Short? How many shares?"

"Fifty thousand," I said quietly. "And I need your finger on the trigger."

Nicole stared at the TV screen, suddenly grasping that something terrible was about to happen to Horizn stock. "My God, Jack. Oh, my God."

"Exactly, sweetheart. Just do it, please."

"Fifty thousand? Oh, God, Jack. What is this?"

"Get it on your screen, but don't send it until I tell you." Billy kept talking, his mouth moving silently in the corner of Nicole's monitor. I glanced over the trading numbers; the buying was still brisk. The next fifteen seconds were agonizing. They passed in slow motion, the way seasons change. I thought I was going to explode if Billy Little didn't shut up.

Finally, just when I thought we were screwed, Billy raised his eyes from his prepared statement. Hands went up from the reporters, and Billy pointed at one. I looked at Nicole. "Now, please. All of it, every share, and this second."

Nicole blanched. "Jack, listen to me . . ."

"*Now.*"

Nicole pressed enter on her keyboard. Nightmare put his head in his hands, trying to steady himself. Robinson walked over beside me, and together, we watched our bid sit in the electronic ether, waiting for a buyer. *Fifty thousand shares, sold short.* The size of the bid stopped the day traders; they sniffed trouble. The bid sat flashing, lost in a financial demilitarized zone. For a terrible moment, there was peace, the combat ceased. I glanced at the TV screen; Billy was handling a flurry of questions. Before he could finish one, a dozen hands were up in the air. *Come on, baby. It's now or never.* Suddenly, our bid was greedily snapped up in one bite by an institutional firm. The flashing little square on Nicole's screen turned red, and it was gone. Robinson gasped, then exhaled.

"Is it okay?" Nightmare asked. His voice was quaking, and he was washed out, like a junkie.

I turned and smiled. "Old economy, Michael," I said. "You really ought to try it sometime." I looked at Nicole. "You can turn up the volume now."

Nicole pressed a button on her computer, and we heard Billy Little's voice. "That's right," he said. "There's no evidence that any other officers at Horizn were involved. We're only charging the two principals, Charles Ralston and Derek Stephens." Nicole gasped, and I put a hand on her shoulder.

"Is that first-degree murder, Detective Little?" a voice from the press room asked.

Billy Little nodded. "That's right. Eight counts, murder in the first degree."

I squeezed Nicole's shoulder. "You can turn it off now. And you might want to lock your door."

Nicole looked up at me. "God, Jack, you knew. It's insider trading."

I shook my head. "You sold after the announcement was made. The information was public at the time of the trade. The trading records will back that up. By definition, the trade was *not* insider."

Nicole looked down at her monitor; there was already some light selling. It would be a matter of minutes before the stock went into free fall. "But, Jack, a lot of people are going to get hurt. You could have saved them millions."

I took her hand, pulling her up out of her chair. I kissed her cheek. "No matter where I went, a lot of people were going to get hurt. But this way, I could protect you."

Nicole leaned back heavily in her chair and stared at her monitor, watching Horizn stock already crashing downward through the 30s. "You bastard," she said, quietly. "You are such a bastard."

I smiled. "You knew nothing, you broke no law, and you made your new clients very rich. All in all, quite a good morning."

Horizn responded within hours, flooding the airwaves with denials. But the damage was done. By the time the dust settled, Horizn was trading at four dollars and twelve cents. Thomas Robinson made $2,604,000, all in about two hours. Nightmare—who, no doubt, would soon begin to refer to himself as Mr. Michael Harrod, made $46,000.

I made nothing. I had given Thomas Robinson back his self-respect and a measure of revenge. I had already regained the former, and I had no further need for the latter. Robinson was fighting a bitter battle, and I was glad to help him find his life again. But I would never make a dollar off anything that had ever touched Michele Sonnier. Others had done so, from her managers to concert halls around the world. Even her husband, after a fashion; he had traded on her gift to gain entrée to a part of society otherwise closed to him. But I would rather die. She was my dark angel: conflicted, tortured, and still brilliant as the sun.

Only one other person benefitted from those hours of trading at Shearson Lehman. The money that Nicole had spotted me against my life insurance netted Briah Fields $72,280. Of all the victims in the story, in the end, she was the only one who truly deserved no pain.

CHAPTER THIRTY

ROBINSON, NIGHTMARE, AND I stood outside the Shearson Lehman offices in a bright, warm sunlight. The traffic flowed briskly by as people lived their good lives, their bad lives, their in-between lives. Their loves and hates and ambitions traveled along with them, filling Atlanta with the noisy, multicolored crush of a very imperfect humanity. I turned to Robinson. "You're a good man," I said. "A good doctor."

Robinson smiled. "Maybe they'll let me do some research again. That would be nice."

"Things are going to get hairy for a while," I said. "Reporters, cops, probably the SEC. But don't worry. You have a good lawyer."

Robinson nodded. "One hell of a lawyer."

Michael—still reeling with the idea that he wasn't broke—said, "Go to bed, will you? You both look like hell."

Robinson turned toward him. "If you still want that job, let me know. You've got a good mind, and I have a lot of software-intensive ideas."

"What about it, Michael?" I asked. "You'd have to pay taxes. On the other hand, you'd probably be a lot less likely to end up in jail."

Nightmare flushed and stood up a little straighter. "Yeah. That would be good."

"Glad to hear it," I said. "Now you and the doctor get some rest."

There was much to grieve, and I needed quiet to do it. I called Blu and gave her the rest of the week off, with pay. She was concerned, but I wouldn't let her come over. I needed the time alone. I didn't leave my apartment for a couple of days. There was sleep, but it was troubled, and full of dreams. I awakened each time ravenous, eating whatever I could find, ordering in when I ran out of food.

I had loved Michele, but in a whirlwind. She had blown into my life, disturbing everything in my world. It would take time before I could regain any stillness within myself, any peace after her storm. While I looked for quiet, the city heaved under the news that one of its heroes had turned against it, trading the lives of eight people for the promise of money. Soon there would be grueling depositions, and the certainty that every shred of Michele's past would be exposed, no matter how personal.

When I finally ventured out, I stood outside my apartment on the street, coming to terms with my city once again. The neighborhood was quiet in the midafternoon, but I knew that it was an illusion. To the east crowded the urban life of Atlanta's lower middle class, pressed together like worker bees in a hive; to the north were the thriving megabusinesses of the southeastern United States. In every direction, the ceaselessly expanding suburbs stretched, filling with the people who poured in from every part of the world.

One memory remained to be released, a lingering wound to dress before that chaos descended. Three days after Michele's death, I went alone to my familiar stop at the flower shop on Woodward Avenue. I purchased my usual red tulips, and drove toward the silent retreat where two years earlier I had left a piece of my soul. I rolled through the iron gates of Oakland Cemetery, opening my windows to let the scented, summer air inside the car. I parked and sat in the tranquil quiet, leaning back in my seat, breathing deeply. The grass shimmered green in the breeze, the leaves making a serene, intermittent rustle around me. I thought of Thomas Robinson, and how he had risked everything—even his own life—to redeem his work. Courage and desperation are close cousins, and he had drawn on both to break open what would otherwise have been one more story of the evil prospering. And I thought of Michael, and how he had found himself at last. Once out of his dark cave, he was capable of anything. But my thoughts only stayed with those two a moment. A few yards away, a woman rested. I counted the six gravestones, and saw her. *La flor inocente,* her gravestone said, but I knew it was only a romantic vision. She was not innocent. She had chosen to love a violent man, and in so doing, she took on his evil. But I have spent my days and nights with the refuse of my city, and I sit in no judgment seat. I saw her beauty, fell captive to it, and set into motion events that haunt me still. Nothing truly evil could possibly have lived behind her eyes. She was only conflicted, like everyone, struggling to find love and security in a changing world.

I opened the car door, walked quietly across the familiar names in stone, and found her. *Bella como la luna y las estrellas,* her gravestone said, and of that, there could be no doubt. Violeta Ramirez, lovely as the moon and stars. I knelt down before her grave, laid my flowers across her plot of earth, and said goodbye. If her ghost revisits me, it is only in the place of memory, no longer in my conscious, waking hours. The time had come to let her go, and I felt her fall away, freed from the concerns that made her life so hard.

I rose, feeling the warm air on my face, breathing in the urban compounds of life—automobiles, plants of every kind, people, industry, love, and sin—that permeate my city. Missing at my side was Michele, brilliant artist, brilliant lover, failed, tragic mother. What can I make of her, now that her light has gone out, or at least left this world? My heart opened up to her, but our love was cut short. For that, I feel both cheated and saved. There are a thousand nights I never got to feel her hand in mine, and a hundred more I never got to hear her sing. Love is part possession and part happenstance. Would I have loved Michele if I had met her in McDaniel Glen? Would my eyes have been open to see her spectacular gift? Or would I have simply walked past her, summing her up as one more victim of the projects? I will never know.

None of this has the power to unmake me, not anymore. Life doesn't yield nicely to logic, in the end. Or perhaps it yields only to this logic: *L'amore non prevale sempre.* Grayton was saved, and with it, Robinson and Nightmare. But Michele was gone, separated from her daughter by eternity. Love does not always prevail, not always, not in this life. Shakespeare knew that, and every generation has to learn it again. Doug knew it. Deep in his damaged soul, he must have sensed he was doomed by love the second he spoke those words to Michele. They were his greeting, and they were his goodbye. And I know it now, never to be forgotten. We breathe, we risk. We make our peace. We strip it down, and we let it go.